ASCENDANT

A Mira Raiden Adventure

Dark Trinity
Book One

Sean Ellis

Gryphonwood

Gryphonwood Press

ASCENDANT- DARK TRINITY BOOK 1. Copyright 2012, 2014 by Sean Ellis

Published by Gryphonwood Press.
www.gryphonwoodpress.com

ISBN 13: 978-1-940095-16-5

BOOKS BY SEAN ELLIS

Magic Mirror
Ascendant

The Nick Kismet Adventures
The Shroud of Heaven
Into the Black
The Devil You Know
Fortune Favors

The Adventures of Dodge Dalton
In the Shadow of Falcon's Wings
At the Outpost of Fate
On the High Road to Oblivion

Secret Agent X
The Sea Wraiths
Masterpiece of Vengeance
The Scar

With Jeremy Robinson
Callsign: King
Callsign: King – Underworld
Callsign: King- Blackout
Prime

With David Wood
Hell Ship

With Steven Savile
Wargod

PROLOGUE

Somewhere in the South Pacific, 1944

The grave robber stared out across the sun-dappled water of the lagoon, anxiously scanning the horizon for movement. In a world at war, even in this remote part of the globe, planes and submarines could deliver death without warning, without provocation. Though he was not a soldier, he had seen his share of war and knew that in a combat zone there were no innocent bystanders.

Not that he was innocent.

He had knowingly struck a deal with the devil—the devil always had the shiniest gold and, contrary to what the Good Book said, usually came out on top.

But this time it looked as if the devil was going to lose. The last report the grave robber had heard before leaving civilization confirmed what he had suspected for some time. Germany was fatally wounded, crippled by the economic and human cost of supporting a war on two fronts. While the scientists of the Third Reich were arguably the most brilliant in history, there was simply not enough time for their superior weapons to be perfected and deployed. Their generals and admirals and spymasters were unparalleled in their respective crafts, yet their supreme commander was a madman, whose mercurial temperament had consigned thousands of young men—the cream of Germany's youth—to death on the frozen threshold of Stalingrad.

The grave robber shook a Camel from a nearly empty pack and lit it with a single wooden match, struck on his thumb and cast into the lapping waters of the lagoon, where it died with a hiss. As he drew in a deep breath of nicotine-laced smoke, his fingers felt the outline of the artifact concealed beneath his shirt and wondered if that simple circle of metal and crystal might change that inevitable outcome.

"*Guten Tag,* Herr Tarrant."

The voice startled him, nearly causing him to drop his cigarette. He whirled, unconsciously recoiling like a frightened animal, and searched for its source. A dark figure, a man wearing an overcoat in spite of the tropical humidity, stepped out from concealment behind a coconut palm directly opposite the lagoon. His sudden appearance almost startled Tarrant a second time.

"How in the hell did you get over there?" he grumbled, trying to repair his tattered dignity.

The German smiled icily. "These are dangerous times. One cannot be too careful."

Tarrant nodded and took a deep breath. "Tell me about it."

The German strode out onto the sandy beach, fully exposing himself to the sun's glare. The grave robber idly wondered if the man would burst into flames, like a vampire in a horror film. He did not, though his pale skin and gaunt features certainly evoked such a comparison. "Do you have the item, Herr Tarrant?"

"You know I do."

"Ah. And you wish for some assurance that I have your money?"

Tarrant affected a surly shrug. "You could put it that way."

The German cocked his head sideways. His smile sliced downward like the blade of a scimitar. "I would have thought a man like yourself would expect treachery at every turn. Why, for argument's sake, would I surrender a fortune in gold to you when I could simply kill you and take the artifact for myself?"

Tarrant was used to the Nazi's mind-games; they had done this before. "Because," he answered in a tired voice, "you want the next one. There's always a next one. And you know I'm the only man who can find it."

The Nazi's smile slipped a notch. "You said that there were only two—the Twins, you called them. Our scholars agree."

Tarrant backhanded the cigarette to his lips, dragging deeply as he watched beads of sweat trickling down the other man's forehead. He blew out a perfect smoke ring, which quickly fragmented in the moist air, before answering. "When you touch these things, especially after they've gone undisturbed for a while, you see things. Visions of the past. And sometimes of the future."

"Yes, you've reported that, though our scientists cannot verify your claim."

The grave robber jerked a thumb at his chest. "I am the proof. How do you think I found them? The remains of lost cities that you thought were only myths. I saw them in a vision. And this time, I saw something else."

"Tell me."

"There's another one of them. Three in all. Individually they're powerful beyond imagination, but if they're all brought together in a certain place . . . limitless power."

"Power." Something changed in the German's eyes as he echoed the words, and Tarrant felt an inexplicable rush of fear. He kept talking to hide his trepidation.

"The antediluvian world was just as advanced as our own; maybe more so. They spread their civilization over the entire globe, not just Asia. There were at least three separate empires, an Axis of power if you will. Each ruler bore one of these." He lifted the circular relic, still depending from the chain around his neck, to emphasize his point. "Trinities are everywhere in ancient religions, the embodiment of ultimate power. That's the answer to all this. The whole is greater than the sum of its parts. The ancients ruled the world with it. I believe that is your ambition as well."

"Our destiny." For a moment, the Nazi seemed lost in thought, then his expression hardened again. "You say that this ancient trinity ruled the world with these talismans of power. But they are not among us today. Do you know why?"

Tarrant licked his lips, which in spite of the humidity had become very dry. His heart was racing, as if his body had experienced a premonition that his brain was only beginning to grasp. "What are you talking about?"

"They did not know when to stop." Suddenly, the scimitar returned to the Nazi's lips. "As with you, Herr Tarrant, you believe there is always one more piece of the puzzle to be found. And you imagine that by finding it you can extract a king's ransom in gold from the coffers of the Third Reich.

"You imagine incorrectly."

Tarrant raised his palms in protest, but before he could say a word, the Nazi raised his hand as well. Clenched in one gloved fist was a Mauser P08 pistol.

"Wait. . . ."

Tarrant's protest fell on ears deafened by the roar of the pistol. He felt a sharp hammer blow to his chest and he was knocked backwards. The cigarette flew from his fingers as he splashed onto his back in the shallows where the lagoon met the beach.

Though it was midday, twilight seemed to fall over the island. Tarrant struggled to rise, but no amount of effort yielded the slightest result. He heard the sound of his attacker splashing toward him, felt the gloved fingers tear open his shirt to search his body and discover the relic, but saw only the descending fog of premature night.

Tarrant awoke on the tide. A mouthful of tepid seawater triggered his gag reflex and he rolled onto his side, retching. The sudden, violent movement stirred the embers of pain in his wound, but the unpleasant sensations produced a welcome revelation; he was still alive.

He struggled to his hands and knees, grimacing as the blossom of pain in his torso threatened to render him unconscious a second time. The water stroked his exposed chest and the ragged flesh of the wound as gentle waves brought the tide in. He realized with a start that he had only been unconscious for a short time, perhaps less than an hour.

He rocked back onto his haunches and felt the wound. Blood had begun to trickle afresh since his waking, but he intuited that the nine-millimeter slug had miraculously deflected off one of his ribs. It had burrowed under the skin, but done little more than fracture the bone at the point of impact. It hurt like a son of a bitch, but he would live. He fumbled for a cigarette, but found that the remaining two were sodden from his submergence. Casting the ruined pack into the water, he rose to his feet.

The Nazi had double-crossed him.

His assailant's final words haunted him. He had indeed played the game once too often. The outcome of dealing with the devil was inevitable, yet he had truly believed that the Nazis would spare no effort to recover every last vestige of the ancient power manifest in the relics. They were desperate for anything to turn the tide of the war. In hindsight it had been a foolish notion; what good was a thrice-powerful talisman if it arrived after the war had been lost?

The pain in his chest was beginning to subside and with that recession, his cognitive abilities began to flow. A line of footprints led away into the sparse forest, marking the path taken by his assailant. With steps uncertain at first, but quickly becoming more determined until he was almost running, Tarrant chased after the Nazi agent.

The footprints disappeared as sand gave way to loamy soil, but the trail remained evident in the trampled underbrush. The Nazi had followed a path that circled back to the beach two miles north of the lagoon. Tarrant slowed his pace as the thicket gave way once more to bare sand, in which the footprints of the Nazi were plainly stamped. The trail led directly into the surf, where wave action had erased the final destination.

A boat, Tarrant surmised. Probably a small motorized launch, which had conveyed the man to a waiting ship. He scanned the horizon, hoping to catch a glimpse of the parent vessel. This close to sea level he realized that his horizon was severely limited, so he dashed back to the forest and scaled a coconut palm. From there, his visual range was extended by several miles.

A black column stood monolithic in the distance. He squinted, minimizing the glare of the sun, and saw more detail. It was a submarine, a German *Kriegsmarine Unterseeboot*. The grave robber did not know a great deal about naval vessels, but he studied what he could see of the submarine carefully. There were numbers painted along the conning tower, the letter "U" followed by four digits. Tarrant squinted harder, trying to distinguish them, but the waves slapping against the tower made this a nearly hopeless task.

The U-boat was sinking—*No*, he corrected. *It's diving*. His surveillance took on new urgency as he strained to catch at least catch part of the submarine's designation. "Two—Five—" The lapping water touched the base of the painted numbers. The next digit was two or three, but he could not be sure which. A moment later, the black column was gone.

Tarrant closed his eyes and sighed through a sudden flare of pain in his chest. He had aggravated the injury with his sprint through the forest and the scramble up the tree. It bled freely now, a throbbing ache pulsing in time with his rapid heartbeat. With due restraint, he slid down from his perch and sank to his knees in the coarse sand.

He didn't really know what had motivated him to chase after the Nazi. He had escaped with his life, which was certainly more than the double-crossing German had intended to leave him with. Now the Nazis had two of the relics; they could join them and use that power to . . . Well, what couldn't they do with it?

Though they did not yet realize it, the Nazis now had the power to boil the seas and shake the earth from its orbit. The relics could even raise an army of the dead to lay low the enemies of whoever wielded it. Even if he one day encountered the man whose treachery had almost killed him, what could he do?

Gazing at the sea, at the very spot where the U-boat had vanished, Tarrant made another deal with the devil. Though the cost would no doubt be higher in an eternal sense than his deal with the Nazis had proved, he swore he would not be so easily taken when his next chance came.

Panama, Present Day

"*¡Alto!*"

The laborer froze in mid-swing, the point of his machete aimed at the heavens.

Marquand Atlas rushed forward, exertion and excitement putting a dangerous strain on his already overtaxed heart. The morbidly obese billionaire panted for several seconds, bent over at the waist with his hands on his knees, in order to get enough breath to finally speak. "You've found it!"

Mira Raiden didn't know what she had found; didn't know if she had in fact found anything. She only knew, with a certainty that she could not put into words, that something very bad would happen if the laborer blazing their trail through the dense undergrowth allowed his blade to fall. She gestured for the man to back away from his task. Evidently, something in her demeanor conveyed what speech could not, for the man retreated from the thicket as though it were squirming with vipers.

Mira glanced briefly at her benefactor, then behind him to meet the gaze of Curtis Lancet, Atlas' executive bodyguard and general factotum. Lancet, a former Green Beret and decorated war hero, was everything that Atlas—for all his wealth—could never be: handsome, athletic, charismatic, and a damn good lover.

"What is it, Mira? What do you sense?" Lancet's concern was genuine and typical of his good nature. Where his employer saw Mira and her unique abilities merely as one more resource to be exploited and discarded, Lancet had always shown a deep fascination with her as a person as well as with what she could do. Over the course of their journey she had become much more than just a working partner to him.

She shook her head uncertainly, trying to get a handle on the premonition. In some cultures her gift was called 'second sight,' but in sensorial terms, it was nothing at all like vision. Having lived with it all her life, she could not explain it any more than she could explain her other five senses, but the closest comparison she could offer was the olfactory sense.

Second smell, she had once told one of her Agency handlers with a chuckle, but that was exactly what it was like. Sometimes, a rosy 'smell' hinted that something good was about to happen, while other situations just plain stank. This one, however, was harder to pin down.

It was neither good nor bad. It was just . . . potent.

She directed her words to Lancet. "Send them back to camp."

Atlas' eyes began to dance with anticipation. "Yes, send them back. If they catch even a glimpse of what we've found, we'll be fighting off tomb robbers for weeks."

Mira hid a frown. She wasn't worried about protecting the discovery from the looters that she knew were dogging their steps; her concern was for the safety of the hired workers. She didn't know what lay beyond that curtain of foliage, but she was certain that it was as dangerous as a loaded gun in the hands of a child.

She held Atlas back with a raised hand until Lancet finished sending the laborers back to their camp a few miles back. Only when their murmured conversations were no longer audible did she advance along the freshly blazed trail, stopping exactly where the workman had been moments before. The indescribable feeling grew with each step forward.

"Curt, let me borrow that sword of yours."

Without question or hesitation, Lancet drew a large Pathfinder knife from the sheath on his belt, right behind a holstered SIG Sauer 9mm semi-automatic pistol. He casually flipped the knife and caught the fourteen-inch blade between thumb and forefinger, proffering the hilt to Mira.

Mira was less cavalier about her handling of the knife. She did not hack at the brushy barrier, but rather used the blade to probe the thicket, gently bending vines and branches out of the way. Her surgical precision gradually laid bare the object that the laborer would have discovered with his next cut.

It was a stone stele, standing shoulder high to the petite Mira, adorned with what looked at first glance like Mayan glyphs. Maintaining her calm demeanor, she continued to clear the remaining growth away, fully exposing the carved bas-relief message.

"It's Mayan, all right," Atlas announced. From the moment she had revealed the first glyph, he had commenced scanning the image into his palmtop computer.

"What's it say?" Lancet asked in a breathless whisper.

"'Abandon hope, all ye who enter here,'" Mira muttered, not quite joking.

Atlas chuckled. "That's a pretty close translation actually. It is indeed a warning, from our old friend Storm Jaguar."

Though she was no expert on the Maya, Mira knew more about Storm Jaguar than any classically trained pre-Columbian archaeologist. The truth of the matter was, due to a series of unfortunate circumstances beginning with the actions of an opportunistic Dominican friar and extending forward five centuries, no one in the scholarly world had ever heard of him at all.

Storm Jaguar—the name was a literal translation of the ancient pictographic script—had been the king of an early city-state in western Honduras, well to the south of what most historians believed was the limit of Mayan expansion. His life story had become the basis for the Mesoamerican equivalent of an epic poem, committed to paper—or *huun*, as the Maya called it—in the fifth century.

A thousand years later, and several centuries after their civilization had mysteriously vanished, most surviving examples of the ancient texts were destroyed by Spanish conquistadores who believed the writings would inhibit conversion of the native population to Christianity. A scant few books, bound and folded into codices, survived the purge, preserved by Spaniards who recognized their worth, but remained hidden and forgotten for hundreds of years thereafter. Experts now knew of four authentic Mayan codices and had used these in combination with the relief carvings in Mayan ruins to develop a fairly comprehensive translation matrix, but none of the known writings mentioned Storm Jaguar. That name was found only in a codex that Atlas had purchased on the black market.

A translation of the document yielded, among other things, the Mayan equivalent of the Epic of Gilgamesh, a tale of how Storm Jaguar left his kingdom and journeyed to Xibalba, the Mayan Underworld. The tale expanded on the creation myths found in the *Popul Vuh*—a collection of folklore based on oral tradition passed down in the Quiché language—but the provenance of Atlas' codex had been impossible to establish through conventional means. Which left only unconventional means.

Enter Mira Raiden.

Four months earlier, the closest Mira had ever come to a tropical jungle was the Rain Forest Café at the MGM Grand on the Las Vegas strip. She had been making the circuit of Sin City casinos, winning big, but not too big, and gradually but determinedly feathering her nest. Gambling afforded her no addictive thrill. With her intuition guiding her bets, it was merely working for a living.

One night while playing colors at the roulette table, she had felt the tingle of someone watching her. Surprised that she had been noticed so early in the evening, she had nevertheless taken that as her cue to cash out her winnings and head for the door. The watcher in this case was not the pit boss, however, but rather a sweaty, smiling, little fat man who spoke to her as if they were already old friends.

"My dear Mira," he had said, grinning cryptically. "You have a gift."

Her "gift" told her that, where Marquand Atlas was concerned, looks could be deceiving, but she sensed nothing threatening about him. And that, coupled with the fact that he had correctly recognized her abilities and seemed impressed by them, was enough for her to accept his offer of a drink.

They made an unlikely pair in the cocktail lounge. Her elfin physique and features were not exactly glamorous, but she knew that most men found her attractive. Under normal circumstances, she could have had her pick of companions, and at first she had imagined that onlookers would wonder why she had picked the portly Atlas. Only later, when she finally began to get an inkling of his net worth, did she realize that the jealousy she had sensed was actually directed at her.

For his part, Atlas had never tried to impress her with his wealth, much less make any sort of sexual advances. From the outset he had focused solely on her unique attributes, all but interrogating her in an effort to define exactly what she was capable of doing. Later that night he had shown her the codex.

Without even knowing what it was, physical contact with the brittle, discolored pages had filled her with certainty regarding the codex's authenticity. More than that, it had triggered what she could only describe as a homing instinct, a powerful urge that over the course of several weeks would lead her, with Atlas in tow, to a buried Mayan temple in Honduras more than three hundred miles from the ruins of Copan near the Guatemalan border and from there even farther south to the rugged wilderness of the Darien Gap in search of the legendary Mayan underworld.

But that night in Vegas, as her fingertips brushed the decorative leaves of the codex, she understood for the first time the thrill that made ordinary people gamble away their last dollar on the promise of what the next roll of the dice might bring.

"Is it a warning?" Lancet asked.

"A 'No Trespassing' sign, of sorts. It's a boundary marker. Beyond this point, we are in the realm of Xibalba." Atlas made a dismissive gesture. "From the looks of it, the lords of Xibalba have been gone for a long time."

Mira wasn't convinced. When they had discovered the tomb of Storm Jaguar in the catacombs beneath the temple in Honduras, she had felt only an overwhelming desire to press on, to retrace the steps of the ancient Mayan king. Now, however, on the threshold of that final discovery, her urge to move forward was being countered by a more primal instinct. It wasn't exactly panic, but something pretty damn close.

Atlas evinced no such inhibition. Drawing his bush knife, he began clumsily breaking trail beyond the stele. Ever loyal to his employer, Lancet reclaimed his own blade from Mira and joined the effort, with considerably more effectiveness. As the two men hacked at the verdant barrier, Mira remained vigilant, sniffing for any hint of imminent peril.

In a matter of minutes, the jungle yielded up another carved stone—not a stele, but rather an entire wall peeking through the growth. The markings on it were definitely not Mayan hieroglyphs.

"It's Atlantean," gasped the billionaire.

The ambient sensations presently inundating Mira's precognitive abilities could not quite hide the subtle change in Atlas' aura. The very sight of the strange markings—a language that was far more reminiscent of a phonetic alphabet than any pre-Columbian pictograph—had awakened something deep inside the man, something buried so deep that she had never sensed it before. The only word to describe it was "hunger," and the impression was so sudden and overwhelming that the irony was lost on her.

What have I done? she thought. *I shouldn't have brought him here.*

Atlas continued chopping away the vines to uncover more of the unique text, and where he did, his fingers brushed at the recessed letters lovingly, his lips moving silently as he read whatever was written there.

Lancet stood paralyzed in disbelief. "You can read this?"

"It is the language of Atlantis. I had long suspected that what Storm Jaguar called Xibalba was really an outpost city built by refugees from that fallen civilization. This"—he patted the wall reverently—"is the tomb of the king of Atlantis."

"That doesn't explain how you are able to read it," Mira countered.

"Tsk, tsk, my dear. Did you think you knew all my secrets?"

Actually, I did, she thought.

"Atlantis is just a . . . ." Lancet looked to Mira, perhaps for confirmation that he was not going insane, but stunned by her own inability to detect Atlas' hidden agenda, she could offer no such assurances.

He's been looking for this all along. He knew what it was. He knows what it means. Suddenly the potency she had sensed from afar took on a dire implication. "Mr. Atlas, I think we should proceed with a little more caution."

"Nonsense. We must find a way inside, and quickly, before the looters get wind of this." As if to emphasize his newfound urgency, his next cut exposed the edge of a doorway. Beneath the artistically executed arched lintel, utterly unlike anything she had ever seen. T in her brief experience with Mayan ruins—the passage was choked with rubble, but even this did not slow Atlas down. Sheathing his knife, he reached in with both hands and began pulling out broken blocks of cut stone that were twice as large as his own head.

Lancet tapped him on the shoulder. "Take a break, Mr. Atlas. I'll get this."

The billionaire, red-faced and panting, mopped his brow with a shirtsleeve. "Very well, but you must hurry. We're so close."

"We're *too* close," Mira murmured, but even in the grip of her newfound anxiety she was not immune to the thrill of discovery. After all, it wasn't every day that a person found proof that Atlantis really existed.

With half of the blockage cleared away, it became apparent that the passage beyond was wide open. Eager to be inside, the billionaire squirmed his massive body through the narrow gap. A tiny spot of light blossomed in the darkness beyond and immediately began moving deeper into the interior.

"Damn him," Lancet growled before scrambling through the aperture in pursuit of his headstrong employer.

Mira's slight form slipped through without even significantly shutting out the sun's rays, and in the circle of daylight that illuminated the first few feet of the passage, she caught a glimpse of Lancet, already on the move.

Like the others, she carried a tiny squeeze light clipped to a breakaway chain around her neck. The powerful light emitting diode threw out a brilliant cone of illumination, but as she hastened after her companions, she felt such a sense of familiarity about the place that she probably could have negotiated the buried ruin in total darkness. She was starting to think that Atlas probably could have done so as well. Despite his bulk, he was flat out running ahead of them, drawn inexorably toward the center of temple.

There was no time to examine the halls and rooms through which she now raced. Flashes of light danced on the walls, revealing brightly colored human figures, veristic images, faintly reminiscent of the style found on the walls of Pompeii. The constant motion and vibration at the source of the illumination made it seem like the pictures were coming alive, and then it occurred to her that perhaps the movement glimpsed in her peripheral vision had nothing at all to do with the interplay of shadow and light. She hastened on.

The tunnels wound back and forth through the underground complex like a mystical labyrinth, and while she often lost sight of the flickering lights carried by the two men, she never faltered in choosing her path through the maze. But there was no escaping the grim reality that Atlas would reach the goal—the unknown prize at the heart of the ruin—before she caught up to him.

Then, inexplicably, she skidded to a stop. The goal, she realized, was not merely at the center of the ruin. Storm Jaguar had called this place Xibalba, the underworld, and just like Orpheus and Dante, his journey had taken him far beyond the first level of Hell. The prize Atlas sought lay somewhere below, in the bowels of this ancient subterranean temple. More importantly, there was a shortcut.

Whether Atlas knew about it or not was irrelevant. The most direct route to the temple's core had not been constructed for the purpose of passage. It was a vertical shaft less than two feet in diameter that stabbed through the center of every layer of the temple, allowing sunlight from the surface to filter down into the deepest catacombs. The ancient architects had not designed this to be a ruin, but rather a living place of worship, and such a place needed light. The roof of the superstructure had long since collapsed, shutting forever the oculus, which had permitted the sun's rays to enter, but the shaft remained.

At the next junction she turned away from the sound of footsteps and quickly found the opening, a shadowy void in the floor, surrounded by the rubble of the fallen roof. She trained her light into the shaft, verifying with her eyes what her mind already knew; the hole penetrated every descending level of the temple. Motivated though he was there was no way Atlas would ever be able to shove his girth through that orifice. Mira faced no such limitation.

Effortlessly, she lowered herself feet first into the void, gradually but confidently letting her extended arms take the burden of her weight. The floor of the next level was perhaps another four feet below her dangling toes, but she knew better than to simply let go. Directly beneath her, the deep shaft continued, and while she was in a hurry to get to the bottom, she wasn't in that much of a hurry. Instead, she spread her feet apart, straddling the opening as she landed. With increased confidence, she repeated the process three more times until, above the fifth level, her small light showed something other than a hole in the floor beneath her.

With each successive layer, the intensity of the sensation she had first encountered at the marker stele grew, and now that she was at last face to face with her destination, it was impossible to distinguish anything else. A blanket of psychic white noise emanating from the lowest stage of the temple left her precognitive faculties completely numb. But like a gambler, certain that the cards were about to break her way, the thrill of imminent victory compelled her onward.

From her overhead vantage, it was difficult to say exactly what the object occupying the center of the temple was. She thought it was an altar of some kind, positioned to lie in the beam of sunlight that had once reached into the depths of the temple at midday. If so, the altar was merely a showcase for something else, something that she could not quite make out with her tiny flashlight, but which she knew unequivocally to be the object of Atlas' mad dash into the ruin.

"Jackpot," she whispered, her lips curling in a triumphant grin as she proceeded to lower herself down onto the altar and then onto the supporting dais, where she got her first good look at the tomb of an Atlantean king.

The room was a circle, perhaps fifty feet across, and its single, continuous wall was adorned with a narrative mural executed in the same style as the frescoes she had glimpsed in the tunnels above. She took a moment to circumscribe the room with the beam of her light, and what she saw took her breath away. Protected from the elements, the images were perfectly preserved, the pigments still bright and vivid. Unlike the flat, two-dimensional images that adorned most ancient ruins, the artists who had decorated this tomb understood perspective and had created a remarkable illusion of depth. And while she was no expert on history or folklore, she recognized instantly the subject of the visual sequence. It was the story of the fall of Atlantis.

The tale began and ended with the only break in the circle, a vertical protrusion that stretched from floor to ceiling. At first she thought it was a door, but the carved relief—a perfect rendering of a man in repose—clued her in to its actual purpose: it was a sarcophagus.

Her brief examination of the life-sized sculpture revealed a nude male with exaggerated musculature and exquisite aquiline features. Unlike the death masks of Egyptian pharaohs, this figure wore only one piece of ornamentation—a circular diadem with a single hexagonal shape positioned in the center of his forehead.

The sculpted form on the sarcophagus featured prominently in the mural, and in most of those depictions, the circlet floated above his brow, the hexagon a white gemstone blazing with supernatural fire. Only the first scene was different; in it, the king struggled with another man—an oddly familiar figure that Mira felt she should recognize, but could not—for possession of the crown. Though she could not read the strange writing that framed the picture, it was evident that the battle between the two men directly contributed to the catastrophic collapse of the kingdom, shown on the subsequent panel.

From that point onward, the king wore the talismanic crown, leading the refugees of the doomed civilization to a new life in exile. The cycle ended with the king's death and burial, and in the profound sadness displayed on the faces of the anonymous mourners, she saw written the final doom of Atlantis. She didn't need to be psychic to know that the refugee city had not survived long following the death of that last king.

Remembering the purpose for her hasty descent, she turned at last to the altar at the center.

The stone pedestal stood on an upraised podium directly beneath the aperture. What she had first taken to be an object on display, she now saw was actually a fixed part of the altar, an irregular tableau with a recessed, ring-shaped groove at the center. There seemed little question that the niche was meant to display the crown, but the headpiece was conspicuously absent. Frowning, she glanced about the room, and only then realized that there was no other means of entering or leaving the tomb.

She was trapped.

Panic washed over her and with it a surge of adrenaline. She had never experienced fear on this level. Her preternatural intuition had always provided ample warning of dangerous situations long before they reached a critical stage, but that sensory organ had been muted by . . . by whatever it was that she was supposed to find down here.

She took a deep breath, remembering how her abilities had guided her here in the first place. There had to be a way in and out of this chamber. Atlas knew it, and when she had been on the upper levels, she had known it as well.

When I've got what I came for, the way out of here will be obvious, she told herself. Then she laughed as she realized that this was probably how all those gamblers felt as they put their last chip on the table. An all-or-nothing bet. . . . Luck, be a lady tonight. *No, it's nothing like that. I was meant to be here. Something called me here. That's what I need to focus on.*

It was the crown. It had to be.

She turned back to the upright sarcophagus, looking past the life-like effigy, scanning every inch of its surface for some indication of where the lid had been sealed into place, but found nothing. There was no way to open the tomb. Frustrated, she hammered her fists against the unyielding stone and was rewarded only with a dull pain in the heels of her hands.

Think! It brought you here; it wants to be found. There has to be a way.

Willing herself into a state of calm, she attempted something she had never before tried; there had never been reason for it. With her eyes closed and her breathing deep and steady, she attempted to reawaken her quiescent sixth sense. Whether or not it worked, she could not say, but after a few moments, it dawned on her to look for some kind of mechanism.

She returned her attention to the sarcophagus, now using her fingertips as well as her eyes to search for the trigger that would unlock the ancient casket. As she did so, she realized the answer was staring her in the face.

The crown.

Or rather, the carved likeness of the crown that adorned the face of the statue. She reached up to the hexagonal shape in the center and pressed firmly.

There was a grating sound followed by a whoosh of air, and the entire block of carved stone began to move, sliding down into the floor. She took a step back and then directed her light into the depths within.

"You don't look anything like your pictures," she muttered as the beam illuminated the mummified remains of the Atlantean king. Indeed, the handsome, athletic figure had become merely a leathery, discolored shell. His skin had dried out and was stretched taut over his skeleton. His strong nose had shrunk into his skull. And where once he had gazed out at the world with intense dark eyes, there were now only empty sockets. There was one element, however, that remained consistent: the mummy still wore the silvery circlet with its single strange jewel.

Breathless with anticipation, Mira reached for the crown. . .
.

Time abruptly jumped forward—how far she could not say—but in that lost bubble of memory, everything changed. She was no longer standing before the remains of the king, but instead lay supine in near total darkness. An instant later, pain stabbed through her skull, and was especially intense in the area just behind her right ear. When she gingerly probed the spot, her fingers felt something damp—her own blood.

A light flared off to one side and she reflexively turned toward it, wincing as the motion brought another throb from her wound. She fumbled for her own light, still turned on but hanging uselessly from the neck-chain, and raised it just as Curtis Lancet burst through a breach in the tomb wall. The opening had not been there before, she was certain of that. Someone had opened it from the outside, the same person that had cold-cocked her from behind. And if Lancet was only now arriving, that meant . . .

She twisted around just in time to catch sight of Atlas' grotesquely fat fingers closing around the mummy's neck.

"I promised you this day would come." His words were for the ghost of the king alone. He was oblivious to everything else. "My hands at your throat once more, but this time, I will triumph. The Trinity is mine."

Through the fog of pain, something clicked in Mira's mind, and she realized why the figure struggling with the king in the mural looked so familiar. *Atlas! But that must have been thousands of years ago.*

For just a moment, Mira thought she saw the mummy's hands start to move, as if to wrestle free from Atlas' grasp. *No,* she told herself. *It's just an illusion, caused by Atlas shaking him.*

Sputtering with maniacal laughter, the obese billionaire wrenched the corpse's head from its torso, letting the lifeless body fall back into the sarcophagus. He cradled the severed head to his chest and pried off the crown. As his fingers made contact with the metal circle, the jewel flared to life, filling the tomb with penetrating supernatural radiance.

"What the hell?" gasped Lancet, staring in disbelief at the unfolding apotheosis. His gaze then dropped to where Mira lay, and as he spied the fresh blood streaming from the gash on the back of her head, his visage grew hard. With one hand raised to shade his eyes from the quasi-solar discharge, he wrestled his pistol from its holster and raised it toward the man he was sworn to protect. "I don't know what the hell's going on here, sir, but I think you'd better put that thing down."

Atlas' eyes showed not even a whisper of fear as he regarded his bodyguard. "Mr. Lancet," he said, barely able to enunciate through his laughter, "your services are no longer required."

Mira didn't need a premonition to know what would happen next. "Curtis, run!"

Her warning came too late.

A spear of brilliant light burst from the crystal and sizzled through the tomb, blasting Lancet back and pinning him to the wall. His gun was knocked from his hand and clattered impotently to the floor. Though it took only an instant for him to die, his agony seemed to stretch out into eternity.

Mira gasped in horror as her friend, her lover, the only man for whom she had ever dared to let herself feel more than just infatuation, was ripped from existence. But in that moment she felt no grief. That would come later.

With cat-like grace, she rolled under the still crackling tongue of energy. Her fingers closed on the discarded SIG, and in a single fluid motion, she brought it up in a one-handed grip, aimed and fired.

During the weeks they had been together, Lancet had decided to teach her how to shoot his pistol. She had smiled demurely and accepted his offer simply because it made him happy to teach her things and she had very much enjoyed pleasing him. She never let on that she already knew at least as much about firearms, weapons and unarmed combat as he did. Mira had been trained by the best, and for more years than she cared to remember, had been shaped and honed, physically, mentally and psychically into an unparalleled living weapon.

She had given up that life, but some things you never forgot.

A lone nine-millimeter round from the Swiss-made automatic split the air, a microsecond ahead of the thunderous report. Compared to the supernatural light-energy Atlas wielded the bullet was ponderously slow, but it moved faster than he could react.

The six-sided crystal did not shatter as the ballistic projectile slammed into it, but the blazing fire within was instantly extinguished.

Despite the sudden darkness, Mira remained poised to fire again, but the heavy thud of Atlas' corpulent form hitting the stone floor told her that her first shot had done the job.

Nevertheless, it was a long time before she lowered the gun.

After the blinding radiance of the strange crown it took her eyes several minutes to recover to the point where she could make anything out in the comparatively dim glow of the squeeze light. Yet, even before her vision returned, she discovered that another of her senses had fully reawakened.

Atlas was dead, a shapeless blob of flesh, soiled in his own filth. When her bullet had struck the crystal, the force had been sufficient to deflect the talisman away without significantly affecting the trajectory of the round which, as luck would have it, passed through the billionaire's left eye. The fat bastard might have somehow survived for thousands of years after losing his confrontation with the Atlantean ruler, but evidently he wasn't immune to lead poisoning.

She felt no sense of victory. Curtis was dead. Only a charred, vaguely human outline remained, burned into the middle of one of the mural scenes. Lancet had been erased from existence, and when all the extraneous details were stripped away, the whole thing was her fault. Without her help, Atlas would never have found the tomb or unleashed that unholy power. And she had been so blind to his fundamental nature; how could she have missed it? Had the thrill of hunting something so completely lost to human knowledge blunted her keen intuition?

The price for her failure felt unbearable.

She brushed away the tears and shone her light on the newly opened passage leading back into the temple maze. A section of the wall had slid down into the floor, just like the lid of the sarcophagus, to reveal a secret exit. For all she knew, they might have opened at the same time, both triggered when she had activated the mechanism. It felt like one more accusation leveled against her.

As she took a step toward the doorway, her foot struck something on the floor and sent it skittering ahead of her.

It was the crown. What had Atlas has called it? The Trinity.

She knelt and reached for it, and as she did, something indefinable whispered in her consciousness.

The strange circlet was unquestionably the source of the

power that had drawn her all the way from the tomb of Storm Jaguar in Honduras—perhaps even from that first encounter with Atlas' codex. It was silent now, but was it truly dead?

Would it awaken for her as it had for Atlas? As it had for the Atlantean king? And if so, what would she become?

Her fingers closed on the cool metal.

Nothing. It was dead. She sensed nothing from it but the memory of a great power, lost forever, just like the ancient civilization that had brought it into being.

Mira stuffed the Trinity into one of her cargo pockets and began the long trek back to the surface.

PART ONE
SINGULARITY

ONE

New York City, Six months later

Walter Aimes sat patiently in the spacious interior of the limousine, saying nothing until Mira was seated across from him and the chauffeur had closed the door. She was grateful for his forbearance. Climbing into the low-slung vehicle, wearing the skintight, full-length sheath dress and three-inch sling-back stiletto heels was, she discovered, more complicated than crawling around the Atlantean temple. She had discovered the hard way the danger of catching a heel in the hem of the dress, which in addition to tripping her up, posed the added threat of revealing even more of her décolletage to passers-by. The strapless gown already showed off just about all that she could legally get away with.

She had not chosen the dress to advertise her body, but neither did she now experience any degree of self-consciousness. It simply wasn't in her nature to worry overmuch about what sort of impression she would make with her physical appearance. The gown, bought off the rack at Bloomingdale's that afternoon, had more or less been a random selection. She was too preoccupied to stress over her wardrobe choices.

I do look pretty good in it though, she thought as she caught a last glimpse of her reflection in the side window.

Once seated, she looked over at Aimes' smiling face. If the older man was entertaining any lewd fantasies, he did not allow them to taint the humor in his eyes. "Mira," he sighed, approvingly, "you look like a princess."

"I don't think I'm cut out for royalty. All this publicity is driving me nuts. They've turned me into some kind of pop star."

The older man chuckled. "You are a star, tonight at least, and you deserve to be put on a pedestal. You've rewritten the history of our planet."

It was an odd conversation, uncharacteristic of the man she

had known virtually all her life. Her earliest memory was of a much younger Dr. Aimes visiting her in a foster home, interviewing her for the program. Even then, he had always had a friendly, avuncular disposition, and she had never sensed even the slightest duplicity from him. At the same time, he had always held her at a distance; he could not be the father she never had, and he wasn't going to permit her any illusions to that effect. For him to lavish praise on her now . . . it just didn't seem like the Walter Aimes she knew.

Because she had never really known the sort of life that people called "normal," it was only in hindsight that she saw the true nature of their relationship. She had always been his lab rat, a well-tended specimen to be sure, but always a lab rat.

Back then, Aimes had been a behavioral psychologist working under contract with the government, combing the child welfare system looking for dispossessed children who exhibited a certain range of unusual abilities. At five years of age, Mira had displayed exactly the aptitudes he'd been looking for, and within a few weeks of discovering her, she had been relocated to a farm—"The Farm," as everyone called it—in rural Virginia, where she was subjected to a regimented and insulated, albeit pleasant, existence. Aimes was a frequent visitor to the Farm, and really the only link to her previous life, but his role in her upbringing—in her schooling and training and the endless tests she had been subjected to—was, from her perspective at least, incidental.

As she grew to maturity, her future path in life became clear. She would have the privilege of using her unique abilities in the defense of her country against the evils of communism. From her trainers and instructors she sensed only an absolute certainty of purpose, and there had never been any cause to doubt the fundamental rightness of the cause in which she had been enlisted. But when she went into the field, exposed for the first time to the complexities of the real world, seeing the human struggle not as a Manichean battle between good and evil, light and darkness, but in all its varying shades of gray, she had proved to be a spectacular failure.

Aimes, ever her guardian, had managed to convince the

Agency that she could be salvaged, so they shunted her to the research and development section, where people with similar endowments were being trained for long-distance psychic surveillance—"remote viewing" they called it. But soon thereafter the Cold War had ended, and the Agency, under intense political scrutiny, disbanded the entire department. Virtually turned out onto the street, Mira had once more looked to her protector, Walter Aimes.

Even then, he had not allowed her to make him a father figure. He did not take her into his home—though in a weak, tearful moment, she had all but begged him to—did not give her money or a place to live or help her find suitable employment. But in a way, he had given her exactly what she needed when he had calmly suggested that she could use her precognitive talents to make a very comfortable life for herself. And she had done exactly that, first in Atlantic City, and then in Vegas. It wasn't a special, exciting, or even particularly meaningful life, but it was her own. There was no agency claiming ownership of her, no constant supervision or endless testing and training; she was her own person. And, ultimately, it had led to this, arguably the most important discovery in human history.

When she had crawled out of the temple, still bloodied from Atlas' betrayal, she had instinctively known to call on her former benefactor.

With Aimes both coaching and shielding her, she took the discovery public. The trustees of Atlas' estate were eager to keep the scandalous nature of his demise forever buried—she had told no one of the possibility that he might have been a centuries-old survivor of Atlantis—and they had provided the legal and logistical means to launch a more professional exploration of the ruin. In the months that followed, the academic world had been turned on its ear as the site yielded an endless trove of treasure and knowledge about a period previously relegated to prehistory.

For her part, Mira finally felt that she had discovered her niche. Though she was not classically trained as an archaeologist, her intuition, and perhaps more importantly, her dogged determination, kept her always in the forefront of the ongoing exploration.

Meanwhile, back in the civilized world, Walter Aimes had also found a new purpose in life.

The limousine slowed as traffic around Central Park grew thick. A banner hung from the stone battlements of the museum, draping the entire distance from the roof over the fourth story to just above the windows of the ground level. In gilt letters, against a scarlet background, it announced the exhibit's opening.

"'Treasures of Lost Atlantis'?" Mira shook her head disparagingly.

Aimes gave a guilty smile. "I know it's a bit over the top, but it's not completely inaccurate. Some of the pieces in the collection really do seem to have been carried away from Atlantis after its untimely demise. And then of course there's the Trinity. . . ."

"Don't remind me," she replied, unable to hide a scowl.

"Mira, I know that you are worried about the Trinity, but I swear to you, there is no cause for alarm."

"Marquand Atlas tried to use the thing to turn himself into a god. And he very nearly succeeded. What makes you so certain that somebody won't try to follow in his footsteps?"

"I know you believe that the Trinity is a talisman of great power, but it's dead now. The damage to the crystal cannot be repaired by any technology known to man. There is simply no way for anyone to unleash its power as Atlas tried to do."

"But what's to stop someone from trying? Museum security? That's a joke. The Trinity is a very tempting target. I wish you'd taken my warning more seriously." She felt a twinge of excitement at having the temerity to reprove Aimes, but it was just as quickly extinguished by a childish guilt at having talked back to a parent.

The limousine pulled to a stop and the driver hopped out. Aimes waited for Mira to get out before answering from the shelter of the car. "The Trinity is the highlight of the collection." His voice was the soothing tone of a politician. "It is what will bring the crowds; the most precious artifact of the prehistoric world. The power of the god-kings of Atlantis, and it's right here in the Big Apple."

She didn't answer. It was already an old argument. Months of negotiations between the American Museum of Natural History, Aimes, the Atlas Trust, represented by Mira herself, and even the United Nations Global Heritage Commission, the de facto custodians of the treasure inasmuch as no single modern government could rightfully claim ownership thereof, had ironed out every point of contention but one. Mira knew that her account of the crown relic's supernatural nature would be regarded with amusement and even contempt, but she had nevertheless implored Aimes, the one man who she knew would not be put off by her tale, to find some pretext for removing the Trinity from the collection. But as Aimes had reminded her, the relic had been quiescent, even to her own psychically endowed senses, and there was no real basis for her concern. In the end, the UN, bowing to financial need and political pressure, had agreed to allow the Trinity to tour with the exhibit.

Aimes offered his arm and together they ascended the steps of the museum. The gathering of paparazzi quickly shifted to greet the darling of the exhibit, momentarily mimicking a lightning storm with their camera strobes. Mira kept her displeasure hidden, showing only a wry smile. She didn't like being on display, and she certainly didn't think of herself as a celebrity, but resisted the urge to quicken her steps, knowing that the eighty-one-year-old Aimes would have difficulty keeping up.

As if observing an unseen barrier, the photographers held back at the top step, turning away as Mira and Aimes pushed through the revolving doors. Despite the elite caliber of the guests that would be attending the exhibit, all visitors were required to file through the revolving doors of the museum at the Central Park West entrance, beyond which each had to present their official invitation. Mira waited for Aimes on the other side, and when he stepped out of the slowly turning door, he flashed twin pieces of parchment, stamped with a hologram of the museum's logo. The uniformed guard nodded perfunctorily and ushered them through.

The after-hours party began in the grand foyer of the museum, the Theodore Roosevelt Memorial. Men wearing immaculate tuxedoes and women in extravagant evening gowns were scattered throughout the lobby, sipping from bottomless glasses of champagne and engaging in meaningless gossip. Most of them were present only because they perceived that they were supposed to be there, that it would somehow advance their social standing. Mira found it appalling that she and the treasures of the Atlantean king's tomb were now the latest episode in the great social drama of American culture.

Exerting a gentle tug on Aimes' accompanying arm, she rushed through the lobby toward the elevators, just outside the Hall of North American Mammals.

One of the spacious exhibition halls on the third floor had been painstakingly turned into an enormous diorama of the Tomb of the Unknown King, as they had taken to calling it. As she entered, Mira found the similarities a little too familiar. The designers had done their job well. Thankfully, they had rendered the mural as it had been when she first saw it, and not as it had looked after Atlas incinerated Curtis Lancet.

The artistry, both of the architects of the exhibit and their source material, seemed lost on the crowd of spectators. They were too self-involved to appreciate the significance of the Atlantean king's place in history, which was, in fact, a prologue to all known history.

A cluster of people, who perhaps were not totally immune to the spectacle of what the exhibit represented, gathered around an upraised dais in the center of the hall. Mira knew without looking what was kept there: the Trinity of Atlantis. It was displayed on an enclosed altar that was, but for security measures, an exact replica of the one in the king's tomb. Unlike the tableau she had found, the Trinity had been placed on the altar in an adjoining room, under the constant glare of an overhead high-intensity light bulb and, more importantly, under a thick pane of glass and dozens of other protective mechanisms. Usually she felt a faint tremor in its presence, the ghost of a memory, but tonight, not even that.

Mira guided Aimes forward, past the Trinity, and through a doorway into a replica of the tomb. Passing through the doorway, she felt a tingle of apprehension—*Just bad memories*, she told herself—as she entered the mock vault where the very real mummy was on display.

The vault was empty of visitors, but Mira could feel a presence nevertheless. A perfect replica of the mural, its written narrative only partially decoded, decorated the circular walls. She stepped closer to the half-opened sarcophagus.

"Hello again, old friend," she whispered softly.

The restoration team had succeeded in repairing the damage Atlas had caused, but the ancient king looked incomplete without the circlet.

"A great man," Aimes offered, standing respectfully near the doorway. "Almost lost forever to history. You see there, Mira? He had the Trinity, yet it availed him naught. He could not save Atlantis from the cataclysm that wiped it away and, in the end, died like any other man."

Another figure moved into the crypt, and though the churning sensation in her gut only deepened, Mira did not look away as she responded. "It was the attempted theft of the Trinity that caused the cataclysm that destroyed Atlantis and wiped away nearly every vestige of the pre-historic world. Marquand Atlas might have created a second catastrophe with the same power."

"Power is a tricky thing."

"Power corrupts . . ."

"And absolute power corrupts absolutely. But the Trinity does not represent absolute power. It was merely a tool. And it wasn't enough for him, or for Marquand Atlas—"

A sudden concussion, deafening in the tiny enclosure, caused Mira to jump. It was a noise all too familiar. Whirling around, she dropped into a low, defensive crouch.

Aimes leaned against one wall of the vault, slowly sliding down. The rough sandstone behind him was stained dark red, and a brighter shade of the same color was creeping across the white fabric of his dress shirt.

Mira sprang across the short distance, catching him in her

arms as he fell. He was impossibly light, like a frail skeleton ready to turn to dust in her hands. He opened his mouth, as if to finish the sentence that had died on his lips, but no sound issued. Instead, a stream of crimson flowed from between his teeth, followed by a rattling exhalation. His sightless eyes seemed to lose focus, and Mira knew without feeling for a pulse or listening for a breath that Aimes was gone.

The impossible symmetry of the experience stunned her. Curtis, the first man she had ever dared to love, had died in the real tomb. And now Aimes, the only man she had ever thought of as a father, lay lifeless in a replica of the same.

A shadow fell over her as a half-glimpsed figure moved between her and the source of ambient light. She looked up and saw one of the uniformed security guards, his gun drawn, standing in the doorway as if in response to the shooting.

Her eyes settled on his bland features; a young man with a wispy goatee and tufts of bleached-blonde hair escaping the confines of his patrol cap. His face bore the signs of multiple flesh-piercings, but he had evidently removed the silver studs and hoops for the sake of his job. Her gaze dropped down, past the indigo tattoos on his forearm to the drawn weapon in his fist.

Tendrils of blue smoke drifted from the barrel. The sting of sulfur burned in Mira's nose as realization dawned. Staring into her eyes, the guard saw it too.

As if in slow motion, the gun arm started to rise, coming level with the place where Mira knelt beside the fallen Aimes. But even as the man's cool blue eyes tried to focus on the living target, Mira launched into action.

She crossed the distance to the guard in a single leap. In the split second before springing at the shooter, she had slipped out of her high-heeled shoes, leaving the left one behind and gripping the other in her right hand. With almost the same motion, she hiked the confining evening gown up to her thighs, allowing her greater freedom of movement. Both actions were instinctive, decisions reached and executed in an instant that was stretched out of proportion by the adrenaline coursing through her veins.

As the guard started to exert pressure on the trigger of the snub-nose .38 revolver, Mira struck. The metal tipped heel of her shoe slashed across his forearm like the sting of a scorpion, knocking the gun hand aside as the weapon discharged, the bullet striking the solid stone of the sarcophagus, chipping away a divot of rock the size of a quarter. Mira's attack drew blood, and the guard let out a surprised yelp of pain.

Though he outweighed her by a good fifty pounds, the momentum of her follow-through charge was concentrated in the leading corner of her shoulder, and she slammed into him like a sledgehammer, driving the breath from his lungs in a whoosh.

It ended with both of them sprawling forward into the Trinity room, where a stunned audience was only beginning to comprehend that an act of violence had occurred in their midst. The human sea parted as both Mira and the assassin crashed onto the floor and slid toward the dais where the relic was displayed.

The guard thrashed on the ground, ineffectually grabbing at his chest. Mira did not relent in her attack; the man was a killer, and she was not about to let him regain the advantage. She chopped down across his throat with the edge of her hand.

A collective gasp passed through the spectators, followed by pandemonium. Mira could pick out one or two of the more strident observers and instantly divined their importance. The assassin was not working alone.

She looked up through the tumult of frantically fleeing aristocracy to see the second gunman. He stood at the entrance to the exhibit, wearing a tuxedo and was, but for one small detail, indistinguishable from the high society guests. That detail, however, was significant. Cradled in his hands was an Ingram MAC-10 light machine pistol. As the business end of the firearm swung toward Mira it began to spit flame, and chaos ensued.

Ducking low, Mira pulled the prone form of the ersatz guard over her as a shield. Right away she felt the impact of rounds punching into his flesh.

Thrusting the fatally wounded assassin forward, she rolled

away, behind the cover of the Trinity altar. Something hard struck her in the small of the back, followed by a blast of cold. Fearing the worst, she flipped around to confront this new threat.

She found herself facing a young man crouched on the ground with his face against his knees and his hands covering his head. His white jacket and gloves identified him as one of the waiters, and only then did Mira realize that the cold spreading across her back was from the champagne that had spilled when the hapless young man had dropped his tray. The silver platter lay upside down beside him, along with the fragments of several shattered champagne flutes. Mira's eyes fixed on the tray and inspiration dawned.

In a fluid motion she snatched up the serving disc and rolled back into the open. The tuxedoed assassin was firing the machine pistol in short bursts at the ceiling, frightening the crowd and fanning the flames of confusion. When he saw her move out from cover, he brought the gun down, ready to finish her off.

Like an ancient Greek discus thrower, Mira hurled the tray. The platter spun through the air like a flying saucer as it flashed across the room, a streak of light reflecting from its polished surface, and struck home. The edge of the tray smacked into the tuxedoed gunman, catching him at the bridge of the nose. He flew backward, arms windmilling, and the gun slipped from his fingers. Mira was already sprinting after him, intent on seizing the weapon before he could recover.

The man fell back against the wall, but quickly recovered his equilibrium and crouched into a fighting stance to meet her second charge. Blood gushed from the wound on his face, yet neither the pain nor the hemorrhaging seemed to sap his ferocity. Mira feinted with her right hand, but as the man raised his fist to block, she dropped to one knee and knocked the man's legs out from under him with a sweep of her right foot. As he crashed heavily to the floor, her fist, followed by her elbow, hammered across his jaw. The double-strike repeated twice more, throwing up a spray of blood that stained the carpet and the wall of the exhibit. She was prepared to continue raining blows on the defeated man, but his head lolled off to the side, indicating that further punishment would serve only as a vent for her rage.

She leaned back on her haunches, faintly aware of how gruesomely ridiculous she probably looked: streaked with the blood of three men, her dress hiked up around her thighs and barefoot. It was doubtless something the Manhattan elite would discuss over cocktails for many months to come. She grinned triumphantly for the benefit of the many shocked onlookers and brushed a stray wisp of hair away from her face.

A sudden explosion of gunfire brought her to her feet. Although the source was not readily visible, the spectators were again scattering. Mira snatched the fallen MAC-10 off the floor. Smoke still curled from its muzzle as she ejected the ammo clip into her hand. It felt light; she reckoned less than a third of the load remained. With a grimace, she shoved the magazine back into the pistol. A quick search of the man's jacket produced two full magazines of nine-millimeter ammunition for the weapon.

"That's more like it," she murmured. With nowhere on her person to stow the magazines, she would have to hold them in her hands while firing the gun; an awkward arrangement, but preferable to running out of ammo after a short volley.

The gunfire seemed to originate from the direction of the Reptile and Amphibians exhibit, part of the museum's standing collection. She had once thought it an odd segue from dioramas of stuffed lizards and frogs to the tomb of an Atlantean king; now she thought of it only as a battlefield.

She inserted herself into the flow of fleeing spectators. A few steps beyond the mock-up of the tomb she found the shooters. Two men, dressed in the uniforms of a hired security service, wielded machine pistols identical to the one she had liberated from the tuxedoed assassin. They fired short bursts into the air, shattering light fixtures and ripping apart the acoustic tiles to create a rain of debris and pandemonium that scattered the guests. Though the objective of their rampage was lost on Mira, her response to their actions was unequivocal.

"Everybody down!"

Somehow, her shout pierced even the decibel level of

gunfire. The high-society guests, already in a frenzy, did not question her authority. Mira's field of view cleared immediately. The two bogus security guards lowered their weapons in momentary confusion, then their eyes locked on Mira.

About sixty feet separated Mira from the two shooters. It was too great a distance for conversation or negotiation. Mira did not even attempt to shout for the men to surrender. Yet, from where they stood, suddenly confronted by the blood streaked warrior goddess opposing them, both men could see her left eyebrow arch ever so slightly, a harbinger of their fate if they elected to fight her. They slowly turned to each other and, in a silent melding of minds, reached their decision together.

They ran.

Cursing under her breath, Mira sprinted across the Hall of Reptiles and Amphibians. She winced visibly when a shard of broken glass slashed her bare foot, but did not slow her pace.

The two guards cut left and dashed for the marble stairs outside the gallery. Mira exited the hall in time to see their retreating backs on the descending flight. She fired a blind burst over the balustrade, then took off after them.

Their lead was too great. They would be able to muscle through the frightened guests and gain the exit before she could catch them. As her feet hit the mid-point landing, she gripped the railing with her left hand and swung her hips onto it.

The fabric of her dress created almost no friction as she slid down the banister at a speed approaching free fall. She hit the second floor and somersaulted out of what would otherwise have been a headlong crash, coming up with the gun ready. The sound of footsteps on the stairs below was audible in the sudden quiet. Mira again flung herself onto the descending rail and slid after them.

The fleeing shooters reached the first floor in that instant. Mira saw them darting toward the Theodore Roosevelt Memorial Hall and brought her MAC-10 to bear. Two quick, three-round bursts splashed in the path of the fleeing guards. Hot brass blasted from the sliding mechanism and flew back at her, burning the exposed skin of her shoulders, but the pain barely registered on her battle-heightened senses.

The two men stumbled over each other, then quickly reversed and headed back into the museum. Mira chased them with bullets as she completed her slide, hearing the clank as the pistol's open bolt mechanism slammed shut on an empty firing chamber. She rolled off the railing, ejecting the spent clip as she stood, and slammed one of the spare magazines into the butt of the weapon.

Gunfire erupted from the Hall of North American Mammals. Bright muzzle-flashes scorched the air from within the dimly lit exhibit, forcing Mira to dive behind the wall near the entrance. She worked the slide action, chambering a round, then stuck the MAC-10 around the edge and squeezed the trigger. The gun jumped in her hand, unleashing three rounds at random. She fired again, but her foes did not answer with a return volley.

Nine-millimeter Parabellum slugs from three different machine pistols had savaged the display of North American wildlife. Animals felled by hunters' rifles decades before were wounded afresh, their hides torn with broken glass and stray bullets. The display windows were scattered in fragments across the floor.

They know I'm barefoot. They did this on purpose.

Mira moved with quick caution through the ruined exhibit, placing her feet down carefully, but still at a pace that could easily be considered a sprint. She reached the far end, a display corridor lined with dioramas of small mammals, just in time to see the blue shirt of one of the guards flash around a corner. When she reached that bend, she almost died.

The guards had split up. One of them had turned left, heading down an empty gallery toward the main entrance facing 77th Street, where an enormous, authentic Native American boat dominated the lobby. The other guard had continued straight, toward the IMAX theatre. After taking only a few steps toward those destinations however, both men turned, waiting to catch her in the crossfire.

Mira had no time to think and barely even a moment to react. She threw herself flat, diving into the gallery where the first shooter stood. Though she was removed from the line of fire of his companion, she was completely visible to this man. Thinking that he had the advantage, the guard walked a constant stream of automatic fire toward the place where Mira lay prone.

Bullets stitched the carpeted floor and ricocheted harmlessly back into the corridor. Mira rolled away from the barrage, trying in vain to bring her own weapon up against the shooter. All of a sudden, the incoming gunfire ceased. She did not hesitate.

A three-round burst took the guard in the chest, knocking him backward. Mira was up in an instant and crossed the distance to where the fallen guard lay, his smoking, empty weapon still clutched in his out-flung right hand. Spent brass cartridges were strewn all around him, an epitaph to his poor shooting skills. She added the man's remaining magazine to her own supply, then darted back toward the corridor.

There was no sign of the other shooter. She ran past the doors to the IMAX auditorium, toward the site of the closed Eskimo exhibit, expecting at any moment to be fired upon, but found nothing. He had somehow evaded her.

Not satisfied with that conclusion, she backtracked. The assassin could not have slipped past her. That meant he had either ducked into the Northwest Coast Indians exhibit or into the IMAX Theater.

She stood at the intersection, weighing both options. If the man had gone into the exhibit, then she had truly lost him. He would already be on the street, outside the museum, and probably in a waiting getaway car. Although that choice made the most sense, something about it didn't seem right.

Four men had contributed to the night's mayhem: three wearing the uniforms of security guards and one posing as a guest.

"Why?" she muttered to herself.

The first gunman had boldly killed Aimes right in front of her. The second man was conceivably his back-up, ready to shoot the place up in order to cover the first gunman's escape. It wasn't a bad plan, just poorly executed.

Why had the other two men entered the fray? With both

assassins down, they could have simply slipped away. Instead, they had chosen to fight, leading Mira on a wild chase through the museum. Something wasn't adding up.

"The Trinity," she gasped. Of course. It made perfect sense. The running gun battle had been a diversion, drawing both her and everyone else away from the real target of the scheme.

Without further consideration she pushed through the doors of the auditorium, ready to fire. Only floor lights on the ends of the aisles illuminated the theatre, but she could still distinguish the ornate facade along the walls and the towering sixty-foot-high projection screen.

She strode directly toward the screen, her gaze weaving back and forth in case the gunman was concealed in one of the rows of auditorium seats, waiting for a chance to spring up and fire.

When the edge of the balcony was directly overhead, she executed a shoulder-roll and came up facing the rear of the auditorium. She brought the MAC-10 up, sweeping it back and forth across the balcony, searching for a target, then whirled back to the screen. She double-checked the balcony again, hopping backwards down the aisle.

The theater was empty.

The trail was growing colder by the second. Mira believed she knew where the gunman was headed, but there were too many variables for her to simply double-back to the Trinity sanctuary. She had to follow the man's footsteps, surprise him from behind.

She turned down one of the rows of chairs, walking sideways with her eyes always darting into the shadows. She still half-believed that the assassin would spring up at any instant, catching her unaware with a burst of nine-millimeter rounds.

There was a good chance that the man had secreted himself in one of the two stairwells on either side of the theater, leading to the balcony. If she chose the wrong one, she would be dead before she even realized her mistake. Glancing up at the balcony, a better idea dawned.

She climbed up on the back of a seat positioned directly

beneath the balcony and launched herself straight up, pitching the machine pistol and its spare magazine over the rail, and in the same motion caught the balcony rail in her outstretched hands. She swung her legs up and managed to hook one foot on the banister, from where she had little difficulty heaving herself over.

Bullets glanced off the railing in a shower of sparks to Mira's left as she dropped onto the balcony floor. Upholstery stuffing and splinters of wood and plastic showered her as she crouched down to grope for the gun. She crept left, trusting that the gunman would expect her to move away from his line of fire.

Another burst tore up the seats on Mira's right. She popped up and swept across the back of the balcony with a steady stream of gunfire. The assassin swiveled toward her position, forcing her to duck back down, but two of her blindly fired rounds struck him in the abdomen. When his pistol emptied, she heard his muted curses and knew that she had drawn blood. She waited for the next burst of gunfire, but heard only the click of a door latch resetting.

Mira straightened her dress, and then sprinted for the exit the guard had used.

She slipped through the door, dove forward and rolled, scanning for a target, and hopped lightly to her feet, ready to fire. The assassin had fled, but a trail of blood spatters marked the path he had chosen. With a triumphant grin, she sprinted after him.

A line of crimson splatters led straight through the Hall of African Mammals toward the flight of stairs that she had used earlier. The drops grew closer together, indicating that the man was slowing, perhaps fatally wounded, but still out of her visual range. The marble steps were similarly marked with bright red; the injured man had ascended to the next flight.

She charged up the stairs, taking two at a time, but maintained constant readiness to fire. Although she expected the trail to lead back into the Atlantean exhibit, the splashes of blood continued around the bend and up the flight of stairs leading to the fourth floor. She could hear his labored breathing and footsteps echoing down the stairwell, almost lost in the cacophony of noise from sirens and shouting rising up from below.

At the fourth-floor landing, she discovered that her quarry had jumped the rope barrier and continued upward, toward the roof. Genuinely perplexed, she charged up the final flight, catching a glimpse of the roof access door swinging shut. Moments later she burst through that door onto the roof of the museum.

The city noise was sudden and almost overwhelming. The thick stone walls of the museum had effectively insulated her from the almost constant orchestra of honking horns, police sirens and screeching tires. But there was another element to the melody, a deep bass tone that was far more immediate.

The imposter guard was still on his feet, but only just. Mira could tell by his aimless staggering that he was not long for the world. Yet the goal toward which he was moving was all too apparent. Fifty yards from the access door, a Bell 206-B JetRanger III helicopter rested on the roof, its rotor blades beating the air with a noise that hammered at her gut and all but overwhelmed the sounds of the city.

Two barely visible figures occupied the aircraft. One of them was female, her head capped by an extraordinary mane of blonde hair. The other was a man, a hulking figure with a shaved head. Mira inferred that the woman was piloting the craft; helicopters, unlike airplanes, had no autopilot and required constant attention, even when sitting on the ground, if the rotor assemblies were engaged. The woman had to be at the controls, because her large companion slid open the door and stepped out of the aircraft, hefting an AK-47 assault rifle.

Mira rolled for cover as 7.62mm rounds chewed up the roof in a deadly stream that quickly curved her way. She leaped into the air, taking herself momentarily higher than the flow of lead, and twisted her body to return fire. The gunman in the helicopter seemed unconcerned as her bullets danced harmlessly off the metal and fiberglass shell of the JetRanger.

Mira hit the rooftop rolling, seeking what little shelter she could from a protruding vent cover. She dove away an instant later as rounds from the Russian-made Kalashnikov shredded the aluminum without even slowing.

Her next barrage from the MAC-10 was only slightly more accurate, but a lucky shot found the interior of the helicopter and got the attention of the pilot. Mira could see her turning to her companion, unrestrained rage clouding what were otherwise beautiful features. Though the large gunman apparently believed himself invincible, the woman did not seem to share the sentiment.

Mira ineffectually emptied the clip at the helicopter. The MAC-10 rounds simply didn't have the muzzle velocity to do much more than scratch the paint at that range. Nevertheless, her unrelenting assault forced the pilot to flee the scene prematurely. While the wounded guard was still twenty feet from the rescue aircraft, the skids lifted from the flat surface, kicking up a sudden windstorm.

The gunman in the JetRanger ceased firing at Mira, giving her a moment to slam the last magazine into the grip of the MAC-10. She got to her feet and, throwing caution to the wind, charged toward the ascending aircraft.

The wounded man took another step forward, a betrayed look mixing with the agony on his countenance. Suddenly, a ragged hole appeared on his forehead as his head snapped back. Mira caught a final glimpse of the gunman in the helicopter. He wore what could almost pass for an expression of grief as he lowered the rifle after administering the coup de grace to his comrade. Then the airframe swiveled beneath the rotors and he was lost from her view. The helicopter turned ninety degrees on its central axis as it moved forward over Central Park.

Despite the sheer futility of the gesture, Mira could not simply stand by and watch as the last two members of the murderous conspiracy fled the scene. She charged to the edge of the rooftop, emptying the captured weapon with surprising, but impotent, accuracy. A frustrated howl escaped from between her clenched teeth as the MAC-10 spoke for the last time and the final bullet sparked harmlessly against the whirling tail rotor blades.

The running lights of the JetRanger shrank into the

shadows of the park, the beat of its rotors similarly fading. A moment later, the sound of footsteps on the roof behind her indicated that a new potential threat had arrived.

The shout from behind her was authoritative, but there was no concealing the undercurrent of uncomprehending panic. "Drop the weapon."

Without turning, Mira extended her arm and let the empty gun fall to roof.

TWO

Detective Michelangelo DiLorenzo looked across the table at the woman in custody. Beneath a mane of cropped, spiky auburn hair, her brown eyes, like chocolate mixed with honey, matched his gaze, a piercing stare, from which he was forced to look away after a moment. He fumbled with his papers in an attempt to appear nonchalant.

"Miss Raiden—Mira—May I call you Mira?"

"Whatever."

DiLorenzo raised an eyebrow. "Well, Mira. I want to apologize for having kept you here so long." He gestured to the bleak environs of the interview room. "As you can imagine, we had a lot of people to interview in order to get some idea of what happened last night."

He waited, watching her eyes for some hint of how to proceed. Mira stared back coolly, saying nothing. She still wore the black evening gown, torn and streaked with dust, though her feet were bare. DiLorenzo knew that she had been waiting in the interview room for nearly six hours, yet had not succumbed to irrational antics of the caged. She had not even asked for a bathroom break. Instead, she had merely sat quietly, meditatively, refusing to be "softened up."

"Well?"

DiLorenzo started, as if waking from a daydream. "Pardon me?"

"Were you going to ask something, or just keep staring?"

He chuckled nervously, glancing behind him at the one-way glass through which his partner was doubtless observing the interrogation. "I'll ask the questions when I'm ready," he said, realizing as the words escaped his lips, how foolish he sounded. She was getting to him and he hated it; there was no place for feelings like that in police work.

"Let me know when you *are* ready."

DiLorenzo's cheeks flared red in embarrassment. He saw

her full lips curl ever so slightly at the ends, a smile at his expense. "Right. Okay, Mira, we've talked to everybody that survived last night's little brouhaha at the museum, and they all agree about one thing. You killed two men."

Her smile slowly melted away and DiLorenzo found himself regretting that he had initiated its disappearance. Mira waited several seconds before speaking a single syllable. "And?"

"What?"

"You keep making statements, detective. I'm not quite sure how I ought to respond."

DiLorenzo sighed in exasperation. "Miss Raiden. Would you like to tell me your version of what transpired last night? Please?"

"Since you used the magic word . . ." Mira's smile returned, but now it was merely a polite smile. She started talking, recounting the events at the museum, starting with the moment she and Aimes had entered the exhibit and ending with the disappearance of the helicopter over the park.

When she finished, he glanced back at the first page of his notes. "Okay. Back up a second. It sounds like Aimes was the target here."

"I agree. Whatever else they hoped to accomplish, assassinating Walter was their first priority."

The detective maintained a neutral expression, having composed himself during the long narrative. She was, after all, the suspect in a shooting spree that would likely occupy headlines for weeks to come, not some girl in a bar that he was trying to impress. Although he couldn't simply turn off the emotions that the sight of her stirred in him, nor suppress the bio-chemicals that were responsible for that reaction, he was a professional; he knew how to deal with it. "But you think they were also after this Trinity?"

"The Trinity is an immensely powerful artifact. People will kill for it."

"Hmm." He tapped his pen against his notepad. "Why is it called a 'Trinity'? I saw a picture of it, and there's nothing triune about it. I'm Roman Catholic, I know a thing or two about the real Trinity."

SEAN ELLIS | 52

"That's what they called it in Atlantis. The concept of triune godheads is much older than your Christian religion, detective. Perhaps something about this powerful talisman implanted the concept of worshipping trinities into the collective unconscious."

"You keep talking about how powerful it is. What the hell is this thing anyway?"

Mira shrugged. "From what we can tell, it was created several thousands of years ago by a race of superior humans—"

"Superior?" DiLorenzo knew it was irrelevant to the investigation, but he was curious in spite of himself.

"Their technological advancement makes our progress seem pitiful by comparison. They were on the brink of evolving into a new level of existence. The Trinity may have been the key to that leap forward."

"I don't get it. What does this thing do?"

"No one has been able to explain how it worked, but my theory is that it could amplify the thoughts of its user. It could literally do almost anything that the person possessing it wanted."

"You mean like turning lead into gold or something?"

Mira chuckled dismissively. "That would be a trifle. A person controlling the Trinity could easily manipulate the elements, but that's only the tip of the iceberg. The Trinity could make a person virtually immortal."

DiLorenzo raised a skeptical eyebrow, but did not pursue the issue. "So, you think that what happened last night was also a bungled robbery attempt? That they were really after this Trinity?"

She shifted in her chair, pausing thoughtfully. "Those men were professionals—mercenaries. A single sniper could have killed Walter at any time. They were definitely after the Trinity. You should take immediate steps to secure it. It must be removed from the exhibit."

It was the detective's turn to laugh. "No need for that. Thanks to you, the exhibit is closed indefinitely. Besides, you're getting ahead of yourself. By your own admission you killed a man last night. That doesn't count the one that was apparently finished off by his buddy on the helicopter. You've got other things to worry about."

"You can't be serious." Mira's tone was incredulous, but she did not appear as concerned as the detective had hoped she would. At this point in the interview, suspects were usually fidgeting nervously, or begging for their lawyers. "That was clearly a case of self-defense."

DiLorenzo smiled like a serpent, poised to strike. "Well, that's not up to me—"

He was interrupted by a terse knock at the door, which opened a crack, and a head peaked in. "Mike, could I have a word?"

DiLorenzo's eyes rolled back in annoyance at the interruption; Winslow should have known better. He brought his facial expression back under control and stood, his arms crossed over his chest. "This will only take a minute. Don't go anywhere."

Mira denied him the pleasure of a sarcastic retort and simply folded her own arms, to better advantage than he, and remained silent. DiLorenzo sighed, perturbed, and headed for the door.

Mira remained motionless, a regal sphinx awaiting the detective's return. Almost as soon as he was through the doorway, shouting was audible from the hallway. DiLorenzo's voice was not the only one in the argument, but it was the loudest. The wait was mercifully short. A few seconds later, the door virtually exploded open and a clearly irritated detective stormed into the interview room. His face was a mask of barely controlled rage through which a tight, but by no means contrite, voice escaped.

"Thank you for your assistance, Ms. Raiden. You're free to go."

Mira couldn't resist taking a jab at the detective's wounded ego. "Just like that? No bright lights and torture?"

DiLorenzo actually seemed to soften, as if trying to convey that she was not the focus of his ire. Though his words still burned with acid, Mira got the impression that he was speaking for the benefit of those listening over the intercom. "It seems that the politician elected to be our District Attorney was at the gala last night, and he feels that your actions were justified, or at least that it would not be politically expedient to pursue a case against you. Like I said, it's not up to me. As far as I'm concerned, you committed a crime last night."

Mira rocked forward slightly. It wasn't an entirely unexpected development. Indeed, the shootings had been completely justified, and it irked her to be counted with the real villains of the previous night. But there was no longer any point in stating her case, and she didn't have the energy to expend in such a futile endeavor. She rose from the hard chair, determined not to let the detective see how tired and sore she was, and walked with determined steps toward the door, ignoring the stinging pain that burned in the cut on her bare foot. The door seemed to open of its own volition as she approached.

She paused on the threshold. "If you want my opinion detective, you've spent the last several hours investigating the wrong crime."

DiLorenzo continued to face the empty chair where she had been sitting. "Thanks, Ms. Raiden. But I don't want your opinion."

Mira shrugged, then pushed past a heavyset man in a stained dress-shirt hovering near the door. He regarded her with a contemptuous leer but said nothing. While she was still within earshot, he entered the interview room. "'If you want my opinion . . .'" His attempt at mimicking Mira was hopelessly thwarted by his Bronx upbringing. "Can you believe the nerve of that bitch?"

DiLorenzo turned to his partner, resignation overcoming his earlier rage. "She's right, Jeff. We're investigating the wrong crime. We should be trying to figure out why someone wanted to whack the doc."

Winslow was taken aback. "Okay, smart guy. Where do we start?"

DiLorenzo turned and went to the door. Mira's back was visible as she approached the stairwell leading to the ground floor of the precinct, but he reckoned she could still hear him if he spoke loud enough. "Jen, could you please have a sector car drive Miss Raiden to her hotel. It's the least we can do after inconveniencing her."

"A car?" blustered Winslow. "What, are we running a damn taxi service?"

DiLorenzo shrugged. "If the politicians like her so much, I'm sure they won't mind our using city vehicles to shuttle her around town." He tried to sound sarcastic, but a part of him that he couldn't deny felt something for the tough but nonetheless beautiful woman walking on bloodied feet down the stairs of the precinct station house. And he wished he could do more.

He turned to his partner and tried to put a conspiratorial spin on his act of mercy. "Whoever killed Aimes was after that thing in the exhibit, too. Mira Raiden seems to be the resident expert on it, and whoever did this knows it. I also have a feeling that she won't just let it go. In fact, my gut tells me that if we stay on her, she'll go right to the heart of whatever is going on."

As if by some psychic premonition, the concierge was waiting for Mira with a pair of complimentary hotel issue shower slippers the moment she stepped through the doors into the spacious lobby of the Park Lane Helmsley Hotel. On the surface it seemed like a thoughtful gesture, but the slippers made little or no difference to her bare feet on the carpeted floor, not after walking on the abrasive concrete sidewalks. She suspected that the offer of the footwear had more to do with protecting the hotel carpets than any concern for her personal comfort. She pushed through to the row of elevators without exchanging a word.

Somehow she maintained her unflagging exterior until, at long last, the door of her suite was closed and locked. Only then did she stagger toward the freshly made bed and collapse.

She lay there for a long time, hoping for sleep to steal over her, but her mind would not turn off. In spite of a fatigue that seemed to reach to her very bones, she was jittery.

Rising from the bed, she dragged herself into the bathroom and started drawing a bath in the Jacuzzi tub. She turned the hot tap until the water temperature was almost unbearable, then let the tub fill up. It seemed to take forever for the water level to rise above the movable jet nozzles, at which point she activated a timed switch on the wall to turn the bath into a frothing cauldron. Finally, at long last, she took hold of the dress and pulled it over her head. She broke into uncontrollable laughter when the fabric tore apart in her hands.

"Well, I guess you served your purpose." She tossed the ruined garment in the wastebasket, and slipped out of her black bikini briefs and dropped them in as well.

Leaving a folded towel on the floor beside the Jacuzzi, she took a tentative step into the nearly scalding water. The sudden flash of pain was an almost welcome contrast to the numbing ache that had settled into her muscles. She eased herself down onto the edge of the tub then slipped her weary body into the frothing water. Extending a toe from beneath the surface, she turned off the flow from the spigot. It only took a moment for her body to adjust to the temperature. Almost immediately, she could feel the tension and soreness seep away. She stretched beneath the raging water, leaned her head back and closed her eyes.

In spite of the fact that she had chased down Aimes' killer and co-conspirators, she knew that her part in the drama, which had begun with the assassination, was far from over. She remained certain that the killers had been after the Trinity and was not entirely ameliorated by DiLorenzo's assurance that the artifact was secure. She would have to check it out for herself.

She found her contemplation suddenly sidetracked by the thought of the detective. She thought him an inflexible bureaucrat who probably cared more about getting a conviction than seeing that justice was served. Nevertheless, something in his intense dark eyes had appealed to her on a level that she rarely visited. Perhaps it was simply animal magnetism or the mythic lure of the Italian Romeo. DiLorenzo was by no means unattractive. She found herself wondering if her attempts to bait him had not been a subconscious attempt at flirtation.

With a shake of her head, she thrust the detective's face from her thoughts and forced herself to concentrate on the mystery behind the attack at the museum.

The helicopter was a clue that would surely leave a trail, as were the automatic weapons. Getting access to such hardware was far different than stealing a car or buying a Saturday night special in a back alley or a pawnshop. However, DiLorenzo would surely pursue such obvious leads.

She chuckled at how quickly he had returned to her thoughts.

"Why kill Aimes?" she said aloud, without opening her eyes. Maybe the sound of her own voice would help her concentrate.

Why indeed had the mercenaries targeted her old friend? Aimes had not been merely a target of opportunity. What had he done or known that warrented his assasination? Therein lay the key to unriddling the conspiracy.

Mira shifted under the surging foam, trying to redirect the massaging action of the Jacuzzi jets to other aching muscles. Already she was feeling better, restlessness being replaced by relaxation. She stretched again, welcoming the heat into her pores.

She realized suddenly that her assumption about the Trinity was in no way founded. The timing of the attack on Aimes might have been a coincidence; perhaps the elderly researcher had racked up a gambling debt to some shady underworld figure. She quickly frowned at that idea. The complexity of the assassins' scheme did not support such a mundane scenario, though upon closer examination it was difficult to conceive of any plot that would require such a wanton display of force.

Aimes was the key. She could not escape that conclusion.

The bath worked wonders. She raised up enough to pour some liquid soap onto a loofah and commenced scrubbing away the blood and sweat of her ordeal. When she was done, she felt alive and refreshed, but at the same time, ready to surrender to the need for sleep.

On an impulse, she twisted beneath the still frothing surface of the bath, pressed her body close to the massaging jets of water, and shifted until they were positioned in just the right place. Then, as the pulsating water worked its magic, she closed her eyes again and let her thoughts drift.

Not surprisingly, Michelangelo DiLorenzo found his way into her daydream, and this time she did not send him away.

Three hours later, Mira stepped out of the elevator and crossed the lobby of the hotel. The concierge stepped forward, offering to call for a cab, but she dismissed him with a shake of her head.

She now bore little resemblance to the woman that had trudged through the foyer earlier, or to the person that had left the hotel room the night before. Despite the autumn chill, she wore a pair of tan cargo shorts, turned up once into a cuff on either thigh, along with a short tank top of clingy, powder blue fabric that didn't quite reach her belt. When she walked, the hem of the garment exposed her midriff. Except for the well-worn Dr. Martens boots, tied with bright red laces, she looked like somebody on her way to the park for a jog.

She quickened her pace on the sidewalk, more out of impatience than urgency. Despite, or perhaps because of their long relationship, the impact of Aimes' death had not really sunk in at an emotional level, but the prospect of shedding light on his murder and protecting the Trinity filled her with a sense of purpose. She was in a hurry to get started, and as she strode toward her destination, the last vestiges of lingering tension in her limbs melted away.

She hiked north on Central Park West, the golden leaves of deciduous trees in the park a constant companion on her right, counter-pointing the pervasive odors of rubbish, urine and automobile exhaust that marked the experience as singularly urban. Adding to the sensory feast was a cacophony of honking car horns from the paralyzed flow of traffic that started at 59th Street and stretched all the way to the museum.

As she drew closer to the source of the problem, Mira found that pedestrian traffic was also bunching up. Crowds of idle spectators had gathered around the barricades that cordoned off the sidewalk and grounds of the museum. Numerous police cars and other emergency vehicles were haphazardly parked on both sides of the street, along with a small army of vans bearing the logos of different network affiliates and satellite news services.

Mira pushed through the throng, ignoring the murmurs of recognition. She soon found herself at the front of the gathering, facing the same impediment as everyone else: a series of blue and white wooden barricades presided over by a row of unblinking New York City police officers.

An annoyed frown touched her lips. The prevailing circus atmosphere had caught her off guard and she was irritated by the delay. As she turned her head from side to side, looking for some member of the museum staff to recognize her and sanction her presence, a soft voice reached out from directly in front of her.

"Ms. Raiden?"

She turned to find one of the police officers gesturing to her, and she removed her sunglasses to make eye contact.

"Are you here on official business, ma'am?"

She grinned ruefully at being called "ma'am." "You could say that."

He nodded and waved her forward, pushing one of the barriers aside to permit her passage. "We thought you might put in an appearance. Detective DiLorenzo requested that you not kill anybody."

She arched an eyebrow as she passed the young man in uniform. "Then would you be so kind as to let the detective know that he is a smart ass?"

"That's common knowledge," replied the officer with a chuckle. "I guess I don't need to tell you to watch your step in there."

She thanked him and proceeded up the concrete steps to the familiar entrance into the Theodore Roosevelt Memorial. A swarm of activity that began on the steps carried over into the museum itself. Functionaries scurried about like drones, giving the perception of accomplishing something, though what exactly that was remained a mystery to Mira. She passed them by and headed for the stairs.

It was there that she began to see the aftermath of the previous night's chaos. Bullet gouges in the floor and walls of the hallway and on the steps themselves had not yet begun to be repaired. She saw workmen carrying debris away, bringing in replacement panes of glass and working in nearly every part of the museum. A pang of guilt at having contributed to the ruin made her want to put her sunglasses back on.

The mock-up of the Atlantean king's tomb seemed to be the focus for all the activity. As soon as she entered, a bookish middle-aged man rushed over to greet her.

"Oh, goodness. Miss Raiden, it's so good to see you. What a nightmare this has been."

His name was Jonathan Overby, the museum's liaison to Aimes, and evidently a closer friend to the octogenarian than she had realized. Mira was moved by his obvious grief. She shook his proffered hand. "Jonathan, I'm truly sorry for your loss."

Overby pressed his hands to his chest, as if overcome with emotion. It was a decidedly feminine gesture. "He was like a father to me. And he loved this project."

Something about the way he used the word "father" struck her. Throughout her childhood she had entertained fantasies of just such a relationship, but Aimes had never deigned to let her into his life. Even though Aimes had always been there, she knew next to nothing about him as a person. "Did Walter have any family?"

Overby nodded, grateful for a listening ear. "A daughter, Rachel. The police are trying to track her down."

The knowledge stung her at a deep emotional level, but she filed the information away, focusing on the matter that had drawn her to the museum. "What is the status of the exhibit?"

Overby seemed to brighten at the opportunity to perform his sole function. "Well, the museum is a shambles, and that, of course, includes the exhibit. However, if the police would stop getting in our way, we'd be able to have things up and running in a matter of days."

"What about the Trinity?"

"Safe and sound. It has a dozen different security measures: infrared, thermal and motion sensors; pressure triggers; lasers; multiple cameras. No one got near it. We know how important it is, Miss Raiden. You made sure of that."

"May I see it?"

"Certainly. This way."

She followed him onto the dais where the Trinity altar was situated. Though the artifact had been at the forefront of her thoughts for several weeks in anticipation of the exhibit, she had not actually seen it in its display during that time. Neither had she had the chance to get a good look at it *in situ* the previous night.

The designer of the altar had incorporated the security system into the presentation, and though the setting wasn't strictly authentic, the end result was fascinating. Suspended in a magnetic levitation field above an array of blinking laser lights was the ultimate artifact of the Atlantean civilization: the Trinity.

The Trinity's six-sided crystal was no longer white, but rather a dull gray, its perfection marred by a fracture that bisected it from one corner to another. Mira involuntarily recalled the moment she had fired a bullet into it, putting an end to Marquand Atlas' second attempt to usurp the throne of Atlantis, and his misbegotten existence as well. Cracking the crystal had silenced the relic's display of supernatural energy, but the net effect to the power of the Trinity was anybody's guess. That uncertainty had been at the heart of her argument to keep it out of public view. What if there were other men like Atlas out there who knew how to awaken it yet again?

Yet despite her concerns, despite the fact that there had been a direct and violent attack against the museum, centering on the exhibit, the Trinity seemed to be, as Overby had stated, safe and secure. And yet, her intuition told her that something was not quite right about the tableau.

"Can you open the case?"

"Open? I, ah, well . . . yes, I can. But why do you want me to?"

She unleashed the full potency of her smile. "Humor me."

Overby walked around to the other side of the altar and fumbled with one of the stones until it popped open on recessed hinges. Underneath was a numeric keypad. He entered a sequence of ten digits, then waited for tone indicating that the system was deactivated. Another button raised the transparent cover. A whoosh of air indicated that the interior of the case had been sealed in a vacuum.

She tentatively reached for the artifact, seizing it out of the magnetic field with a gentle tug. The repelling forces caused it to twist in her grasp as if it were alive, and for just a moment she was afraid that might be the case.

Overby watched without comment as she felt it carefully with her fingertips and held it up to the light for a close visual inspection. Her face was unreadable, creased with a deliberate frown of intensity. She paid careful attention to the damaged crystal where her bullet had struck the essential blow to end Atlas' mad apotheosis. Then, as if satisfied with her scrutiny, she handed the relic to Overby without a word and turned away.

He hurriedly replaced the Trinity in the magnetic field, then reactivated the complex security systems. When the final beep signaled that all the measures were armed, he raced after her.

He caught her as she was beginning her descent of the stairs. "What did I tell you? Nothing at all is amiss with the Trinity."

"Nothing at all," Mira echoed, without looking or slowing. "I don't think you'll have anything more to worry about."

Overby had to yell to reach her with his voice. "Why do you say that?"

"Because the Trinity in that case is a forgery."

THREE

The noise of the city did not decrease with twilight or the subsequent fall of evening. Yet, at the onset of her third night in Manhattan, Mira had already begun to tune out the din. She filtered through the racket, straining for the sounds that might signal the approach of an unwelcome visitor, and glanced down at the alley below to verify the message her ears—and her intuition—were receiving, namely that her activities continued to go unnoticed, then swung her attention back to the matter at hand.

She looped in several yards of the woven kernmantle climbing rope so that the end of the line would not be visible to anyone walking along below where she now dangled. The climb had been fairly easy, but the specter of imminent discovery by a passerby had haunted her from the moment she lofted the lightweight grappling hook over the parapet above.

She tied a loose figure-eight knot around the excess coil of rope and, with her feet planted against the brick exterior of the building, gripped the framework of steel bars that blocked access to the fourth story window of Walter Aimes' apartment. The bars were spotted with rust, but otherwise solid. She didn't think she would be able to bend them apart with the carbon-steel pry bar tucked in her climbing harness like a dagger. However, where the steel was joined to the brick, screwed in with thick bolts of similarly hardened metal, there was a chink in the building's armor. The metal may have been impervious to her assault, but the masonry in which it was embedded was old and brittle.

She slipped the pry bar under the cage-like gate near the lower left-hand corner, gripping it with hands protected by black leather fingerless gloves, and pushed with her legs for maximum leverage. The screw, along with a fastening bolt at the other end, exploded out of the brick, leaving a hole about an inch in diameter. The operation had not exactly been silent, but the noise was no louder than a distant car backfiring.

"One down," she murmured.

Before continuing, she loosened the extra length of rope and threaded a section of it through the bars, securing it with a gated carabiner. If the bars came loose prematurely, this would prevent their fall to the pavement below, though Mira found herself wondering if the rope, or the hook on which it depended, was strong enough to bear a sudden increase in weight. She silently resolved not to let that happen.

Using a pair of Jumar ascenders, she ratcheted her way up until she was level with the top of the window. Anyone inside would easily distinguish her silhouette, but the interior of the apartment was dark. It was her understanding that Aimes had lived alone, so there was no reason for anyone to be at his residence.

The bolt securing the upper left corner was more stubborn than the first but nevertheless yielded to her straining exertions. She slipped the pry bar back into her belt and pulled on the left side of the frame. The metal eyeholes where the right side of the frame was joined to the building bent like hinges, permitting easy access to the glass.

She dropped down a couple feet and slipped into the gap. Compared to the bars, getting through the window would be a challenge. The wooden frame held panes of glass as old as the building itself. Rippling distortions, where the glass, molecule by molecule, had succumbed to the pull of gravity, showed the pane's age and frailty. Doubtless, only a simple swivel latch kept the vertically sliding lower panel secure, though she had heard of city dwellers at lower elevations nailing their windows shut due to high crime rates. Either way, there seemed to be no means of getting through without shattering the glass and taking the chance that the noise might raise an alarm.

Taking the pry bar in one hand, she drew back, preparing to smash through the window.

Suddenly, the curtain behind the glass was thrown back, revealing an indistinct figure. Mira gasped in surprise and her veins filled with ice water. The pry bar slipped from her fingers as her feet lost their purchase. Though the nylon mesh harness around her hips kept her from falling, it did not prevent her from turning uncontrollable circles in the air. The lost pry bar clanged noisily on the pavement below, even as she fumbled with both hands for the taut rope in a frantic effort to right herself.

The window was thrown open with a piercing shriek—the sound of old warped wood being manhandled—even as she continued spinning at the end of her rope. A firm grip caught her shoulder and held her motionless before she commenced another pummeling somersault. Grateful for the assistance, she caught hold of the line, and pulled herself upright.

Before her eyes could register completely on the face that now smirked from inside the apartment, a familiar voice drove a nail of dread into her heart.

"Need a hand, Miss Raiden?"

With both feet firmly on the carpeted floor of Aimes' living room, Mira unclipped from the nylon rope. She turned to face her unexpected savior.

"Great minds think alike, eh, Mira?"

"One of us ought to feel flattered, detective." Her voice kept an ironic edge that neatly masked the adrenaline still pumping through her veins. The biggest surprise to her was that she had felt no precognitive warning concerning the lurking visitor. Perhaps the simple fact that he was "safe" had shielded his presence from her. "Here to arrest me again?"

DiLorenzo only smiled. "What's the use? Your fan club would probably try to give you an award for your ingenuity and bust me down to walking a beat."

"Then what are you doing here?"

"Ah, ah. You first."

She studied the detective's countenance in the glow of the single overhead light, switched on now that the subterfuge of her covert entry was irrelevant. DiLorenzo seemed to have become immune to her jibes, gazing back with dark eyes and an inscrutable smile. Which only added to his mystique.

She brushed a strand of hair away from her eyes. "Somebody wanted Walter dead. I was hoping that something here might reveal why."

He nodded, as if she had confirmed his original statement. "But you also think this has something to do with that thing at the museum?"

"The Trinity. Yes, I'm sure of it. I went to the museum earlier. . . ."

DiLorenzo waved dismissively. "Oh, yes. You claimed it's a forgery. The curator called in a panic the moment you left. Of course, he doesn't have a clue as to how you made that determination. Or any way to authenticate the claim. It seems there aren't very many experts on the antiquities of Atlantis."

"That Trinity is a forgery," she reasserted.

"How can you tell?"

Mira's tongue unconsciously darted across her lips, moistening them to a ruby sheen, as she studied his face carefully. She wasn't ready to trust the detective with the knowledge of her unusual abilities. "I know more about that thing than anyone living, detective. You'll just have to trust me."

DiLorenzo laughed without condescension. "Well, if you're right, it would mean that the forger had access to the exhibit in order to switch them."

"Exactly. But who had that kind of access?"

DiLorenzo's smile fell as he weighed the implication of her words. "An inside job. Do you think Aimes was involved? That might give us a motive for his murder."

She pondered this. A deep-seated loyalty to the old man warred against an instinctive belief that there was a deeper mystery surrounding his life. The discovery that he was a family man had shaken her view of him and colored all her memories of their time together. "Walter and I argued endlessly about the danger of its being stolen. If he took my advice, he may have commissioned a replica without telling anyone and put that in the exhibit, while keeping the real one in a safe place."

"Then it might be here somewhere."

"I doubt he would have kept it in a cookie tin on the mantle. However, there may be some clue here that will point us in the right direction." She shrugged. "The alternative is that it really has been stolen."

The detective kept at the thread of supposition. "If somebody found out about the switch, it might explain why Aimes became a target. Maybe they wanted him to tell them where it was and he wouldn't play ball."

"A plausible scenario." She stopped looking at the detective, instead allowing her eyes to sweep the room. It seemed very much like the residence of a bachelor or lonely widower. Generic watercolor paintings hung in cheap frames from the walls, with no correlation of styles, colors or themes, or any connection to the tasteful but mismatched furnishings. A bookshelf stood guard near the front door, packed with dusty leather-bound tomes. Mira peered at the gilt letters of the titles and saw that the books were part of a collection of classic works spanning everything from Plato to Melville. They appeared to be decorative, though it wasn't too hard to imagine the elderly researcher reclining in the overstuffed chair with a snifter of cognac and a well-read copy of *Great Expectations*. But that was an image fabricated from suspect memories; she really didn't know Walter Aimes at all.

A musty atmosphere hung about the room, and it took her a second to recognize the odor of cigarette smoke. She had not known that he was a smoker, but the telltale yellowing of the walls told of many years devoted to the habit.

DiLorenzo seemed to understand the focus of her search and wandered into the dining room. "Guess he ate out a lot," he remarked. She looked around the corner for clarification.

The dining table was stacked with books and loose papers. There wasn't a patch of bare surface big enough to set down a saucer or mug, let alone a dinner plate. She picked up one of the books and examined its cover.

Unlike the collection at the door, this book had been used extensively for its intended purpose. The paperback binding was creased along the spine, almost to the point where the title print was illegible. The printed cover was ratty and separating, and the style of artwork and lettering was at least three decades old. She read aloud the title. "*Atlantis, Lemuria, Mu: The Prehistory of the World.*"

"Atlantis I know, but I've never heard of those last two," remarked DiLorenzo, glancing down at the other titles. "There seems to be a theme developing here. What the hell is Lemuria? Sounds like some kind of rodent."

"Lemuria was a legendary lost kingdom, named for the lemur, a kind of monkey, said to inhabit the ruin. Spiritualists in the early 20th century believed they could channel the spirits of ancient Lemurian kings."

"Lost kingdom. You mean like Atlantis?"

She nodded. "Something like that. Mu is one of several Pacific versions of Atlantis. Apparently Walter had an interest in legendary lost civilizations."

"An interest? I'd say he was obsessed."

The dining room had become a de facto study, but nowhere on the table could Mira find any notes written by Aimes himself. The books themselves ranged from the popular works of Charles Berlitz and Graham Hancock to photocopied newsletters from contemporary New Age movements dedicated to unlocking the mysteries of Mu, Shambala, Argatha, and at least a dozen other lost civilizations of which Mira had never heard. The sum total of the information on the table seemed to indicate that the entire planet had at one time supported a culture advanced beyond the wildest dreams of modern man, existing now only as a psychic echo. But for her own experiences in the ruins of the Atlantean temple, Mira would have dismissed it all as a load of rubbish. Now, she could not help but wonder which myths held a nugget of truth. As if to underscore the idea, Aimes had tacked a map of the earth to the wall opposite the chair where he had apparently sat while conducting his investigations.

DiLorenzo clapped a book shut and cast it back into the pile. "These people have way too much free time."

Mira nodded absently. "If he left a clue, it's not here."

"Maybe we should check the bedroom?"

"You'd love that."

He grinned, but conspicuously did not defend his suggestion. "I'll just go have a look."

He walked away, leaving her alone with the impromptu

research library. Mira watched his departing back and found herself wondering what the tall detective was really thinking. She shook her head to focus her meandering thoughts and looked back at the stacks of books.

Aimes had apparently collected any printed material that had anything at all to do with Atlantis and other legendary lost civilizations. The problem with academic research in that particular field was that there was nothing authoritative to be found. Until the discovery in Panama, a bare half year ago, Atlantis, and to a lesser degree the other cities and civilizations mentioned, had always been referenced in myths rather than historical documents.

The earliest account of Atlantis, if apocryphal references were discounted, was in the dialogues of Plato. In that context, it seemed to be more of a political parable, not unlike More's *Utopia*, rather than an attempt at chronicling the fall of a true ancient superpower. The Atlantis myth was often considered an alternate telling of the Great Flood story, which could be found not only in the Biblical account of Noah's Ark, but in almost every culture on the planet in some form or another. It was an explanation Mira herself could easily have accepted had she not actually stood in the tomb of an Atlantean king and seen a contemporary painting of the disaster that had ravaged the antediluvian world and hidden Atlantis itself for millennia.

What plagued the authors who hoped to offer some new theory on a legend so deeply ingrained in the human consciousness was the lack of scientific methodology; how could their theories possibly be tested? Without fear of being proved wrong, the pseudo-scientists and scholars could write whatever they pleased. Aimes' exhaustive study would never have brought him nearer to the truth about Atlantis, only closer to an understanding of the human need for mystery.

She turned her back to the table, moving through the apartment to see if DiLorenzo had uncovered anything significant. She found him kneeling in front of Aimes' bureau. His efficient search technique allowed him to thoroughly examine the contents of each drawer then return it to almost exactly the same state he had found it.

"You look like you've had some practice with that."

"It's the job," he chuckled, sliding shut the last drawer. "Nothing."

She nodded absently. "So, I told you why I'm here. What are you doing here?"

"I knew you'd end up here eventually."

"Don't you have other leads to chase? Or am I still a suspect?"

"Oh, I suspect you of a lot, Miss Raiden." He smiled again, as if to assure her that he meant it only as playful innuendo. "But I'm afraid all the leads have been chased, and they've led nowhere.

"The three dead guards were identified. One of spent a few years in the Army, and his brother and the third guy did time together. Apparently they and some other buddies formed a little mercenary venture—I guess the correct term for them these days is 'private security contractors'—and put a classified ad in a popular military magazine. As you can imagine, a business like that doesn't keep much in the way of records."

"The guns? And the helicopter?"

"Stolen. The helicopter is probably the same one that was reported stolen from a helipad in Wall Street earlier this week. Homeland Security is working that, but no leads yet. Now obviously, whoever took it has to have access to fuel and a place to land, not to mention a pilot, all of which suggests that they didn't need to steal it; they just didn't want to use their own. The guns were all part of a private collection stolen from a gun shop owner several weeks ago. Just between you and me, we suspect the owner of having brokered a deal for the weapons and then turned them in as stolen for the insurance money. He's being investigated, but I doubt that will yield anything soon."

"How did these mercenaries pass themselves off as museum guards?"

"They were guards. Somehow they all got hired on with the temp security agency that landed the contract to guard the exhibit at the museum."

"Now that's interesting. Who was in charge of that

decision?"

"Several people, but all of them are above suspicion. Aimes was one." He straightened from his kneeling position and turned to face her. His expression seemed genuine. "The guy that you brained, the one in the tuxedo, we haven't identified yet. He's at the hospital with a concussion. Conscious, but not saying a word. He doesn't appear to have any direct connection to the mercenary brothers though."

"Then he must have been their employer. And they must have slipped him through security."

"Maybe not. The guy had an authentic invitation, though the name on it turned out to be an alias."

"Those invitations are almost impossible to duplicate."

"This one was probably forged from a stolen blank."

Mira's eyes narrowed in thought. "That adds credence to the idea that this was an inside job."

DiLorenzo inclined his head. "And our friend Aimes seems always at the heart of the conspiracy except for one tiny detail—"

"Namely his being dead."

"Yup. Now, the suspicious sort of guy I am, I wonder: could he have faked his own death? Maybe it was all a trick with fake bullets and stage blood. Maybe he paid off a doctor to sign the death certificate—"

Mira whirled to face him, as if the idea was suddenly very plausible. "Where's the body?"

"I'm getting to that. I had to know for sure, so I went down to the morgue to have a look for myself. Got to watch a few minutes of the autopsy."

Mira's expression sank. If Aimes had faked his death, a lot of loose threads would have come very neatly together. "I suppose that sort of thing only happens in the movies."

DiLorenzo shrugged and picked up a small picture frame off the top surface of the dresser. He flashed it toward Mira. "And then his daughter had the remains sent to a funeral home to be cremated."

Mira was about to respond when her gaze fell upon the blonde-haired woman in the picture DiLorenzo was holding:

Aimes' daughter Rachel. After a moment, her deep brown eyes flashed up to lock with the detective's. "That's the woman who was flying the helicopter last night."

DiLorenzo's eyes also grew wide, but before he could say a word, a shuffling noise behind Mira distracted them both. The detective's sidearm was out in a heartbeat, and he raised his finger to his lips, beckoning Mira to silently wait while he checked out the source of the disturbance.

Mira, responding to her own internal warning system, was already moving.

The intruder had his back to them when she got her first look, but her approach was not sufficiently stealthy. He whirled around, dropping into a defensive stance before she had crossed half the distance to the dining room.

She recognized him instantly even though a jet-black balaclava in the same hue as the military style fatigues and boots he wore covered his face. The clothing could not conceal his bulky frame, nor could the mask hide his lethal eyes. He was the shooter from the helicopter who had so savagely murdered his own comrade to prevent him from revealing any information to the police.

He had left behind his assault rifle, but he was not unarmed. In addition to his overpowering physical strength, he held a short object in his right fist; a device that telescoped to four times its original length when he pressed a button.

"Damn it, Mira!" DiLorenzo was shouting. "Get down."

The big mercenary laughed through the fabric of his mask, swiping the air with the cudgel. The tactical baton was a flashy choice of weapons, but realistically no more intimidating than anything else he might have brought to bear. Its chief advantage was that it was easy to conceal, and that had ceased to be a factor. Nevertheless, Mira eyed the baton warily, knowing that the brute who held it was certainly capable of breaking her bones with it.

DiLorenzo was still shouting for her to get out of the way, but Mira did not hear him. The rush of adrenaline in her bloodstream roared through her head like a waterfall.

The mercenary lunged at her, sweeping toward her head

with the baton. At half his mass, Mira ducked under the assault and lashed out with a kick to the giant's midsection. Her booted foot struck what felt like a bag of cement, and she rebounded away to land on her rear.

DiLorenzo seized the opportunity to brandish his pistol. "Freeze!"

The big man ignored the threat as he advanced on Mira. He raised a foot to stomp on her, but she rolled underneath him, driving her foot into the back of the mercenary's knee. His supporting leg folded, and he pitched backward like a felled tree, crashing into the dining room table. The nearest legs of the table snapped under the sudden load, and the man was buried in an avalanche of musty-smelling speculative literature.

Thunder roared in the small room as DiLorenzo's weapon discharged a split-second too late to hit his target. The bullet passed through the space where the man had stood and smashed impotently into the kitchen wall. DiLorenzo spat a curse, lowering the barrel and taking aim again. As he was about to fire, Mira popped up directly in the line of fire.

The mercenary had lost his baton when he fell and made the mistake of looking for it. He was still fumbling through the scattering of books when Mira's gloved palm slammed into the bridge of his nose.

At the proper angle, with sufficient force, the blow might have been fatal. Mira, however, did not want the man dead. She knew what he was: a hireling for somebody with greater resources and a more dangerous agenda. As a soldier of fortune, he might be compelled to see that the path of greatest reward lay in cooperating with the police, but to do so, he would have to be physically subdued. The brute obviously wasn't afraid to take a bullet, and Mira suspected DiLorenzo wasn't afraid to give him one. That meant it was up to her to bring him down.

She heard the cartilage in the man's nose pop as she made contact. The faint protrusion beneath the fabric of the balaclava was now visibly asymmetrical. Moisture soaked through the fabric, dripping crimson onto the scattered pages.

The mercenary howled in frustration, but if he felt the pain of his broken nose it in no way slowed him down. He swung at

Mira, striking her on the left side with his forearm. It was a reflexive blow, without any real purpose behind it, but it knocked her flat a second time.

The mercenary came to his feet, roaring and waving his arms like an angry ape. DiLorenzo did not hesitate. His pistol roared three times in quick succession, drowning out Mira's cries of protest. The .38-caliber rounds punched into the mercenary's chest and knocked him back onto the wreckage of the table.

"No!" Mira was up in an instant, hurling accusations at the detective. "We needed him alive."

DiLorenzo's eyes were blazing with unexpected emotion. "I needed *you* alive."

She opened her mouth, but found his simple answer too compelling to argue against. She turned and took a step toward the fallen man. "Call an ambulance," she said, unable to muster the urgency she wanted. She had seen the fabric of the man's shirt erupt as the lead missiles struck home. DiLorenzo's rounds had struck dead center over the man's heart. "Maybe there's time to save him."

The detective reached her side a moment later, staring down at the motionless figure. A sprinkling of blood had fallen around the man's head, but there was less than Mira would have expected to see. She turned to comment on this, but was stopped by the expression on DiLorenzo's face. In a sudden rush of comprehension, she intuited that the detective had probably never killed a suspect before, that he had probably never even fired his weapon in the line of duty.

She sucked in a deep breath and let it out slowly to calm her racing heart. "Thank you."

DiLorenzo's pained eyes caught her own, and for a moment, there was a silent connection between them.

A heartbeat later, their legs were swept from beneath them as the fallen giant arose from the dead. Protected by an undergarment of woven Kevlar fibers, he had been hammered hard by the bullets, but they had not penetrated his chest cavity.

They fell into each other, a tangle of limbs, each struggling to help the other stay upright. Mira glimpsed the mercenary, pulling himself erect and scrambling across the room. He made no further attack, focusing all his energies on escape. She could tell from his gait that he was hurting, but he reached the window where she had made her entrance before she could regain her feet and pursue him.

DiLorenzo was still struggling to rise as she reached the windowsill to stare out into the alley where she had made her ascent. The mercenary was free rappelling down the vertical surface on the rope she had set. She looked down and made eye contact with him, just as he reached the end, still a good 15 feet above the pavement. The excess rope she had earlier gathered in and tied off now delayed his flight.

He gazed back up at her, hesitant to surrender to what would surely be a painful drop to the ground, and curious to see how she would respond. There was only one way down for the man. It was just a matter of how long he would dangle helplessly before surrendering to the fall. Once he recovered from the drop, providing he broke no bones, there would be no preventing his escape.

Mira stared at the taut rope, wondering how she might use the situation to her advantage. The section she had gathered up had pulled tight into a hopeless Gordian knot. Eighteen inches higher, the line threaded through the bars which now formed the fulcrum from which the mercenary hung like a pendulum.

Inspiration dawned. Without hesitation, she swung into the window frame and braced her boot heels against the steel cage. The first two-footed blow sent a shiver down the climbing line. She could hear the man shouting for her to stop in between the percussive sounds of her heel strikes. On the fourth, the bolt securing the upper righthand corner tore free with an eruption of masonry shards. The entire steel frame then flipped forward, dropping the mercenary a few feet lower and slamming him against the wall of the building. The steel eyehole, through which the remaining bolt was threaded, seemed to quiver as the load placed on it strained it to its breaking point.

In that moment, the mercenary might have escaped without any further injury. He was within safe falling distance of the pavement, and the threat from the steel grating was not yet imminent. Nevertheless, acting on the instinct of a falling man to cling to whatever safety was available, he passed up his chance to let go of the rope and get away.

Mira leaned out the window. The full weight of the giant was now pulling on that single bolt. Even without further action on her part, the bars were going to break free at any moment. When they did, the rope she had secured around the steel rods would prevent them from falling to the alley below. That was the part of Mira's plan that required some adjustment.

She slipped a thin, fixed-blade knife from her right boot and held it at the ready. A final kick caused the framework of steel to break free with a tortured shriek. In that instant, she slashed the blade of the knife across the rope. The fibers parted with a whispered popping noise, followed by a clatter of steel on brick as the frame plunged down the side of the building.

The mercenary hit the ground hard, flat on his back, driving the breath from his lungs in a gasp. He could only stare as the rope coiled haphazardly onto his chest, followed about one second later by the tumbling steel grid. The heavy frame impacted with a muted thump, followed by a jangling of metal on stone. When Mira next saw her assailant, he was motionless beneath the grating, his head lolling to one side.

She whirled to find DiLorenzo at her shoulder. "Come on. Let's get down there before he comes to."

"Hang on a sec," DiLorenzo was shouting, as if standing still would somehow help him to grasp all that had transpired in the space of a few seconds. Mira was already moving.

She burst through the front door into the hallway and was suddenly confronted by her unfamiliarity with the building. Her intuitive gift did not translate into instant knowledge, but in tandem with a logical appraisal, she determined to head for the center of the corridor.

The door to the stairway was just opposite the entry to the elevator shaft. She darted into the stairwell and hopped down three steps at a time.

She reached the front lobby on the ground floor less than thirty seconds after leaving the apartment and did not slow down as she flew into the lobby. Out of the corner of her eye, she saw a man in a generic uniform standing in one corner, speaking urgently into the telephone. The doorman was probably summoning the police after hearing gunfire from the upstairs apartment. Mira was already on the sidewalk before her brain had begun to process that information. She turned right and raced for the corner of the building, and the entry to the alley where she had made her covert ascent.

As she rounded the corner, she was suddenly bathed in the harsh glare of twin halogen headlamps and brought up a hand to shield her eyes. The roar of a revved-up engine and squealing tires told her a vehicle was driving straight at her. She leapt backwards, swinging her arms to get the most distance out of the hasty maneuver, and reached the cement sidewalk as a white van, with windows only in the cab end, raced by. The van turned right in a screech of rubber on pavement, then accelerated away down the street.

Mira's blind jump had almost sent her sprawling backward. She caught the edge of the building with her right hand and steadied herself for a moment before chasing back into the alleyway. She was not surprised by what she discovered there. The metal grating lay more or less where she had seen it fall, but there was no sign of the mercenary. His comrades in the van had swooped in for the rescue in the half-minute it had taken her to reach the ground floor. She muttered useless curses as she gazed up at the window of Aimes' apartment.

She heard the noise of labored breathing in the alley and turned to find DiLorenzo running toward her. His face was strained by the exertion of following her down the stairs. In the back of her mind, she wondered why the detective wasn't in better shape; didn't policemen routinely chase suspects on foot? It was a passing thought that owed more to her irritation at having failed to capture their prey, and she let it slip from her mind as he drew close. She now saw that in addition to his sidearm he held a cellular telephone.

He paused at her side to catch his breath, gesturing silently to the place where their assailant had lain only a minute before.

"His friends showed up," she explained. "They took off in a delivery van. And no, I didn't get a license number or a good look at the driver, but I've a fair idea of who it was."

"Rachel . . . Aimes," he wheezed. "I'll put . . . an alert out."

A few moments later, the distant noise of police sirens became audible and steadily drew closer. Patrol cars, summoned either by the doorman or by DiLorenzo, were responding, too late, to the scene of the crime. Mira gazed back up at the window, wondering what she was forgetting.

DiLorenzo took a final deep breath then let it out slowly, after which he attempted to breathe normally. "You took a big risk," he accused.

"What was he after?" she wondered aloud, disregarding the statement.

"I thought that was obvious. He was after you."

She shook her head. "Then why didn't his friends stick around to finish the job? No, I don't think that's it. Come on."

DiLorenzo's expression fell. "Where?"

"Back up there," she shouted over her shoulder, already breaking into a jog. "Don't worry. I'll send the elevator for you."

DiLorenzo scowled, then willed up the energy to chase after her.

Mira saw what had changed almost right away. The wall map, opposite the dining room table, had been taken. A rectangle of white, a shade lighter than the smoke-darkened paint of the wall, exposed its absence. In each corner of the outline, a tiny hole revealed where a thumbtack had fastened the paper to the wall.

She stared at the emptiness for a moment, trying to recall details about the map, and wondered how the mercenary had known of its presence and importance. The answer to that was obvious; Rachel Aimes had doubtless supplied that information.

She could hear DiLorenzo's voice speaking into his cell phone in the other room. "Well, why can't they transfer him tonight?" he was asking, his tone one of disbelief. "Still no idea who he is? . . . No. But they hit us here— . . . Mira— . . . I don't think I'd go that far. . . . Well, she's a lot easier on the eyes than you are."

Mira chuckled at the turn the conversation had taken, then focused her attention on the task at hand. In her mind's eye, she could see the map of the earth. It was the kind of thing one could purchase in any bookstore. Aimes had probably bought his in the museum's gift shop. With closed eyes, she could not recollect any sort of modification. There had been no marks on the map to suggest that it held the key to some hidden secret. Why, then, had the mercenary taken it? She opened her eyes and looked again.

There it was.

In what would have been the lower left quadrant of the map, there was another tiny hole, identical to the tack marks in the corners.

"Well?"

It took a moment for Mira to realize that the detective was addressing her. She turned to face him. "There was a map here. A map of the world that Walter had used to mark a specific location. That's what he was after."

"Do you know where?"

She turned back to the blank wall, trying again to summon a mental picture of the map. She extended a finger, seeing it in her mind, and placed it where she would have imagined South America to be. When she opened her eyes, the pinhole was scant centimeters from her fingertip.

"Somewhere in the South Pacific. Or possibly the tip of South America."

"South Pacific? Do you think he figured out where that Lemur place was?"

"Lemuria was probably an ancient name for Madagascar in the Indian Ocean." Mira shrugged. "The map could mean almost anything. But whatever it was, they have it now."

"And they've got a head start. But the question is a head start on what?"

"Hopefully, I'll find out when I get there."

DiLorenzo coughed in disbelief. "Just like that? You're going to jet off to the South Pacific?"

"That's where the answers are." She turned to face him again. "You know, I almost wish Walter had faked his own death and was secretly orchestrating all of this."

"Why?"

"Then, at least, I would know who the bad guys are"—she looked down at the chaos of books scattered on the floor—"and what they're looking for."

FOUR

Although the austral spring was in full bloom, carpeting the lowlands in lush verdant foliage and vibrant multi-hued blossoms, a harsh wind off the Pacific Ocean was Mira's constant companion from the moment she began descending the western slopes of the Andes.

Her route led her either head on into the tempest or presented her for a broadside hammering as she negotiated switchbacks on the mountain roads. She was burning through her supply of gasoline much faster than she had anticipated and was forced to refill both the tank on the Harley Davidson and the twin 20-liter jerricans in panniers slung over the front wheel at every outpost of civilization. Such outposts were few and far between, especially after her unheralded crossing of the Argentine border with Chile.

She had fixed her destination before leaving Aimes' apartment that night, now four days in her past. Though she had not had access to a map at the time, she had taken accurate measurements of the distance from the pin mark to the perimeter of the outline of the map utilizing a string and a paperclip to form a plumb line. She had then made an assessment from the point where the string intersected that imaginary line to the corner of the map. Utilizing those two distances, she had purchased an identical map early the following morning and plotted her next move. The tiny pinhole represented an area of the earth's surface of several square kilometers, but there could be no disputing that it fell squarely on the Chilean coast, just to the south of the Gulf of Penas. In a remote fjord, somewhere between Wellington Island and Hanover Island, Walter Aimes had determined that a secret lay, and his murderers had judged that secret more valuable than his life. Mira had pledged to discover it first.

The long journey by motorcycle had given her plenty of time to ponder the significance of Aimes' research. It seemed unlikely that the map coordinates could be anything but connected to Atlantis; Aimes had appeared to be interested in little else. Yet, this location was far too remote to have been an Atlantean outpost. While it was true that the refugees of Atlantis had indeed brought the Trinity to the Americas, the location of the temple ruin was thousands of miles away on the Central American isthmus. Two days of hard riding, during which there had been plenty of time to ponder the mystery, had brought her no closer to answering the question of how she would even begin her investigation.

Her meditations on the subject were not the only matter to occupy her mind during the long trip. There had been reports of bandits and armed revolutionaries inhabiting the mountain regions away from civilization, and extreme vigilance had been required. With her intuition safeguarding her, she had made contacts in the Argentine underworld who had been able to equip her to face the dangers of the road. The Beretta nine-millimeter semi-automatic pistol had cost her more than double its market value, but the added expense insured that there was no paper trail.

She wore her pistol in a shoulder rig, which also contained two spare magazines. The reason for the open display was two-fold; not only did it afford easy access to the firearm, it also served as a warning that she was not toothless prey. And while it was true that anyone lying in ambush would get the first shot, she was confident that her intuition would give her the advantage. That said, throughout the long journey she had not experienced the slightest hint of impending danger.

Mira had not spoken with DiLorenzo since they'd gone their separate ways following the arrival of police patrol units at Aimes' apartment. He had been caught up in official procedures, and she had been focused on determining the map coordinates. Though she occasionally felt a pang of regret that circumstances had not allowed her a moment to relax and enjoy his company, she was already relegating the experience to the archives of distant memory. She recognized that her path would not have ever crossed the detective's if not for Aimes' murder that night at the museum and, as such, saw it as no great loss that the encounter was already behind her. Both of them deserved better than a fling based on a chance encounter.

But deep down she knew there was more to it than that. When she looked at DiLorenzo and felt the stirrings of desire, she could not help but think of the last man she had loved. Curtis Lancet's death was a wound to her heart that was healing, true, but in DiLorenzo she saw the potential for a replay of that tragedy. The job of a New York City police detective was not exactly the safest career choice, and she wasn't about to invest her heart in someone who might just that easily be taken from her. Not again.

Her journey ended without incident. As the last gently sloping hillside gave way to flat coastal plain, she eyed the readout of the handheld global positioning satellite receiver, taped to the handlebars of the motorcycle. According to the GPS unit, she was there. She squeezed the clutch lever and tapped the gear selector with her foot until the bike was in neutral. As it coasted to a stop, she put out her left foot to balance it upright.

She could hear the sound of the Pacific Ocean, not too distant but hidden behind a curtain of trees. The dirt road on which she traveled was deeply rutted, indicating at least occasional traffic by trucks and buses, but she thought it unlikely that many of the people who lived in the region owned their own vehicles. The track continued parallel to the ocean, then dove into the heart of the forest, presumably toward some kind of seaside settlement. If she allowed for certain tolerances in her estimation of the map coordinates, whatever kind of town lay ahead would certainly make the ideal starting point for her search.

She started again and emerged from the wind-sculpted forest into the full fury of the blow. She had to gear down in order to make any headway, and as soon as she saw the loose collection of dilapidated buildings, she pulled behind one, grateful for shelter. Dropping the kickstand, she eased off of the big Harley.

She had purchased the motorcycle, a classic if battered 1958 Harley Davidson XLH, outright in Buenos Aires, bargaining its owner down to where she was paying only fifty percent more than its actual value. Between the motorbike, the gun, and the cost of air-travel to Argentina she had burned up nearly all of the money she had earned since leaving the Agency. Her deal with the Atlas Trust entitled her to a regular stipend, but she was loath to use their money, especially since they were connected, albeit in an indirect manner, to the Trinity. Fortunately, casino winnings were a renewable resource.

She left the motorcycle behind the first building, with only the fuel cans presenting any sort of target of opportunity for thieves. Everything else was in her nearly empty North Face backpack, which held only her passport and traveler's cheques, a change of clothing almost identical to what she was currently wearing, extra ammunition for the pistol, a well-provisioned first-aid kit, and a few energy bars, which were all that remained of the food supply she had brought along. She stuffed the GPS unit into the bag, and then slipped her arms through the comfortable padded straps.

She had not seen a single soul since motoring into the little village and found herself wondering whether it was altogether abandoned. The relentless wind was visibly eating away at the structures, stripping off sideboards and roof shingles with every gust. There were about a dozen buildings in all, lining either side of the dirt road. The forest lay to the rear of the village, on her left, while the ocean pounded the rocky shoreline not far from the structures on her right. She turned toward the shore and discovered a tiny harbor sheltered in a cove etched out of the rock.

A stairway led down to a rickety wooden pier where two boats, one in surprisingly good shape, rocked back and forth in the swells. Though the cove was protected from the wind, the energy it stirred up on the surface of the water found its way in and repeatedly threw the boats against their moorings. Only the makeshift truck tire bumpers on their gunwales prevented them from being battered into splinters. She made her way to the boats, again thankful for any respite from the wind.

The pier itself rocked up and down, though it was anchored to pilings at each corner to prevent any lateral movement. Nevertheless, Mira had to find her sea legs in order to approach the nicer of the two boats. The 40-foot-long fiberglass hull was green with algae a meter above the water line, presumably the difference between a hold full of cargo or fish and its present, unladen state. Barnacles were also visible through the murky water, indicating that the boat, though nicer than its companion, had not been especially well cared for.

She walked along the length of the boat, but saw no evidence of anyone aboard. Hesitant to trespass, she chose instead to survey the other boat. As she crossed over to its moorage, a voice reached her from behind.

"Looking for someone, Miss?"

The man that stood at the beginning of the pier, like the boat that he doubtless skippered, had seen better days. His accent, though thick with alcohol, sounded Irish at first blush, but she quickly pegged him as an expatriate from Down Under. He stood a hair over six feet and could probably have added to that if not for his slovenly posture. His grizzled head hung over a prodigious beer gut, which strained the tattered fabric of a cable-knit fisherman's sweater, yet despite his run-down appearance, he looked strong and able.

"I'd like to speak to the owner of one of these boats."

"You want to charter a fishing trip?" The man guffawed derisively at the notion.

"Something like that."

The quiet confidence in her voice stopped his sardonic laughter. "Well, then, you'll want to talk to me. The name's Muldoon. Hank Muldoon. I own these boats. I own the whole town. So if you want something, you have to take it up with me."

She looked at him, feeling a vague hint of despair. There was nothing duplicitous about him, but his general manner and the overall appearance of his operation did not instill her with much confidence. Without any idea of where to begin, asking Muldoon for assistance seemed like the epitome of futility, but what choice did she have? In the absence of an intuitive cue against such a course of action, she would have to trust him.

"Lovely," she said through a tight smile. "Let's get started."

Muldoon made his office in a small shack under the stairs that led up to the village main. The word "office" was perhaps too grand for the refuse-strewn room, but it did have at its center a magnificent desk of teak wood, worn and battered, but still an antique of obvious value. Mira suspected it once might have occupied the cabin of a China Clipper captain from before the age of steam. Like everything else that fell within Muldoon's realm of influence, the desk was suffering from neglect. A scattering of old magazines and newspapers adorned its intricately carved surface, held in place by empty beer bottles. Mira had taken a seat on an upturned banana crate opposite her host at his desk and given a detailed and mostly false explanation of her reasons for visiting the remote location.

Muldoon listened thoughtfully, never taking his eyes off her, even when he reached into a drawer and brought out a square bottle of brown glass. He waved it toward her without interrupting her narrative and, interpreting her nod as assent, fumbled for a rusty tin cup and splashed in a copious amount of clear liquid. He pushed it across the desk until it was within her reach, then fished around for a second cup.

Mira finished recounting her cover story—in which she claimed to be on the trail of a scholar who might have visited in years past—as she regarded the offering of spirits apprehensively. Although the cup appeared to be the breeding ground for an unidentifiable black fungal growth, Mira did not doubt that Muldoon's potent liquor had killed anything organic on contact. That did not necessarily translate into eagerness to drink.

Muldoon showed no such antipathy, draining his portion in a bored gulp. "Aimes, huh?" He belched thoughtfully. "No, can't say's I heard of him. But I can hazard a guess why he's interested in my little hamlet."

Mira watched with growing dread as Muldoon started pawing through the haphazard collection of pornographic magazines and Chilean newspapers on the desk. It seemed doubtful that he could produce anything of merit from such an accumulation. Her suspicions only deepened when he abruptly held up a dog-eared, decades old copy of *National Geographic* magazine. Muldoon paged through it until he found what he was looking for, then turned the magazine around and pushed it across the desk to her.

Mira leaned forward on her crate, glancing down at the periodical without touching it. The two pages showed a single photograph, taken underwater, though obviously not by a professional. Through the murky water, a distinct knife-like shape was discernible. Leaving her ambivalence behind, she picked it up and scanned the text printed in the inset. "A submarine. You found a Nazi U-boat?"

"Oh, aye. And for a while, all kinds of folks were trying to get me to tell where it was. But see, I was too smart for 'em. I gave 'em a phony fix. They never found it. Eventually gave up."

"I don't understand. Why didn't you want them to find it?"

Muldoon gaped at her, and when he spoke, his voice was strident with emotion. "Salvage is a cutthroat business, lass. As soon as I give up the location, fortune hunters will swoop in like vultures and I won't get squat for my discovery."

Mira smiled in spite of his tirade. "And if that happened, you'd have no means to support this extravagant lifestyle."

"Laugh if you like, missy. But I'll have the last laugh when I get my salvage finished. There's riches down there—Nazi gold! But if I were to show up rich all of a sudden, someone might take note, if you follow my meaning."

"I'm afraid I don't."

Muldoon leaned over the desk, close enough for her to smell the vapors of alcohol still on his breath, and whispered conspiratorially. "Odessa."

Mira did a mental back-flip at the all too familiar word. In the context of their discussion, "Odessa" could have meant only one thing; Muldoon lived in fear of something that had existed primarily only in the minds of imaginative espionage novelists. "Odessa," she echoed. "The organization of escaped Nazi officers who sought refuge in South America after World War II. But it's been nearly seventy years. How many of them could possibly still be living?"

"They've got heirs. Some say they even cloned themselves to keep the legacy alive. And you can bet they want what I've got. Right now, they think I'm just a foolish old pirate who stumbled on the wreck once, but was too drunk to find my way back."

Mira rocked back until the crate was square on the floor. She had not expected the map to lead to something so completely unrelated to Aimes' quest for prehistoric civilizations. Yet it seemed improbable that he could have found another event as significant as Muldoon's discovery in such a remote location. She swung her gaze back to him. "Have you recovered anything besides gold?"

"Ah, well. You see, I haven't actually salvaged anything yet. Keeping a low profile, you understand."

Realization dawned, and Mira fixed him with a stare that brooked no further deception. "There isn't any gold, is there?"

Muldoon scowled irritably, but did not meet her gaze for long. "Damn it, of course there is. But it's hidden all clever, see? And the currents—" He looked up again into her unwavering stare and dropped his hands in surrender. "Ah, missy. You found me out. I've dived on her a hundred times and not found the gold. Now I'm too old and too broken down to dive on her myself, and I don't dare take on a partner who'd likely stab me in the back as soon as the treasure was found."

The potential significance of the U-boat remained a mystery, but Mira was becoming convinced by degrees that the wreck of the Nazi vessel was indeed the clue that had prompted Aimes to put a pin on his map, pointing the way to Muldoon's forgotten seaport. The solution to that puzzle would not be found in an old photograph, however. Mira leaned close to the drunken wreck of a man, closer than he had been a moment before.

"Listen, Hank. I don't care about your gold, but I want to see what else is on that U-boat. If you'll take me there, I'll dive on it, and you can keep whatever gold I find."

Muldoon grinned, then grabbed the dark bottle and raised it in a mock toast. "I'll drink to that, missy."

Mira chuckled softly. "My intuition tells me you'll drink to anything."

A rare calm visited the Pacific Ocean the following morning. The constant gale, which had rattled the rafters overhead in the draughty hostel where Mira spent the night, had subsided in what her new partner would doubtless have called "the wee early hours." She had risen shortly after the onset of the calm and hastened down to Muldoon's boat, rousting him out of an alcoholic slumber. He came awake more easily than she had anticipated; evidently, he had grown accustomed to the effects of the liquor. He had grumbled over the cup of coffee she had thrust into his hands, but showed no other signs of physical impairment.

With Muldoon at the helm, the forty-footer pulled away from its slip and charged out into the gray waters of the Strait of Magellan. Distant shapes seemed to wink in and out of view on the horizon, islands that formed the final barrier between the South American continent and a stretch of empty water that, if one traveled due west, ended almost six thousand miles later at the twin islands of New Zealand.

With Muldoon bellowing about his lucidity, Mira left him on the flying bridge and went below to inspect the dive gear. The SCUBA tanks were at least twenty years old, faded from what was once a bright yellow hue and streaked with algae, but otherwise seemed in good repair. The gauge showed one fully filled—roughly eighty cubic feet of air at 3,000 pounds per square inch—and the other was about three-quarters full. The mask and wetsuit were likewise worn but intact. She played with the rubber straps of the mask, adjusting them to fit her head, then turned her attention back to the SCUBA gear.

The regulator seemed to function correctly, and a cautious breath showed no indication of dry rot in the lines. However, the twin tanks did not seem adequate for an extended dive, and this concerned her. There was no compressor to refill an empty bottle, which meant that one and three-quarters tanks was the limit on her dive time. Depending on the depth there might not even be time to reach the wreck, let alone explore it and still observe decompression tables. Muldoon had offered no clue as to the depth at which they would find the wreck, but the article in the *National Geographic* issue he had showed her the previous day told of a harrowing descent to depths of "inky blackness."

Setting aside the matter, she knelt beside the tanks and unlaced her boots. She had not brought along any sort of bathing suit, so in order to have dry clothes to change back into, she would have to make the dive with nothing at all between her skin and the heavy wetsuit. She tried not to think about the suit's usual occupant as she pulled on the neoprene garment, one leg at a time.

The wetsuit was an awkward fit in almost every way, bunching up in clumsy ripples of excess material, but there was nothing to be done about it. Though it would hamper her swim strokes, the insulating properties of the suit would not be greatly affected. Once her body heat warmed the thin layer of sea water trapped against her skin, it would keep her, if not exactly comfortable, at least comfortably away from hypothermia. A pair of dive booties that fit like clown shoes completed the ensemble.

Mira went back up to the deck to check on their progress. She found Muldoon consulting a chart and compass and realized with a start that the boat was no longer heading west, but rather north, parallel to the coastline. The magazine article had led her to believe they would find the wreck of the U-boat far to the west, in open water. She shook her head in amazement as Muldoon's deception became clear to her.

For close to thirty years, the old man had been telling tales of a dangerous dive in the Pacific depths. He had taken journalists and treasure hunters far out to sea and swept the area where he claimed to have first laid eyes on the wreck with every sort of detection device available, but the dark waters had yielded nothing. The repeated failures convinced the relentless fortune seekers that the U-boat wreck was a clever fraud, designed to bilk them out of their money, and after a while, they left him alone.

It had all been part of his plan. Paranoid that the descendants of the Third Reich would murder him and steal his treasure, he had intentionally misled two decades' worth of treasure seekers into believing that he was delusional.

Muldoon noticed her expression. "Almost there, missy.

Right where I left it."

"No one ever thought to look for it this close to the mainland?"

"Ah, there was one or two. But treasure hunting is a flavor that sours quickly."

Mira grinned. "Not if you're doing it right."

As she had expected, the rush of cold water into the ample cavity between the wet suit and her naked skin was bracing, to say the least. Her muscles involuntarily constricted, followed by a tooth chattering spasm of shivers that lasted several seconds. She bobbed upright in the water, feebly raising a hand to return Muldoon's wave, then slipped the airflow regulator between her lips and ducked her head beneath the chilly waters. Breathing pressurized air, with a faint oily taste, she began kicking and stroking into the deep.

Depth was a relative term. Muldoon had dropped anchor over an uncharted seamount where the ocean floor rose to within twenty fathoms of the surface. It was upon the spine of this rise that the U-boat had reefed herself, rupturing the pressure hull and flooding all compartments before a single man could think to blow the ballast tanks or attempt a free ascent. More importantly, it was a depth that could be reached and explored without overextending her limited supply of air.

Following the creation of their partnership, Muldoon had produced a surprisingly accurate diagram of the U-boat. It was drawn from his own experience rather that any technical information relating to the Walter XXI Electric Undersea Boat design. During the previous night, Mira had used her Internet-capable satellite telephone to do a little research on the history and design of the model XXI; experimental U-boats fielded toward the end of the war. The actual record of service for the XXI boats was somewhat less spectacular and, according to the available documents, all of them were accounted for. Evidently, however, those records were incomplete. If Muldoon was correct, then at least one of the submarines had carried out an unknown mission, which had brought it to its final resting place off the coast of Chile.

Using Muldoon's diagram, she planned her dive. She would

enter through the gaping wound in the U-boat's hull and proceed into the flooded lower deck of the sub. Muldoon claimed to have searched the captain's quarters, the only private space on the submarine, but found nothing. Mira, though uncertain of what it was she was supposed to be looking for, decided to begin her search there as well. Perhaps Muldoon, in his lust for gold, had overlooked something of greater, though less obvious, value.

Beneath the surface of the Pacific, however, diagrams and well-laid plans had very little relation to reality. The chill of the water and the stale taste of compressed air sapped her enthusiasm for the search before it had even begun. The litany of dangers, everything from nitrogen narcosis to shark attack, paraded through her mind, causing her to second-guess almost every decision as she kicked her legs up and down, thrusting deeper into the heart of the sea.

She kept her arms at her sides, moving them only when the growing pressure against her eardrums required her to press the diving mask to her face and snort through her nose to pop her ears. The bottom rushed up at her, bringing with it shadows and trepidation, but it was difficult to say whether her concerns were a psychic premonition or simply a natural fear at entering such an alien environment. SCUBA training had been just one more part of life on The Farm, and, she mentally reviewed those lessons, keeping her breathing steady so as not to hyperventilate, and got her dread under control.

The U-boat lay on its side atop the seamount, looking not much different than the two-decade-old photograph Muldoon had showed her in his office. The encrustation of prolific oceanic life forms could not mask the knife-edge keel of the submarine. The vessel's narrow-beam design represented naval architecture from a forgotten age. Modern submarine hulls were round, not unlike the torpedoes they carried, allowing for greater maneuverability beneath the ocean's surface. Submarines and U-boats of the World War II era and earlier were built along the same lines as surface ships and were quite agile above the depths where they spent nearly eighty percent of their sailing time, but less able beneath the waves, which should have been their primary environment. The XXI boats, designed for extended voyages underwater, represented a step in the right direction for submarine engineering, but were developed too late in the war to make a difference for Germany.

Muldoon's sketch had showed a breach amidships, a long gash that tore through pressure hull, opening the guts of the U-boat to the sea. However, while the outline of the boat was unmistakable, a gently sloping angular plane about seventy-five meters long, the cavity that permitted access was not so easy to distinguish. Mira kicked toward the region of the ship where she expected to find the hole, hoping that it would be easier to discern up close. Schools of fish darted away with her approach.

In spite of the colorful flora and fauna that had taken up residence on the hull of the U-boat, it remained a rust-colored hulk. She reached out to it tentatively with one neoprene-gloved hand, almost fearful that it would evaporate like a ghost before she could make contact. Instead, her touch stirred up a cloud of brown silt that did indeed cause the wreck to vanish, though for a more mundane reason. She continued pushing through the silt until her fingers found the unyielding surface of the boat's outer hull. Her probing hands continued to work up a cloud of sediment and algae, but she soon found what she was looking for: a ragged edge breaking up the otherwise smooth face of the hull. Mira pressed her mask close against the skin of the submarine, trying to get a look at the fissure.

The tear was horizontal along the keel, ten feet long, but less than three feet high. Mira found herself wondering how the bulky Muldoon, with two tanks of compressed air strapped to his back, had managed to slip through the narrow opening. The answer seemed dreadfully obvious; like almost everything else in his tale of Nazi gold and salvage, he had exaggerated. She wondered if he had ever actually ventured inside the wreck.

With her face still close to the hole, she reached to her waist where a mesh bag was secured to her weight belt. The bag contained half a dozen magnesium flares, which along with the SCUBA gear and the dive knife strapped to her right calf, represented her entire array of equipment and weapons. She extracted one of the flares, pulling the nylon drawstrings tight before striking the chemical light. Brilliant white illumination pierced the veil of sediment, giving her a clearer glimpse of the passageway into the U-boat.

The mottled brown of algae or rust seemed unchanged where the flickering rays of the torch cut through the cloak of darkness. Mindful of catching a hose or pranging the valves on the tanks, she eased forward into the hole. The flare continued to emit a rough sphere of illumination, but it took Mira several seconds to make sense of anything she was seeing.

Sixty years of immersion in salt water had disintegrated the wood panels and beams that comprised all non-structural bulkheads and surfaces in the U-boat to reveal an intricate maze of corroded pipes and gauges. Mira eased cautiously into the narrow space and moved toward the forward end of the vessel. There was more room to maneuver than Mira had expected. Nevertheless, she pressed low against what would have been the port-side bulkhead, careful not to snag the tanks or lines on overhead protuberances.

She quickly located the access hatch Muldoon had described and pulled through into what had once been the forward torpedo room. The uniform blight of corrosion made it difficult to distinguish the machinery and framework of the weapons system, but a haphazard cluster of gray sticks scattered throughout the compartment was easier to identify; the skeletal remains of German submariners.

A circular hatch less than three feet in diameter led out of the torpedo room. Why the crew had not secured the watertight doors as soon as the collision alarm had sounded was a mystery that would never be solved. For reasons known only to the brittle bones of the *Kriegsmarine* sailors, when the belly of the U-boat had ruptured, the flood of seawater had inundated every deck, rolling the vessel onto its side, before any damage-control measures could be initiated. Perhaps the sailors had preferred a quick death by drowning to the slow suffocation of being trapped on the bottom of the ocean.

Following her mental sketch of Muldoon's map, she soon located the niche that had been the captain's quarters. A wooden panel had at one time partitioned the small room from the rest of the ship. Only the commander of the vessel was privileged with private quarters, while the officers were accorded semi-private lodgings, and the crew shared the bunks that lined the corridors of the boat. Muldoon's notion that the treasure, if it existed at all, was to be found in the captain's quarters certainly made sense. A submarine did not have any sort of cargo hold. Foodstuffs for a prolonged journey were usually stored in the companionways, forcing the sailors to crawl through the corridors during the early days of a voyage. Yet, as she stared into the closet-sized space that by submariner standards was considered luxurious, she realized the fallacy in Muldoon's reasoning. There was not enough room in the captain's berth to conceal a meaningful quantity of treasure.

Floating in the surreal light of the flare, Mira pondered this revelation. Of course, there was no gold, and Aimes would not have been interested in mere fortune hunting. What, then, was the connection between Atlantis and the wreckage of a U-boat off the coast of Chile?

The captain's desk had fallen prey to the ravages of time and salt water, disintegrating and leaving only a vague outline of metal runners, fasteners and knobs. A shapeless lump that had once been an article of clothing or perhaps several garments hanging in a small closet now rested against the bulkhead, sprouting several rusty coat hangers. Muldoon claimed to have thoroughly searched the cabin, but nothing appeared to have been disturbed. Curious, Mira pushed at the sodden lump of rotting cloth.

A glimmer of gold caught her eye, and for a moment, she almost believed that she had found the elusive treasure. A moment later, however, her gloved hand drew back only a small lapel pin, gold indeed, but decorated with a cloisonné inlay that was all too familiar. A red and black swastika adorned the coin-sized pin, the insignia of the Nazi party.

Not all Germans had been loyal party members during the era in which Adolf Hitler ruled supreme. In fact, most of the rank and file in the German armed services were not Nazis. Only the upper echelons of the military, the generals and admirals, held that dubious distinction. Favored members of the

National Socialist Party were rarely sent into combat. It seemed very improbable that a mere U-boat captain would have received the Nazi badge.

Her probing fingers soon found another pin, though this one was badly discolored from exposure to the elements. Nevertheless, the silver insignia was unmistakable. It was the double-lightning bolt of the *Waffen Schutzstaffel*, the notorious SS guard.

The U-boat had been carrying a distinguished passenger.

Mira knew enough about maritime tradition to know that a captain rarely surrendered the privileges of his rank, but it was easy enough to imagine one of Hitler's elite officers demanding the privacy of the captain's quarters for himself. It was admittedly a minor aberration, but the presence of an SS officer aboard the submarine certainly lent credence to the idea that the U-boat concealed some darker riddle. She quickly probed through the remains of the cabin, searching for anything else that might shed light on that mystery.

Nothing.

The dive chronograph Muldoon had loaned her, an antique in its own right, revealed that she had spent nearly half an hour in the water. And she was already eating into the time reserved for her decompression stop. If the U-boat did not give up its secret soon, she would be forced to abandon the search and return to Muldoon's boat. No more answers would be found in the captain's quarters, but she had no idea where to turn next. Closing her eyes, she tried to imagine what must have happened in the minutes following the collision.

The SS officer would not have been in the control room in the seconds preceding the disaster. Likely, he would have steered clear of the boat's essential areas, keeping to the privacy of his appropriated lodgings, venturing out only to take his meals. Yet, there were no human remains in the captain's cabin.

In her mind's eye, Mira could almost see the arrogant SS officer, startled perhaps out of a nap by the sudden collision. As alarms rang throughout the boat, heralding a torrent of rushing water, he would have fled in terror.

No, there was more to it than that. The SS man had been in

possession of something, some hidden knowledge or discovery that had been his to protect. Walter Aimes had learned about it decades later, suggesting that the Nazi had held something pertaining to Atlantis. In his final moments of life, the SS agent would have sought to protect that secret.

Backing away from the captain's berth, Mira quickly reoriented herself and continued down the passage. As she entered the galley, she was forced to navigate a corkscrew path around tables and fixed benches. Skeletons littered the area, but she did not slow to examine the naked remains. Farther down the companionway, she found what she was looking for: a ladder-like stair that accessed the uppermost deck of the U-boat. Using it as a handrail, she pulled herself into the narrow cavity.

Here she found the greatest concentration of bones. Apparently death had not come swiftly enough to prevent a human stampede, frantic sailors trampling one another in a mad, but futile, rush to the top hatch. The skeletons all but choked the passageway, yet in the light of her flare, Mira could distinguish nothing extraordinary about any of them. Uniforms had long ago rotted away—a final equalization of rank. If the SS officer had lain among them, he would have gone forever unidentified. More than that, her intuition told her that this was a dead end for her as well. Frustrated and running short on time, she backed out of the passageway and returned the way she had come.

As she swam through the now familiar companionways, she tried again to replay her version of the U-boat's final seconds. She could almost see the SS officer, a cardboard cutout lifted from a World War II movie, bursting from the captain's quarters onto the heaving deck. As water rushed around his knees, threatening to overwhelm him, he would have looked about frantically for some way to protect . . .

If only she knew what secrets the SS officer had carried into his watery grave. Perhaps he had possessed nothing more substantial than a bit of knowledge, the location of Atlantis or one of the outposts founded by her refugee survivors. Such knowledge might have caught Aimes' interest, but Mira already knew where once-mighty Atlantis had fallen into the sea. It was hardly information worth killing the elderly researcher over.

I'm missing something, she thought again. *The answer has to be here.*

Unable to fight his way through the panicking seamen, the SS officer would have looked for some other means of salvation. Perhaps he knew that the sub's top hatch could not have been opened with tons of seawater weighing down upon it. Where, then, would he have gone? The torpedo tubes seemed a logical answer. The only practical way to exit a submerged U-boat was to get in the torpedo tubes, then close and flood them, equalizing the pressure. She wondered if, in the heat of the crisis, the SS officer could have planned such an egress rationally.

Suddenly the answer literally broadsided her.

As she attempted to pass through the maze of obstacles in the galley, an unexpected collision stopped her dead in the water. The unyielding barrier was a wall of algae-slicked stainless steel that had survived the corrosive march of time in remarkably good shape. Mira stared at it for a moment, trying to guess its function. Only when she turned her head sideways, looking at it as the crew would have when viewing it aright, did she resolve the mystery. She had run into the freezer.

Unlike most submarines of her day, the XXI U-boats were equipped with extraordinary creature comforts, not the least of which was a deep-freeze compartment for storing meat and other perishables. Though Mira had no way of ascertaining when the submarine had left port fully stocked, it wasn't a stretch to believe that the crew would have consumed most of the boat's frozen goods by the time it had reached the Pacific coast of South America. Nor was it difficult to imagine the frantic SS officer seeking shelter in the sealed compartment in the moments following the collision. It was a theory easily enough tested.

Twisting around to brace her flippered feet against the doorframe, she gripped the latch handle and pulled. Though the mechanism yielded to her effort, the door did not budge. She continued straining against the handle for several seconds until, without warning, it snapped off in her hand, sending her backward into a sideways table edge.

Tossing the useless handle aside, she returned to the freezer door and inspected the damage. The entire latch mechanism had separated from the door, leaving only a ragged cavity in the metal and foam insulation visible within. Separating the metal hatch from the compartment was a thin, partially decomposed rubber gasket, but it was difficult to imagine the door becoming fused shut with the passage of time. That left only one explanation: the freezer compartment was watertight. The pressure of thousands of tons of water at depth was holding the freezer door shut, preserving the dry environment within.

Mira drew the Tekna knife and rotated to a position beneath the freezer. The carbon steel blade easily pierced the sheet metal, and though more effort was required, she soon drew a meter-long diagonal cut in the side of the freezer. She worked the blade back and forth until it was free, then repeated the process, cutting a large X in the metal. Cautiously peeling the metal away revealed the insulation underneath, likewise scored by the blade. Using the blade, she quickly removed all of the foam from the area exposed by her cut and uncovered another metal wall.

As soon as the tip of her blade pierced the freezer's inner wall, a rush of water streamed in through the cut. Heartened by the realization that whatever lay inside the freezer had escaped the despoilment caused by more than sixty years of salt water immersion, she hastily cut another X in the inner wall and bent the metal inward. As she pushed into the freezer, a compartment that was at least as big as the captain's quarters had been, she saw that her assumption was at least partially correct.

A human form sat unmoving on the sideways bulkhead not far from where she had entered. An inch or so of water had flooded the lowest portion of the compartment, dampening the remains, but the air pocket within kept the rest at bay. The sealed crypt of the freezer had preserved the corpse remarkably well. Mira carefully pulled herself over the sharp metal edges of her cut, and knelt in front of the body. She continued breathing the compressed air from her tank, realizing that the man who had sought refuge here so many decades before had likely died of suffocation after consuming all of the oxygen trapped with him in the compartment.

The man had perished with his head resting against his knees, his arms protectively clutching a leather briefcase to his chest. He wore a simple white shirt and dark trousers, rather than the uniform of a *Kriegsmarine* sailor or officer, and no indication of rank or identity except for a silver ring bearing the likeness of a skull and crossbones.

With a triumphant grin, Mira realized that she had found her man.

Careful to avoid too much contact with the corpse, she took hold of a lower corner of the case and tried to pull it from his eternal grasp. His lifeless limbs remained unusually pliable, and he almost seemed to shrug his shoulders as the parcel slipped past his elbow.

Her eager fingers were unwieldy in the confines of the gloves, and it took her several attempts to loosen the catch. Once the fastener relented, she all but dived into the recesses of the bag to see what secret the SS officer had been so desperate to protect. She was almost disappointed when the briefcase yielded up nothing but papers. A rapid flip through the documents, several pages written in German block script, revealed little about their contents. Her grasp of the Teutonic language, courtesy of The Farm, was adequate, but the volume of text was too great and the verbiage too tedious for her to even begin to get a grasp on what was written in the papers. Deciphering the contents of the case would require at least a few hours and a decent bilingual dictionary.

One of the papers, however, required no translation. A large map, folded by eighths, showed a detailed relief of South America. Several notations had been made suggesting that something of importance might be found somewhere in the remote wilderness near the border of Chile and Bolivia. Behind the glass of her dive mask, Mira's eyes lit up. The U-boat did not conceal a treasure, but perhaps this was a treasure map.

She refolded the map and stuffed it, along with the other

papers, back into the case, then crammed the entire parcel into the mesh bag along with the flares. Hopefully, the stiff leather would minimize water damage during the brief ascent, but it was the best she could do to protect the documents under the circumstances.

Feeling a rush of triumph at the apparent success of her mission, Mira turned back to the long-deceased keeper of the knowledge, wondering what other secrets had died with him.

With his burden removed, she could see his features more clearly. A pale, gaunt man, he barely resembled the Hollywood version she had imagined. His short dark hair and whiskers had continued to grow for a while after his death, leaving him with uncharacteristic stubble. Ironically, German submariners did not shave when they were at sea, and the SS officer's attention to personal grooming surely added to the ideological gulf between himself and the crew.

A dim reflection of the flare's light caught her eye; the German was wearing something around his neck. A gentle tug on his collar revealed a necklace of heavy golden links, dropping in a V into the hidden depths beneath his buttoned shirt. Curious in spite of the urgency she now faced due to her rapidly diminishing air supply, Mira took the chain in her fingers and drew the hanging ornament into the light.

Her eyes grew wide as she focused on the impossible yet familiar relic the man wore as a pendant. Then, her heart froze as a hand gripped her wrist and she found herself looking into the eyes of a man who had been dead long before she was born.

PART TWO
DUALITY

FIVE

She reacted without thinking, slapping the restraining hand away without a second thought for the impossibility of what she was witnessing. Mira Raiden had long ago learned how to avert the paralysis of fear. Dead or alive, the man had become both foe and threat. As the reanimated Nazi drew back his lips in a silent, feral howl, she struck. The heel of her right hand slammed into his jaw, snapping his head back. The well-preserved skin seemed to slough away from bone to reveal the curve of his skull. There now seemed little question that the SS officer was still dead; all that remained was finding a way to return him to his eternal slumber.

Recovering from her blow, the dead man began to uncurl from his seated position and rose to his full height, a head taller than Mira. Though apparently possessing supernatural strength, he had only his hands to use as weapons. With a swift slash of the dive knife, she removed one of them, but her foe seemed unconcerned.

As the initial shock of the attack subsided, part of Mira's thought process turned to the other impossible thing she had just witnessed: the object dangling from the necklace of gold links around the German's neck was—without a doubt—the Trinity.

Accepting that the SS officer she now faced was a sort of zombie was not without precedent. In the ruins of the temple in Panama, she had witnessed a supernatural display of power from the Trinity, so it wasn't too much of a stretch to accept that the relic could reanimate mummified corpses.

But how did it end up here, in a sealed compartment, on a submarine lost more than six decades before?

Simple answer: there's more than one. Now you know why Atlas called it the Trinity.

The undead creature darted forward, using its maimed arm as a club, while the remaining hand tore at her mask. Ducking under his attack, Mira swept a foot at his legs, unbalancing him, but only for a moment. The Nazi recovered with unnatural agility, hopping over her kick, and dropped down into a crouch to renew the attack. The stump arm struck a blow to her mid-section that knocked her against the upturned floor of the compartment.

There seemed only one practical means of defense. The Nazi would pose little threat if he were reduced to a pile of disconnected, undead parts. Yet his attacks were too swift to allow her to wield the small knife effectively. Parrying another thrust, she aimed a kick at his chest.

As her foot made contact, the zombie closed his jaws on the end of her flipper. The momentum of the kick knocked him away, but several of his teeth and a fair amount of flesh were ripped loose from his decomposing face. When he came at her again, he resembled death incarnate.

Heartened by the success of her defense, Mira sprang erect once more, slashing with the knife in a double-handed grip. The blade of the Tekna drew a bloodless line across the German's throat, its tip catching for a millisecond on the neck vertebrae before severing them completely. A thin ribbon of flesh still connected the Nazi's head to his body, but it was not enough to keep it from rolling backwards to dangle impotently between his shoulder blades.

Even that was not enough to halt the attack.

The undead Nazi continued to flail at her, sensing her presence, though his desiccated eyes could no longer find her. Ducking under his thrashing limbs, she thrust out her right hand in a stiff-arm blow that would have left a linebacker gasping for breath. The undead SS agent staggered back with the force of the connection, but did not seem otherwise affected. As her foe staggered back, now precariously close to the hole through which she had entered, her hand closed on the shape of the circlet beneath the cloth of his shirt. Wrenching her arm back with all her might, she tore the fabric off of the reanimated corpse. The golden necklace pulled taut for an instant, then, like the blade of a chainsaw, cut through the remaining cords of flesh that held the German's head on his shoulders. The severed head vanished through the opening, but the decapitated form did not relent.

Neither did Mira.

Spinning on her left heel, she brought her right foot, flipper and all, in a roundhouse kick that struck the zombie just below its left elbow. The impact of the blow knocked Mira off balance, but as she struggled to right herself, she caught a glimpse of the German dropping through the cut in the freezer wall.

With her opponent vanquished, Mira felt a preternatural calm come over the silent crypt. She could almost see the vibrations of her heart beating wildly in the grip of adrenaline overload, against the rubberized fabric of the wetsuit. She took a deep breath of air from the mouthpiece, hoping that in the heat of combat she had not overtaxed her oxygen supply. A glance at the wrist chronometer revealed that only a few minutes had passed since her last time-check; her battle with the undead SS officer had lasted mere seconds, but every breath brought her precariously close to an empty air tank.

Nevertheless, she contemplated the cloth-wrapped article in her right hand as if detached from the urgency of her situation. Almost reverently, she pulled back the impromptu shroud, exposing the relic. It was unquestionably a twin to the Trinity she had brought back from Panama. The ring of silver-colored metal unlike any alloy known to modern man, and the white hexagon of unnatural crystal—this one undamaged—were features both eerily familiar.

Yet much about this development was unprecedented. In Panama, the Trinity had blasted her with a psychic assault that had ultimately numbed her precognitive faculties. From this relic, however, she sensed only a faint tingle of background energy, and that only with physical contact.

Where on earth did you come from? She thought to the talisman, unable to speak the words past the mouthpiece. The Trinity offered no illumination.

The papers in the dead Nazi's case, however, might, but those answers would have to wait. As she stuffed the Trinity piece in her mesh bag—owing to a flash of intuition or maybe just plain old deductive reasoning—she realized that Walter

Aimes had somehow known about the presence of the artifact on the U-boat. It was the only explanation that made any sense, yet in the larger context it made no sense at all. She wondered if the mystery of her elderly benefactor's impossible knowledge would ever be uncovered.

Before dropping back into the chilly waters, Mira struck a fresh flare, leaving the sizzling stub of the first to burn itself out. Though the water was only a few feet deep beyond the opening, it was shrouded in shadows, hiding the remains of the enemy she had just defeated. Holding her mask tight against her face, she jumped out into the center of the opening and was instantly immersed in cold darkness.

Before her eyes could register the surrounding images in the sudden illumination provided by the flare, she sensed movement off to her left. She twisted around in time to dodge yet another attack from the relentless reanimated Nazi. As his arms closed on empty water, she kicked at his torso with both feet, shoving him into the maze of tables and benches. Even as he thrashed, his flesh seemed to boil off his bones. The wasted skin and muscle tissue peeled away in the salt water until nothing remained but an impotent skeleton of bones, cartilage and ligaments. The grotesque headless form remained impossibly upright, but there was no fight left in him. However, the zombie's final attack gave her the edge of adrenaline that enabled her to survive what happened next.

She was just turning over to swim out of the galley area when a flash of light and motion struck out of the shadows. She twisted away instinctively, her psychically attuned reflexes saving her life, but nevertheless felt a sudden rush of frigid water as a blade sliced along her left arm, opening both the neoprene suit and the flesh along her biceps. The icy water and the sharpness of the knife dulled the pain of a wound.

Her new assailant was revealed in the light of her torch, not a reanimated submariner, but a living man, breathing compressed air from a SCUBA tank. His gray eyes narrowed behind the glass of his mask, and Mira sensed that another thrust of his blade was imminent. She remained motionless, as if petrified with fear, waiting for his arm to draw back, but as his torso twisted in preparation to strike she spun away. The blade stabbed through the rotting steel bulkhead up to its hilt.

The diver tried to pull it out, adding both hands to the effort, but the blade was lodged firmly in the pressure hull. Mira kicked her flippers vigorously to right herself, then darted toward the momentarily distracted diver. Her wounded arm left a ribbon trail of blood in the water, but she ignored the growing ache, driving like a spear at her assailant. An instant too late, the diver surrendered in the battle for his knife and turned to meet her charge, but a swipe of Mira's right hand removed his mask. The man howled in an instinctive panic as the mouthpiece of his SCUBA system ripped away. A rush of bubbles filled the companionway as Mira's Tekna sliced the man's hose in two. As the doomed diver's terrorized thrashing grew to a fever pitch, she darted past him and began threading the labyrinth in her own desperate bid for survival.

Despite her haste, she was wary. Battling the supernatural guardian of the Trinity had caught her completely by surprise, but this secondary assault from a more ordinary source was not so easily hidden. There were more attackers lying in wait. She took a deep breath as she approached the hull-breach, holding it in lest her air bubbles announce her approach. Gripping the ragged edges of the broken pressure hull, she drew in like a coiled serpent, then launched herself at the fissure.

Right away, she saw two more divers, their generic black wetsuits stark against the dimly illuminated surface above. Both men swam patrol circles, perhaps fifteen feet above the wreck, holding spearguns at the ready. One of them, startled by her sudden appearance, triggered the release on his weapon, sending the barbed spear harmlessly into the depths.

The moment in which the divers struggled to verify that it was their quarry, not their comrade, emerging from the wreck was one Mira used to her advantage. Turning a quick circle in the water, she spied a third diver lurking near the still-clouded waters by the gash in the U-boat's keel. Rapidly inverting herself, she kicked furiously toward the lone diver, knife extended in her right fist.

Something tugged at her right calf and then flashed past

her. The narrow tunnel view of her mask did not allow her to see the object, but she knew by the sudden stinging on the back of her leg that the remaining diver above had scored a glancing hit with his spear gun. Unrelenting, she continued her torpedo assault on the frogman below.

Comprehending his danger more readily than his comrade inside the wreck, the man immediately started swimming away from the target zone. Mira struck an instant later, driving the point of the weapon into the back of his thigh. The tip struck bone and the rubber grip of the knife was wrenched out of her fist as the wounded diver thrashed in agony, a trail of blood darkening the water around him.

At least now, Mira thought morbidly, *if the neighborhood great white shark puts in an appearance, I won't be the only dish on the table.*

Like his friends above, the wounded man carried a harpoon launcher, but the weapon now dangled uselessly by a nylon strap that was itself attached to a quiver full of harpoons secured with elastic cords to his air tank. Forgetting the lost knife, Mira made a grab for the spear gun. Bracing her feet against the man's back, she wrestled the weapon free and whirled to find a target.

Both of the divers were closing on her position, so she brandished the weapon left to right, watching to see which direction they would break in order to avoid her spear. The nearest diver reacted frantically, twisting away from her feint and unwittingly exposing himself. Mira did not hesitate. The harpoon gun shuddered in her hands as the energy stored in its elastic band snapped the projectile forward. The spear itself slipped noiselessly through both the water and the abdomen of the unlucky diver. His final confused thoughts were almost audible: *It wasn't supposed to happen like this. . . .*

The remaining diver capitalized on his comrade's misfortune to take careful aim with his own weapon. Mira abandoned her efforts to thread another harpoon into the gun and kicked to the right. Her foe's barb struck too close for comfort, piercing through the leather case in the mesh bag and lodging midway through. The tip remained dangerously close to her hip as she swam away.

Suddenly her view of the battle vanished in a splash of frigid water. With so many threats from so many different directions, she had missed this one.

An unseen foe had ripped her mask away, blinding her with stinging salt water. Before her vision could resolve the blurry image of the seascape, she felt the assailant attacking again, this time trying to rip her mouthpiece from between her teeth. Like a horse fighting the bridle she resisted, thrashing from side to side and swinging the impotent spear gun like a truncheon. One of her blind attacks scored, and she felt a muted impact as the makeshift club clipped her attacker.

Through the haze of seawater pressing against her eyeballs, she could see the figure of the man she had stabbed with the dive knife. The blade remained firmly planted in his thigh, but apparently he had worked through the pain, intent on accomplishing his mission and avenging his comrades. Before he could recover his equilibrium, Mira clutched the hilt of the knife with both hands and tried to wrench it free.

Agony flared in her left arm where the first attacker's blade had cut deep. Her traumatized muscles rapidly failed, but the momentary exertion yielded favorable results. Though her left hand slipped away, the knife broke loose, gouging a divot of flesh and bone that sent the diver into a state of shock.

Her triumph was short-lived. The other diver slammed into her back, finishing what his friend had started. Rather than wrestle the air hose from her mouth, he attacked the line itself, hacking into it with his knife near the junction with the tank. Mira felt the sudden change in pressure and spit the mouthpiece out as a flood of brackish water rushed into her mouth.

The SCUBA gear on her back, which a moment before had enabled her to endure the alien undersea environment, now represented nothing but a bulky, heavy liability. She sensed that her foe had backed off, content in the belief that her fate was all but sealed. For a moment, she, too, almost accepted that judgment. Hanging in the water, surrounded by the last gasps of air that rushed from the tank on her back, she frantically searched for a better answer.

An experienced swimmer, Mira could easily hold her breath

for over two minutes under ideal circumstances, but this situation was far from ideal. She had not even been given opportunity to draw one final good breath before losing her air supply. The ocean surface was more than a sixty feet above, a virtually impossible free ascent, even for someone of her skill. Willing herself calm, Mira chose to make better use of that final gasp of air.

A couple of quick cuts with the knife severed the straps that bound her to the useless SCUBA tanks. Another cut sliced the line of lead weights free of her belt, sending the gray blocks spiraling downward. Unencumbered by the heavy apparatus, she pirouetted in the water like a dolphin, the full power of the long swim fins propelling her rapidly toward the retreating diver.

At the last second he saw her approach and brought his hands up defensively. His blade slashed menacingly to warn her off. Agilely evading the knife, Mira darted around behind the man and snared hold of his air tank with both hands. The diver spun in circles, trying first to find his attacker, then to throw her off.

Immediately, she wrapped her legs around his waist, locking her ankles together to free her hands for the rest of her plan. Anticipating her next move, the man dropped his knife, throwing both hands up to hold his mask in place. Mira was faster by a heartbeat. After ripping the mask away, she began tearing at his eyes and nose. Though her gloved fingers did little real damage, the terrified diver was too caught up in protecting his face to launch any kind of counter-attack. He barely resisted as she tore the breathing apparatus out of his mouth.

The first thing she did after capturing the mouthpiece was to press it greedily to her own lips, filling her lungs with a fresh breath of air. She could feel the desperate frogman, still captive in her embrace, holding his breath as his flailing hands tried to pry her loose and knew that he was still not out of the fight. A few yards away, the remaining diver was struggling to propel himself to his comrade's aid, his viciously wounded leg trailing uselessly.

Her immediate antagonist somehow seized hold of the air

hose, beginning a tug of war with Mira for control of the business end. She fought back, succeeding only because her position gave her the leverage needed to overcome his superior strength. It was a battle she would ultimately lose if the man received assistance from the injured diver.

Instead of fighting to keep the mouthpiece between her teeth, she spat it into her right hand and pulled hard, ripping it from her opponent's grasp. Wrestling it over his right shoulder, she found the valve of his buoyancy compensator and after only a moment of fumbling joined the two. The bladders of the vest-like apparatus immediately filled with compressed air, causing the diver's chest to swell like a balloon. The transfer of air from the compressed environment of the tank to the external air bladders of the buoyancy vest did not change his actual mass, causing him to shoot uncontrollably toward the surface, but it hampered his ability to resist what Mira did next.

Slipping her knife from its sheath, she cut away his weight belt. She immediately felt the change in pressure as their shared buoyancy caused a gradual ascent. The hose and mouthpiece now dangled out of reach for both of them, but Mira ignored the urgent demand of her lungs for air, focusing instead on the end-game of her bold assault.

Biting down on the back edge of the knife blade, pirate-style, she freed up her hands. She closed her left over the diver's nose and lips and used her right forearm and elbow to lock her hold in place. The frogman, already desperately holding his breath, did not comprehend the danger he was in. Mira abruptly relaxed the grip of her legs and began kicking vigorously toward the surface.

As they shot up through the water, ascending more than three feet per second, Mira steadily exhaled the breath she had been holding, sending a stream of bubbles skyward. If her foe now understood what she was doing, he was helpless to resist. As they left behind two atmospheres of pressure, the volume of air trapped in his lungs expanded in a matter of seconds, rupturing the fragile membranes of his bronchial tubes. She felt a tremor of agony pass through the doomed man and a final, silent scream shouted into her gloved hand, and then the man went limp.

She stopped kicking as soon as her foe became motionless, but the momentum of her ascent was not so easily arrested. Snatching the knife from her teeth, she reached around and slashed the blade across the inert man's chest, rupturing the pockets of air in the buoyancy compensator. The sudden release of air was sufficient to slow the deadly express ride. She soon had the unmistakable sensation of dropping once more.

Releasing her grip on the lifeless diver, she swam a tight circle around his slowly descending form. Her fingers slipped capriciously on the quick release buckle of his waist belt, but once it was free, it took only a couple tugs on the shoulder straps to loosen the SCUBA gear.

The gear she had borrowed from Muldoon was of an older generation than that being used by the unknown assault team. Her bib-style buoyancy compensator was considerably less effective than the vests used by the opposition. Nevertheless, a quick jet of air into the bladder, combined with a few gentle kicks, halted the downward plunge long enough for her to get her bearings.

Through blurred vision she could just make out the last surviving diver, the one she had wounded in the leg, struggling to make his ascent. Too distant to pose a threat, she ignored him and focused on more urgent matters.

The captured SCUBA rig was equipped with a digital depth gauge, which indicated that she had risen to four fathoms, missing an essential decompression stop. There was no way of knowing if she had expelled enough of the nitrogen from her blood stream to avoid the painful effects of decompression sickness. Hoping to take back some of what she had lost, she treaded water where she was for several minutes, breathing away the excess nitrogen and recuperating from the exertion of her battle.

The hazy outline of Muldoon's boat was visible overhead. The thirty feet of water separating her from the surface magnified the view, compensating for the blurring of the image. Harder to distinguish were the four small keels that bobbed just off her fantail. *Too small to be boats*, she ascertained. *Jet skis?*

From the onset of the attack, she had been subconsciously working through two scenarios. The first, admittedly difficult to accept, was that Muldoon had double-crossed her, sending his buddies down to finish her off as soon as the treasure was revealed. She hadn't really considered that to be the case; it was more of a niggling suspicion without any basis in reality. In fact, the more she saw, the less she believed that the crusty old Aussie could have possibly marshaled the commando-style attack force. No, if Muldoon had ever had access to divers and equipment of that caliber, he would not have waited twenty years for her to come calling.

No amount of rationalizing could absolve her from the inescapable conclusion. The unknown conspiracy that had slain Walter Aimes, and perhaps stolen the first Trinity from the museum exhibit, had found her. Worse, they had played her. The stolen map was just so much cheese at the end of the maze, an obvious puzzle that she had counted herself clever for solving. In winning over Muldoon she had bridged the final chasm that prevented them from capturing the second Trinity.

What they hadn't counted on was a mouse with teeth. She still possessed this new Trinity and perhaps with it the element of surprise.

Impatient to get to the surface, she skipped the last thirty seconds required by the standard decompression tables and began kicking for the surface. The current had not carried her too far from the bow of Muldoon's boat, and she broke the surface thirty feet from the vessel.

Wiping the seawater from her eyes, she got her first clear look at the boat since losing her mask. Four brightly colored Yamaha Wave Runners drifted on tether lines from the aft railing, but there was no sign of movement aboard the vessel. If the divers had utilized the personal watercraft, one rider for each, then perhaps they had left the boat unguarded. Nevertheless, she was wary, and something told her that this wasn't over yet.

In capturing the diver's SCUBA gear, she had also liberated another harpoon gun to replace the one she had lost, along with half a dozen barbed spears. Before surrendering the tanks and apparatus to the deep, she cut the quiver loose and looped the spear gun over her shoulder. The single-shot weapon was a poor substitute for a firearm, but it was better than nothing. Her Beretta, secure in her backpack in Muldoon's office, wasn't going to do her any good.

Keeping her head above the waterline and her eyes on the boat, she side-stroked quickly to the fantail, threading her way past the dormant Wave Runners. Before ascending the short ladder onto the bow, she kicked off her flippers. With any luck, she wouldn't be swimming again for a long time.

She raised her head slowly until just one eye peeked over the gunwale. There was still no sign of activity. Emboldened, she hefted the spear gun and rolled over the rail, dropping into a crouch. The deck lay more or less completely exposed. A few paces away, a descending gangplank led below decks, and right beside it a ladder rose to the flying bridge. Mira thought she could see the top of Muldoon's head over the backrest of the captain's chair. She crept forward, waving the gun back and forth, her finger tense on the trigger. This was a trap and she knew it.

Mira felt her dread increasing by degrees. She crept toward the ascending ladder then quickly climbed to the flying bridge. At the top, she spun around, covering the deck once more with the harpoon gun, but there was still no sign of activity. A backward step brought her abreast of Muldoon. She knew without looking that he was dead. The cause of his death was not immediately discernible, but his sightless eyes bespoke the agony that had preceded it. His assailants had tortured him; perhaps his heart had given out.

"Damn you," she whispered, kneeling before him. "He was a harmless old man."

"He kept the secret to the bitter end, for all the good it did him."

The unexpected voice chilled her like another immersion in the deep. She rolled back from Muldoon's corpse, scanning for the unseen speaker. It had been a woman's voice, and Mira had a pretty good idea of who it was.

"Rachel Aimes, I presume." She spoke in a low tone, but

loud enough to be heard on the deck in the area immediately below the bridge.

Menacing laughter was the only answer. Mira eased forward, staying low. Rachel's minions had not hesitated to use lethal force below the waves; it was doubtful that she would meet with anything less above. They had already killed one innocent man, or two if Walter Aimes was included, to achieve their goal. Now that Mira had done all the work, there was no reason left to keep her alive.

"We offered him money," Rachel volunteered, the voice definitely coming from the starboard side of the boat. "But that just convinced him that the treasure was worth even more."

Mira crawled forward to the lip of the ladder then risked a quick look in all directions. No one. With as much stealth as she could manage, she gripped the ladder, holding her insteps against the outer railings, and slid down. As soon as she landed, she spun around, ready to fire the spear gun.

"It's ironic really. He trusted you and ended up leading us right to what he protected for so long. A sucker for a pretty face, and it cost him his life."

The voice hadn't come from the same place. Rachel was moving as she talked, stalling, trying to lure Mira into an ambush.

Forewarned is forearmed, she thought grimly, then risked an answer. "You didn't have to kill him."

Rachel's manic laughter echoed in peals off the ocean's surface, just around the edge of the cabin on the port side. "No. But I wanted to."

Mira somersaulted forward toward the sound of the voice, coming up with the harpoon tip aimed at the place she imagined Rachel to be, but her opponent had already fled. She caught a glimpse of Rachel's blond hair trailing around the forward end of the superstructure.

A premonition told that she had indeed fallen into the trap. She threw herself to the right, twisting about and firing the harpoon. At the same instant, the deck ahead of the place where she had been a moment before erupted in a spray of splinters.

Her harpoon sailed over the head of the target that her eyes had not even seen. Had the man been standing, her spear would have struck dead center in his chest. Of course, given that the bulky mercenary she had encountered twice before in New York usually took the precaution of wearing Kevlar armor, better marksmanship probably would have counted for little. He was not, however, standing, but lying prone in a sniper's crawl, wielding the familiar AK-47 assault rifle.

The unexpected resistance startled the mercenary, causing him to relax his finger on the trigger of his weapon for only a second. Without time to reload, Mira simply hurled the useless spear gun at him. When he threw up his hands to prevent the metal tube from striking his face, she leapt into motion.

Using her legs like coiled springs, she launched herself backward into a shoulder roll, spinning one hundred eighty degrees on her back as she went, so that when her feet touched the deck, she was again facing away from the gunman. Rising up into a sprinter's crouch, she rounded the corner of the superstructure before the mercenary could find the trigger of his weapon. She heard his primate voice cursing as he struggled to rise and give chase.

Suddenly her path was blocked. As Mira skidded to a halt, nearly stumbling in the oversized diving booties, she found herself facing Rachel Aimes. The statuesque blonde stood four inches taller than Mira, slender and athletic, but without a trace of femininity in her stance. Like her comrade, she wore a one-piece black wet suit. Rachel's suit was also far less cumbersome out of the water than the antique Mira was wearing. Yet it was not the superior maneuverability of her antagonist that caused Mira to stop dead in her tracks, but rather a Heckler & Koch MP5K-PDW—a nine-millimeter submachine gun that was a favorite of anti-terrorist operatives and SWAT teams—held in a two-handed grip, ready to fire.

A humorless smile touched Rachel's full lips, a death's head grin on a runway model, then her eyes dropped to the mesh bag slung over Mira's shoulder. "Give it up, sister dear. You can't win."

Mira's eyes narrowed defiantly. She heard the thumping of footsteps behind her as the Rachel's companion closed in to complete the trap. Defenseless and caught between two heavily armed opponents, she had only one answer for the woman demanding her surrender.

"Guess again."

SIX

Rachel's smile slipped a notch. Their trap had backfired. Turner, the leader of the mercenary group that had, in spite of considerable but acceptable losses, pulled off the museum job, had now stupidly placed himself directly behind the target. She could not fire at Mira without hitting him, nor could he make use of the assault rifle, of which he was so fond, without killing his employer in the process. Her indecision unconsciously translated into a slight relaxing of the muscles in her arm, and the barrel of the machine pistol dropped imperceptibly.

In a blur of motion, Mira spun, throwing a roundhouse kick that hit the other woman's jaw with an audible thud. Rachel's head snapped to one side, followed immediately by the rest of her, and the MP5 clattered to the deck.

Turner had barely restrained himself from emptying the AK-47 as he rounded the corner, and now suffered from the same hesitation that had given Mira the advantage over his boss. But with Rachel down, he had a clear field of fire. Bracing the stock of the rifle under his arm, he pulled the trigger, spraying the transom with 7.62mm ammunition. Mira was already gone, however, having sprung over Rachel's dazed form and out of his line of fire.

Turner released the trigger and ran to the edge of the deck just in time to see Mira arcing gracefully out over the water. He swung the AK-47 over the side and pulled the trigger at the same instant she pierced the gently rippling swells, vanishing again from his view. The water erupted in a sprinkling of impact splashes until the magazine went empty and gun clicked in silent impotence.

With the target lost from sight, Turner knelt to assist Rachel. His actions might have seemed more chivalrous had she not been paying him so well. The dazzling blonde woman did not look quite as lovely with blood trickling from the corner of her mouth. There was a rough abrasion on her cheek where Mira's foot had connected, a dark bruise would later color her jaw line. She stared uncomprehending for a moment, then her eyes widened in rage. "Where is she?"

"Over the side."

They both rose and stared across the gunwale into the place where Mira had dived. The blank serenity of the spot was shattered as one of the Wave Runners roared along the side of the boat, the rider instantly identifiable by her spiky auburn hair.

Turner reflexively raised the assault rifle, but he had forgotten to reload and the trigger simply refused to move. Helpless, he turned to his companion.

"After her!"

Rachel's strident voice put both of them in motion. Ignoring the fleeing Mira, they rushed to the stern of the boat, ready to mount the remaining watercraft and give chase. Even before they arrived however, they could see the three Wave Runners adrift, more than a dozen yards off the fantail.

Rachel drew up short, turning to stare in the direction Mira had gone. In a voice that dripped with cold menace, said simply: "Call our friends."

When high-velocity bullets strike the surface of water, they react the way they would if striking concrete. The lead is disfigured by the impact and often fragments completely. Once in a while, they might continue on for a few feet or so, but their lethal properties are almost completely negated in the liquid medium.

Mira's dive took her deep enough to avoid Turner's parting barrage, though that consideration was only incidental. She had another goal and immediately turned back toward the boat, staying about a fathom below the keel until she reached the fantail. She could hear the voices of her foes, only beginning to recover from her desperate escape and reckoned that time was on her side.

She contemplated starting up all of the Wave Runners and sending them away under their own power, but the mini boats were specifically designed to turn in circles if no one was at the controls. She had to settle for simply cutting them loose and giving each a good shove, trusting wind and sea to do the rest.

Only when all four of the craft were bobbing free of their tethers did she risk firing up the engine on the one she had chosen to ride.

Keeping her stance low to avoid being thrown from the craft, she opened the throttles to full and roared away from the boat. She caught a brief glimpse of Rachel Aimes and the hulking mercenary that accompanied her, but did not look back.

Once out of the lee shadow cast by the boat, the chop increased dramatically, causing the deck of the Wave Runner to bounce violently under Mira's feet. She kept her knees flexed, riding out the jolts like a skier in mogul field. Leaning to her right, she angled the watercraft toward shore, carving a ninety-degree turn that put her on a direct heading for Muldoon's harborage.

The larger geographical details of the coastline, the fjords, crags and even the snowy skyline of the Andes, were easily discernible, but the smaller details were a blur. Trees were indistinguishable from shadows; specks in the foreground floating on the surface could have been rocks or anchored fishing boats. But as the separating distance decreased, the clarity of her vision improved. She could easily make out the three small shapes, and another that dwarfed its satellites, rocketing out of the inlet on an intercept course.

In a heartbeat, the approaching objects resolved into more recognizable forms: a trio of personal watercraft, more or less identical to the Wave Runner Mira had commandeered, riding ahead of a sleek, black cigarette boat. Though the larger jet powered vessel could have easily outpaced the smaller craft, its operator chose to hang back, letting the Wave Runners take the lead like pawns on a chessboard.

The gap between the opposing forces diminished rapidly. Mira could distinguish the silhouettes of the riders and two human forms in the jet boat, and then even their features and expressions became visible. The driver's face was eerily familiar.

As if on cue the three Wave Runners broke formation, peeling off in different directions in an obvious attempt to flank her and close in from all sides. She surmised that Rachel was in radio contact with the cigarette boat, if not all of her henchman, and had informed them that their prey was unarmed.

Unarmed, thought Mira with a grim smile, *but not defenseless*.

Rather than veering off to evade the trap, she chose instead to hold her course, aiming directly at the approaching prow of the black jet boat. She crouched low behind the vertically swiveling control column, presenting the smallest possible target. The reduction in drag, coupled with the steady wind blowing from out of the west and against her back, resulted in a substantial increase in speed.

A collective grasp of her strategy caused each of the men on the Wave Runners to hastily alter course, but their gambit had already cost them the initiative and momentum to catch her. The pilot of the boat, disbelieving the message of his own eyes, kept the nose of the sleek vessel lined up with her approaching Wave Runner. Only when the low torpedo-like silhouette of Mira's craft was eclipsed from his view by the cigarette's high-riding bow did he comprehend that his opponent was playing an old-fashioned game of chicken, and playing to win.

The pilot frantically jammed the rudder hard to starboard, hitting the face of an approaching swell like a ramp. The jet boat soared out of the water, its turbines screeching as the intakes sucked air. The rash maneuver caused the boat to twist in mid-air, and when it landed, with enough force to send a spider-web of pressure fractures shooting across the immaculate black fiberglass, it almost flipped over. However, as the starboard gunwale cut into the ocean, the rush of water into the jet intakes forced the boat into motion again, miraculously righting her without any help from the stunned man at the helm. The craft hit another swell head on, lofting clear of the water again, but this time landed on an even keel. The pilot didn't see one of his comrades vanish under his prow, but the noise of the larger vessel crushing the Wave Runner and its rider shuddered through the hull.

Mira grinned in satisfaction as the cigarette boat mowed down one of its own, but she knew it was only a minor victory. The boat was the real threat. Its larger twin engines could easily overtake her before reaching the relative safety of the harbor.

She had to find a way to take the jet-powered craft out of the equation.

The two remaining Wave Runners quickly recovered from the momentary confusion, turning wide circles in the choppy ocean in order to find Mira and give chase. They searched the horizon in every direction, looking for the telltale streams of water spray that might indicate a low-riding craft hiding in the swells, but saw nothing. The jet boat joined the search, turning a broad high-speed circle around the other two craft, but there was no sign of her; it was as if she, like the *Unterseeboot*, had hidden beneath the surface.

A brightly colored oil slick marked the place where the jet boat had destroyed one of the watercraft. The broken form of its rider floated in the midst of the debris, bobbing with the swells, but was otherwise motionless. As the search for Mira grew more futile, one of the Wave Runners veered toward the wreckage. The pilot of the craft eased off the throttles as he drew near, allowing the ski-like craft to coast the remaining distance.

Without warning, the debris field erupted in a wave of spray. A fully intact Wave Runner burst from the heart of the oil slick only a few meters from the approaching craft. Before the driver could even raise a protective hand, Mira's Wave Runner broadsided him, breaking bones and fiberglass as her hull rode over his.

She turned hard to port, easing back on the throttle to cut a tight circle, and came up on the newly wrecked craft. As she slowed, the hydroplaning resistance against the hull diminished, causing the craft to sink until the sea lapped at her ankles.

Despite his injuries, the rider of the Wave Runner broken by Mira's charge was trying to bring his weapon to bear with his left hand, his broken right arm draped over a piece of floating debris. Before he could get his finger through the trigger guard, however, Mira reached down and plucked the weapon from his grasp.

"You'll float better without this," she remarked, ignoring the agonized whimper as the strap snagged momentarily on his wounded arm.

The gun was identical to the one Rachel Aimes had been wielding. Mira gave it a cursory inspection, shook droplets of salt water from the barrel, and then looped the strap around her neck.

Two down. And now I've got some teeth.

The Wave Runner shot away from the spreading oil slick, revealing her presence with an eight-foot-high plume of spray. The remaining pursuers immediately converged on her location and soon were bouncing back and forth across the wake of Mira's craft. This time, the cigarette boat driver did not cede the vanguard position to his comrade, but chased ahead at full speed. The man on the remaining watercraft swung wide to prevent Mira from slipping past.

A glance over her shoulder revealed the nearness of the pursuit, but this came as little surprise. What did come as a surprise was the sudden staccato crackling of gunfire from the jet boat. Mira's foes had not taken advantage of their superior firepower, leading Mira to believe that their intent was to take her alive, or at least subdue her in such a way as to avoid losing the treasure in her mesh bag to the depths once more. There was no way of knowing if the shots were simply being fired in warning or if the gunman on the boat meant business. She had to assume the worst.

Once again, she wheeled about and set a collision course with the jet boat. From her low crouch, she laid the MP5 on the control column and squeezed the hard plastic forward grip of the gun and the handle bar of the Wave Runner together in her right hand. Then, as she hit a swell and the little jet powered craft rose out of the ocean, she squeezed the trigger with her left hand.

The machine pistol bucked in her hand, but a short burst of nine-millimeter ammo flashed ahead of her, punching a trail across the hull of the cigarette boat. If her volley had found flesh, she could not tell, but the panicked driver abruptly steered the boat away before she could close the gap. As he presented the boat's port side to her, his passenger returned fire.

Staying low, Mira altered her course only by a few degrees, locating the remaining Wave Runner and challenging its rider to a joust. Bright flashes, followed by a noise like fireworks, warned her of an incoming fusillade and she ducked low again, answering with a couple short bursts.

It was evident that there was no way to shoot accurately while piloting the Wave Runner. Instead of wasting her limited supply of ammunition, Mira chose to use the latter skill to full advantage. She let the gun fall against the web sling to dangle under her right arm, and tightened her hold on the control grips as she drove headlong toward the other craft.

The driver of the jet boat came around, chasing down her wake, but it was obvious that the two smaller watercraft would meet before he could re-enter the battle.

As the gap closed, Mira intentionally drifted to the left. The opposing rider did not correct course to meet her head on, choosing instead to brace the folding stock of his weapon under his right arm in order to fire a killing burst as they passed each other. Unable to effectively operate the controls, his Wave Runner immediately slowed. Mira sensed the deviation and knew that she had won.

With fifty feet between them she turned sharply across his bow, cutting to his left side. Without thinking, her opponent brought the muzzle of his weapon around, twisting his torso and overextending his left arm across his body in a futile attempt to keep control of the craft. In the instant that he squeezed the trigger he realized his mistake, but it was too late. Unbalanced, he tumbled backwards into the sea. Before he could even think about trying to catch his errant vehicle, the muzzle of Mira's captured gun crashed into the back of his head, knocking him senseless.

The cigarette boat reached the scene within moments, but Mira was already speeding away. Nevertheless, the pilot of the larger craft idled close to the floating form of his comrade long enough to retrieve the dazed man from the water. It gave her a few extra seconds of lead-time, but it was obvious that they would still catch her before she could hope to reach the safety of the harbor. The head start she had gained improved her odds of surviving the next five minutes dramatically, but unless she found a way to defeat the jet boat, it would be in vain. Her eyes scanned the shoreline, then the horizon, searching for options.

A devious grin parted her lips as she realized what she had to do.

From the flying bridge of Muldoon's boat, Rachel and Turner had an unrestricted view of the battle their comrades were waging against Mira Raiden. Their countenances had grown grim as one of their number was crushed beneath the jet boat. They had shouted impotently when Mira had concealed herself in the wreckage caused by that accident in order to ambush another of their friends. And they had hurled curses across the water when the third rider went down. But when they saw the object of their rage do an about face and aim her little watercraft at the boat where they now stood, they fell silent with incomprehension. Only when it was obvious that she was indeed returning to Muldoon's boat did Turner lurch into action, ejecting the spent magazine from his AK-47 and slamming in a fresh one.

"Put that down," admonished Rachel without looking at him. "All this will be for nothing if we lose what she has."

Turner disregarded her warning, raising the stock of the weapon to his shoulder and tracking Mira through his sights. "We can recover it from her corpse."

"Not if you destroy everything with that cannon of yours," Rachel hissed, her tone brooking no defiance.

Turner lowered the weapon but remained anxious. "What the hell do you think she's doing? Is she trying to attack us?"

Rachel shook her head uncertainly. "Get on the radio to Jorge. We need him here. It's time to end this once and for all."

The cigarette boat resumed its pursuit moments after picking up the wounded Wave Runner riders. Mira saw the column of spray as the pilot of the craft opened the throttles to full and gave chase. She turned her eyes forward again, still grinning.

She reached Muldoon's boat a few seconds later, quickly picking out the moving forms of Rachel Aimes and her burly companion. The mercenary fired a few rounds over Mira's head, but it was clear that he wasn't aiming to hit her. Her scheme hinged upon the fact that her enemies needed her more or less intact, and the warning shots provided the final confirmation she needed.

As she cruised past the boat, she slowed enough to maintain control of the craft with only her left hand. Her right braced the machine pistol under her arm as she fired several short bursts that ricocheted off the superstructure, driving Rachel and Turner for cover.

Pulling even with the stern of the boat, Mira swung her Wave Runner around. She released the control grips in order to hold the MP5 with both hands. When she found her target in the sights, she squeezed the trigger.

The clip all but emptied in a matter of seconds, but most of the nine-millimeter slugs went exactly where she wanted them and perforated the fuel tanks. As gasoline spewed from dozens of jagged holes, she sighted and fired until one of the hot rounds sparked against the surface of the tanks and ignited the spilled fuel in a flash of heat and black smoke.

The constant wind flattened the column of fumes against the surface of the water, providing Mira with cover for her escape. She did not wait around to see the fire quickly spreading, or her enemies leaping from the doomed craft. The cigarette boat slowed to an idle as it neared the burning craft so that its crew could hastily pull Rachel and Turner aboard.

Now it was simply a race to shore.

The added weight of extra passengers caused the jet boat to ride a little lower in the water, slowing it considerably. Nevertheless, the driver pushed the engines to a feverish whine in order to close the gap with his prey.

A few seconds later, Muldoon's boat erupted in a pillar of fire. Though she was already several hundred yards from the boat, Mira felt the shock wave against her back and ducked reflexively lest any airborne debris reach that far as well. The jet boat, much closer to the explosion, was pummeled by the force of the blast and pelted with burning shrapnel. In the momentary confusion that followed, Mira's lead continued to increase.

She held a straight course toward the inlet, staying low and not looking back. As the rocky shoreline drew close, she leaned to her left, adjusting slightly to line up with the channel, but did not slow. A few seconds later, the walls of the fjord seemed to close around her like a crypt. The jet boat was less than two hundred yards behind her.

Muldoon's neglected harbor loomed ahead, and with it an end to the water-borne chase. The old boat still rocked in its slip, but there was no other sign of activity in the harbor or in the little town above. Mira's eyes narrowed into grim slits as she lined up on the wooden pier. Without slowing, she lifted her feet and crouched on the Wave Runner's seat like a sprinter waiting for the starting gun.

From the perspective of those on the cigarette boat, Mira's approach appeared suicidal. Though they had closed to within fifty yards, the pilot was already easing back on the throttles. Boats, unlike land vehicles, could not simply put on the brakes and come to a complete stop. Mira. however, was already past the point of no return; a collision was inevitable.

That was when Mira began to fly.

Releasing her grip on the handlebars, she uncoiled her legs, springing into the air above the doomed Wave Runner. Arching her back like a skydiver, she sailed forward in a gentle parabola over the planks of the pier. A millisecond later, the small watercraft smashed into the rickety wooden deck, annihilating both itself and quite a bit of the dock with a sickening crunch.

Before the destruction of the Wave Runner was complete, gravity ended Mira's flight. At the last possible instant, she tucked in, lowering her shoulder to the rapidly approaching surface. Though her forward momentum had carried her safely past the timbers shattered by the crash, it was now the force that would hammer her against the unyielding planks.

Her right shoulder met the surface of the pier in a collision that was, she imagined, something like being hit by a bus. She rolled through two complete somersaults, the hard metal of her captured guns whipping against her like truncheons as she turned over and over again. Mira halted her uncontrolled tumbling by extending her palms, but her body mass had not completely given up its inertia to friction, causing her to skid on hands and knees.

Even as she came to a complete stop, she knew she had to keep moving. Her muscles and joints screamed in protest as she tried to lever herself upright, but the sudden crack of gunfire, originating from the slowly approaching jet boat, drowned out the objections of her flesh. An overriding sense of self-preservation got her through the agony, and she hauled herself erect and launched into a full run.

None of the shots from her foes found their mark, but she could see the outside walls of Muldoon's office splintering with each impact. As round after round punched into the weather-beaten shingles, the little shack seemed on the verge of disintegrating altogether. Nevertheless, Mira sprinted headlong toward the crumbling building, diving at the crosspiece of a smashed out window frame.

For a few seconds, the gunfire relented. Though she could not see what was happening outside, she had a good idea why the barrage had ceased. Rachel and her crew were disembarking from the cigarette boat to bring the battle to her.

On hands and knees, both splintered and bleeding, she crawled across the floor. She almost made it to her goal before the shooting resumed. The air above her head was suddenly filled with the noise of bullets ripping through the walls of Muldoon's office. Though one of her weapon still held a partial magazine, she knew that a prolonged gunfight was a battle she could not win.

A moment later she reached the shadow of the elegant antique desk. The beautiful, dark wood had already taken several hits, perforating the side panels, but the top was fashioned from a slab of tropical hardwood three inches thick. Mira rolled onto her back, braced her feet underneath the desk, and pushed it forward.

A few shots found the makeshift barrier, but did not penetrate. Mira lay supine for several seconds, searching for some kind of solution, but discovered that the adrenaline coursing through her blood was beginning to make her nauseous, and she knew that the longer she remained inactive, the more her pain and despair would paralyze her.

She took in a deep breath, struggling in vain to hold it, and then repeated the exercise three more times until she was no longer on the verge of hyperventilating. Her heart continued to pound in her chest, the blood roaring in her ears as loud as the gunfire, but she had found her will to succeed.

Rolling once more onto her battered knees, she braced her left shoulder against one of the legs of the desk and pushed it across the floor. The heavy desk scraped along the worn floorboards, crunching through glass splinters, until it ground to a stop near the cabinet where she had secured her possessions before leaving with Muldoon. She snagged her backpack and pulled out the shoulder holster rig, which she laid on the floor beside the bag. Rather than removing anything more from the bag, she crammed in the mesh bag with all its contents.

Mira spun off her knees and rested her back against the table as another heavy torrent of heavy gunfire assaulted her shelter. She didn't need to look outside to know that at least a couple of her enemies were probably sneaking in close, under the cover of the constant barrage of gunfire. Though the noise of the shooting was deafening, making it impossible to distinguish one gun from another, the intensity of the shooting had diminished to the point where she was almost certain that Turner, with his AK-47, was doing all the work.

Come on, Mira. Get moving.

She threaded her arms through the holster straps, then through those attached to the backpack, and waited. The second the gunfire stopped, she would expect at least one, maybe two, attackers to come through the front and side doors. There would be no second chances.

Mira's thought was cut short by the sudden intrusion of silence, followed by the side door exploding off its hinges. She took a deep breath as she bolted to her feet and hit the wall running, diving through the riddled gap her foes' bullets had chopped in the back of the building. Beyond the structure, however, there was a solid earthen wall, which sloped outward and disappeared beneath the floor of the building.

The staircase leading from the harbor up to the streets of the village passed directly above the office shed, and between the edge of the steps and the cliff there was almost enough room for someone of her size to squeeze through. *Almost*, thought Mira ruefully. *It'll have to be good enough.*

Wedging herself into the narrow space, she forced her way up the outside of the shack until the bottom of the staircase was in reach. Though she was hidden from the view of her enemies, stray rounds continued to burst through the wall, smacking into the unyielding stone and spraying her with dust and rock chips. There was no protection from the bullets; only luck and speed could save her. Somehow she found enough of the latter to compensate for any deficiency in the former.

She quickly shed her backpack and fought her way through the narrow gap between the wooden risers and the cliff, until after what seemed an eternity, she succeeded in hauling herself onto the exposed staircase.

It was difficult to tell over the ringing in her ears, but Mira was certain that she heard the sound of men shouting. Slinging the backpack over one shoulder, she drew her pistol and took off running up the steps.

She reached the halfway point before anyone on the dock below spotted her. When the railing and steps around her began erupting into splinters, she returned fire in their general direction, but some of her assailants were already chasing up the steps behind her. When the Beretta was empty, she shoved it back into its holster and spun around on her heel, the MP5 now held in a two-hand grip, aimed low. The two men huffing up the stairs barely had time to register shocked expressions before a burst from the weapon swept them away.

Suddenly the wooden steps around her began to disintegrate. Rapid fire from Turner's assault rifle was systematically shredding the staircase. Fragments of wood battered against her as she leapt for the uppermost landing, the force of impact driving the splinters deep through the fabric of the wetsuit and into her skin. She hit the ground above the staircase running, bolstered by the evident escape.

Three new Chevrolet Suburban heavy-use vehicles, their immaculate silver paint jobs masked beneath a layer of dust and mud, sat side by side twenty yards from the approach to a precarious dirt track leading down to the water. Each was linked to a boat trailer, two of which had been modified to carry multiple personal watercrafts. Mira fired a series of quick, controlled pairs into the radiator of each vehicle and then sprinted down the village main toward the hostel and her waiting motorcycle.

She barely slowed as her hands reached out to take hold of the Harley's handgrips, squeezing the clutch lever in her right fist. With all of her weight behind rigidly locked elbows, she shoved the vehicle forward off its kickstand and set the bike rolling. She continued pushing off with her feet until she was almost running again alongside it. Only then did she leap into the broad tractor-style seat, releasing the clutch and feathering the throttle. The bike jerked almost to a standstill as the clutch engaged, but its momentum drove it onward, turning the engine over in the process. As the motorcycle roared to life, Mira accelerated away.

Rachel Aimes and her surviving companions finished ascending the staircase that had almost been destroyed by their own bullets just in time to see their quarry race through town on her motorcycle, the front tire lifted in a mocking wheelie. She leveled her MP5 at the shrinking figure, but Mira had already vanished into the forest.

SEVEN

Detective Michelangelo DiLorenzo stood on the street corner, casually munching a pastry and drinking coffee from a paper cup. To an onlooker, he appeared to be waiting for a bus, but his dark eyes, which seemed to be looking nowhere in particular, did not stray far from a building across the street, halfway down the block.

With what might have seemed like an impatient brusqueness, he crumpled the empty bag that had contained his breakfast roll and crossed the street, where he bought a newspaper. Immersing himself in its contents, he stalked down the sidewalk, slurping from the coffee cup with every fourth step.

He paused in front of the building he had been covertly surveilling for nearly half an hour, glancing through the window with the gilt letters that spelled out the name of the establishment: Hotel Imperial. The name was too grand for the roach-infested flophouse—an Armani suit worn by a beggar. It was the kind of place he had been in more than once during his years as a New York City police officer and criminal investigator. What difference did it make if he was in Argentina, half a world away from the Big Apple?

The bottom floor of the Imperial was devoted to a small café, lifted right out of 1950's Middle America. Cracked red vinyl upholstery covered the round metal chairs scattered haphazardly around a handful of tables, and a squadron of grossly enormous flies buzzed around the remains of a meal, left by an earlier patron and ignored by the proprietor. DiLorenzo batted one of the insects away from his face as he approached the apathetic man behind the counter.

"*Busco esta mujer*," he said haltingly, unsure of himself in the unfamiliar language. He laid a photograph on the counter, sliding it surreptitiously toward the man. Underneath the picture, the corner of a twenty-peso note, worth roughly an equivalent amount in US dollars, protruded invitingly.

The man moved only his eyes, glancing down at the photograph then back up to lock stares with the detective, apparently disdainful of the monetary offer. DiLorenzo frowned, then laid another bill alongside the first. The man folded his arms over his chest, then turned away, passing through a curtained doorway into a storeroom. He returned a moment later and laid a discolored brass key on the counter, never uttering a syllable.

DiLorenzo picked up the black and white photograph—a copy made from newspaper monochrome showing Mira Raiden looking spectacular, if a bit uncomfortable, mere moments before entering the American Museum of Natural History and going to war with a bunch of gun-toting party crashers—and returned it to his coat pocket. He left the money where it lay and picked up the key. The number "5" had been written on it with a permanent-ink marker, but was barely visible against the tarnished metal. Sensing that further taxing his limited Spanish vocabulary would be fruitless, he nodded to the man, then moved toward the stairs.

Like any major city, Buenos Aires had its seamier side. Although DiLorenzo had previously never ventured outside of the tri-state area, much less left the borders of the United States, he felt strangely in his element as he combed the streets of the Argentine capital, looking for any trace of Mira Raiden. Despite the language barrier, his skills as an investigator had shone through. Some inquiries at the banks had set him on the trail of Mira's traveler's cheques. He next learned that a significant amount of the substitute tender had been redeemed, which in turn led him to the previous owner of a vintage Harley Davidson

Between that discovery and his arrival at the Hotel Imperial, there was a lot of footwork and bribery, the latter of which was now seriously depleting his travel funds. But with any luck, the end of the search was finally at hand.

He cautiously hiked up the stairs, watching for the telltale signs that might reveal trouble ahead. He had no reason to suspect an ambush, but he was an outsider in a strange city. The hotel proprietor could just as easily have sent him to the room of an accomplice who would mug him and make sure that the body was never found.

The hallway was quiet, but this did little to allay his concerns. He found the door marked with the same digit as his key, but manners dictated he announce his presence rather than enter of his own accord.

He knocked loudly, then stepped to one side. It was a habit he had learned back home; he knew of too many officers that had been shot through closed doors. He waited several seconds then repeated the knock. Without waiting for an answer, he used the key and swung the door wide open.

A bare hotel room greeted his eyes. The space was small and roughly finished, with a single, made bed and a partitioned lavatory area near the door. He eased inside, first glancing into the bathroom, then gazing around the protruding inside corner wall. A small alcove lay just beyond the bathroom, with a horizontal rod for hanging clothes and a luggage stand on the floor. There was no indication that anyone had used the room in some time.

Breathing a curse for forty lost pesos, DiLorenzo put his hands on his hips and stared at the empty closet.

Five seconds later—five seconds that somehow passed without his conscious awareness—the New York detective found himself prone on the floor. His lower back was numb from the impact that had driven the breath from his lungs and flattened him. His ribs ached from the collision with the floor, and his chin, which had smacked the floor hardest of all, was scraped raw and smarting. Though the weight that sat squarely across his shoulders was not heavy enough to keep him from getting up, the hard metal object pressing into the flesh below his ear and the faint, familiar smell of gun oil, were an implicit warning against such a course of action.

"Not your lucky day, amigo."

The voice, a sonorous blend of bird song and huskiness, tinged with a serious tone of authority, was very familiar, but it was the accent that gave it away.

"Believe it or not, Mira," replied DiLorenzo, as soon as his ability to draw breath returned, "my luck is finally changing."

In room number six of the Hotel Imperial, Detective DiLorenzo lay back on the bed, an instant cold compress from Mira's first-aid kit pressed against his abraded chin, waiting for the ibuprofen tablets she had given him to go to work. Despite her petite size, the blow she had dealt him called to mind his high school football days.

"Expecting someone else?"

Mira paced impatiently at the foot of the bed. "What the hell are you doing here?"

"It's a long story."

"I'd like to hear it. If you found me, then it's only a matter of time before they do."

DiLorenzo sat up, wincing. "Then you already know about them."

Mira stopped in front of him, resting her hands on her hips and leaned forward. "What do *you* know?"

"Well, since you asked so nicely . . ." He lowered the ice pack. "New boots?"

Her chocolate and amber gaze intensified for a moment, then she broke into unrestrained laughter. "It would seem that I underestimated your skills as a detective."

After her escape from Rachel Aimes and her gang of mercenaries, Mira had ridden nonstop for several hours, putting about two hundred miles between herself and the village where she had, hopefully, stranded her foes. Nevertheless, she had exercised considerable caution when deciding to pull off the dirt track for a short break.

A ways off the road, behind a forest thicket, she had located one of the most beautiful places she had ever seen—a clearing around a crystal clear pool at the base of a fifteen-foot waterfall. The natural spring, apparently the end of an underground river, provided not only deliciously pure drinking water, but afforded her the opportunity to take a bracing shower. She had peeled off the wetsuit, which now reeked of stale perspiration, old neoprene and seawater, and plunged into the pool, resurfacing directly beneath the frigid downpour. Standing on rocks worn smooth by erosion, she had scrubbed away the sweat and grime, massaging splinters of wood gently from the torn skin of her knees and palms. The torrent reopened the wound in her upper left arm, but she had allowed it to bleed freely beneath the cold water, hoping to sluice away any lingering infection.

Although she had left her enemies behind, she had not completely lowered her guard. Nevertheless, the three wandering Shining Path rebel soldiers who stumbled across the siren-like figure standing in the midst of the waterfall nearly got the drop on her. Had they not, captivated by her beauty, decided to attempt relieving their lingering sexual frustrations with her, she would have been helpless to defend herself. Laying their weapons aside, they had tried to subdue her with their bare hands, and paid dearly for that mistake.

Always one to find the silver lining, Mira had determined that one of the men had approximately the same shoe size as she. With her Dr. Martens gone to the bottom of the Pacific, trapped forever in the burned-out remains of Muldoon's boat, she took advantage of the unexpected victory over the three bandits by liberating the military issue boots from the rebel's corpse, along with a set of olive drab fatigues, all of which she washed thoroughly in the pool. The three men had carried Type 56 rifles, Chinese-made versions of the AK-47. But a closer inspection revealed that neither of the weapons had any ammunition and had suffered so much abuse and neglect that they were unlikely to work anyway.

Before leaving the clearing, she had stitched the long gash in her arm, wrapping it in a thick layer of gauze and waterproof tape, and treated all of her wounds with antiseptic. To protect her myriad wounds from further infection, she had dressed in the confiscated clothes as soon as they were marginally dry and strapped the still sodden boots on her feet. Sore and tired, but with the worst behind her, she had climbed back on the motorcycle and continued her journey, leaving the castoff wetsuit in the care of the dead rebels.

Fearing the long reach of her adversaries, she had avoided commercial centers or any places in the city where she might be remembered or recognized. For the same reason, she had not been able to purchase new clothing and used only cash, from her very limited reserves, when purchasing food or securing lodgings. She tracked down the black market gun dealer who had sold her the Beretta and convinced him to take one of the Heckler & Koch machine pistols in exchange for several boxes of nine-millimeter 115-grain, hollow-point ammunition that would work equally well in her pistol or in the MP5. She had signed only one of her traveler's cheques, giving it to the hotel owner and promising him another like it upon her departure if he kept a constant vigil in her behalf, alerting her to the presence of anyone looking for her. It was in this capacity that the man had misdirected the detective after alerting her to his arrival.

She did not reveal any of this to DiLorenzo, despite his insistent inquiries. Instead, she directed him back to the lingering question of his presence in South America.

"I guess it started when I left you that night at Aimes' apartment. Jeff—my partner—had called to say that they were transporting the prisoner—the guy that you brained with that serving tray at the museum—to Riker's . . ."

Mira's jaw dropped. "The man driving the boat. I knew he looked familiar."

"Boat?" DiLorenzo's voice was uncharacteristically strident. "You mean you've seen him? He's here?"

"In a minute. Please continue. I have a feeling you're about to tell me how he escaped your custody."

"Oh, yeah. He just waltzed away." DiLorenzo spat derisive laughter, then jumped up and matched Mira's pacing. "I went to the hospital where he was being kept. It was me, Jeff, and a couple uniforms. I mean, it was a prisoner transfer and the guy was practically comatose. It should have been a walk in the park.

"Then everything went to hell. Jeff never—" DiLorenzo faltered, and he turned away quickly. "I don't know how they missed me. Maybe their guy was in front of me or something. I don't remember it all that well. All I know is that they hit us hard and fast."

Mira weighed the detective's words. "I'm very sorry about

your friend."

The detective tried to shrug his emotions away. "They got him to the roof and onto that damn helicopter. I'm surprised that you didn't hear about it. A shootout and escape at the hospital—knocked you right off the front page."

"I haven't had a chance to follow the news. However, I saw that man again a few days ago. He's here—" Mira stopped suddenly, finally connecting the pieces of the puzzle. "But you already knew that. That's why you've come."

"Not exactly." DiLorenzo turned to face her. "A few hours after the escape, we finally got a positive match on the guy's ID. His name is Jorge Montero, an Argentine national. He's the heir to a pretty substantial cattle ranching fortune. But there's more to the Montero family than just the beef."

"Let me guess. He is a grandson of an escaped Nazi war criminal."

DiLorenzo's jaw dropped. "Maybe I should just let you finish the story."

"Lucky guess, I assure you. Please continue."

"Actually, the Montero's are pure-bred Old World Colonial Spaniards. Joauquin Montero, Jorge's grandfather, fought with the fascists in the Spanish Civil War, and reciprocated the support given by the Nazis during World War II. The Simon Wiesenthal Center has been investigating the Montero family for years, trying to find a connection between them and SS officers that might have escaped with plundered gold to South America after the war."

"Odessa," muttered Mira, remembering Muldoon's paranoia.

"Right. So far the case is purely circumstantial, but we do know that Montero and his buddies are killers."

"But you aren't here to take him back?"

DiLorenzo sighed, pacing in a circle. "No. As a matter of fact, I'm on vacation. 'Administrative leave' is actually the official term for it. Apparently, the department psychologist thought that watching my partner die might have traumatized me."

Mira felt a momentary pang of sympathy, but then the last

piece of the puzzle slid into place. She turned abruptly, accusing: "You think you're here to protect me."

DiLorenzo frowned, betraying the truth of her words. "Obviously you don't need my help. But you had no way of knowing that you would be on this guy's home turf. I thought the least I could do was warn you."

Mira turned away, shaking her head. "Prince Charming, come to rescue me."

"Oh, well excuse me for being concerned about you." Before she could parry, he became contrite. "I'm sorry. I didn't mean it that way."

Confused by his sudden reversal, she turned to him again, unable to hide the conflicting emotions in her expression. "How did you mean it?"

He shrugged. "You left without saying good-bye."

In spite of her ire, she found herself laughing at the simple statement. "You're right, I did. I'm terribly sorry."

"Good." He grinned weakly and stared at her for a moment. "I guess you've had another run in with Montero."

She nodded. "And Rachel Aimes and our friend from Walter's apartment."

"It's a regular family reunion down here. Any clue as to what it is they want?"

"Actually, I've got a pretty good idea."

Over a light meal delivered from the café downstairs, Mira recounted her misadventures off the Chilean coast. Although she omitted mention of her battle with the reanimated remains of the SS officer, she grudgingly showed the detective the Trinity relic she had recovered.

"Can I touch it?" When she did not forestall him, DiLorenzo extended a cautious finger, acting as if he expected to receive a shock from the artifact. "I still don't completely understand what all the fuss is about."

"I think there were originally three of them, and that when they were joined together—three in one, a true Trinity—they produced staggering supernatural power."

"I know, you told me." DiLorenzo continued to evince

skepticism. "But if it's all that, then how did they get lost for so long?"

"A fair question. Clearly, the pieces were separated at some point, but they were still individually quite powerful. One of them stayed in Atlantis, where it became the center of a revolt that ultimately destroyed the entire civilization."

DiLorenzo reached out for the relic again, this time without hesitancy. "But this isn't that Trinity?"

"No. According to the notes I found with it, this one is from a culture in Asia that paralleled Atlantis. It seems that in the years leading up to World War II, certain elements in the Nazi hierarchy devoted themselves to a search for occult knowledge—"

"Mmhmm. I saw the movie."

Mira laughed dryly. "Well, the movie may have exaggerated a little, but for a while, some of the high-ranking members of the Nazi party were convinced that they could find Atlantis.

"There was another legend that caught their fancy as well; a myth about a kingdom hidden in the interior earth that was home to a superior white race known as the Aryans."

DiLorenzo's eyebrows went up in disbelief. "Now why does that sound familiar?"

"It was the key to their doctrine of racial purity. The Nazis, and by extension all Germans who fit into the mold, could claim to be descendants of that supposed 'master race.' Finding proof of the existence of the hollow earth was, you can imagine, of great interest.

"There was a particularly unscrupulous man named Tarrant—an American fortune hunter—who brought the Nazis artifacts, which he claimed to have recovered from an Aryan dwelling in Southeast Asia. Despite his ethical shortcomings, Tarrant came pretty close to finding it."

"Wait a minute. You mean this Aryan kingdom really existed?"

"Not as Hitler imagined it. There was no white master race living in a hollow earth. But after Tarrant found the first Trinity—he didn't actually use that word—he told Mann, the SS officer who was running him, that there was another just like it somewhere in the South Pacific—"

"The lemur place!" DiLorenzo exclaimed.

Mira flashed a smile. "Very good. At that point, Tarrant began calling the talismans 'the Twins' evidently evoking dualities common in folklore: the Gemini twins, Castor and Pollux; Romulus and Remus; the Mayan hero twins Hunahpu & Xbalanque; as well as oppostire pairings, God and the Devil, Yin and Yang, and so forth.

"When they studied the first relic, the Nazis realized that they had found something of unbelievable power—the kind of power that might actually change the outcome of the war.

"Mann funded Tarrant's second search and then rendezvoused with him on a remote island. Tarrant then claimed that there was a third artifact, but Mann didn't believe him. Instead, he killed Tarrant and took the second Trinity—"

"This one?" DiLorenzo held out the artifact.

"Exactly. But Tarrant was right; there was a third piece, the Trinity of Atlantis, hidden in a temple in Panama."

"Which you found."

"Which I found," Mira confirmed.

"So the Nazis had two of the three Trinities. Why didn't they use that power to win the war?"

"The war was already lost. It was no coincidence that Mann was in the South Pacific when he was. It seems that in addition to searching for the entrance to the Aryan kingdom at the center of the Earth, he was also in charge of building the Nazis' last redoubt; an underground bunker where they would be able to nurse their war wounds and plan the Fourth Reich. After killing Tarrant, Mann returned to his U-boat, planning to unite the Twins in the secret facility he had built in South America."

"Where the escaped Odessa Nazis have been hiding out for the last sixty years."

Mira shook her head thoughtfully. "I don't think the Nazi survivors or their heirs ever made it there. Apparently, only Mann knew the exact location. Like the Pharaohs of Egypt, he used slave labor to build his stronghold and executed everyone when it was done. He was to have led the way when the evacuation began, but he never made it. The sub foundered off the coast and the location of the refuge died with him, along with one of the three relics."

The last piece of the puzzle clicked into place for the detective. "So Montero and Rachel Aimes are just the last in a long line of Nazis who have been searching for this lost refuge, doubtless hoping to find a mother lode of Nazi gold."

"Along with the other Trinities."

DiLorenzo relinquished the talisman. "So what do we do now?"

"'We' don't do anything. You can finish your vacation anywhere you like—"

"While you traipse off to this hidden fortress and grab the other Trinity. You make it sound so easy."

She raised an eyebrow. "I have had some experience with this, thank you very much."

"Come on," he chuckled. "You know you need me."

Despite her firm conviction that she would be continuing on alone, Mira found herself compelled to let the handsome detective attempt to convince her otherwise. "I need you?"

"Well, for starters, I'd be an extra pair of eyes and hands. Montero and the gang will still be looking for you. Looking for *you*. Not the two of us. This is their turf. If you go cruising through the city on that motorcycle, how long do you think it will be before they spot you? I can rent us a car or something, and while you keep your head down, we can drive away, right under their noses. And you do know that they will be expecting you to lead them to this Nazi refuge, don't you?"

"That's how the game usually plays out."

"Yeah, well anything we can do to escape their notice right now, will put them off the scent."

Mira unconsciously chewed her lower lip. DiLorenzo's logic was unassailable. In fact, she knew that teaming up with him was probably the course of wisdom. But something prevented her from encouraging his participation in the quest, something she was not quite ready to admit to herself. The brief infatuation she had flirted with during their encounters in New York had returned with a vengeance, as did all the guilt that had resulted from the last time she had let herself entertain those feelings. . . .

Before she could sort out the dilemma, a premonition of danger snapped her back to reality. Her face took on a razor sharp intensity, and DiLorenzo paled beneath the sudden harsh glare. He fumbled to apologize for whatever he had said or done to warrant the abrupt metamorphosis, but before he could utter a single word, Mira snapped erect, the Beretta in her right hand. "Down!"

"Jesus!" gasped DiLorenzo, rolling out of his seat and sprawling out on the floor in a panic.

The gun roared in the tiny room, a deafening thunderclap to accompany the tongue of flame that erupted from the muzzle, scorching the air where DiLorenzo had been standing. Before the spent cartridge could hit the floor, Mira sprang forward, reaching out with her empty left hand. In the periphery of his vision, he saw her thrust clawed fingers into a newly created void where a windowpane had been an instant before. When Mira drew back her hand, her fingers were curled around the loose cloth of a dark military-style shirt.

The shirt adorned the staggering form of a man, gasping for air as he flailed his arms uselessly. DiLorenzo almost missed the oblong metal object clutched in the man's right fist, a long-barreled .22-caliber semi-automatic pistol, equipped with a suppressor which, like a car's muffler, baffled the sound of the exploding gases in the firing chamber. Mira had detected his presence and preemptively silenced him with a single shot. The man's eyes, barely visible through the slit in the ski mask-style balaclava that hid his features, glazed over a moment later, and his dead weight pulled his shirtfront from Mira's fingers.

In a fluid movement, like a dancer executing a ballet step, Mira plucked the pistol from the dead man's fingers and tossed it to DiLorenzo, who caught it, more out of reflex than intent. She spun on a heel, sweeping Mann's papers and the Trinity into her backpack, and then she was gone, plunging through the smashed window. DiLorenzo stared at the weapon in his hand, waiting for the incredulity of the moment to pass.

Mira peeked through the opening, her eyes ablaze with intensity. "Coming?"

The alley below the second-story window was empty but for Mira's Harley Davidson and the usual flotsam of daily urban life. There was no sign of reinforcements or transportation for the lone assailant that now lay dead on the floor of Room Six, but Mira knew the man was not alone. After quickly urging her new companion to follow, she holstered her gun, turned back toward the window frame, and stepped off.

Her fingers caught the outside sill, arresting her fall, after which she safely dropped to the street below. The detective's face appeared in the window frame, a bewildered expression distorting his otherwise attractive face.

"Unless you want to entertain his friends," Mira stage whispered from the alley below, "I suggest you get moving."

DiLorenzo muttered a stream of disbelieving profanity as he clumsily crawled over the window frame, awkwardly lowering first his left leg, then his recalcitrant right. Unwilling to surrender to gravity, he lingered there, his torso teetering on the sill. Shaking her head in frustration, Mira turned and sprinted toward her motorcycle.

In some remote corner of her mental process, a flicker of resentment toward the detective began to smolder. Already he was proving to be a liability. How he had prospered in the police force tasked with patrolling the reputedly mean streets of New York City was a mystery to her. His languor endangered both of them. While she waited, concerned for his safety, she was as much a target as he.

Curtis would have . . .

She banished the thought before it could lead her down a dangerous path. She trusted her psychic gift to keep her one step ahead of a bullet, but she couldn't extend that protection to DiLorenzo any more that she had been able to protect Curtis in Panama. She could try to warn him, but he would hesitate and he would die, and she would be left to carry the guilt for another lost lover.

She contemplated simply leaving, diverting the pursuit away from him and drawing the assassins after their real target. That she did not abandon him was a further source of irritation to her. Had she already gotten so attached to him that her emotions were clouding her judgment on a subconscious level?

The motorcycle roared between her legs, a single downward stroke of the kickstarter sufficing to bring it to life. The glass-pack mufflers, a flashy addition by some previous owner, did little to dampen the noise, but the idling of the Harley's engine was unquestionably quieter than the earlier gunshot. It would, however, reveal her intent to escape to the slain man's accomplices. She figured the detective had about five seconds to grow a backbone and catch up to her, or else she would leave him behind forever.

DiLorenzo finally got his nerve and dropped awkwardly to the pavement. The silenced pistol was threaded between his belt and the waistband of his trousers; that it would become entangled if he attempted to draw the weapon was a foregone conclusion in Mira's mind. She prayed that she would not have to rely on his shooting skills to survive what lay ahead.

Mira scooted forward as far as was possible, contorting her leg in order to manipulate the shifter, and made room for DiLorenzo. He straddled the rear fender, instinctively wrapping his arms around her narrow waist, and let his toes drag on the ground. As soon as his hands clasped together, his chest pressed tight against her back, she released the clutch lever and the motorcycle shot forward.

Riding with the extra weight of a passenger required her full attention. The center of gravity had changed, and the bike felt sluggish and wobbly, but the gyroscopic effect of the spinning tires quickly compensated. And after a few seconds, she knew how to handle the bike efficiently in spite of the added mass.

The motorcycle roared into the street that intersected the alley, skidding sideways in a carefully controlled maneuver that caused DiLorenzo's grip to tighten. Mira righted the bike immediately and charged straight ahead down the nearly empty street. Before she had gone a block, however, two parked cars rumbled to life behind her. She didn't have to look back to identify them. She had noticed the Suburban the instant they left the alley; the ragged holes in its fiberglass grille marked it as one of those she had disabled after escaping Rachel Aimes' trap at Muldoon's port village. Almost as conspicuous was a sleek black Volvo S80 T6 sedan parked facing in the opposite direction, obviously out of place in the rundown neighborhood where the Hotel Imperial was situated.

Vehicle traffic on the streets around the Imperial was light. Mira wove the Harley in between the meandering cars and the odd delivery truck, eliciting vocal responses from a few drivers, but scarcely impacting the flow of the mid-afternoon commute. All that changed in the instant that the Volvo squealed through a broad U-turn and created instant pandemonium. The Suburban slipped into the void created when half a dozen vehicles abruptly stopped, scattering to the sides of the avenue in a desperate attempt to avoid a collision with the Volvo. Both chasing vehicles left trails of smoking rubber on the macadam as they screamed after Mira and her passenger.

Mira pushed the Harley as fast as she dared, cutting in and out of traffic and dodging down surface streets in search of a new place to hide. They worked their way through rambling neighborhoods and were eventually shunted into the arterial thoroughfares that crisscrossed the city. The two pursuers rapidly closed the distance, out-muscling the overburdened antique Harley Davidson engine, and only the motorcycle's maneuverability kept Mira and DiLorenzo ahead of the chase. On the more heavily traveled *avenidas*, however, the game turned in favor of the prey.

Midday congestion, the first wave of urbanite Argentines escaping the workplace, had snarled traffic in their path. Long streams of automobiles, belching heat and noxious vapors without making any discernible progress, seemed to stretch ahead forever, broken only by an occasional intersection mechanically regulated by a traffic signal.

Mira drove into the current without slowing, leaning to the right as the rear tire skidded into line. She felt her passenger flailing and leaned a little further to compensate for his erratic movements. There was no time to teach him how to survive the ride—barely enough for the split-second decisiveness that would keep them from spilling onto the crowded pavement. DiLorenzo, she decided, was on his own.

As he regained his equilibrium Mira aimed the front wheel into the narrow channel between the stagnant rows, down the painted line, and goosed the throttle. The Harley shot forward, the speedometer needle marking thirty . . . forty . . . fifty miles and hour. This was going to be the trickiest driving she had ever attempted.

The detective from New York thought that he was getting the hang of riding on the backseat. He glanced back over his shoulder, and saw that their foes had been momentarily thwarted by the gridlock.

"Duck!"

Though he had spent only a few hours in her company, DiLorenzo had already begun to learn how to respond to his new traveling companion's orders. In another life, he would have questioned her, demanding clarification or explanation. But with the adrenaline surge that even now lingered as a numb tingling in his fingertips, he had learned how to simply react, following Mira's lead and directions without question.

He ducked.

Something bright flashed over his head, passing behind him before he could put a name to the object that had missed him by a hand's breadth. The protruding side mirror of an oversized pick-up truck, stretching out almost as far as the midpoint between the two lanes of traffic, had nearly taken his head off.

His amazed relief at the near miss quickly gave way to a different sort of awe. Though the two chase vehicles were eclipsed from his view, a sudden cacophony of horns and screeching metal, strangely audible over the roar of the motorcycle's engine, reached his ears, giving testimony to the fact that the hunt was far from over.

The Volvo had initially led the pursuit, weaving in and out of light traffic more effectively than the bulky Suburban. But upon reaching a main street—*Avenida del Libertador*—it had become entangled in the traffic jam, barely able to merge with the stagnate flow, to say nothing of closing the gap. Where the Volvo's finesse failed to accomplish the task, however, the cumbersome Suburban was the perfect tool for creating an opening.

Linked to his counterpart by hands-free cellular phone, the driver of the Chevrolet hastily explained his strategy. After only a moment of consideration, the driver of the Volvo, one of the upper-echelon soldiers of an organization descended from the refugees of the fallen Axis powers, quickly assented.

Rather than force his way into the snarled traffic, the Suburban veered away from the idling cars and angled toward the street's edge, where a string of unattended automobiles were parked. The driver geared down, reining in the engine's considerable horsepower, then moved slowly, steadily forward into the narrow gap between parked and idling vehicles. The space between was only about three feet, less than half of the Chevy's width. All that changed a heartbeat later when the Suburban plowed forward.

The shriek of metal on metal was audible more than two blocks away. The reinforced steel bumper guards, driven by a 300-horsepower, 6.0-liter V-8 engine, rammed into the cars like a tank, thrusting them negligently aside. The steel cage around the headlights and grill took the brunt of the collision, leaving the Suburban unscathed. Immediately, a dissonant outcry of automobile horns, peppered with screamed obscenities from outraged drivers, added to the symphony of chaos.

The Suburban's assault was relentless. It pushed cars out of its way in either direction, creating a ripple effect of secondary collisions. A wave of panic soon overtook those in its path of destruction, with startled drivers struggling in vain to get out of the way of the approaching juggernaut.

Mira eased back on the throttle, risking a glance over her shoulder. The motorcycle was more versatile on the choked streets, but she doubted it could provide escape from an enemy that did not hesitate to wreak total havoc in their efforts to capture or kill her. Moreover, she was playing on their field, and she didn't doubt her enemies were already summoning additional firepower to intercept her. On the plus side of the equation, DiLorenzo seemed more at ease on his precarious perch, anticipating her movements and minimizing his tendency to overreact.

A major intersection loomed ahead. The sign hanging from a traffic signal indicating that *Avenida Sarmiento* lay down the left-hand path. Red-lining the tachometer in a sudden burst of speed, she shot ahead of the cars entering the junction and cut across their path. DiLorenzo's hold around her waist barely tightened.

Avenida Sarmiento traveled northeast through the park that contained the city's zoo and botanical gardens, then hooked due east, where the horizon was broken by the jagged outlines of industrial loading cranes. To their left lay the open space of the Municipal Airport, but Mira did not alter her course. Instead, she raced at full bore toward Puerto Nuevo, the four-mile-long strip of port facilities on the Rio de la Plata.

The river was actually more of a large bay at the terminus of several major waterways, flowing from the interior of South America and emptying into the Atlantic Ocean. During the era of Spanish conquest, the Rio de la Plata had seen cargoes of silver and gold loaded aboard large galleons for transport back to the Old World. The name "Argentina" was in fact derived from the word "argent," an adjective often associated with silver. Though very little of the earth's precious metal remained to be harvested, the port continued to be a focal point of Argentine wealth, with an almost unrivaled volume of beef cattle and cereal exports to global markets. However, Mira's interest in the docks that lay ahead had little to do with the state of Argentina's economy.

A sudden eruption of noise in their wake signaled that one or both of the pursuing vehicles had reached the intersection and turned after them. Her lead was not nearly great enough to run the gauntlet on the crowded riverfront, but alternatives were in short supply. Leaning forward to reduce wind drag, she twisted the throttle handle wide open, merging onto the *Avenida Obligado Rafael*, which paralleled the waterfront. This time she surprised her passenger, and the suddenness of his grip all but drove the breath from her lungs.

Though the street ahead was broad and fairly open, Mira

immediately recognized that this would work to their disadvantage. Overburdened, the motorcycle was no match for the Volvo. They could not outrun the pursuit. She was going to have to outfox them.

With almost mechanical efficiency, she began gearing down, letting the torque of the engine carry the burden of braking. The Harley lurched as second gear engaged, at which point she squeezed the hand brake and turned sharply to the left. The Harley crossed the *avenida* and speared toward a side street that ran between two large warehouses, appearing to end at an open wooden dock. A few moments later, the front tire hit the boardwalk, generating a violent tremor that quickly traveled into the handgrips and up her forearms, setting her teeth rattling.

The smell of the riverfront, a mélange of things organic and artificial—the aroma of live cattle and the scent of offal from meat-packing houses, the unique tang of algae from the river, diesel and grease from the industrial complex—assaulted her senses at a visceral level, but barely registered in her battle-heightened brain. A hundred yards onto the boardwalk, they passed the end of the warehouses, and Mira steered right, turning parallel to the river. All too soon, they heard the rattling sound of the Volvo's tires hitting the planks, and Mira knew that their lead was almost gone. She brought the Harley to a skidding halt, leaving a swipe of rubber on the weathered boardwalk.

She turned her head sideways, her cheek almost touching DiLorenzo's chin. "Get off!"

She felt his hold loosen automatically, but he stopped short of letting go. "Why?"

"There's no way we can get away if we stay together," she shouted over the noisy Harley engine.

DiLorenzo nodded, unclenching his knotted fingers and sliding back over the rear fender. "Gotcha. Split up and lose 'em. Where should we meet up?"

"We don't. Go home to New York, and watch your back."

She saw the protest instantly register in his countenance, but silenced his denial by revving the throttle and letting the clutch slip. The Harley, almost two hundred pounds lighter, burst forward in second gear. From the corner of her eye, she watched in the side mirror as DiLorenzo shrank to a mere spot in the distance. The decision stung her as much as it did him, but she took consolation from the fact that she had probably just saved his life.

She wished she could be more confident about her own fate.

The clopping sound of the Volvo's tires quickly replaced the noise of the motorcycle, and the detective's instinct to survive overpowered his disappointment at being abandoned. He dashed toward the warehouse and ducked behind a stack of wooden crates as the front end of the sedan rounded the corner.

The Volvo passed by his hiding place without slowing. In fact, the driver put on a burst of speed once clear of the narrow alley. Dock workers, still recovering from Mira's sudden appearance, scattered as the black sedan charged into their midst, some fleeing into the warehouse while others were forced to choose between a three-story plunge to water below or going under the Volvo's all-season radial tires. Their panic was compounded when the passenger side window lowered and a masked man with wielding a machine pistol leaned out and fired short bursts at the retreating motorcycle.

As quickly as the wave of panic had risen, it subsided, the laborers venturing back onto the dock to gaze after the speeding car in wonderment. Though many of them had watched DiLorenzo's concealment with quizzical glances, he now seemed to have been forgotten. Worming his way deeper into the maze of shipping crates, the detective was thankful for that small blessing.

Three hundred yards away, Mira ducked her head as a near miss from the shooter in the sedan showered her face with splinters. Without DiLorenzo's added mass, the Harley Davidson was more responsive—feeling more like a natural extension of her mind and body—but the damage was already done. She had wandered into a place where speed and maneuverability would only count for so much, a maze that might not have a way out, except through her opponents. Praying that her luck would change, she drove deeper into the tangle.

Removed as he was from the immediate struggle, DiLorenzo's ego, like any other part of the body that suffers a trauma, began to smart. Though he could not fault the logic of her decision, he was irritated at the implicit lack of faith in his abilities. Between the two of them, there was surely enough firepower to make a stand, but Mira obviously didn't trust him, and did not yet think of him as an equal in their venture.

He knew that he was being unreasonable; she had not asked for his help and had every right to disdain his company. Nevertheless, he was invested in the struggle against Montero and his allies, if for no other reason than to avenge his partner's murder. Surely that was something she could understand.

Who're you trying to kid? accused his conscience.

The thumping noise of car tires on the boardwalk grew again, reminding the detective that there had been two vehicles pursuing them. He wrestled the silenced .22 from his belt, inspecting the weapon for the first time. Though the design seemed familiar, a stubby, angled grip hung beneath a half-slide and fixed barrel, the name of the manufacturer, embossed on the slide was one he had never encountered: TALA (*Talleres Armas Livianas Argentinas*). A locally manufactured gun, it resembled the weapons often used by the bad guys in spy movies; the suppressor, nearly doubling its length, completed the picture. If he'd had the time and the tools, he would have attempted removing the silencer. The additional length and weight would doubtless skew his already questionable ability with semi-automatic firearms—he preferred the less visually appealing Colt .38 Cobra—but the set screw that secured the cylindrical sleeve around the barrel would not yield to the efforts of his fingers to loosen it. Thumbing the safety off, he eased out his hiding place.

The silver Suburban rolled slowly down the dock, the

occupants scanning the path ahead. They appeared to be searching the boardwalk and the open warehouses, and DiLorenzo realized with a start that they were looking for him. Likely, the driver of the Volvo had called his counterparts in the Chevrolet, informing them that Mira had dumped her passenger. Though he was well concealed, he caught himself holding his breath as the Suburban rolled by.

The multi-use vehicle passed him without slowing, continuing past a small mountain of shipping crates and out of his view. Hesitantly, he moved in the direction of the crates, edging toward the open dock. He peered around the corner, glimpsing the rear end of the Suburban, still creeping forward.

The immediate threat had passed, and he was safe for the moment. All he had to do was lie low and wait for a chance to hail a cab, or for that matter, simply hike the short distance to the airport, where he could change his flight reservations for a nominal surcharge and return to the relative safety of New York City. He knew that was exactly what he should do. It was the smart thing to do.

But it wasn't what Mira Raiden would do.

With an almost manic gleam in his eye, he started forward. He made a quick dash toward a double stack of waxed cardboard shipping boxes, his dark hair easily visible above the topmost container if anyone in the Suburban happened to look in that direction. They did not. From there, he sprinted another fifteen yards, reaching the rear bumper of the vehicle, and jogged along behind it, too close to be seen by either the driver or his companion. The passenger had his head and shoulders through the window frame, gazing back and forth in search of their quarry. DiLorenzo remained in the blind spot until the man's gaze roved forward, then he made his move.

He ran forward, seizing hold of a conveniently provided handle beside the door, and hopped onto the running board. At the last second, the man in the passenger seat saw his approach, but it was too late. DiLorenzo roughly thrust the silencer end of the pistol against the man's ear, his finger ready on the trigger.

"Stop the car," he shouted, then hoping he remembered the correct Spanish word, added: "¡Alto!"

The driver's eyes grew wide in the narrow slit of his mask. DiLorenzo, anticipating that the man would try to slam on the brakes in order to dislodge him, flexed his knees while tightly gripping the handle. As if on cue, the driver stomped the pedal, throwing both himself and his passenger forward against the dashboard. DiLorenzo felt the strain in his biceps as the momentum yanked his arm straight, but he held on, the muzzle of the pistol never losing contact with the man in the passenger seat.

In that moment, in spite of his disadvantaged position, the passenger, perhaps believing that DiLorenzo would falter, turned and made a grab for the gun. The New York detective then did something that he never would have believed himself capable of. In a moment of pure, uncontrolled reflex, he squeezed the trigger.

The .22 round punched into the skull of the masked passenger, killing him instantly. The force of the gases expelled from the muzzle blew tissue and fluid from every orifice, showering the windshield with gore.

Instinctively, the driver let go of the wheel and hurled himself across the interior of the vehicle toward DiLorenzo. The Suburban, still idling and in gear, began rolling forward as soon as his foot left the brake pedal, veered off on a tangent when the man's hip struck the steering wheel. The automatic clutch did not accelerate the vehicle, but the gentle force it transmitted to the wheels was enough to nudge it toward the edge of the dock.

Though killing a man in such a gruesome fashion had rattled the detective, he still held the gun tightly, and was ready to use it again. But his new opponent somehow wormed under him, thrusting his gun hand up. His finger again tightened on the trigger, releasing several rounds, with a noise that was no louder than a cough, into the upholstered headliner. Abandoning the idea of shooting the man, DiLorenzo instead threw himself back, wrestling the weapon free.

Barely keeping his hold on the Suburban, he again pulled himself back toward the door. Inside, the driver was fumbling with his own gun, an MP5K-PDW. DiLorenzo did not even bother trying to shoot him, but instead brought the TALA .22 down like a club on the side of the driver's masked head. As his second foe slumped unconscious between the seats, DiLorenzo realized the vehicle was rushing toward the edge of the boardwalk.

The Harley Davidson was barely moving now, crawling along only slightly faster than a normal person's walking pace. Mira clenched her teeth in frustration as she rounded a corner in the warehouse maze and found yet another dead end. She almost cursed aloud at her own stupidity.

Like a chess player realizing that a checkmate was inevitable she could only look back on the opening moves and berate herself for having followed her heart instead of her head. Seconds wasted waiting for DiLorenzo to flee the hotel . . . the escape hampered by the added load on the old Harley's engine.

This was why she preferred to work alone.

Wheeling the Harley around, she faced back the way she had come. A long corridor of large wooden bins, stacked three high, stretched to the front of the warehouse. As she started to roll forward, the nose of the black sedan crept into view at the opposite end, slowly turning until it was face to face with her. The wide-bodied Volvo moved into the channel, barely clearing the irregular wooden walls on either side. Mira doubted that the sedan's doors could be opened enough for the occupants to exit the car.

She squeezed the clutch lever, watching the Volvo make its approach, and weighed her options. She could not go around. She could shoot, but in an escalating gun battle, she would surely lose. She had no cover, while her opponents could duck behind the dashboard, waiting for her to run out of ammunition. As if to jump-start her mental process, she unconsciously revved the throttle, which caused the glass-pack muffler to roar like a challenge. With a grim smile, she realized what she had to do.

Before the rumble of the engine subsided, Mira dumped the clutch and the motorcycle shot forward. The sudden burst of speed lightened the front wheel and Mira pulled back on the grips, crossing the distance to the car with the front tire raised like a battering ram. The driver of the Volvo barely had time to apply his brakes before the front tire of the Harley smashed down on the Volvo's hood, crumpling the metal and demolishing the immaculate paint job. The undercarriage of the Harley grated against the grill and snapped the fiberglass grid as the rear wheel climbed up the bumper of the car and shot Mira forward again.

The windshield of the Volvo miraculously bore the weight of the vintage motorcycle, but as soon as the front tire settled onto the roof of the car the glass fractured into a spider web pattern, radiating from the center where the sedan's roof had folded in half like a taco shell. The Volvo was engineered with a reinforced steel cage to withstand the worst imaginable crashes, but it had not been built to survive bisection by a motorcycle. Nonetheless, the upright posts held, bending only slightly as the weight of the bike rolled down the length of the car.

Mira leaned back as the leading tire dipped suddenly, crashed past the shattered remains of the rear window, and slammed against the boot cover. Another jarring drop put her on the floor, the demolished remains of the Volvo behind her. She opened up the throttle, knowing that the men inside the car might still be able to shoot, and that her only refuge lay in getting out of the deadly canyon of crates.

No shots were fired, but the fifty yards remaining to be crossed seemed like a killing zone where death might descend at any instant. One by one, the uneven planks rolled beneath her tires, speeding her closer to salvation. She was so intent on escaping the killers behind her that she barely sensed anything when a masked figure moved from behind the end stack. She did not even have time to raise a hand in defense.

The attacker swung a long board like a bludgeon, smashing across her upper torso, just barely missing her lowered chin. The plank slammed hard into her upper arms, instantly breaking her grip on the handlebars, and followed through with a solid collision just below her collarbone. A dull moment passed, followed by an awareness of pain, but worse a numbness that prevented her from acting.

The attack had swept her off of the motorcycle, laying her out on the floor of the warehouse. The Harley Davidson continued on, keeping an arrow-straight course out of the building and across the dock. Without any intelligence to guide it, the motorcycle sailed unhesitatingly over the brink, vanishing into the Rio de la Plata with a loud splash and the hiss of steam.

Mira lay on her back, struggling to rise even though she was too disoriented to remember where she was or why it was important to keep moving. A figure interposed between her and the dim overhead lights—a man wearing a dark balaclava, holding a two by four.

She could tell he was laughing behind his mask, grinning in triumph beneath the knit fabric as he tossed the broken length of wood behind him. Mira made a silent vow to wipe that smirk of his face if it took her last breath, and through a supreme effort of will she rolled over onto her stomach.

Her arms refused to work. A tingling numbness spread across her chest and down her arms, intercepting the commands sent from her brain to the muscles and tendons of her extremities. Somehow, she brought her knees up, rolling into a ball from which she was able to raise her upper body. It wasn't much of a defense, but she could see that it had given her assailant reason to hesitate.

Gritting her teeth, she willed her right arm into motion. Her hand flopped onto her thigh, then crept toward the butt of the pistol holstered under her left arm.

The eyes of her attacker grew wide through the slits in his mask. She could see the awe, the disbelief . . . the fear. The smirk was gone.

Did it, she thought.

Another vehicle rolled slowly into view, opposite the place where the man had lain in ambush. It stopped, equidistant from both Mira and her assailant, forming the third point in a loose triangle.

Mira's fingers curled around the grip of her gun, but she knew it was an act more of defiance than defense. Her attacker hastily brought his own sidearm to bear. She could tell by the way that he fumbled with the safety that her unwillingness to accept defeat had him rattled. Small comfort. But she refused to bow her head in acceptance of her fate.

The suddenness of the shot surprised her because the man was still trying to work the action to advance a round into the firing chamber. She felt no different after the ear-splitting thunderclap of the gun's discharge—the numbness in her arms was slowly turning into a throbbing ache—but she was pretty certain that the shot had gone astray. She looked for the gunman's eyes again, but this time they were different.

The masked gunman toppled forward like a felled tree. As he went down, Mira could see a moist shadow spreading across the black cloth of his combat blouse.

"Need a lift?"

DiLorenzo stepped out from behind the Suburban, looking strangely out of place wielding a sub-machine gun. The barrel of his weapon—a commandeered MP5, not the silenced .22—was still smoking from the three-round burst that had felled Mira's assailant. He laid the gun on the hood of the vehicle and rushed to her aide.

"Now, aren't you sorry you tried to get rid of me?" he murmured softly, helping her to her feet.

Actually, I'm glad I did, she wanted to say, but though her mouth could shape the words, but her lungs denied her the breath to make them a reality.

Somehow, DiLorenzo understood. "You're welcome."

Rachel Aimes leaned back in the overstuffed chair, closing her eyes against the coming storm. "Tarrant," he had said. "I gave the name up all those years ago. Now I'm taking it back."

Tarrant would not be happy about the unsanctioned attack, or its subsequent failure. She was only thankful that she had been left out of the loop by their Argentine counterparts, and thus would bear none of the blame.

Montero paced nervously, waiting for the figure in the shadows to respond to his disclosure of the afternoon's disastrous events. His anxiety at their de facto leader's reaction was only one of the burdens weighing on his conscience; two encounters with the intrepid Mira Raiden had put a dent in the paramilitary arm of his organization. Tarrant, all but invisible in the shadowy niche where he spent most daylight hours, was eerily silent for a long time, heightening the anxiety.

"Nothing changes," he sighed, startling both Rachel and Montero in spite of the softness of his tone. "Sixty years ago, your predecessor's lack of patience cost him and his empire the privilege of reuniting the Trinity. His insistence on treachery and violence has, it seems, been handed down to his heirs."

Montero's head sank lower, but his eyes revealed that his shame stemmed not from recognition of his own poor judgment, but from the fact that he would have to continue looking to the old man for guidance. "So what do we do now?" he asked in heavily accented English, the same language Tarrant had used.

"We do as I directed at the outset. Your failure at the U-boat should have underscored the need to leave our enemy to find the treasure for us. The cost of openly opposing her has been too high. Better to let her brave the uncertain path ahead, follow in the trail she blazes, and seize the artifact from her once she has cleared the way."

"And if she eludes us again? We don't even know where to begin looking for her. Or the sanctuary."

"That signifies nothing. She has the Trinity of Lemuria. I am attuned to it in ways that you cannot imagine. Even now, I see her clearly as if she alone carried a torch through the darkest night. No, my friend, if you are to find the treasure you seek, you will have to learn from the failure of your predecessors. You will have to learn to trust me."

EIGHT

DiLorenzo paused to catch his breath, shouting down his body's incessant demand that he beg Mira to slow down and wait for him. After thirty seconds of labored panting, he lurched into motion and attempted to scramble up to the next turn in the switchback trail in a single push. Mira was already rounding that bend and seemed to have hardly broken a sweat.

The five days that had passed since their narrow escape from Montero's goons in Buenos Aires had been a whirlwind of activity. Though Mira appeared to thrive under such conditions, DiLorenzo found himself counting the moments until his next brush with total physical and emotional breakdown.

He had been so pleased with himself for rescuing Mira from the menacing gunman in the Puerto Nuevo warehouse. He had been so calm, so focused in that instant when he reached across the interior of the Suburban, steering it away from an almost certain plunge into the harbor. His confidence bolstered, he had slipped behind the wheel of the big vehicle and wandered into the maze of stacked crates, searching for Mira. He had not hesitated at all to fire a burst from the machine pistol, killing the man that was a heartbeat from shooting Mira, and he had felt no guilt after the fact. For a single shining moment, Michelangelo DiLorenzo had become a hero.

It had pretty much gone downhill from there.

After ditching the Suburban a few miles down the highway from the densely populated metropolitan area of Buenos Aires, he and Mira had hitched a ride in the back of an empty cattle truck. Despite her injuries, Mira seemed incapable of slowing down. He could see her wincing with every breath, the pain of bruised and cracked ribs making every inhalation an ordeal, yet she had made climbing onto the elevated platform of the truck look easy.

It had been well past dusk, with Buenos Aires several hundred miles behind them, when the driver had stopped the truck long enough to open a gate that appeared to lead directly into the untamed expanse of grass collectively known as the Pampas. DiLorenzo was shocked when the man returned to the cab and unhesitatingly drove the truck into the field, somehow locating the twin grooves of an overgrown track. By the time they arrived at the hacienda, where the owner of the ranch and his gauchos resided, the detective could have sworn that his innards had been pounded to jelly.

Things had not improved with the morning light. Though the owner of the ranch, Diego Cordova, was the epitome of hospitality, DiLorenzo found himself with only the clothes on his back; he did not have even a single change of underwear, to say nothing of a toothbrush, razor or deodorant. His discomfort multiplied when, adorned in the previous day's apparel, replete with the odor of cattle manure from the long truck ride, he joined their host at the breakfast table, where Cordova's son, also named Diego, appeared to have become obsessed with Mira.

Upon later reflection, he would admit that Diego, Jr., was merely infatuated with the lovely adventuress—what sane straight man would not be?—and that his judgment stemmed more from jealousy at the attention showed her than from any sort of malicious intent on the part of the young man. However, as he sat at the table, watching the handsome and clean-smelling Diego Cordova, Jr., fawn over Mira, DiLorenzo's distrust for the man grew out of all proportion to the threat he might have posed. When Mira announced that Diego, also an accomplished pilot, had agreed to fly them on to Bolivia, he almost exploded in rage and frustration.

Perhaps, he thought staring up the trail, panting like a tired dog on a hot day, *I should have indulged that urge*. Mira certainly would have rejected his companionship at that point, but it would have spared him the hell that followed.

Without being consciously aware of it, his feet heaved into motion and he trudged ahead, up the trail. The dull throbbing behind his eyes had grown by an order of magnitude over the past few hours, but he had striven to hide his discomfort from Mira, not wanting to call any more attention to his shortcomings.

Their benefactor had flown them safely, as promised, to the remote city of Ouros in Bolivia. The town, like the mining industry it had once supported, appeared to be on the verge of drying up altogether. It was a rough and inhospitable place, desolate and underdeveloped. Mira had seemed to know exactly where to go, so DiLorenzo had kept his mouth shut and followed blindly. His relief at parting company with their pilot was short-lived, for the headache that had settled in shortly after taking off from the private airstrip on Cordova's ranch had not relented upon landing. Instead, it had continued to grow with each passing hour. DiLorenzo had never heard of altitude sickness, but at nearly ten thousand feet above sea level, his ignorance afforded no protection from the affliction.

Mira had been forthcoming with information about their goal, but the detective had retained little of what she had told him. The documents she had recovered from Mann's case contained rough directions for finding the Nazi refuge, located in the Altiplano region of Bolivia. The papers were not designed to be a guidebook to the redoubt, but rather a chronicle of Mann's achievements, both in recovering the artifacts of the antediluvian world and in building an underground city worthy of the ancients.

There was mention of an underwater entrance from the Pacific coast, which could accommodate several U-boats, connected to the refuge by a long tunnel equipped with an electric trolley to speed the trip along. The distances involved made the tunnel sound like more of a long-range plan than a reality, but if such a submarine base did exist, it would help to explain the demise of Mann's U-boat. Perhaps the captain of the vessel had blundered onto the seamount while negotiating unfamiliar waters in search of a submerged entrance to the base. If such an underwater passage did indeed exist, the only record of its location was in the sodden remains of the captain's logbook, deep beneath the Pacific.

Finding the alternate entrance into the Nazi stronghold would require some legwork, but there were sufficient clues in the narrative to put their goal well within the realm of possibility. Mann had mentioned using existing mineshafts and naturally occurring tunnels for ventilation purposes. To top it off, he had harnessed the power of steam, tapping into geysers to produce electricity for the entire underground complex. There were enough clues to flesh out the bare bones directions to the refuge, and Mira seemed confident that they would find what they sought.

DiLorenzo snapped out of his reverie as he reached the crest of the hill they had been climbing for what seemed an eternity. Mira knelt there, her eyes roaming over the landscape below. Though his headache clamored for attention, he found the sight of her gazing serenely toward the horizon more refreshing than a cold beer or a dose of aspirin.

When their eyes met, she treated him to a sincere smile that conveyed no sense of frustration at his plodding pace. "We'll camp here."

No one in Ouros knew the old man's name. Some wondered if even he remembered the name he had been christened with. To most of the people in the city, he was simply a crazy old man, wandering the streets with his burro. To the occasional tourists, mostly adventure-seeking Europeans and a scattering of American backpackers, he was the local colour; a toothless Quechua in a straw hat and stained white cotton garments, always willing to bare his gums in a smile for the camera. To the handful of people with whom the man regularly had dealings, he was know as "El Borro"—a nickname derived from the Spanish word for drunkard. The appellation was accurate, as the man did love intoxicating beverages of any quality, so long as the quantity remained copious. Since he appeared to have no form of employment, those who did not know him other than to see him sometimes wondered aloud at how he had managed to stay alive—and constantly pickled—through the years. Those that knew him as El Borro, however, did not have to ponder this riddle. They knew the answer well.

El Borro was roaming the streets of Ouros, much as he did every day, when the airplane descended into the city. Aircraft were not uncommon in the backwaters of Bolivia, but the old man decided to investigate anyway.

The plane returned to the skies before he could complete his journey, but this did not trouble him, because he was no longer looking to the skies. His rheumy eyes were fixed on the road and on the cars that periodically passed by. He did not have to wait long.

A battered orange car of indeterminate make rumbled past the him less than five minutes after the mosquito buzzing of the airplane's single engine had faded into the distance. Black stenciled letters identified the vehicle as a local taxi, but this was something that the old man already knew. His attention was fixed on the passengers in the rear seat. Strangers were easy to spot in the remote city, and these two could not have looked more out of place. *Especially the man*, thought El Borro. *He looks like he is sick or scared to death. Or both.*

The woman seemed surer of herself, gazing out the window with an almost lackadaisical disinterest. *She's a looker. If I were twenty years younger* . . . He didn't allow himself to finish the thought. Alcohol was his mistress, and a jealous one at that.

The arrival of the strangers was not really a noteworthy event, but El Borro made a careful effort to remember everything he could about the pair in the taxi. Delacortes would ask many questions before paying him for the information.

As Bolivia's mining industry withered, the rural peasants had soon found a different resource to tap for their livelihood. They had always grown and harvested coca, chewing the leaves as a mild stimulant when they worked as their ancestors had for untold generations, little realizing that it would prove to be the cash crop of their age. A growing global demand for refined coca—cocaine—had arisen just in time to rescue them from the economic blight that had settled over the region. That it was illegal made it all the more lucrative.

Rafael Delacortes was one of a handful of local businessmen who had grown fat from the labors of the *campesinos*. He did not grow, harvest or refine the coca, nor did he smuggle the cocaine out of the region. He was simply a middleman, taking advantage of other people's willingness to break the law to become wealthy.

Delacortes maintained a network informants like El Borro. In his profession, ignorance could prove deadly. The arrival of the strangers described by the old man troubled him.

They did not sound like tourists. Narcotics agents from the American DEA perhaps? One could never be too cautious.

A couple of discreet phone calls had helped him track down the plane and its owner and had revealed the flight's point of origin in Argentina. Soon he possessed enough information to alleviate his concern that the strangers might be drug enforcement agents, but their presence concerned him nonetheless.

The man that Delacortes had contacted in Argentina had not been completely forthcoming. He knew a great deal about the pair the old man had described to Delacortes, especially the woman, and as soon as he had ended the conversation with the Bolivian cocaine merchant he dialed another number.

Within one hour of her arrival in Bolivia, Jorge Montero knew where to find Mira Raiden. The handsome heir to both a prodigious cattle-ranching fortune and the mantle of leadership for the reborn Odessa smiled haughtily as the news was relayed over the telephone lines.

"Tell your man in Bolivia to follow them," he instructed, not entirely comprehending the relationship between the corrupt government official and the cocaine baron. "But under no circumstances are they to approach. I will be there very soon. Your loyalty will be remembered."

Returning the handset to its cradle, Montero leaned back in is chair, gleefully triumphant.

"The Raiden woman has been found?"

The voice belonged to Guillermo Petronilo, Montero's foremost lieutenant and lifelong friend. His roguish good looks had been marred by a bandage over his left ear, the result of a pistol-whipping suffered at the hands of Mira's companion. They had identified the police detective, but remained unsure of his role in her quest. Petronilo nevertheless looked forward to meeting up with DiLorenzo in the near future.

"We do not need that old meddler's help. We will reach the

prize ahead of him and take back what should have been ours all along."

Petronilo echoed his superior's laughter, the shooting pain along his jaw reminding him of his personal motives in the matter. Montero allowed his mirth to subside and picked up the telephone. There was much work to be done.

In the dim orange glow of the campfire, DiLorenzo seemed almost at peace. A long period of fitful tossing had eventually given way to a deep, healing sleep. Mira had insisted that the detective drink a great deal of water. He was obviously dehydrated and suffering from altitude sickness. Though there was nothing she could do to alleviate the latter, keeping him hydrated would at least help him to cope with the symptoms until he was better acclimated.

Her eyes lingered on him a while longer, half-heartedly pursuing random thoughts about the man and her feelings for him. Their trials together had done little to build any sort of romantic bond between them. His adolescent antics at the Cordova ranch hacienda had been more irritating than endearing, but a part of her that she could not begin to explain was secretly pleased that he had felt so threatened. Perhaps when they were back in familiar surroundings, without an army of malcontents trying to kill them, she would slow down long enough to address the riddle of her emotions.

A distant sound, probably nothing more than the movement of a small animal through the brush, broke her out of her meanderings. The noise had not startled her, but served as a reminder of a conclusion she had reached earlier when they had thrown down their bedding: they were being followed.

She remained awake, careful not to stare at the fading coals of their campfire, and focused on what she could hear, rather than trusting her sight. If they were indeed being shadowed, their pursuer was either very skilled or hanging back some distance. She prayed the latter was the case.

As the moon dipped below the horizon, she rolled stealthily from her bed. Starlight afforded little in the way of illumination, but her eyes were already becoming accustomed to the darkness. DiLorenzo snored lightly, obliterating any chance she might have to pick out distant noises in the night, but she did not disturb him. With any luck, she would be back before he knew she had gone.

She stayed low, sometimes crawling on hands and knees, working her way back down the route they had blazed. It was impossible to make out any details of their earlier passage, but she knew the signs were there; boot prints and displaced foliage carved a path that even a modestly skilled tracker could follow. She had not been overly worried about leaving a trail, initially believing that their enemies could not possibly have picked up the scent so quickly, then later realizing that keeping DiLorenzo moving would demand all of her attention.

In the darkness, she had to rely on her memory of their ascent, but soon found herself picking out notable landmarks, familiar outcroppings of rock or uniquely gnarled trees. Her visual acuity continued to improve, and soon she was moving down the slope almost as fast as she would walk under normal circumstances. Nevertheless, it was neither her eyes nor ears, nor even her sixth sense, that tipped her off to the location of their pursuer.

A faint whiff of smoke, not burning wood but the sweet aroma of tobacco, drifted across her path, stopping her instantly. Reflexively, she knelt into a defensive crouch, her right hand seeking the butt of her holstered automatic. She sniffed cautiously at the air, trying to find the source. There was virtually no wind, so she knew she was close.

She found the campsite within two minutes of first scenting the cigarette smoke. The men had camped almost exactly on top of the trail she and DiLorenzo had left during their climb. There were two of them, rough looking men whose dark complexions revealed both their aboriginal ancestry and a lifetime of toil in one of the harshest places on earth. She doubted that they were Montero's soldiers, but it seemed reasonable to believe that the men were working under his direction.

The men had pitched bedrolls, eschewing the comfort of a campfire doubtlessly to maintain the secrecy of their pursuit.

They had cloaked themselves in wool blankets, hand-woven, with geometric patterns in ochre and indigo. One of the men appeared to be sleeping while his companion kept a failing vigil. Not only had indulging his nicotine habit betrayed their location, but the man also appeared to be dozing off. Every few seconds, he would jerk spasmodically, trying in vain to raise himself back to wakefulness.

Mira pondered her options. Killing them outright was an obvious solution, but one that would not rest easy on her conscience. If the men had been overtly linked to Montero and his neo-Nazi group, she might not have hesitated. She had long ago learned that sparing an enemy simply postponed an inevitable life or death struggle. However, it was evident that these men had not been sent to kill her, and acting preemptively against them would tread too closely the fine line between war and murder, a line she had been unwilling to cross during her days as an intelligence agent.

As she watched, the sentinel's head dipped forward once more, the man's chin coming to rest on his chest. His cigarette had ceased glowing, but tendrils of smoke were beginning to rise at the point where the tip of the cheroot met the rough cloth of his shirt.

"Those things will be the death of you," she murmured, creeping forward in an almost serpentine crawl. Her fingers deftly plucked the smoldering butt from the garment, removing the imminent danger. The negligent watchman offered his gratitude with a gentle snore.

She did not linger in the campsite. Her reasons for daring to move so close were two-fold, and in rescuing the oblivious sentinel from his own stupidity, both for the sake of altruism and to prevent a rude awakening, she had accomplished one of those tasks. The other promised to be more profitable.

Lying haphazardly between the sleeping men were two large packs. Mira crept past the nearby guard, entering into the heart of their campsite, and eased the packs onto her back. Each weighed about twenty pounds, a difficult burden to bear when crawling, but she kept her breathing soft and shallow as she slipped silently away from the camp.

Hiking back up the trail, her calves and thighs burning from the exertion of the added weight, she contemplated how the men would react when they awoke to discover that their camp had been raided. Their upbringing in the harsh country had likely imbued them with the necessary survival skills to survive by foraging, but with any luck they would simply turn around and head back to the city. Meanwhile, she and DiLorenzo would profit from their loss.

The sky was beginning to lighten in the east by the time she reached their campsite. A smoky odor lingered in the air, the only remnant of their fire. The thin atmosphere had quickly smothered the coals once the fuel was expended, eliminating the small corona of warmth that DiLorenzo had unconsciously huddled close to in his sleep. Though he continued snoring loudly, his fingers had pulled the sleeping bag tight around his shoulders, and were visibly clenching the fabric. Weary from the nocturnal trek, Mira eased the packs to the ground and then collapsed on top of them.

Anxiety and adrenaline prevented her from sleeping. Her eyes continually roved across the indistinguishable landscape for some sign of pursuit. Nevertheless, the rest from physical activity was hungrily welcomed. Her ribs still smarted from the blow she had taken on the Puerto Nuevo docks, only the latest in a series of scrapes and contusions that were slowly eroding her stamina. For all the discomfort, however, she could not deny the feeling of vitality that her adventures had awakened. She was also eager to learn the fate of the third Trinity relic and prepared herself to do whatever was necessary to keep Montero and Rachel Aimes from seizing its power.

Her intuition gave her no insight into the Trinity's strange nature. That it was a talisman of supernatural power was evident, but the source of its energy was problematic. Did it derive power from the traditionally recognized sources of magic: gods and devils, angels and demons, spirits and ghosts? Or was it in actuality the product of a technology so advanced as to be indistinguishable from sorcery?

Did it matter?

Without realizing it, she found herself staring at the piece of the Trinity that she had recovered from the U-boat. Though it had been securely stowed away in her backpack, she had unconsciously taken it out, lightly caressing the hexagonal gemstone. In the twilight, it almost seemed as if the crystal was glowing.

When she had been working with Atlas on the trail of Storm Jaguar and then later in the temple in Panama, the Atlantean Trinity had exerted a gravitational pull on her, drawing her like a moth to flame across thousands of miles. And when she had stood in its presence, the "noise" from the relic had overwhelmed her prescient sensory organ, a noise that had gone silent when she damaged the crystal. By contrast, the Lemurian Trinity, as Mann had dubbed it, had not revealed its presence to her, at least on a psychic level, even though it was clearly active—active enough to reanimate Mann's corpse.

The Trinity was proving to be a fickle conquest.

She had told DiLorenzo that there were abundant clues in Mann's journal to lead them to the entrance of the hidden Nazi refuge, but that was only partly true. She did not need Mann's directions; the Trinity was speaking to her again.

She held the circlet in her hands, trying to remember the sensations that had come from its Atlantean counterpart, and she felt the same kind of homing instinct that had pulled her toward the tomb in Panama. More than that, she felt attuned to the location, not only of the remaining Trinity relic—Mann had linked it to the ancient myth of Shambala, chief city of the Hollow Earth empire known as Agartha—now secreted away in the Nazi redoubt, but also the stolen Atlantean Trinity. She couldn't fix their exact locations, but like the needle of a compass, she could track a straight line directly to either one of them. And in the case of the Shambala Trinity, she knew that she was very close.

The Trinity sensed that a reunion was near, and it was beginning to sing to her.

Abruptly, a discordant tone insinuated itself into that urgent and insistent song, compelling her to gaze toward the horizon. There she spied the blinking light of an artificial star—an aircraft, probably a helicopter, moving across the sky and descending into Ouros.

In the remote frontier of Bolivia, air travel was more a necessity than a luxury, and the arrival of an aircraft should not have been noteworthy. Even the unusual hour of arrival could be explained rationally, considering cocaine smugglers didn't always keep banker's hours. However, her intuition was telling her otherwise.

She nudged DiLorenzo with a booted foot. "Wake up. We're going to have company."

NINE

Though he was the closest thing to nobility for several hundred miles, Rafael Delacortes was deferential to the point of sycophancy. Montero strove to conceal his contempt for the half-breed drug lord as he offered thanks for the man's cooperation. Delacortes in turn promised to continue providing whatever assistance Montero might need. Although the Argentine had brought a dozen of his best recruits—survivors of earlier skirmishes with Mira Raiden—armed to the teeth with the finest weapons money could buy, Montero did not refuse the contribution. In the uncertain terrain and altitude, it only made sense to place the local rabble in the vanguard.

Within two hours of their arrival, the sun now climbing out of the eastern sky, the expedition set out in a loose formation of jeeps and pickup trucks. Almost immediately, the impromptu caravan turned into the jungle, treading deeply rutted, smuggling roads.

In the passenger seat of Delacortes' Ford Explorer, bathed in the cool breeze of a surprisingly functional air conditioning unit, Jorge Montero closed his eyes and tried to imagine what they would find. The relic that Tarrant hungered for was unquestionably significant, but it was a mere fraction of the wealth and power that his forefathers had likely secreted away in the subterranean fortress. Not only had the Nazis cached their plunder in the hidden redoubt, but the accumulation of their scientific knowledge was most certainly archived there as well. Although both America and Soviet Russia had plumbed the depths of Germany's progress in the fields of atomic science and rocketry, squeamish sentiment had prevented them from making use of the information gained in medical experiments conducted in the relocation camps. Doubtless, what they had taken after Germany's defeat was the merest tip of a juggernaut iceberg of knowledge.

Making wise use of what they would find in the Nazi fortress was perhaps more problematic. After a lifetime—make that nearly three lifetimes—of searching for the hidden treasure, the imperatives that had once driven the members of Odessa were no longer so clear. Global domination was not as attractive as it had once perhaps seemed. The world was overflowing with undesirables, too many to eradicate but of little value as subjects or even slaves. No, the real power at work in the world derived, as it always truly had, from controlling money. Though ultimately he could only begin to guess at what they would find in the Nazi redoubt, Montero was confident that he could parlay both physical riches and the treasure of knowledge into an iron fist of wealth and power that would make both superpowers and mega-corporations kneel to kiss his ring.

"Señor." The soft voice, intentionally unobtrusive, barely broke through Montero's grandiose idlings. He raised his eyes to find that the convoy had stopped in the middle of the wilderness road, and Delacortes was standing in front of the open door of his car.

"What is it?"

"Señor, my humblest apologies, but the men I have sent ahead to follow the woman . . . There has been no radio contact since last evening."

"What does that mean? Are they dead? Has the Raiden woman killed them?"

Delacortes shrugged, bringing his hands together as if he were genuflecting. "I do not know. They were good men." Montero could only assume that the cocaine seller spoke of their toughness and reliability, rather than their moral character. Delacortes continued: "I do not believe that this woman could have overwhelmed them."

"She's a resourceful bitch," snarled Montero, flashing back to his encounters with Mira, one of which had left him in a New York City hospital under police custody. "The question is, can we find her without them?"

Delacortes shrugged again. "We know where they last sighted her. Perhaps we can pick up the trail from there."

"Good. Then let us proceed with all haste." Tarrant would soon see through the subterfuge by which he had left

Argentina, and it was imperative that Montero be in possession of the Trinity relics before the old grave robber caught up to him. Though he could tell himself that he was unafraid of the old man and his mystical talismans, he knew that he was fooling no one, least of all himself.

DiLorenzo followed the invisible line, leading from the tip of Mira's finger to a point on the rock face roughly sixty feet above their heads. A faint plume of steam was creeping from a barely discernible crack in the vertical stone wall.

"You're kidding."

She shook her head grimly. "It's the only way in."

"How can you know that?" DiLorenzo's tone was tinged with panic. "Wait. Don't tell me. I don't think I want to know." He leaned back against the wall, sinking into a tired squat, and massaged his temples in search of courage.

His headache was mostly gone, conquered by hydration and acclimatization. In its place was a sort of total body ache, but even that felt good in a macho sort of way. Since rising, he had almost kept pace with Mira—a more hurried pace than the previous day.

Shortly after waking, she had passed him a steaming mug full of a rich brown liquid. Though he usually took his coffee with two creams, two sugars—regular by New York standards—he had gulped it down straight, welcoming the flow of warmth into his veins.

"Thanks," he murmured. A moment later he spied a stack of tortillas and an array of fruit, and looked back at her in wonderment. "Did you run to the corner store for this?"

She flashed a wry smile. "In a manner of speaking."

The provisions she had raided from the camp of their pursuers were a mixed bag indeed. The men had carried coffee, fruit and tortillas, but no fresh water. Their packs had also included a small arsenal of weapons and ammunition, from which DiLorenzo had taken a .38 revolver, while Mira had added a single-barreled pump-action shot gun to her armaments, along with a score of buckshot shells. The only other item of interest was a military-style radio. They had listened warily since dawn to the repeated inquiries from some distant source, demanding a reply.

Upon breaking camp, Mira had navigated more precisely, as if following an unseen beacon. DiLorenzo had tried to solve the mystery without asking, but soon the pace she set cleared his mind of everything but exertion. It was almost noon when they reached the vertical rock face, where a wisp of vapor marked the presence of a geyser, at which point Mira had announced that they had arrived.

Though her face and manner betrayed no anxiety toward the ascent, Mira was hiding a deep-seated dread. Her concern stemmed primarily from the fact that she would have to guide her companion, doubtless a rank beginner in the world of rock climbing, up what appeared to be a very technical route. Adding to the predicament was her lack of any safety equipment, not counting the fifty feet of hemp rope, a gift of the Cordova family. She sorely missed the gear she had purchased in New York for her clandestine entry into Aimes' apartment.

The ascent did not appear impossible by any means—Mira had trained on much more difficult routes back on the Farm—but to a neophyte like DiLorenzo, difficulty was measured on a completely different scale, on which failure meant pain, serious injury or even death.

"I'll go up first," she announced, trying to mask the hesitancy she felt. "I'll take the rope with me and set a belay at the top. I won't be able to pull you up, but it will help you make the climb."

DiLorenzo nodded silently, unable to completely conceal his trepidation behind a brave smile.

Mira nodded in return, then slung the rope coil over her shoulder and turned to the rock. The first few steps would be easy. The base of the cliff was littered with large boulders, forming a platform from which to launch her ascent. After that, however, the angle of the stone face was just a few degrees off vertical, though thankfully the degrees were in her favor.

"Watch what I do carefully. Pay attention to where I put my hands and feet. You will need to do exactly the same." She sucked in a deep breath, painfully aware that anything she failed to tell DiLorenzo might cost him his life. "A basic rule is to always keep three points of contact. Always keep both hands and one foot, or both feet and one hand, in solid contact with the rock. Don't move until you're sure your new hold is secure.

"Once you start up the rock, two things will happen. You will get fatigued very quickly, and you will be overcome with an almost paralyzing fear. Under no circumstances are you to stop moving. It won't get any easier if you cling to the rock, afraid to move."

DiLorenzo nodded again, swallowing a dry lump in his throat. "Lead on."

She turned briskly back to the cliff and scampered up the boulder pile. Without further preamble, she extended her hands to the rock, placing her left on a small protrusion about the size of her fist, situated at shoulder height. She lifted herself just a few centimeters, dividing the weight between her tiptoes and her left hand, then thrust her right arm up as far as she could reach to snag a horizontal crack with her fingertips. Remembering her own admonition to DiLorenzo, she resisted the urge to pull herself up, waiting until she found a step for her right foot. Only then did she loft herself upward.

Though the climb was easier than most, the challenge of keeping to the simplest possible route for DiLorenzo's sake proved more involved than she had anticipated. She forced herself to pass up opportunities to make quick, dynamic advances in favor of handholds that were more pronounced and closer together. Within a few minutes she felt the familiar burn of lactic acid buildup in her forearms and thighs, a warning sign of approaching fatigue. Days of hard travel and combat were taking their toll; she needed this climb to be over quickly. She rested for a moment, breathing slowly as she shook the soreness out of first her right, then her left arm.

Her brief respite did little to alleviate the burn in her extremities. If anything, the sensation seemed to be increasing in intensity. She could feel warmth spreading through her fingertips, a virtual impossibility since there was no musculature in the digits to store lactic acid. She pondered this paradox as she reached up with her left hand, thankful that her muscles had not yet begun to quiver from the sustained exertion.

Her hand froze mere centimeters from the rock. Directly over her head a white plume was blossoming skyward. At first glance it seemed as if a cloud had reached down from the sky and taken root in the stone. "The geyser," she murmured.

Almost unconsciously, she looked at her wristwatch—the antique dive chronometer that she had inherited from Muldoon—noting the time and the sweep of the second hand. The eruption continued to build silently above her, the water vapor, superheated by subterranean geothermal forces, refusing to dissipate quickly in the thin air.

She had known about the geyser, both from Mann's writings and from her own observations of the rock face, but the eruption had nevertheless caught her off guard. She had not been expecting something so spectacular. The wisps of steam she had glimpsed upon approaching the cliff were merely a herald of the explosion to come.

The warmth in her arms and thighs, she now understood, was also attributable to this natural phenomenon, and not anaerobic fatigue. Heat rising from the earth's mantle had saturated the rock surrounding the vent, making it warm enough to cause discomfort with prolonged contact.

The geyser continued to spew hot steam for nearly two minutes. When the eruption ceased, it was with an abrupt finality, as if an energy-conscious god had turned off Mother Nature's hot water spigot.

Two minutes spent frozen in place, watching the spectacular column of vapor, had allowed a very real fatigue to creep into her muscles. There was no longer any time to waste in searching for an easy, if meandering, route up to the crevice. She quickly picked out a series of holds and articulated her way upward in a fluid ascent that lasted mere seconds.

Wisps of vapor continued to trickle from the vent, marking the location of the geyser. The horizontal slash was much larger than it had appeared from below, easily big enough for her to crawl inside the fissure and turn around. She leaned out and peered down at DiLorenzo, barely able to make out his expression.

"Made it," she called. "Think you can do that?"

"Piece of cake," he returned. Even with the intervening distance, there was no mistaking the quaver in his voice.

Mira nodded grimly then unlimbered the rope. With no means of fastening the line into the rock, she was forced to improvise. Tying a large knot in one end of the hemp cord, she proceeded to wedge it into the seam where the fissure began. When her fingers could press it no further, she jammed the toe of her boot into the crack and continued forcing it in. Satisfied that the rope would not quickly become dislodged, she wrapped a length of it around her hips, then cast the remainder out into space.

"Tie it around your waist," she shouted. "Then bring it up between your legs and out to the sides. You remember what my climbing harness looked like, right?"

She saw the nod of his head as he reluctantly complied, and she talked him through the steps to tie a Swiss-Seat harness. She had no idea if his makeshift knot-work would save him in the event of a fall. The hemp rope was considerably stiffer than the nylon lines used by professional climbers and lacked the necessary elasticity. There was a good chance that, if DiLorenzo did fall, the shock of hitting the end of the safety line might prove as damaging as a fall to the rocky ground below. The purpose of the rope was primarily a psychological crutch to help the detective overcome his fears. He looked up again when he had finished, waiting for the next cue.

"Come on up. And whatever you do, don't fall."

After two false starts, DiLorenzo committed to the climb, rising completely out of the horizontal world. He quickly grasped the concept of finding the subtle protrusions of stone, and was soon climbing with the same confidence he might display ascending a vertical ladder. As he gained elevation, Mira pulled in the slack, spooling it around her lower body. It was a dangerous belay. If DiLorenzo fell, his mass might pull her out of her perch and catapult her from the vent. Or, it might work exactly as she intended. It was impossible to predict what would happen, and therefore was a scenario she hoped would never be tested.

DiLorenzo's initial enthusiasm quickly paled as the ground shrank away. The fear that he had managed to suppress reasserted its grip, causing him to hesitate before each movement, sometimes pondering a handhold for several seconds before reaching out to it with quivering fingers.

"It will only get harder if you take too long," she chided, trying to motivate without pushing him to make a foolish mistake. "You've got to keep moving, or you'll exhaust yourself."

DiLorenzo wisely saved the breath that might have been wasted in an empty retort. Mira checked the face of her watch again. The detective had already spent twice as much time on the rock face as she had, and was only about halfway up. It seemed doubtful that he could endure the strain of such a slow ascent.

An abrupt change in the air distracted her from these concerns. It took a moment for her to isolate the change, a fractional rise in the temperature and a gentle wind brushing at her back, accompanied by a pungent odor of sulfur and freshly turned earth. But in the instant that she divined the significance of these clues everything changed.

"Hang on!"

Mira dove forward, twisting as her body slipped past the edge of the fissure, and snared the stone lip with her fingertips. As her full weight succumbed to the lure of gravity, the loop around her waist pulled tight against the makeshift belay, burning painfully into her abdomen. If DiLorenzo fell now, the rope would cut her in two, but this dark thought was eclipsed by a something far more immediate.

A belch of superheated steam erupted without further warning from the ragged frown of rock where Mira had been perched only an instant before. Though the hot vapor rose up and away from the desperately clinging figure, she nevertheless felt the skin of her knuckles and fingertips blistering from the sudden exposure. Gritting her teeth, she did the only thing she could: she endured.

As the initial shock of the moment passed, she became

aware of DiLorenzo, motionless against the rock face, no more than six feet from her dangling boots. He had heeded the frantic warning and held his position without panicking, though she could not begin to guess at the toll such an exertion was taking on his already fatigued muscles.

Almost unconsciously, she remembered that she had been looking at her watch a few seconds before the eruption. The second release from the geyser had followed the first by an interval of about twenty minutes. The implications of that fact stunned her like a physical blow.

Though most geyser eruptions were random and unpredictable, some, like the renowned Old Faithful in Yellowstone National Park, kept a constant schedule. The subterranean chambers fed by invisible rivers and springs filled up at a constant rate, reaching the boiling point like an enormous underground tea kettle every few hours, sometimes so reliably that one could set a clock by them.

If this geyser was as dependable, there would be precious little time to complete the ascent and find the hidden entrance to the Nazi fortress.

The eruption ceased as abruptly as it had begun, with the last gasp of boiling hot steam dissipating into nothingness. Despite the adrenaline in her veins and the time dilation of unending agony, Mira reckoned that no more than two minutes had passed since the beginning of the eruption. The two geothermal events had lasted for an equivalent span, suggesting that the interval until the next would be similarly measured. There was no time to lose.

Bracing her toes against the rock, she pulled herself once more into the fissure, sighing aloud with relief as the noose around her waist loosened. Her fingers flared with the pain of a severe scalding, but the skin was not as badly traumatized as she had expected, which was fortunate, as she had neither the time nor the resources to treat the injury.

Before she could regain her earlier position within the seam, DiLorenzo, in a last-ditch, heroic effort, ascended the remaining section. As his fingertips grazed the lip of the fissure, Mira reached out and helped him up onto the horizontal surface.

Her scalded fingers unriddled the knot he had tied around his waist. The detective obviously had never been a Boy Scout. His belay would certainly have failed had he fallen against it. As he struggled to prop himself up on his arms left weak with fatigue, Mira hastily drew in the rope, coiling it in a butterfly pattern with an urgency that barely allowed her the time to keep it from tangling.

"Let's go," she stated in a tone that brooked no argument. "We don't have much time."

By her best estimation, in fact, they had about eighteen minutes before the fissure filled with boiling steam. If they had not located the entrance to the Nazi fortress by then, the geyser would cook them alive.

For Rachel Aimes, the failure to retrieve the Trinity from Muldoon's U-boat had proven to be a blessing in disguise. Though both physically and emotionally battered by the defeat, the intervening days had afforded an opportunity for rest that she had postponed for too long. In the palatial surroundings of Montero's villa, it was easy to almost forget about the quest that had consumed her life for too many years to remember.

Following Tarrant's wishes, she had relented from combing the Argentine streets for their enemy, filling her days instead with exercise and relaxation. Though it had been difficult at first to sit idly by and wait, she soon found enough pleasant distractions to pass the time. This day, for example, had begun with a strenuous swim in Montero's Olympic-distance pool, followed by an hour-long massage, after which she had stretched out her invigorated limbs on a chaise lounge beside the pool, wearing only sunglasses and a bikini brief that would have made a stripper blush. She knew that Montero's house servants were probably watching her, and the thought of being on display was strangely tantalizing.

Indulging her exhibitionist fantasies had awakened her to emotions kept dormant for too long. Though she was conscious of her beauty, aware of her raw sexuality, she rarely took any pleasure from her natural gifts. Sex was a tool she used to gain control of, or favor with, men. It was a talent that had served her from the time of her earliest memories as she moved through a succession of foster homes until, at age twelve, a benevolent man named Walter Aimes had drawn her out of that personal hell, showing more interest in her mind than in her body.

The thought made her chuckle. "A pity we had to kill him," she mumbled.

"*Perdón, señorita?*"

Behind the mask of her sunglasses, her eyelids flashed open. The response startled her, but she did not flinch. It took a moment for her eyes to adjust, revealing the familiar face of the steward that had attended her earlier. She remembered the subtle tremble of his fingertips as he had oiled her skin with suntan lotion.Had he now worked up the impertinence to approach her? A coy smile touched her lips.

"*Disculpe,*" continued the young man. "Señor Tarrant has called for you."

Her smile fell by a degree, but her mind quickly switched gears, squelching her flirtatious impulses. Without speaking she swiveled into a sitting position, then rose gracefully to her feet. She stood nearly a head taller than the pool boy, her bared nipples thrusting forward just below the level of his chin, but she was now oblivious to the fact that his stare was transfixed on her breasts; the moment was gone.

The summons from Tarrant was ominous, but there was no way of knowing if it boded good or bad. Knotting a short silk robe around her waist, she left the young steward in her wake, racing into the villa to find the old grave robber in the shadowy recesses of Montero's library.

Despite her long acquaintance with the man, Rachel could not help but feel intimidated in his presence. This sensation was certainly amplified by recent events; Tarrant's possession of the Atlantean artifact had fundamentally changed him. It was, she imagined, something like having an audience with God.

It took a few moments for her to locate him. Though he had made no effort to conceal himself, his lack of motion caused him to blend into the staid surroundings. His hooded coat, almost like a priest's cassock, added to the mystery that had surrounded him since his acquisition of the Trinity.

"You summoned me?" The words sounded strange on her lips. They were not a part of her ordinary vocabulary.

"She is close."

"Raiden?"

Tarrant nodded imperceptibly. "If she survives the journey, she will find the prize today."

"Does Montero know?"

Her breathless statement elicited a cryptic chuckle from the hooded figure. "He is nearly there as well."

Rachel was dumbfounded. "You sent him without telling me?"

"Perish the thought, my dear. Our radical young friend is operating quite independently of my direction."

The second revelation was nearly as disturbing as the first. "He double-crossed us?"

"It is his nature. He is drawn to treachery as a dog is to its vomit. He could not have done otherwise."

"But if he gets the Trinity before—"

Tarrant waved dismissively. "I doubt that he will survive his next encounter with Mira Raiden. It is also in his nature to underestimate her, and that will prove his undoing. However, even if he should survive long enough to claim the prize, it will avail him naught. He barely grasps its potential. No, it is not Montero's treachery that concerns me. It is Mira. She understands."

Tarrant turned to face her, rising with an uncharacteristic abruptness. "That is why we must hasten there as well. Our time is nearly at hand."

Beyond the fissure, the seam in the rock face opened into a broad cavity, almost high enough to allow Mira to walk upright. That was the good news. The bad news was that the passage turned almost immediately downward at a forty-five degree angle, plunging into the dark heart of the mountain.

Hunched over to avoid striking her head on hanging protuberances, Mira led the way at a brisk trot. In a matter of seconds, the light from the opening in the rock face was swallowed up by the angle of descent, but she deftly plucked a flare from her backpack, striking it on the run. The twenty-foot sphere of pink-orange illumination revealed nothing about their destination, however. The distant end of the passage remained secret in the darkness.

Running was almost impossible. Her stance, bent forward because of the low ceiling, added to the difficulty of maintaining her balance, while every step seemed to promise a headlong plunge. The shaft was thick with heat and humidity, the air permeated with acrid fumes of brimstone. The surreal light from Mira's flare cast a laval glow upon the rough walls, like a web of magma and shadow that presented the illusion of a descent into hell. The real inferno, however, would begin in less than sixteen minutes.

She didn't know whether DiLorenzo was keeping pace and did not pause to look back. Her concern for his safety seemed to express itself best as rage. An eruption of ire to rival the geyser seemed to be building within her abdomen and she had to bite her lip in order to stay focused on the immediate problem.

It was impossible to measure their progress in meaningful terms. Even the passage of time seemed distorted by the proximity of instantaneous death. Mira's mental clock, fueled by adrenaline, seemed to be running twice as fast as the watch ticking on her wrist. How far had they gone in five short minutes? The stifling heat made the journey all the more taxing, further impairing her perceptions. The awkward gait required to make the descent was like nothing she had ever experienced. She could not even begin to guess at the distance they had covered. *A quarter of a mile, at best*, she thought. *We've barely scratched the surface.*

The unremarkable tunnel continued straight as the thrust of a knife into the heart of the mountain, maintaining a more or less uniform diameter. The glow of the flare exposed the origin of the tunnel, black streaks of shadow outlining the tool marks of its original excavation. This, Mira reasoned, was a good sign. The tunnel's architect would have chosen the shortest possible distance for the vent.

She checked her watch again. Eleven minutes until the next eruption, and they had reached the event horizon—it was time to decide. "Go back!" she shouted without turning her head.

"Only if you do."

The blood rushing in her ears effectively drowned out the sound of his footsteps, and she had no idea that he was so close. But his almost immediate response indicated that he was only a step or two behind.

Damn him. She did not waste the breath to make the curse audible. Then, suddenly, it didn't matter any more. The flare's pinkish flame reflected off of a metal surface ten meters ahead in their path, and before Mira could come to a complete halt, the vent tunnel ended.

"This is it," she breathed, extending her hands against the wall, absorbing the last of her forward momentum. DiLorenzo skidded to a stop half a step behind her.

The slope of the passage changed abruptly, opening into a roughly spherical chamber fifteen feet across. The walls, like the sides of the passageway, bore the marks of human labor. The floor, however, was nothing like what she expected.

Instead of rough-hewn stone, they found themselves standing on a grillwork platform of metal, faintly dulled by the passage of time. Wisps of steam rose through the spaces, hiding from view whatever lay beneath the platform.

"It's hot in here." DiLorenzo's offhand comment seemed forced, a breathless attempt to hide his trepidation.

"We're standing on top of the geyser." Mira checked her watch. "Nine minutes until it erupts again."

"It took longer than that just to get here."

She dropped to her knees and probed the hot metal grid with her hands. A flash of pain reminded her of the injury sustained during the previous eruption, but gritting her teeth, she locked her fingers through the grating and lifted.

The metal was heavier than she had been prepared for, and the pain more intense. After a moment of struggling, the section of grating seemed to rise effortlessly, swinging away to reveal a three-foot-square gap in the platform, framed by girders of a similar metal. Only when she let go of the grating, permitting it to fall, did she realize that DiLorenzo had been helping her lift the heavy screen.

The detective let go of the grating, allowing it to crash noisily onto the platform. "Now what?"

Mira gestured at the hole, then shrugged out of the rope coil. "We go down."

"Down? That's your plan?"

She silenced him with a dangerous glance, then extended the flare out over the opening and let it fall. The orange brilliance revealed an intricate web of metal girders and curving surfaces before vanishing completely into the inky depths below. DiLorenzo withheld further commentary, shifting impatiently on his feet as she lit another flare. She then knelt and began feeding a loop of rope through the platform grating, tying it in a simple bowline knot, and allowed the rest to drop into the hole. Only then did she face him again, her eyes flashing dangerously in the flame of her torch.

"Wait for my signal." Before he could even think to question her, she dropped from view, abseiling into the void beneath the platform.

What she had seen the instant before the first flare winked out only confirmed her suspicions. The platform was part of a larger structure, built entirely of metal and designed to harness the energy of the geyser. In an unparalleled feat of engineering, Mann had capped the geyser, creating an enormous boiler and steam turbine. Though it seemed difficult to believe that the machinery constructed sixty-odd years previously was still functional, the lethal power of the geyser itself was beyond question.

The rope burned against the padded leather palm of her fingerless gloves as she squeezed it in her grip, slowing her virtual free fall. An instant later her feet touched another metal grating, forty feet below the platform. She flexed her legs to absorb the impact of her landing but kept a firm hold on the rope lest the walkway collapse under the sudden burden. A ripple of kinetic energy caused catwalk to groan and undulate, but the tremor passed without any compromise to the structure.

The narrow walkway was a bridge spanning the distance from the rough-hewn rock on one side to a curving wall of dull metal. Where it met the surface of the boiler the catwalk split in either direction, taking the immense structure in the circle of its embrace. Mira's destination, however, lay the opposite way.

A short dash brought her to a landing braced against the stone wall of the chamber. Framed in chiseled basalt was a rectangular, metal hatchway about one and a half meters high and half as wide. Her grin of triumph melted when, despite pouring all her remaining energy into the effort, the flywheel latch mechanism refused to move.

The catwalk groaned and shuddered a second time as DiLorenzo crashed loudly onto the metal span. Though the platform where she stood was securely anchored, the sound of rivets bursting from the joints of the walkway and pinging like bullets against the metal and stone prompted Mira to clutch the flywheel until the rocking motion subsided. A glance over her shoulder found her companion lying sprawled on the catwalk, similarly holding on for dear life. He remained motionless a moment longer, fearful that movement might cause the span to collapse beneath him, and then cautiously rose to his feet.

"What was the signal again?" His quip, obviously rehearsed prior to his near-disastrous descent, seemed forced, a desperate and insincere attempt to hide his terror behind a facade of bravado. Mira nevertheless returned a quick smile.

The hatchway was secured with a watertight door of the type used to seal off compartments in a submarine. The flywheel not only controlled four sliding steel bolts, but also served to pull the latch tight against the vulcanized rubber seal that framed the doorway. Years of disuse and corrosion had effectively welded both the wheel and the bolts in place. Though she braced her feet apart, twisting with all her might, Mira could not get the wheel to move.

As soon as he reached her, DiLorenzo wordlessly joined in the effort, gripping one side of the wheel and augmenting her efforts from a different angle, but to no avail. After a few seconds of intense effort, his muscles, already fatigued from the long climb up the rock face, failed, and he fell back shaking with exhaustion.

"It's no good," he panted.

Before she could reply, rebuking him for his defeatism, a low rumble vibrated along the unstable catwalk, followed by a shrieking noise that quickly reverberated in the narrow confines of the cavern, growing to ear-shattering intensity in a matter of seconds. Despite the darkness, both could see the expanding cloud of steam billowing from the top of the boiler. Mira didn't need to check her watch to know that they had run out of time.

TEN

Instantaneously, the air around the catwalk became opaque, distorted by a curtain of steam that billowed from the top of the boiler. Though the vapor was not quite hot enough in itself to scald them, the air temperature was rising rapidly.

DiLorenzo continued to struggle with the flywheel, bunching his shoulders in an effort to break the weld of time and oxidization. Mira however, inexplicably released her hold on the metal ring and took a step back.

"What?" DiLorenzo gasped the syllable in disbelief, and immediately felt the force of his own resolve falter.

In a fluid motion, Mira unslung the pump-action shotgun from her pack, gripping the stock in both hands. She then stepped forward, stabbing the stubby steel barrel through the center of the wheel.

Comprehension dawned quickly as the detective watched her place the full burden of her weight on the end of the makeshift lever. Even so, it was not enough.

"Let me," he shouted, gripping her shoulder and pulling her out of the way. The maneuver caught her off guard and she stumbled backwards as DiLorenzo threw himself onto the butt of the shotgun, driving down with all the mass and power he could muster.

As Mira scrambled to regain her balance, she heard a tortured shriek of metal. Once the resistance was broken, the wheel yielded completely, dumping DiLorenzo forward. His forehead glanced off of the door, and his eyes were filled with a flash of blue light. Then nothing.

Montero prodded the coarse earth with his toe. Years of big game hunting had taught him how to read the subtle signs left by the passing of man or beast, but those skills were hardly necessary to discern that two people had camped overnight on the ground before him. Though they had built no fire, nor left any other permanent spoor, the outline of bodies on the gravely soil was evident even to the least observant tracker in their party.

Delacortes confirmed the obvious. "This is where my men last reported from. They said the people you are seeking had camped up the ridge a ways."

"Then what happened, señor? Where are your men now? There was no fight here." Montero squinted at the soil again, this time looking for foot tracks. "Your men deserted their post."

"They will be punished." Delacortes' reply was hasty, but rang of insincerity. Nevertheless, Montero could hear the agitation in his voice.

"That does not concern me. We can pick up the trail for ourselves."

"We will be unable to use the vehicles."

"Our foe is also on foot." Montero swung his eyes toward the ridge above. "We are very close, Señor Delacortes. But this bitch . . . when she is backed into a corner, she fights. We must be cautious."

DiLorenzo opened his eyes lazily, squinting in a vain attempt to focus. Two blurry Miras floated in his view. "Did I fall asleep?"

She did not smile. "I think you may have a concussion."

The strange quiet of their surroundings, glowing pink in the light of a burning flare, seemed to counterpoint an urgency that DiLorenzo was hard pressed to recall. He gradually remembered that they had been on the verge of death, but the details, like his vision, remained foggy.

"You should be in a hospital," she continued, her tone without a trace of humor. She was kneeling, bent over his supine form and holding an instant cold compress from her first aid kit against his forehead. "But I suppose that's not really an option."

DiLorenzo mumbled a vague reply. There was no pain, but he knew that would follow all too soon. "What happened?"

"You saved us."

"Oh. Good."

The corner of Mira's mouth curled slightly. "Yes. You'll do as a sidekick, but in the future try to avoid cracking your head."

The hissing illumination provided by the flare revealed a narrow corridor similar to the one that had cut diagonally into the heart of the mountain. This passage however was horizontal, leading away from the heavy steel door for a distance of about twenty meters, where it ended at another door. Stenciled letters painted on the steel surfaces announced a message that was wholly foreign to the detective. "German?"

Mira nodded. "Mann's secret Nazi bunker. We've come in the back door, though I'm not certain the front entrance was ever finished."

"Does that mean we'll be leaving . . . ?" He finished the question by gesturing at the closed door behind them.

"Not if I can help it." She glanced back toward the door at the end of the corridor. "First things first. Think you're up to having a look around the place?"

"I'll manage." With her assistance, he struggled to his feet. The passage seemed to be heaving chaotically the closer he came to standing erect. He closed his eyes, bracing one hand against the wall, waiting for the moment of vertigo to pass. "What does the door say?"

"It's a reminder to keep both doors shut. Below that it says: 'Stairs to parade grounds.'"

DiLorenzo raised an eyebrow, instantly regretting the almost unseen gesture as a knifepoint of pain pierced his forehead. If she noticed, Mira said nothing to acknowledge his agony. Instead, she moved down the passage as far as the door and wrenched the flywheel until the bolts slid free. In the relatively dry environs of the access corridor, the mechanism had not suffered from the corrosion that had befouled the first door, nearly at the cost of their lives.

The doorway did indeed lead to a flight of descending stairs, cut directly into the gut-rock of the mountain. Wide enough for only one person to pass through at a time, the low ceiling added to the sensation of claustrophobia, looming ominously like the lid of a coffin. Despite the fact that there was ample clearance, Mira felt compelled to walk in a stooped position. The glow of her flare did not immediately reveal an end to the stairway.

The design made sense, she reasoned. The stairs and their upper terminus served only the most utilitarian purpose. The steam turbine was of necessity situated away from the main excavation, and appeared to have been designed to function without constant supervision. Indeed, the fact that it still regulated itself, bleeding off the pressure on a reliable twenty-minute schedule after more than sixty years of neglect, was a powerful testimony to the brilliance of its design. The stairs had likely been cut only for the purpose of an occasional maintenance inspection. Notwithstanding this, Mira could not help but wonder how much of the mountain Mann's army of slaves had hollowed out in order to create the last bastion of German National Socialism.

The echo of DiLorenzo's footsteps on the stone behind her filled the confined space, a strangely comforting sound. It was the only whisper of noise in the tomb of rock, but it was enough to offset the overwhelming claustrophobia. There was little else to occupy her senses. The light of the flare revealed little, and its sulfuric fumes effectively prevented any naturally occurring odors from reaching her nostrils. Based on prior experience, she knew this to be a blessing in disguise. With so little to mark their passage, Mira could feel a dangerous lethargy settling over her. She shook her head to clear the cobwebs, reflexively letting one hand drop to the grip of her sidearm. Yet, despite her best efforts at restoring her vigilance, the abrupt change in the shadow took her by surprise.

The pistol was drawn in a blur of motion, springing into her hand as if it were a living thing. Her right hand rose, gripping the gun, finger already tightening on the three-pound trigger, though no target was in evidence. In the same motion, she lifted the flare over her head, throwing its pink-orange illumination down on the apparition.

Sensory input gradually began to filter through the suddenness of her reaction. She could hear DiLorenzo, struggling to draw his own weapon, asking for an explanation in a hoarse whisper. She did not answer immediately.

Moving the flare had changed the shape of the shadow confronting them, but not significantly. It remained a razor sharp line of darkness, cutting down the side of the passage to their right and filling their world with impenetrable night. With an almost audible sigh of relief, Mira relaxed the pressure on the trigger.

There was no threat from the lightlessness, only the surprise of the unexpected. The explanation was ridiculously simple. One side of the passageway had abruptly ended and opened into an unfathomable vastness that did not return the limited flickering light of the flare.

"What is it?" hissed DiLorenzo again, his voice urgent as he brandished the pistol at the wall of night.

Mira eased her finger from the trigger as she holstered the weapon. "Sorry. Jumping at shadows. However, I believe we have arrived at the parade grounds."

She took a step forward, past the end of the confined passage, waving the flare to get a better estimation of what lay before them. Despite the grandiose description written on the sign they had earlier found, she was unprepared for what lay at the end of the stairway.

The flare could not begin to illuminate the immense chamber. In fact, its inadequate flame seemed to vanish into the darkness like a drop of rain into the ocean. Only a scant area in the foreground was laid bare to their eyes, but it was enough for them to begin to grasp the scope of what they had found.

The narrow staircase continued down for another twenty yards, hugging the wall of stone from which it had been hewn as it descended away from the end of the tunnel. Beyond lay a landing which turned to the right and opened onto a broad terrace of smooth stone extending in either direction beyond the sphere of illumination. Every descending step toward the terrace reinforced Mira's impression of the sheer size of the chamber, but something else was revealed in the torchlight.

Although the passages through which they had entered the mountain fortress showed the unquestionable impact of human laborers, a history permanently tattooed into the living stone in the form of chisel marks and blast scars, the tunnels and steps had been strangely barren. No dust or debris, the typical litter associated with the presence of real people, remained to give evidence that anyone had ever walked there. The terrace however bore quite a different testimony.

Large patches of the stone were covered in dark stains, likely the excrement of rodents. Mira could distinguish rags of cloth, along with bits of metal and glass mixed in with these mounds. As they drew closer to the landing, even minute details became more apparent. In one dirty heap, Mira could make out the tiny round shape of a brass button. Another step showed the fastener still attached to a sleeve of dark cloth. Protruding from the blue material were two brittle yellow sticks: the radius and ulna bones of a human arm.

The terrace was approximately sixty feet across, butting up against the wall of the chamber on one side and opening once more into the void on the other. Though they could see no end to the broad walkway in either direction, there seemed to be a pronounced curve, suggesting that it probably circled back on itself, ringing the mysterious parade grounds. Mira waved the flare in a broad arc, then stepped off the landing and headed straight across the terrace to its mysterious inner edge.

DiLorenzo drew abreast of her as she peered out over the knee-high parapet that formed the only barrier between the terrace and the empty night beyond. "Well?"

She strained her eyes to pick out some detail in the blackness. Defeated, she shook her head and tried a different tactic. With a throw to rival an Olympian javelin toss, Mira hurled the half-spent flare out into nothingness.

Though she and DiLorenzo were instantly plunged into darkness, the flare revealed a series of images as it traversed the space above the parade ground. The dancing flame sailed out over the edge of the terrace, revealing a strange and ominous landscape in its ephemeral illumination.

Below the parapet at the edge of the walkway where they stood descended long rows of carved stone tiers, forming a vast amphitheater at least thirty rows deep. The sphere of light did not extend to where the seating area eventually ended, but was quenched as the flare dropped into the debris-strewn area. In the final moment before the light blinked out, Mira caught a glimpse of something moving in the irregular crevices formed by the stone steps—something, or rather many somethings, scurrying to maintain their age-old concealment in darkness. Though the illumination was utterly squelched, the sound of skittering across bare stone filled the vast auditorium for several seconds afterward.

"I don't think we're alone in here," she remarked, unaware that her voice had dropped to a loud whisper. She reached back and slipped a flare from her pack, but DiLorenzo's hand found her wrist, gently halting her.

"Look up."

Reflexively, her head tilted back, her unseeing eyes gazing into the invisible upper reaches of the cavern. Then, almost right away, she realized that she could see something—a vague outline barely visible against the high, domed ceiling. As her pupils continued to dilate, growing more accustomed to the absence of the flare's brightness, she realized that the light level in the chamber was nearly equivalent to the twilight moments before the sun's rising.

"How is that possible?" ventured DiLorenzo. "We're deep underground."

"Natural luminescence perhaps." Mira could hear the lack of conviction in her own voice. Though she knew of caverns where lichens produced a phosphorescent orange or green glow, the light that suffused the vaulted ceiling of the cavern was different.

As her ability to perceive the light increased, she got her first real look at the underground chamber. Though her initial response to the title Parade Grounds had been dubious, she now felt a grudging admiration for what the architect had accomplished. However, as was the case with history's greatest man-made wonders, Mann had only been able to achieve such magnificence through unimaginable brutality.

The source of the light was limited to the ceiling dome. The hemisphere, stretching well over a hundred yards in diameter, was the source of the pale blue emanation, and provided the first real measure of the chamber. The illumination ended nearly fifty feet above the level of the terrace, but provided enough light to confirm her earlier speculation that the walkway did indeed form a circle. And now she could discern other details about the terrace.

A series of ornate columns, each crowned with an enormous winged figure, rose toward the dome. At first glance, the standards appeared to be eagles, but in the failing twilight Mira could make out human features as well. "Valkyries," she murmured, thinking aloud. "Norse mythology. Typical."

Her eyes continued to roam the dimly lit chamber, gradually acquiring details that never would have been revealed by the flare's light. Six descending staircases, arranged symmetrically like the rays of light from a star, led down into the amphitheater. As her vision improved, she could see still more. The lowest reaches of the auditorium became visible, though only through a veil of night. Below the last row of seats was a vast open area.

"That parade ground is big enough for a full military pageant," she said, pointing down into the darkness. "Or the Olympic games."

"Hitler liked to show off."

Mira nodded. "Impressing the rank and file with cheap theatrics was the very essence of his philosophy. And was no doubt to be the foundation for rebuilding his Third Reich again. . . ."

Her voice trailed off as her eyes were drawn to a shadow, moving up from the depths of the amphitheater. She squinted into the darkness, trying to discern more detail, but could tell only two things: the shape was large, and it was moving quickly. Out of the corner of her eye, she spied another silhouette, a slightly darker spot, bounding up a different flight of stairs, then another close behind the first.

"Company's coming," she observed, drawing her pistol and flicking off the safety. "Let's give them a proper reception."

Jorge Montero pressed his fists against either side of his head, trying to drown out the screams that drifted down from the opening in the rock face. And although the anguished cries had already fallen silent, mere seconds after the first tortured shriek was heard, the sound Montero could not quiet was merely a memory of that horrible instant, and the realization that he had sent his best friend to his death.

The heir to Odessa stood at the base of the cliff, accompanied by Delacortes, the cocaine baron, and a loose collection of their respective soldiers. Montero's men were dressed in black uniforms and sporting the finest in automatic weapons while the Bolivians working for Delacortes wore jeans, ragged slogan t-shirts and baseball caps, and carried a motley arsenal of cast-off army surplus and other assorted firearms with visibly questionable maintenance histories. In spite of the obvious disparity between the two, there was a uniting factor that, for the moment at least, leveled the playing field: a look of horror that was fixed on the countenance of each man.

Mira Raiden and her companion had left an easy trail for them. That path had led them directly to a sheer rock face, and Montero had easily deduced where the prey had gone. At his order, two of their number, Guillermo Petronilo and one of Delacortes' men, had scaled the rock face, setting belays for the rest of the group to follow. Then they had ventured inside the crevice, scouting ahead as the rest of the group prepared to follow. Less than half a minute later, the screams began, followed by an unexpected eruption of steam. The fate of the two men inside was beyond question.

Montero lowered his hands, still balled into tight fists, and gazed once more at the crack in the rock wall. He was no stranger to sending his soldiers on deadly missions. His recent struggles with Mira Raiden had already begun to harden him to such losses, but Petronilo? His closest friend? Not in his most pessimistic visions had he ever seen himself without Guillermo at his side. And if Petronilo could die, then was not he also vulnerable?

The steam vent continued to loom above them, a humorless grimace, leaking wispy trails of water vapor. Mira Raiden had evidently ventured into the fissure. Was she, too, dead somewhere in the unknown passages beyond their line of sight? Or had the ever-resourceful bitch eluded fate once more, slipping from his grasp to race ahead to the prize? Somehow, he knew the answer was not the former.

Mustering his courage, he turned to Delacortes, his lips already framing the orders that would send another pair of men into harm's way. The cocaine baron stared back at him, an expectant look of dread on his face. The rest of the Bolivian locals shared their employer's palpable apprehension. Worse, he saw the same fear in the eyes of his own men. Drawing back the words with an inhalation, he switched gears. "What do you know about this geyser?"

Delacortes' face went blank for a moment. "We do not come up here, señor. But there are many geysers such as this throughout the region. They are very unpredictable. . . . But señor, they are simply pits of steam and sulfur. They do not lead to anything."

"This one does. It leads to Mira Raiden." He swung his eyes back to the fissure. "And I am going to find her."

Mira sighted down the barrel of the pistol in her right hand, leading the nearest shadow by a few feet. When she was marginally sure of her shot, she squeezed the trigger. Before she could register whether or not her bullet had struck true however, her world vanished once more into darkness.

"Damn it!" Her curse was squelched by the retort of the gun blast, which echoed through the chamber like a crack of thunder.

"I can't see," shouted DiLorenzo, barely audible through the ringing sound in Mira's ears.

She muttered a curse again. Shooting in the dark had been a rookie mistake. She knew better. The muzzle flash of that single gunshot had erased her night-vision, constricting her pupils and leaving a bright spot of color burned into her retinas.

Holstering the pistol, she reached back into the side pouch of her backpack. Her fingers felt the smooth, cylindrical casings of the remaining flares, five in all. She grimaced into the darkness: another amateurish blunder. Poor planning on her part not to bring more, but there was no use worrying about it now. She slipped one of the flares free and struck it.

Illumination instantly filled the area around them, causing another moment of blindness. Before their eyes could readjust, the shadows attacked.

Mira threw her hands up reflexively, her left dropping the flare and in the same instant closing on something warm and rough. The sudden burst of light revealed only a slavering bestial head, with teeth bared in a feral snarl. As her fingers tightened, grasping the loose flesh around the animal's neck, it lunged for her throat. Its momentum knocked her backward, but even as she fell, she twisted, redirecting the fury of the attack away from her face. As Mira and the assaulting beast hit the stone surface of the terrace, she hammered the butt of her pistol against the side of its head, but this only further enraged the creature.

A step behind her, DiLorenzo was clenching his small revolver, waving it around in search of a target. With each indecisive second, more of the attacking animals drew closer, unafraid of the intruders in their realm.

Wild dogs, thought Mira, hammering again with the solid metal of the gun. The weapon broke through the tough flesh protecting the beast's skull, but it continued to twist in her grip, teeth snapping at her exposed jugular. She could taste its hot, carious breath blasting against her face, and knew that the crazed animal would eventually overpower her. Abandoning the brute force defense, she chose a simpler method. A single shot from the pistol, its muzzle pressed under the dog's thrashing jaws, blasted away a large chunk of the animal's skull.

Even as she thrust the carcass away, Mira rolled into motion, staying low to avoid DiLorenzo's field of fire, and searched for another target. Two from the pack were close enough to pose an immediate threat—close enough that one of them would certainly get through their defenses. She sighted on the closest and opened fire, squeezing and holding the trigger, tracking the animal's approach with a volley of lead. The hollow-point rounds exploded against the stone of the terrace, blasting chips of rock and dust that tore into the dog's toughened hide, but none of the bullets found their mark. As the dog bounded across the remaining distance, her gun went empty. The beast launched into air, its teeth bared and seeking her throat.

Mira countered the imminent threat almost without thinking. She leapt into the air, her feet rising three feet off the ground, twisted and whipped her right foot around. The toe of her boot connected solidly with the dog's head, snapping it to the side even as it deflected the momentum, sending it hurtling past like a misguided missile. But in the instant her feet returned to the stone terrace, the tide of the battle turned.

She did not immediately feel the teeth ripping through the cloth of her combat trousers or tearing into the flesh of her left calf muscle. The force of the surprise attack, from a third dog approaching unseen from behind, sent her stumbling headlong.

She recovered quickly, turning her fall into a controlled shoulder roll, and came back to her feet in a low crouch. The back of her leg was starting to throb, but she easily dissociated herself from the pain. There would be plenty of time to worry about that later if they survived. As she completed the somersault, she slammed a fresh magazine into her pistol and fired blindly at the place where she expected the dog to be. Even as the first round exploded from barrel of her pistol, Mira knew she was exposing her back to yet another of the wild pack.

DiLorenzo shook off his hesitation, but his shooting accuracy proved no more effective than Mira's. He emptied the .38 at the dog approaching from Mira's exposed flank, but the rounds zinged harmlessly into the dark shrouded walls of the cavern.

Mira's pistol clanked empty again a moment later, their foes no closer to being vanquished than when the cacophony of gunfire had begun. Four dogs now circled them, chastened perhaps by the noise and fury, but in no way daunted. They had the scent of blood now and nothing would dampen their lust for flesh. The momentary ebb of the battle tide allowed Mira her first good look at the pack.

It was difficult to judge the breed of the dogs. They were large, possibly Alsatians, but the rigors of living in the hostile micro-environment had left them disfigured almost beyond recognition. Their pelts were virtually non-existent, replaced by a network of scars and open wounds from a combination of in-fighting and parasitic infestations. What little mangy fur remained was stretched over lean, almost emaciated frames, and this, combined with the fact that their ears had long ago been torn from their skulls, gave them the appearance of reanimated canine corpses.

Mira felt the slow burn of her wound, pulsing in time with her heartbeat, and growing in intensity with each passing minute. *God only knows what I've been infected with*, she thought, holstering her empty gun without reloading. *No time to worry about that now.*

With a smooth, almost practiced motion, she reached around and grabbed hold of the MP-5K, slung from a web strap underneath her pack. The dogs, unaware of the firepower in her hands, continued to circle closer. Cradling the weapon in both arms, she braced the stock against her right shoulder, and feathered the trigger.

The automatic weapon spewed a burst of rounds in the general direction of the closest dog. Two of the rounds found their mark, blasting the animal sideways. Its squeals of agony continued long after the fight was over.

DiLorenzo took his cue from Mira and abandoned the useless revolver, turning the full fury of his own machine pistol against the pack. The ensuing melee was mercifully short. The cavern came alive with flashes of light and thunder, peppered with the noise of bullets impacting and ricocheting on the carved stone surfaces. The feral dogs continued braying and snarling, but the show of deadly force had thrown them into confusion. Mira and DiLorenzo walked their fire into the scattering beasts, cutting them down before they could think to flee or press their attack. Unfamiliarity with automatic weapons caused DiLorenzo to run empty first, a scattering of spent brass cartridges at his feet, but what he lacked in accuracy he made up for with volume. Two of the pack had fallen to rounds from his weapon. Mira chose her targets with more care, dropping three and wounding two more as they retreated into the impenetrable darkness of the cavern. Almost as quickly as it had begun, the attack ended.

"Are you all right?" shouted Mira, barely able to hear herself over the ringing echoes of gunfire in her ears. DiLorenzo nodded, fumbling with the weapon in order to eject the spent magazine. She tossed him a spare, adding an admonition. "Be careful with it. There's no telling how many more surprises we'll run into, and we don't have much ammo left."

She retrieved the flare from the floor and held it up as a torch to light their way. The battle had curtailed her efforts to grasp the scope of the amphitheater above the parade grounds, but she had no difficulty recognizing the significance of its scale. In designing such a vast auditorium, Mann had revealed the enormity of the Nazi Party's grandiose vision. From the fastness of their mountain crèche, the reborn Reich would have wielded two pieces of the Trinity, more than enough to realize the dream of world domination, which had eluded their *Fuehrer*. Had Mann's U-Boat completed its journey sixty years earlier, the world would have become a very different place.

They turned into one of the stairway alcoves, following the tunnel underneath the uppermost ring and down into the gallery below. The carved stone tiers appeared to offer little in the way of creature comfort. Doubtless, the gathered masses would be too busy chanting with arms raised in salutes to notice that there was nowhere to sit. Mira reckoned that the auditorium could probably hold a standing crowd of nearly twenty thousand persons. She wrinkled her nose, unconsciously imagining the closed environment of the cavern filled with passionate, sweaty, chanting hordes of Nazis gulping down the last gasps of fresh air.

"It doesn't look like this leads anywhere," observed DiLorenzo. Indeed, the final tier of the amphitheater, ringed by a waist-high parapet, looked down on the black cinder floor of the parade grounds two stories below. If there was a way down to the floor, it was hidden in the shadows beyond the reach of the flare's illumination.

"We'll find what we're looking for on that dais," she replied, gesturing toward one end of the parade ground where an ornate stage had been carved. "I'm betting that the leaders of this outfit had their own private entrance in order to avoid mixing with the rabble."

DiLorenzo grunted an ambiguous reply. Mira did not add that she felt an intuitive desire to proceed in the direction she had indicated. The Trinity relics were drawing each other together like a pair of oppositely charged magnets.

Montero gazed down at the small army of men, wondering if any would follow in his footstep, should the worst come to pass. His own men, the loyal soldiers of Odessa, would follow him into hell if he gave the order, but the Bolivian locals were another story. They obeyed him now out of fear and the promise of a reward. Still, the hidden caverns beneath the mountain probably concealed a horde of wealth beyond the wildest dreams of the motley collection of bandits and drug runners. He shuddered to think about the prize treasures of his forefathers in the hands of such uncultured individuals.

He had watched the geyser through three more cycles, establishing the certainty of its pattern, and calculating exactly how long he would have to find a place of safety, provided such a refuge existed. There was every possibility that the tunnel beyond the fissure led to nothing more than a bubbling pit of mud, too far inside the mountain for him to turn back in time. That was the chance he was going to have to take in order to cement the loyalty of his men.

As soon as the next eruption relented, Montero hauled himself up onto the horizontal surface of the fissure. He hastily unclipped his climbing harness from the fixed rope his doomed lieutenant had set, and snatched a large flashlight from a belt holster, stabbing the beam into the sloping darkness. Grimacing in fear, he plunged into the tunnel and followed the bright spot of illumination.

He moved as fast as the slope would allow, shuffling along at a jogging pace, and checked his watch repeatedly. Soon, the light from the fissure opening was swallowed up, leaving him cloaked in night, with only the beam from the flashlight for assurance that he had not unknowingly been struck blind. Four minutes into his descent, he found the bodies of the fallen advance group.

When he first noticed the shapes, he dared to hope that the bodies would belong to Raiden and her companion, but there was no mistaking the dark fatigues his friend had worn. As he drew closer, he realized that the garments would prove to be the only means of identifying the corpse; the flesh had been boiled until it virtually fell off their bones, revealing gleaming white skulls. Montero did not linger with the fallen men lest he share their fate.

His pace quickened as the minutes ticked away. He could not control the panic rising in his chest, nor stem the murmurs of profanity that trickled from his lips. The deeper he went, the more certain he became that he would not survive to see daylight again. Twice, he almost turned back, but it was already too late for that. Then, when there seemed no alternative but to give in to his growing despair, he reached the end of the tunnel.

The platform was exactly as Mira had left it. The grating was pulled back, revealing the sodden length of rope that afforded passage to the catwalk below. Montero stared dumbly at the rope, wondering if he dared to proceed. Completely alone, without any way to communicate this discovery to the rest of his group, or to request back-up, he would be easy prey for Mira Raiden. Shoving aside his hesitancy, he reached into his pack and fumbled for a rudimentary figure-8 rappelling device, which he threaded onto the fixed rope. Hooking the device to his climbing harness, he lowered himself through the hole and descended like a spider on a strand of silk.

As his feet touched upon the lower section of metal grating, it occurred to Montero for the first time since commencing his journey into the mouth of hell that he was standing on the threshold of something Odessa had desired for nearly sixty years. More than once, he had publicly questioned whether the so-called "Last Redoubt" even existed. Now, however, he could not help but be awed by the grandeur of his predecessor's accomplishment.

He correctly recognized the apparatus before him as part of a geothermal generator. He had seen plans for similar devices and knew that they were utilized extensively in Iceland, the most geologically active place on the planet. Yet here before him was a steam turbine built decades before his own birth, operating flawlessly despite the fact that it had been untouched by human hands for all that time. Montero momentarily forgot the urgency of his situation, lingering instead with his appreciation of the technological feat. He knew that most of the device must lay hidden in the depths of the mountain. Only the uppermost workings, the actual generating device, was exposed here at the top. Subterranean caverns formed a natural holding tank, he surmised, building up the steam pressure necessary to turn the turbine fans.

In a rush of understanding, it occurred to Montero that there must be some way to disable the turbine temporarily, in order to prevent the release of steam from the generator, clearing the way for his soldiers to descend. He crossed the catwalk toward the cylindrical turbine housing, scanning the exterior for any kind of control apparatus. He found what he was looking for almost immediately. Stenciled letters, indicating in the German language the need for due caution, marked a hinged cowling on the uppermost surface of the generator. Montero pulled it back, revealing a simple flywheel valve control underneath.

He checked his watch; only a few minutes until the next eruption commenced. If he failed to stop the steam from venting into the tunnel, there would be no escape. Strangely, he no longer felt any fear. Though the flywheel was stiff with age and the beginnings of corrosion, it yielded to his strength. He screwed it in a clockwise direction, noting that each twist seemed to shorten the valve stem, until it would turn no more, then sat back to wait.

Nothing happened.

Almost giddy with relief and the thrill of a minor success, Montero ascended the rope, eager to gather his troops and take possession of that which he had sought for so many years.

ELEVEN

DiLorenzo gazed dubiously over the parapet at the parade grounds below. It looked to be about a twenty-foot drop, roughly the equivalent of jumping off the roof of a two-story house. From somewhere in the darkness above, he heard the low growl of the wild dogs, perhaps gathering their courage for another assault. "A rock and a hard place," he murmured.

Mira flashed a daring smile, handing him the flare, then spritely hopped onto the narrow wall, planting her left hand and dropping over in a smooth, almost practiced motion. Her right hand flashed up, catching the wall to arrest her fall. She lowered herself until her arms were fully extended, then let go, dropping the remaining twelve or so feet—more than twice her own height—to the ground below. The shadows of the parade ground seemed to swallow her whole.

"Huh," observed the detective, with characteristic eloquence, dropping the flare over the side. "Well, it won't be the craziest thing I'll do today."

With considerably less grace and confidence, DiLorenzo heaved himself onto the half-wall and, after a great deal of tentative positioning, lowered himself until he was hanging by his fingertips. The added length of his reach and his height reduced the distance he would have to fall by a bit, but his additional weight and lack of experience more than cancelled out this small advantage. Screwing up his courage, he surrendered to gravity. The cinders that had been scattered on the floor of the stadium absorbed most of the energy of his landing, but he nevertheless hit with a bone-jarring impact that sent him sprawling and reawakened the throb in his skull with a vengeance.

"We'll need to work on your technique," Mira observed dryly as she aided him to his feet.

"A little sympathy would be nice." DiLorenzo feigned umbrage. "I do have a concussion after all."

She ceded the point with a sideways tilt of her head and

then scooped up the flare. In the relatively small sphere of illumination, it was impossible to see their goal or much else. The parapet ringing the stands was now a featureless high wall trapping them in the arena. Mira handed the detective her flare and reloaded her Beretta.

"Expecting more trouble?" he inquired.

"Always."

Trouble, however, did not rear its head as they crossed the floor toward their unseen destination. They reached the carved stone platform in less than five minutes, scrambling up the carved relief figures from Norse mythology in the last flickers of flame from the nearly spent flare. As soon as they were solidly on the enormous podium, Mira pitched the flare out into the darkness. It landed in the cinders at the foot of the dais, quickly guttering and enveloping them once more in darkness.

"Try to let your eyes grow accustomed to the darkness," she advised. "Down here, relying on artificial light could prove fatal."

DiLorenzo squinted into the black. "You know, I think I can see."

"It's the luminescence. Mann must have found a way to stimulate it artificially, perhaps with a low-level electrical current."

"But still working after sixty-some years?" DiLorenzo made no effort to hide his incredulity.

"The steam generator is still working. And you can see with your own eyes the evidence. The light was probably much brighter fifty years ago." Mira's fingers explored the back wall of the dais. At first glance, it had appeared to be nothing more than blank rock, but the darkness revealed what the flare's light could not. A thin blue tracery outlined a minute gap between the stone blocks; the wall was not a single solid piece. After a few minutes of study, she was able to confirm that the center block, roughly three feet wide and twice as high, was not cemented in place with mortar like the other blocks.

"Well?" inquired DiLorenzo, able to distinguish her examination of the wall in the pale periwinkle night, but clueless as to its significance.

"Open sesame." She placed her hands flat against the center block, extending her right leg back, and threw her weight forward. A grunt escaped her lips as she reached into her deepest reserves of strength, then a different noise filled the air.

Grudgingly at first, but then with decreasing resistance, the block slid backward on the stone floor. DiLorenzo stood gaping, not even thinking to add his power to the effort. Mira continued shifting forward, planting her boot soles in short increments in order to gain maximum leverage. The block slid a full meter back before she paused for a moment to catch her breath. It was not enough to afford access to whatever lay beyond—the surrounding wall was almost that thick—but the intensity of the illumination spilling through the crack grew tenfold. The substance or mechanism that caused the dome overhead to glow was considerably more powerful in the passageway beyond the sliding section.

Mira threw herself once more at the block, forcing it completely out of its niche and into a recess in the corridor beyond. Azure brilliance filled the tunnel, spilling from every surface—walls, ceiling and even the floor.

DiLorenzo let out a low whistle. "Do you see stuff like this a lot?"

"Not like this."

The tunnel ran perpendicular to the opening for about fifty feet in either direction, ending at the top of paired descending stairs. Mira felt no urge toward one descent over another, but sensed that the rest of the Trinity did indeed wait somewhere below. Favoring an old superstition, she chose the left-hand stairwell.

The luminescence remained constant as they worked down the long, spiraling steps, sublimating the most instinctive of human terrors—fear of the dark—but did little to assuage the second—claustrophobia. The passages remained cramped, the air stale and hot. The stairs opened onto a landing, from which sprouted another long, constricting tunnel, but also continued descending. The corridor was lined with wooden doors and lintels. Curious, Mira opened the nearest.

The room beyond had at one time served as a luxury

apartment. Time, however, had ravaged the furnishings, leaving only a scattering of debris. A closer inspection revealed the presence of two mummified corpses amid the ruin, withered, leathery limbs still filling out the uniforms of German *Wehrmacht* soldiers.

"Nobody's home," she muttered, backing out of the suite. They returned to the stairwell and continued descending.

There were four more levels devoted entirely to apartments. On the second of these, they began to see bodies strewn about the tunnel. Some wore German army fatigues, while others wore simple pajama-style garments. But whereas the remains in the apartments had been more or less preserved from decay, these corpses were only skeletons, picked clean of flesh. "I'd say we've found the food source for the dogs," ventured Mira.

"That's crazy. Even if they did eat carrion, they would have run out after a few years."

"True. After that, they probably survived on whatever vermin made it down here, or simply ate each other. A closed environment." Gazing at the skeletons, victims of a similarly savage action, but one perpetuated by a human beast, Mira regretted having voiced the observation. "Let's keep moving. What we want will be farther down."

Beyond the residence levels, there were two larger caverns with endless rows of freestanding structures that looked almost like tents. Mira realized that the suites had been designed for officers and high-ranking Nazi Party members, while the foot soldiers for the reborn Reich would bivouac here. These levels had housed the thousands of slaves secretly brought over from the death camps up until the time Mann, like an Egyptian Pharaoh, determined to kill everyone who had labored to hew the stronghold out of the mountain. She didn't want to think about what horrors they might find in those vast chambers.

As they reentered the stairwell, eager to see something other than the lingering evidence of the last great Nazi atrocity, a strange noise echoed down through the depths.

"That's gunfire," breathed Mira. "We're not alone."

"Someone is still alive down here?" DiLorenzo sounded almost ready to believe anything.

"No. We were followed. I didn't think they'd catch up to us so quickly though."

"So what do we do? We're going to be outnumbered."

"We get what we came for and worry about the rest later." She managed a confident smile. "Don't worry. I know what I'm doing."

Montero gazed at the bullet-riddled corpses of the last remaining members of the feral dog pack. The automatic weapons carried by his soldiers had swiftly converted the crazed canines into hamburger. But there were other carcasses nearby that had nothing to do with their brief battle. Mira Raiden had fought the same pack not long before.

He surveyed the carnage with his flashlight, half hoping to find her mangled corpse among the dead. Still, he was not entirely disappointed to discover that she had survived her encounter with the dogs. For the first time, it occurred to him that Mira was an attractive woman. Though Rachel Aimes had been capable in bed, there was nothing quite as exhilarating as taking an unwilling lover by force. Montero now found himself excited by the idea of capturing Mira alive.

He divided his forces into three groups of eight, assigning his own men as leaders over larger forces of Bolivians. "We may not be able to use our radios down here," he concluded, after giving each group an assignment, "so pay attention to where you are and how you got there. Meet back here in half an hour. Don't try too hard to take the Raiden woman alive, but if you do . . . nobody touches her until I'm finished with her." His lascivious grin earned an eager chuckle from the men, who evidently had entertained a similar fantasy.

Montero led his group clockwise around the landing above the parade grounds. A second force went the other direction while Delacortes was part of the third division, tasked with exploring the depths of the stadium. Montero watched as the men moved out, soon becoming nothing more than flickering ghosts of light in the vast darkness of the cavern.

Five hundred yards from the point of entry, Montero found a recess in the outer wall, all but hidden from view. A closer inspection showed a steel accordion gate, blocking access to a vertical shaft. An old-fashioned electrical switch was mounted to a gatepost. Curious, Montero threw the lever. There was a burst of blue sparks as the current flashed through the connection, followed by a whine of resistance and a growing smell of ozone, but nothing helpful occurred. Montero quickly broke the circuit.

"Let's get this open. We'll rappel down."

On the far side of the parade grounds, three of Montero's Odessa soldiers and five local ruffians from Ouros had made a similar discovery. Unaware of their superior's failure, the man in charge of the group threw the switch. This time, the circuit closed cleanly, and the antique system of pulleys, cables and counter-weights was activated. To the amazement of the onlookers, a large elevator car rose slowly from the depths of the shaft.

As the car drew level with the platform on which they stood, the leader reversed the switch to stop the elevator. He then drew back the gate and opened the hinged door to the car. There was room inside for six. After directing two of the Bolivians to stand guard at the entrance to the shaft, he led the rest of the group into the car and closed the door.

Unlike a modern elevator with an automatic system of sensors controlled by push buttons, the old lift car featured a handle similar to the engine controls on a ship. The lever controlled the speed and vertical destination, requiring the operator to be attentive in order to stop the car level with the desired floor. Situated alongside the lever was an unusual numeric keypad—zero through nine—that seemed unrelated to the operation of the elevator. The leader pushed the number "2" experimentally, but nothing happened. Shrugging, he moved the control lever to the right. The lift car shuddered under the load, then began settling downward.

Through a glass porthole in the heavy metal door, they could see only the bare rock of the vertical shaft. As the car descended, they spied markings on the rock face, indicating that something was about to happen. The lead soldier eased back on the lever handle, slowing the already plodding descent as the gated opening came into view. It settled a few centimeters after he released the controls completely, but was nevertheless almost perfectly level with the passage beyond. Smiling, he reached for the door handle.

The inside door was locked. He wiggled the handle in frustration, but the mechanism would not yield.

Someone behind him coughed nervously, suddenly making them all very much aware of where they were: trapped in a closet sized room, with limited air, in a cavern hundreds of feet beneath a mountain.

In a rush of understanding, he divined the importance of the keypad. It was a numerical lock. In order to open the door, he would have to enter the correct sequence of digits to release the pins that held the latch closed. The possible combinations numbered in the millions, perhaps more as he had no idea how many numerals were in the sequence. The idea of being held hostage by such a simple security measure was especially frustrating.

"Forget it," suggested his friend, likewise one of the Odessa troopers from Argentina. "You could spend the rest of your life trying out combinations. Just force the latch."

The leader nodded, drawing a large commando-style knife from a sheath on his combat harness. He inserted the blade into the narrow gap between the door and the lintel, probing for the latch bolt. The tip came to rest against an unyielding bar, at which point he began wiggling the knife, slowly moving the bolt back into the door.

"Got it," he declared triumphantly as the bolt cleared the doorjamb.

All of a sudden, several more bolts sprung out from the doorframe, permanently securing the door in place. Before any man could so much as utter an expletive, an unseen compartment opened beneath the car, exposing pellets of Zyklon B, which immediately reacted with the oxygen in the air to release fumes of hydrogen cyanide gas. The chemical agent swiftly silenced their screams, leaving only bloody claw marks as testimony to the terror of their passing. Though dead for more sixty years in his watery grave, Mann had committed yet another unspeakable act of violence, unknowingly striking down the heirs to his evil ideology.

As Mira and DiLorenzo neared the next level of the fortress, the sound of rushing water grew loud in their ears. The stairs were now littered with both human remains and animal spoor, showing evidence of rodent infestation but not the presence of the dog packs. Evidently, the dogs had been trapped in the upper levels of the redoubt, sustaining themselves on the smaller vermin that found their way up through cracks too small to permit a larger mammal to pass. The placement of the bodies seemed to indicate that they had been dumped by those who survived them.

Mira vaguely wondered what means of execution Mann had employed against the laborers that had allowed some to live long enough to dispose of the rest. Probably poison in the food. The soldiers would have willingly carried out the extermination of the slaves, little realizing that their next meal would also be their last.

The next landing marked the end of the stairwell. The chamber beyond thundered with the echoes of a subterranean waterfall and the air was humid, heavy with warm mist, as Mira and DiLorenzo entered.

The area beyond the final landing was a vast open cavern cut through the heart of the mountain by the force of endless underground floodwaters. It did not appear that Mann had spent much effort finishing the cavern; nature had done the job well enough for his purposes. The gently sloping curve of the floor, scoured clean of stalagmites and other protrusions, ended abruptly midway across the chamber where it dropped off into nothingness. The plumes of spray rising from beyond that brink revealed the presence of a turbulent underground river.

"Hot in here," remarked DiLorenzo.

"This river is probably part of the same geothermal system as the geyser. Some of it is probably effluent from the steam generator."

There was one other feature of the cavern that had initially escaped their notice, one that was unmistakably a construct of the human denizens of the underground fortress. It looked like a city bus, floating above the surging waters of the river. As they drew closer, they saw the cables and pulleys that suspended the trolley car above the water. A wooden staircase rose up to the closed door of the vehicle.

"A tram car," said the detective. "Like the one to Roosevelt Island. But going where?"

Mira's eyes followed the guide cables. At one end of the cavern, they wrapped around an enormous metal wheel, part of the motivating system for moving the tram from one terminus to the other. The cables ran above the river's surface, following the tunnel that continued into the darkness beyond the point where the large chamber closed in. There was likely a second, matching car at the opposite end of the line, along with the primary machinery for operation. It was anyone's guess as to whether it still worked after so many years.

"I'd guess this leads to the U-boat dock," she ventured. "The river probably becomes more navigable further on."

"So this was to have been the main entrance?"

She nodded. "Let's hope there's another. I'm in no mood for a long swim."

Aside from the landing and the river course, there was another tunnel leading away from the chamber, partly concealed behind stacks of wooden shipping crates. A cursory glance showed the cargo containers to be empty, long ago pillaged by human and vermin, and slowly rotting away. The tunnel, however, was pristine, a stainless steel corridor roughly six feet square, leading into the raw stone. There was no gate or door securing the passage, only an incongruous numeric keypad mounted to the metal lintel on the right-hand side. Mira studied this last item carefully, while DiLorenzo peered down the long corridor. The far end was a nondescript square of pale blue illumination. He took a step forward.

Before his foot could settle on the stainless steel floor, Mira's hand flashed out, catching him none too gently across the chest. The blow cancelled whatever momentum he had, throwing him off balance with arms flailing. Her hand clamped around his biceps, steadying him, but she did not allow him to advance.

"Not yet," was all she said. Chastened, he stood aside, leaning against the smooth stone of the cavern wall, waiting as she continued her assessment of the keypad. Because he was facing outward, he saw the men enter from the landing a moment before they saw him.

"Company's coming." His words were louder than he'd intended, spoken from a burst of sudden panic and adrenaline. He hauled up his gun and ducked behind one of the sodden crates. Mira dropped quietly beside him, her pistol likewise drawn.

"They caught up to us a lot faster than I expected," she murmured as six figures spilled from the landing, crouching defensively with weapons at the ready. A moment later, their guns thundered.

One of the men, wearing a black combat uniform, spun in mid-step as a 9mm round caught his upper torso. He staggered into one of his comrades, momentarily taking both of them out of the fight, but the rest of the troop began a murderous return volley.

The crates afforded little protection. The concentrated fire from several semi-automatic weapons, along with shotguns and revolvers, blew gaping holes in the moldy wood, alternately bursting through more solid pieces in a shower of splinters. Mira scored a second hit, dropping one of the Bolivian men with a headshot, before return fire drove her flat against the floor of the cave.

"We've got to fall back," shouted DiLorenzo. "That tunnel is the only way out."

"The devil or the deep blue sea?" She rolled toward the metal corridor, rising into a crouch that left her partially exposed. "Go!"

As DiLorenzo took his first step toward the tunnel, Mira raised her Beretta and took aim at the shiny floor. The pistol thundered in the tight confines, and there was a spark as the hollow-point round ricocheted from the metal surface. What happened next occurred too fast for either one of them to see.

All down the length of the tunnel, at twenty-foot intervals, solid lines of darkness had appeared to block the way. DiLorenzo stopped just short of the first set of what he now saw were steel blades, one about the height of his knee, another just below the level of his throat. A moment later, the blades began swinging away, receding slowly into the almost invisible slots in the wall where they had been concealed.

"Go," repeated Mira, dashing ahead of him. She dived between the first set of knives, though they were nearly out of the way. "Run!"

DiLorenzo felt a momentary panic, realizing how closely he had come to being decapitated by the antique Nazi booby trap. He had no clue as to how Mira had spotted the device, much less known how to trigger it, nor was he convinced that it would not spring again while they were in the tunnel. But to hesitate was to ensure failure and death, either at the hands of the pursuing force or in the bladed trap. Forcing down his fear, he sprinted into the metal corridor.

The gunfire behind them ceased almost immediately. Their foes had surely grasped how the pair had eluded them and were almost certainly advancing. The hallway, nearly forty meters long, would give the fleeing couple no room to dodge the storm of bullets that would surely follow. To make matters worse, the spring-loaded knives had nearly completed their retraction cycle. DiLorenzo put his head down and poured on the speed until he was almost stepping on Mira's heels. When he looked up again, the end of the corridor was in sight.

"Dive for it," shouted Mira, taking her own advice. She hurled herself forward, somehow flattening out in mid-air like a swooping falcon, then curled her body into a protective ball in the instant before hitting the ground. DiLorenzo simply made his best attempt at a slide into home base. Even as his built-up momentum dragged him the last two meters, he heard the click of the trap resetting, followed by the whoosh of the blades slicing through the air once more. He was conspicuously aware of movement scant inches above his head.

As he came to rest, his left foot still touching the metal surface of the tunnel, he became aware of Mira kneeling in front of him and facing down the length of the corridor with both arms extended, pistol at the ready. She did not fire however.

A long silent moment passed before DiLorenzo dared to lift his head and look behind. He saw the blades once more returning to their place of concealment, awaiting the next footfalls that would trigger another deadly, snake-like strike. Then he saw the bodies.

It was difficult to tell from where he and Mira now were, how many of the pursuers had been caught in the second release of the trap. The far end of the corridor looked like a charnel house; the stainless steel walls dripped with dark splatters of blood and there was a jumble of disconnected body parts blocking the far end. If there were any survivors— stragglers bringing up the rear who had not yet entered the kill zone when the first footsteps of their companions activated the pressure-sensitive trigger mechanism—they had retreated from view.

DiLorenzo looked away from the gory scene, sickeningly aware of how close he had come to sharing the same fate. He knew that Mira's instincts alone had saved him from certain death. If he was going to survive to see the end of this nightmare, it would only be through putting aside his macho prejudices and trusting her to get them both out alive.

The chamber in which they now found themselves was once more a joint production of Mother Nature and human hands. The irregular floor had been covered over with diamond-patterned steel decking, as might adorn the walkways of a battleship. The walls were smooth, carved over the course of centuries by the flow of an underground river, but several new alcoves and tunnels had been hewn into the solid rock of the mountain. Some of these were secured with heavy doors, while others stood open but empty beyond. Several large shop tables were arranged in the center of the chamber, but only a thin layer of dust dulled their surfaces. The cavern appeared to be some kind of laboratory, with the side chambers perhaps containing equipment and raw materials. Directly opposite the corridor through which they had entered was another metal passageway, similarly guarded by a numeric keypad.

Mira strode to the edge of the second corridor, but again made no move to enter. "It's down there."

"Another trap?"

"Yes, but I'm betting this one won't be so easy to fool." She studied the keypad diligently. "This is some kind of mechanical combination lock."

"Might as well not even try, then. The number of possible combinations must be astronomical."

She nodded thoughtfully. "Mann designed this in the 1940's. It must have been revolutionary for its time, but why go to the trouble when a key would have worked just as well?"

"That's easy. Keys can be lost or stolen. With a combination lock, you carry the key in your head. And you can give it to other people."

"Exactly. But you need to make the combination something that's easy to remember."

"Just like using your birthday as your PIN number."

A whining noise abruptly cut him off, the unmistakable sound of a bullet piercing the air nearby, followed almost simultaneously by the crack of the gunpowder charge that had propelled it. Mira and DiLorenzo each dived for cover, but the bullet had already carved a chip of stone off the wall and rebounded along an unknown vector. There was no sign of the shooter, but it seemed logical to conclude that there were at least some of that original group of foes who had escaped death in the tunnel trap. Evidently, they were hanging back, shooting blindly through the tunnel and hoping to get lucky. Because the second passage was almost perfectly aligned with the first, they would be fish in a barrel for the length of time it would take to traverse that distance. Providing, of course, that Mira could somehow work out the numeric lock, or failing that, outwit the trap mechanism as she had the first time.

Mira rose up from her hiding place and snapped off several shots down the distant tunnel. Their pursuers must have realized that they too were exposed in the arrangement, and retreated from the opening. Satisfied with the moment it bought her, she returned her attention to the keypad and quickly tapped in eight digits.

There was no visible change, no electronic tones or signal lights to indicate that she had been successful. She threw a glance at DiLorenzo, then drew in a sharp breath. The New York detective realized at that moment that Mira had no idea whether the sequence she had entered was correct.

She paused abruptly, as if spooked at the last instant, and whirled again to face the keypad. More confidently than the first time, she tapped out eight more digits—it was impossible for DiLorenzo to tell how this attempt differed from the initial entry—after which there was a faint, but distinctive click of an unseen device deep in the tunnel wall falling into place.

"That's it." She sagged in relief for a moment and then sprinted unhesitatingly into the tunnel. Nothing at all happened as she ran.

DiLorenzo realized that he had been holding his breath, and let it out in a whooshing exhale. "What was it?"

"Hitler's birthday," she shouted, without looking back.

"Jesus, what did you try the first time?"

If she heard, she did not answer.

The second passage seemed as long as the first, the stainless steel walls dully reflecting light from the pale blue luminescent substance that ran like a paint stripe down the length of the ceiling. The chamber at its end, however, showed no such light source. Instead, only a dark nothingness awaited them, but Mira did not need to see their destination to know what lay beyond. The Trinity in her backpack was vibrating furiously in anticipation of being rejoined with one of its counterparts after so many millennia of separation.

The chamber that lay beyond the steel passage was of indeterminate dimensions, but the room seemed to radiate around a central hub, a stubby cairn of stones that could almost be taken for a ceremonial altar barely illuminated by ambient light spilling from the passage. Mira recognized it right away; it was a Trinity altar.

She struck a flare, and the pink-orange illumination was reflected by a circle of dull metal adorned with a single, six-sided crystal.

"I'll be damned," DiLorenzo whispered, gazing at the talisman, then laughed. "This is probably business as usual for you."

"It never gets to be old hat."

"May I?" DiLorenzo reached for the relic, hesitating to see what her response would be.

For the merest instant, she felt a twinge of panic. It had been in a place very much like this that she had lost Curtis . . . lost him to the very same power that now hovered at DiLorenzo's fingertips. In her mind's eye, she saw power lancing from the Trinity to incinerate the detective, just as it had Lancet. It was not a premonition, she knew, just an irrational fear. Pushing the grim memory away, she nodded.

DiLorenzo treated the artifact like a young man reaching for the chalice at his first communion, eager, but at the same time fearfully reverent. He let his fingers drift along the outer edge, brushing lightly the crystal, and then closed his grip. When he did, the hexagonal gem came alive, blazing with pure white intensity that overwhelmed the flickering illumination of the flare.

Mira cast the sputtering flame aside and took the matching Trinity from her pack. Its crystal was likewise burning with argent brilliance and the metal vibrated against her fingertips as if charged with an electric current.

She extended the relic toward DiLorenzo, nodding silently, confident that he would know what to do.

He returned the nod, his arm lifting almost without his volition, as the newfound Trinity reached out to its long lost complement. Like the opposing poles of a magnet, the pieces leaped into a shared embrace, joining together with crystals diametrically opposed, united again for the first time in over ten thousand years.

TWELVE

The time of the Ascendant Ones was at an end.

That was not their own name for their race; they had no need of names or even of words. It was the name given them by those who watched and jealously waited for an opportunity to usurp the position as foremost species on the planet. An appropriate name indeed, for they had risen as far above their primate origins as the stars were above the earth.

For uncounted millennia, they had roamed, living in herds and foraging for food. Evolution had appointed them well for survival; the development of their brains was rivaled only by the structure of their bodies. Instead of hooves or claws, they had long dexterous fingers, with opposable thumbs. They walked erect but could climb or crawl as necessity or decision dictated.

The herds were strong. The alpha male of each herd carried only the best survival traits in his genetic make-up, passing these on to the next generation. Few other males were permitted to procreate, and in some herds, when the alpha male was young and new to his dominant role, all male children might be put to death at birth or exiled forever to a solitary existence upon reaching puberty.

The Ascendant Ones did not fashion tools, erect buildings or use fire. They had no need of such trivialities. Centuries of natural selection had unlocked mental powers that would, in less primitive society to come, be counted as magic. Game beasts obeyed the command to lie down and bare their necks for slaughter.

The Ascendant Ones could heal infection and disease with a thought. They could even avert the power of the elements, raising heat from the stones on cold nights, or turning rain aside simply by willing it. Though their physical appearance was unremarkably hominid, they were the pinnacle of evolved intelligence.

Such ascendancy could only be maintained at a heavy price, however. In the same fashion that the alpha male in each herd cast out all potential rivals, so too did the herd fall upon or banish any weakling in their midst. Children born with physical or mental defects were quickly cast away and left for the scavenger beasts. Though their minds were tremendously powerful, freedom of thought was severely restricted. The imperatives of existence, though not dictated by instinct, per se, were nonetheless absolute: follow the alpha male wherever he leads and bear him many female children.

The failure of this magnificent species to evolve socially was its death warrant.

No other destiny could have awaited the Ascendant Ones. Though the herds might have continued to refine their mental and physical powers, it is doubtful that they would ever have conceived of aesthetic beauty. The laws of natural selection do not encourage a species to care for its sick and old, or to manufacture that which nature has not provided in order to subdue nature itself. Only less developed minds could value an idea or a thing more than the betterment of the species. Only the underdeveloped psyche of a creature without inherent god-like powers would imagine the existence of a god and build fantastic temples and cathedrals, write transcendent works of doctrine, poetry and prose, or develop the concepts of love, morality or conscience in their behalf.

The Ascendant Ones made one other fatal error in their intrinsic belief in the power of natural selection. They imagined that the exiled ones would fail to thrive. And although most of them did indeed perish, unable to stay the jaws of predators or turn the fury of storms, a few—the fittest of the rejected—survived and prospered. Lacking the mental puissance of the herds, they were compelled to find or fashion the means to defend their existence.

These tool- and fire-users prospered in their enclaves, but never dared to challenge the Ascendant Ones' supremacy. But then, when seven generations had passed, the Wise Father appeared and everything changed.

The exiles did not revere the aged as they later would. Few enough lived even to maturity in their harsh world, and those who did survive to see their hair turn gray were often viewed as a burden to the rest. Although the men were stronger than the women and cherished for their hunting prowess, they could not work the magic of making children, and so the females, with their fertile wombs, were more highly esteemed—worshiped even. Then the coming of the Wise Father challenged the way the outcasts saw their world.

He roamed the earth, seeking out the camps of the exiles, speaking the tongues of these diverse groups as easily as if he had been born in their midst. He did not openly oppose the will of the Mothers, the fertile matriarchs of each clan, but so valuable were the new skills he imparted to *their communities—the understanding of seasons and rudimentary agriculture—that he was soon elevated to a greater stature than the Mothers. Long after his departure, the men scattering seed—whether on fertile ground or in fertile wombs—would make supplication to the Wise Father in order that the resulting harvest might be abundant.*

When he had gained their trust, when the cult of the Wise Father was universal in their scattered enclaves and his archetype imprinted in their collective memory, he returned. And this time with a new message.

The time of hiding is nearly at an end. This world belongs to you, my children, and soon you will take it back from those who spurned you.

He began drawing them from their caves and their crudely fashioned huts to a place of ancient power. It was said by some that the Wise Father was not born of woman, and while he gave no credit to any supernatural origin, their pilgrimage brought them one and all to the great mountain, named for the Earth's navel, the very place from which it was believed the Wise Father had come into existence.

Foreseeing that the Ascendant Ones would one day perceive the exiles as a threat to their hegemony, the Wise Father determined to act preemptively. Under his tutelage, the exiles fashioned weapons and built palisades of wood and stone. But his guidance did not end there. He taught them ways to hunt great beasts, so that their physical bodies became powerful where their minds were not. And even their primal mental energies were made sharper.

From their guttural language, a new form of communication developed, and soon thereafter, the means to record them in soft clay or with pigments upon scraped animal hides. The children learned games of skill that subtly taught them the concept of strategy. The strongest and smartest soon came to comprise a superior caste, honored above all their peers, and beholden only to the Wise Father.

As the power of the enclave that resided at the Earth's navel continued to grow, their benefactor took a bride—a girl child who had never known a man, but was herself descended from the fiercest war-leader and the most revered of the Mothers. In the fullness of time, she came to be with child, though many secretly believed that the seed in her belly had been planted through the Wise Father's magic, a rumor that seemed to be confirmed when the time of the harvest came, and it was revealed that not one but three sons had been conceived.

Three sons, the offspring of the Wise Father; men who were also gods.

Their names—Sham'b'Alla, Le'Mu, Atl'an—would be eternally imprinted onto the consciousness of the human species.

Though they were not alike in appearance or temperament, they were all worshipped alike, and when they reached adulthood, the Wise Father granted them their birthright.

Metalworking was unknown to them, and none could comprehend by what means the Wise Father had fashioned the crowns which he now bestowed upon his children.

The eyes of your enemy are ever on you, *the Wise Father told them.* With this, you will hide your strength as you grow in power and solidarity. *When the crowns sat upon their brows, their understanding of his high-sounding words and complicated gestures increased, as did their comprehension of the ideas he sought to convey.*

Each of you is guardian of a part of this great power, *he explained.* But together, you are greater than the sum of your parts. When this Trinity is joined together, what is the thing that you may conceive, yet not accomplish?

With that unanswered question, the Wise Father left the enclave of the exiles, never to be seen again. Yet his sons knew that when they had completed the Great Work, when the world was made ready, He would return.

For a generation, the three guardians continued to hide their people from the eyes of the Ascendant Ones, even as they explored the intelligence and might bequeathed to them by their magnificent benefactor. Their health and youth were extended indefinitely, granting them the time and vigor to conceive ideas previously undreamed and perform feats thought impossible. Then, when each was at the summit of his individual growth, the next phase of the Great Work began.

The Trinity crowns imparted to them a blueprint for a great city, built of living rock and hidden in a cavern beneath the Earth's navel. That holy mountain, in whose shadow they had dwelt for centuries, would become the foundation cornerstone of a city to rival any accomplishment of man into the distant future.

Using the power of the Trinity, they brought forth a swarm of beetles, as wide as the great river, who devoured stone the way the great mastodon herds devoured grass. In a mere score of years, the passages and galleries were hewn, honeycombing the massive mountain and descending deep into the earth.

Upon the exposed stone, they worked a different magic, and soon walls of crystal began to grow. Transformed molten rock, pulsating with a strange kind of life, grew as well, shaping into structures and passages according to the will of the Trinity, in much the same way that an embryo takes shape according to the master plan written in an individual's genetic code. In the greatest chambers, the roof glowed with light like the sun, and soon crops began to give their yield deep underground, feeding the exiles as they had never been fed on the surface.

Into this city—Agartha—the triumvirate led their exiles.

On the fertile plains of an untamed world, the Ascendant Ones continued as they had for centuries, maintaining a strong gene pool by casting out the weak and crippled. The alpha males of each herd had never imagined that those who had survived the initial days of their banishment would eventually find refuge in the marvelous hidden city. Even if they had cared enough to reach out with their minds, analyzing the potential threat to their status as the dominant intelligent species, the fact of the city's existence would have been blocked from their sight. The power of the Trinity effectively cloaked the cavern city in a haze of mental white noise.

And then the moment they had eagerly awaited came. The Wise Father appeared to the Trinity bearers in a vision, commanding them to enter the Shrine of the Trinity, located on the uppermost level of the great city, where they joined their crowns together upon the altar. Amplified by the unique properties of the Shrine, they expressed a single command in one unified voice.

All over the surface of the globe, the Ascendant Ones took notice. With the psychic equivalent of a lightning flash . . . a shrieking cacophony . . . their superior mental abilities were deadened.

In a collective state of shock, the herds fell apart. Young rivals overwhelmed their alpha males, ignoring the approaching threat of predatory beasts. Unable to collect food or shelter themselves from the elements, thousands died before a season had passed. A few smaller herds drew together out of the chaos, but it was now physical strength, rather than mental superiority, which determined who would lead.

Within three generations, the gene that had once granted this race of hominids virtual omnipotence over their planet had become recessive, occurring in less than one in a hundred births. Even when it did manifest, the blanket of silence cast by the Trinity remained, stifling the growth of the *pineal gland, the organ that produced the unique hormone that accelerated brain activity.*

The Trinity bearers looked out in triumph at their victory over the Ascendant Ones. Though they could not fathom why the Wise Father had given them the opportunity to avenge an aeon of perceived injustice, they were proud to have been the instrument of judgment. Those who lived beneath the sheltering rock prospered, wanting for nothing and rarely spared a thought for returning to the wild spaces where their ancestors had once roamed. Perhaps it was inevitable that a serpent would enter paradise and tempt Eve with forbidden fruit.

As the Great Work progressed, it became evident that the prosperity of the human race could not be contained in the caverns beneath the Earth's navel. Whether at the subtle insistence of the Trinity, or merely the voice of reason, the three brothers determined at long last to divide the Trinity again, and to go their separate ways. The brother whose name was Sham'b'Alla, ventured a short distance from the mountain to a concealed valley and established a city that bore his name. Le'Mu used his Trinity to found a city in a land across the ocean from whence the sun rose. The third brother, Atl'an, established a similar city on an island in the great ocean of the sun's setting. But events would soon transpire there that would alter the history of the world.

Hidden from the eyes of the great king, the high priest, a man named Atl'as hungered after the power of the Trinity. He set forth from the island under the guise of a pilgrim, visiting first the secret valley of Shambala. Using guile, he struck a cowardly blow from the embrace of a supplicant, killing Sham'b'Alla even as he wrestled the Trinity from the fallen king's brow. With his stolen power, he smote Le'Mu. Uniting two of the Trinity talismans, he set forth on a campaign to seize the third, but craven deception would avail him naught against the remaining brother.

In distant Atlantis, the king knew of his brothers' deaths and the betrayal by his own high priest, and readied himself for the siege to come.

The final struggle was a cataclysm so tremendous that it would be imprinted upon the consciousness of the species, both as a memory of an ancient tribulation and as a prophecy of the end of days.

The heavens wept, flooding all but the highest peaks. The Earth split apart, swallowing those that were not burned by the bleeding rivers of lava and fire. The island where Le'Mu had built his city was enveloped in a volcanic upheaval. The sun was darkened in the sky, freezing the floodwaters and ruining the vegetation. At the heart of the apocalypse, noble Atlantis vanished beneath the waves.

The loss of life was unparalleled. Not since the fall of the Ascendant Ones had so many people died in so short a time.

Yet, despite his mastery of two-thirds of the Trinity, Atl'as proved weaker than his noble foe, and in the end he was vanquished, sealed in an abyss beneath another mountain on the edge of a great desert. Uniting the Trinity once more, Atl'an alone struggled to save the last vestiges of life on the Earth. He returned to Agartha, a city unremembered by the survivors of the cataclysm, and entered the Shrine where he silently beseeched the Wise Father for guidance. His prayers were in vain. The burden of preserving the human species would be his alone.

There seemed but one course of action. The Trinity was a threat to the future safety of humanity. How long before the lure of such power, perhaps with noble intent, led to another uprising? How long before another Atl'as arose from the survivors of the cataclysm, and in attempting to wrest control of the Trinity, might utterly destroy the Earth? The Trinity of brothers had already failed; the Great Work would never be complete, but there would be a future for humanity.

As the scattered survivors went forth to every corner of the world, Atl'an sealed up forever the entrance to the mountain city and then led a small group of exiles from Atlantis on one final quest. The Trinity was divided once more and the three relics were hidden away in distant lands, as far from each other as night is from day. Only his own Trinity did Atl'an keep, more as a memento mori *than anything else, and despite the fact that the talisman had kept him vital for centuries, he soon began to grow old.*

As the centuries passed, the truth about the cataclysm and the great migration grew into the myths, legends and religions of the disparate cultures descended from the original trinity of cities. The names of the cities were not forgotten, and their rulers were remembered as gods. Even the Wise Father came to be deified by a people who scarcely knew he had ever existed.

The Trinity talisman passed entirely from the memory of mankind, but the purpose for which it had been forged by an intelligence not of this earth—a task the ancient triumvirate knew only as "the Great Work"— remained unfinished.

For long millennia, the three relics remained hidden in the places so remote that no human could be found to rouse them from slumber. And then, more than ten thousand years after the catastrophe, they were found, and the Trinity was about to be rejoined.

As the three pieces came into close proximity again, thousands of years after the time when the Great Work ought to have been completed, a message was sent. A beacon shining across time and space, into dimensions of existence unimagined by men, warned a slumbering intelligence that its scheme for earth had gone awry.

And the Great Father began to stir.

Mira's eyes flashed open. Still gripping the two joined pieces of the Trinity, she staggered under the weight of knowledge, experienced as vividly as if she had lived those many centuries herself, but was also stunned by the import of that final revelation.

The Trinity was about to become whole again. But that could only mean . . .

Reflexively, she reached for her gun, but froze before her hand could close on the Beretta's grip. DiLorenzo, too, blinked in disbelief as the apocalyptic vision faded, and he became fully aware of the half-dozen gunmen now surrounding them.

Though their reverie had lasted only a moment, it had been enough time for their enemies to find them.

PART THREE
TRINITY

THIRTEEN

For countless centuries, deep beneath the mountain, a collision of water and magma had created sporadic eruptions of super-heated vapor. During that period, geological activity of varying degrees of magnitude had changed the geyser's pattern of behavior, sometimes coaxing it into long periods of activity or alternately blocking its vent with rock and soil, which inevitably resulted in violent, explosive bursts. Such was the power of the steam pressure that not even stone could prevent its release.

In the late 1930's, when an SS officer named Gerhardt Mann saw the potential to harness the geyser's power for his generators, he of necessity had to create a controlled method for storing up that highly pressurized vapor. The steam jet would turn the enormous turbines, which would spin magnetos and create an electrical current. The mechanical elements of the system were state of the art for their time, utilizing the strongest and most durable alloyed steel products from Krups and an innovative self-lubricating process that actually pumped and refined small amounts of naturally occurring crude petroleum before injecting the finished product into the main hub of the turbine. The result was a syncretism of mechanical and geological engineering that performed beyond the wildest expectations of its heinous creator.

Even so, Mann had provided for the possibility that the turbine might one day need hands-on maintenance, and to that end he had created a shut-off valve for the purpose of temporarily capping the geyser so that his engineers might be able to safely perform whatever repairs were needed. This override valve could not, of course, avert the continued buildup of steam pressure in the superior holding tank, nor in the caverns deep beneath the mountain; such was never its intent. Mann had designed the valve to be employed for brief periods of inspection and maintenance only. In the event that a longer shut-down was needed, a second vent shaft was to have been dug at a future date, but events in the outside world permanently forestalled that phase of construction.

It had been nearly an hour since Montero closed that valve for the first time in sixty years—quite possibly for the first time ever. Though neither the steel nor rock yielded so much as a millimeter to the building mass of pressurized steam, the strain against them was growing exponentially. A gauge near the flywheel control, registering the internal pressure both in millibars of mercury and with a simple color code—red for dangerously high—had already ceased to give an accurate measure. The needle had been pegged for over ten minutes when, with an earsplitting crack, the gauge's steel pipe fitting blew off of the tank and blasted through the metal cowling as if it were made of paper. It shot as high as the cavernous ceiling where it drove like an arrow into the heart of the stone.

The steam rushed through the small opening with a shrill whistle, but the net effect on the pressure inside the tank was negligible. Fired by a prodigious volume of water flowing into a volcanic furnace to rival Dante's Inferno, the buildup to catastrophe continued unchecked.

Mira stared dumbly at the ring of armed men surrounding them, her muscles twitching defiantly with the urge to draw her pistol and fight.

"Give it up. We might let you live." The man who spoke looked familiar to her. It was the same man she had fought with in the museum—the tuxedoed gunman that she now knew to be Jorge Montero, heir to Odessa. Once again, he was blocking her way with a machine pistol.

Mira brandished the Trinity. "You should be more worried about whether I'll let you live."

Montero smiled cautiously. "If you knew how to use it, I do not think you would hesitate to kill me."

Mira matched his smile. The twinned crystals seemed to blaze empathetically. "Try me."

Suddenly the Trinity ripped free of her grasp, spinning like a hurled discus across the chamber. Two of Montero's soldiers ducked instinctively, then turned to see where the relic had gone, as did every other pair of eyes in the vault.

A second group of armed men had silently taken station behind Montero's party, entering the vault through the same point of access, a long vertical shaft cut into the mountain to accommodate a mechanical lift. The steel gate securing the entrance had been torn off its hinges, and the web of brightly colored climbing ropes bore testimony to the method by which the two separate groups had found their way into the Trinity vault. The newcomers, like Montero's men, wore military-style fatigues with combat harnesses holding additional weapons and gear. Two of this number were readily recognizable, one for his hulking size, the other for her arresting beauty.

"Rachel." Montero's attempt at appearing pleasantly surprised was stillborn. He could not hide the nervous quaver in his voice; a child caught with both hands in the cookie jar.

Rachel Aimes regarded him coolly, her weapon not quite pointing at him, but nonetheless ready for immediate action. She did not speak, but rather moved smoothly aside to permit another figure to step between herself and the lead mercenary. The man's face was lost in the shadows of the hood covering his head, but Mira's eyes were drawn to the item he held in his right hand: the Trinity, still ablaze with supernatural fire.

"Well, well. The gang's all here." She brought her stare to the eyes hidden beneath the hood. "I don't think we have all been together since that night at the museum. Does that sound about right, Walter?"

The hooded man laughed, reaching up with his left hand to draw back the covering, and a pallid, gray face—the face of a bloodless corpse—was revealed. "Very perceptive, Mira."

DiLorenzo started, visibly shaken. "Aimes?"

"It was the only explanation that made any sense," observed Mira, calmly. "The theft of the Atlantean Trinity had to be an inside job. You were the most likely suspect, except for one almost insignificant detail."

"I was dead."

"I witnessed your autopsy," protested DiLorenzo. "You couldn't have faked that. You were laid open like a fish."

"Such colorful simile. Mr. Turner, please disarm them."

As the brutish mercenary collected their guns, Mira half-turned toward the stunned detective. "He didn't have to fake it. He had the Trinity."

"Not quite as damaged as you believed, Mira, though I confess, it took some doing to reawaken it." Aimes, tapped his chest and smiled knowingly. "It's a part of me now. Surgically implanted after the autopsy."

"You mean he—"

"He brought himself back to life. Only you're not quite alive, are you Walter? Or should I call you Tarrant?"

Aimes' smile slipped. "Well, it would seem that now you do know all my secrets."

"Hang on a second," protested DiLorenzo. He began gesturing with his hands as he spoke, as if trying to physically grasp the ideas which eluded his mind. "Aimes is really Tarrant? The guy who found the other Trinity relics for the Nazis? So everything that happened at the museum—"

"All part of the plan. The shooting at the museum, the map in his apartment—all designed to maneuver me into finding the treasure for him."

"All too easily." Aimes' smug grin reappeared.

"But why? You could have taken off with the Trinity any time you liked. Why . . . um, kill yourself?"

"He had to get my attention," answered Mira, frowning at her own naiveté. She directed her words at Aimes. "As long as I thought I was following in your footsteps, fighting the same enemy that killed you, I wouldn't stop to think about how obvious it had all been."

"Yes, there is that," confessed Aimes. "But death and resurrection—there's something deeply spiritual about it all, don't you think? All the best gods died and came back. Perhaps conquering death is the key to divinity."

"Don't kid yourself, Walter. You're better suited to the opposite role."

Aimes chuckled. "Better to rule in hell, my dear."

"I'll be happy to speed you on your way home, then. You may have played me, Walter, but now the cards are on the table, and I'm all in."

"Enough." Montero recovered from the surprise appearance of his confederates and made an attempt at asserting his authority. "Why are you wasting time talking to her? We have what we came for. Let's kill them and be done."

"I agree," intoned Rachel. "She's dangerous."

Mira studied Montero carefully. The subtle nuances of the neo-Nazi's relationship to Aimes, or rather Tarrant—a man that had allowed himself to be killed in order to possess intimate control of the Trinity—were not lost on her. Montero had no illusions about who was really in control. "I'm dangerous? Have you asked him what he plans to do with the Trinity? If I were you, I'd be more concerned about stopping him."

"What in the hell are you talking about?" Montero tried to sound fierce, but she could sense that he already knew the truth of her words.

"Sixty years ago, a Nazi like you double-crossed him and left him for dead. Do you think he's forgotten that? He's playing you. And when he's finished . . ." She drew a finger past her throat.

Tarrant inclined his head to Mira. "You are good. Mann must have written quite the tale before his timely passing. But consider this, my dear: if I wanted only to rid myself of this Nazi pest, I would have merely had Rachel shoot him. You underestimate the depth of my thirst for justice."

"Don't you mean revenge?"

Tarrant made a waggling gesture with his hand. "Tomato, tomahto."

Montero's eyes widened in surprise as he heard his fate discussed so casually, and in his very presence. The barrel of his firearm swung around to center on Tarrant. "What's she talking about?"

"Absolute power corrupting absolutely," explained Mira, her eyes never leaving Aimes. "He's going to get revenge for Mann's betrayal. Tell us, Walter, what you're going to do now that you have reunited the Trinity."

"I'm surprised you care, my dear. I'm going to balance the scales, something that should have been done long ago. The fascist nations of Europe and their petty squabbles have caused bloodshed beyond Genghis Khan's wildest aspirations—"

"And you mean to do away with the lot of them?"

Tarrant shrugged indifferently. "I'll admit, at first I was content to dream only of one day erasing Germany from the map. Of course, I couldn't very well allow Austria to remain either. Or the spineless French for their complicity. And one mustn't forget Spain and Italy in the equation. Do you know that to this day, the people of the European continent loathe us, considering themselves superior? The cradle of civilization? They were a conquered people, but the Allies let them escape the judgment they so richly deserved. Propped up their governments, gave them new life." Despite his casual beginning, his furor increased as he ticked off the litany of his hatred. "As the years of my forced exile passed, I realized what had to be done."

DiLorenzo shook his head. "I don't believe I'm hearing this."

A hungry gleam alit in his dead eyes. "Ten thousand years from now, children will tell stories of how the lost continent of Europe was swallowed up by the earth."

Only then did Montero grasp Tarrant's intentions. "You are insane."

Before the Argentine could tighten his finger on the trigger, the joined Trinity in Tarrant's hand flared brightly, forcing Mira and DiLorenzo to shade their eyes from its intensity. When the brilliance subsided, they saw Montero and all of the Odessa soldiers crumpled on the floor. The handful of Bolivian locals gasped in horror at the supernatural manifestation; one of the men crossed himself, setting off a brief wave of religious supplications. DiLorenzo found himself joining in reflexively.

Tarrant chuckled, gloating. "Ah, you see? Well begun is half-done. I suppose I shall have to do some house cleaning in other parts of the globe, too."

"Why stop there?" replied Mira, acidly. "Why not clear it all away?"

He feigned a thoughtful pose. "You may be onto something there, my dear."

"Unbelievable," whispered DiLorenzo. "He's unstoppable,

isn't he?"

Mira shook her head slowly, then answered, speaking loud enough for Aimes to hear. "There's more to this, isn't there? You need something else. . . . The Shrine."

DiLorenzo flashed back on the vision they had shared. "That pagoda we saw?"

"Something about that place magnifies the power of the Trinity. Only you don't know where it is, the hidden city of Agartha. You need me to show you the way. Well, I'm done playing for you, Walter."

Tarrant's smile grew cold and menacing, and for the first time, Mira realized she had found a weakness in the resurrected grave robber. He stared at her for a long moment, hefting the Trinity as if to intimidate her with the power he had used to slay Montero. When she remained unbowed, he turned his gaze to DiLorenzo.

He made a claw hand gesture with his free hand, reaching toward the detective with his fingers upraised. DiLorenzo let out a gasp as invisible lines of force radiated into his chest cavity and squeezed the air from his lungs. His feet lifted off the ground. Tarrant curled his fingers, drawing DiLorenzo toward him, then squinted with his eyes, as if peering deep into the detective's soul. "Yes. It's in there, isn't it? We shall have to find out what you know."

Without releasing DiLorenzo, Tarrant turned to Mira. "It seems we won't be needing you after all, my dear."

Mira remained defiant, showing no fear. For a few seconds, nothing happened.

Finally, Rachel Aimes broke the impasse. "What are you waiting for?"

Tarrant's eyes did not leave Mira, but his demeanor changed, becoming almost wistful. "You know, there was a time not long ago when I loved you. Even thought of you as a daughter. You think me a monster, but I have feelings too. I could never bring myself to harm such a thing of beauty."

He smiled and then turned his head imperceptibly toward Rachel. "Kill her."

Mira did not hear her death sentence declared. Even as

Tarrant began speaking, she knew what was coming. Her heartbeat roared in her ears with the sound of a waterfall, her extremities began building up adrenaline for a final fight or flight. Her subconscious condemned her for what she was about to do, abandoning DiLorenzo to Tarrant's machinations, but she knew that any other course of action would assure total failure. There were more lives at stake than just his and her own.

Rachel smiled hungrily, raising the machine pistol in her hands to deliver a long awaited coup de grace. But she was once again denied. Mira shot forward, aiming straight at Aimes' daughter yet somehow staying out of her field of fire. Momentarily flustered, Rachel's aim wavered.

Mira's sudden move gave her the advantage of a millisecond—the reaction time for Turner and his mercenaries to come to Rachel's aid. Tarrant could have permanently ended her flight with a mere thought, but he did not, perhaps trusting his human assets to accomplish what he had already publicly balked at. Whatever the case, Mira remained alive long enough to cross the distance between the Trinity altar and the stainless steel passage through which she and DiLorenzo had entered. Only then did the gunfire commence.

No less than twelve guns blazed after her, the bullets sparking and dancing along the wall of the cavern and into the polished interior of the tunnel. A roar of thunder without end assaulted her senses and a rising wave of heat, the exhaust of so many shots fired in such a small enclosure, buffeted her back.

Somehow, she slipped inside the tunnel without sustaining a single hit. Because most of the shooters were not correctly lined up with the steel shaft, their rounds impacted harmlessly on the cavern wall or struck the mouth of the corridor at an oblique angle, ricocheting harmlessly past Mira. For the handful of Turner's mercenary soldiers who were facing directly down the tunnel however, the target was almost impossible to miss.

Caught up in a surge of adrenaline, Mira barely noticed the stripe that appeared on her upper right arm as a bullet graze left a shallow furrow in her epidermis. A few centimeters below that, another round struck closer to home, gouging a chunk of flesh just above her elbow in a spray of red. Two more rounds superficially clipped her right thigh, then a ricochet passed diagonally through the meaty part of her left calf. She felt the pain distantly, almost a memory rather than an immediate experience, but her injured muscles were quick to respond. Swelling from the trauma, she found her legs no longer striding as far or quickly as they had. A ricochet grazed her back, opening a long, ragged wound that instantly spread a dark bloodstain across her shirt.

The hollow channel formed by the tunnel focused the noise of gunfire to a deafening crescendo. The auditory assault was more painful than the wounds she had sustained, leaving her both unable to hear and mildly vertiginous. Even if she had been able to register sound, the roar of her enemies' guns would still have prevented her from hearing the loud clicks, gradually increasing their pace, that emanated from the tunnel walls, the only indication that the trap she had disarmed with the digits of Adolf Hitler's birthday, was about to reset. She was less than halfway down the tunnel when the clicking became a buzz, then ceased altogether. Her next footfall triggered the device.

Luck and her preternatural intuition saved her. The spring-loaded blades that suddenly materialized in her path were simply obstacles for her to jump over, roll under or dive through. The last element to the trap, however, would not be so easily avoided. She felt it first as a tickling sensation, like thousands of tiny feathers caressing her exposed skin, teasing stray hairs and drawing them away from her body.

Electricity!

The end of the metal corridor remained maddeningly close, blocked only by a pair of parallel blades. The space separating the two knives was less than a meter, a narrow but not impossible margin through which to slip. She was no longer aware of the enemies behind her, nor conscious of the fact that they had stopped shooting.

In the instant that she dove for the gap in the final barrier, an electrostatic charge was released. The entire tunnel was wired, like an enormous bug-zapper. A finger of blue flame reached out to snatch her back, stabbing through her torso to form a vicious triangle between the floor and the wall on her left.

Then she was through.

She lay dazed on the floor of the cavern they had designated the laboratory. Blood flowed from wounds too numerous to count, but the worst of it was the jarring numbness that had seized her musculature. She knew there would be pain later, but the electrical discharge must certainly have left its mark on her skin. For now however, there was only a brief moment of relief that she had survived this far, and the overwhelming imperative to race onward. She knew she was a long way from safety.

Rachel Aimes peered down the smooth metal corridor, watching in faint amazement as the blades quietly retreated into the walls. Mira lay motionless at the far end, a barely discernible lump on the floor. Her disbelief was compounded as that lump began to stir.

"Impossible," she whispered with grudging respect.

Aimes chuckled. "It seems I still underestimated her. A pity she could not have seen her way clear to join us, but then that, too, was never really in question."

He turned to gaze at the unmoving form of DiLorenzo, still suspended in the air by the power of the Trinity. He knew that he could have taken control of Mira in similar fashion—not as easily perhaps, for her mind was stronger and she was much more in tune with her psychic endowments—but somehow he had known that such was never really an option. Her failure as a field officer for the Agency was not a result of any lack of will or wit, but purely the result of a moral conflict. Despite his own best efforts, he had never been able to reprogram her conscience. But regardless of his statement, he had never made the mistake of underestimating Mira Raiden.

"She's getting away," urged Rachel.

The man who once again called himself Tarrant closed his eyes, momentarily caught in the confluence of memories and intentions. He tightened his grip on the Trinity, holding it close to his chest, where the third segment pulsed in time with his heartbeat. "We have more important matters to concern us now."

He extended his free hand, making a clawing gesture similar to the one he had used to seize the New York detective. This time, however, he did not turn his power against the living.

Jorge Montero and his Odessa soldiers had not been dead for more than a few minutes. Their corpses had yet to relinquish a significant degree of body heat, and it would be some time before the stiffening of rigor mortis would set in. Nevertheless, they were indisputably deceased, beyond any hope of resuscitation. With the power of the Trinity, Tarrant had destroyed their life force, slaying every living cell in their bodies in an instant of time. Yet, what the Trinity had taken away it could, after a fashion, give back.

Montero and the others began moving, twitching at first, then sat upright and got to their feet. Their faces were expressionless, eyes staring forward without seeming to focus, but as one they turned purposefully toward the metal tunnel and began running.

Unlike the zombies of Hollywood motion pictures, these living dead men did not shuffle along gracelessly in mindless pursuit of the living. Instead, they moved with an almost cat-like grace, darting heedless of peril into the corridor. Twisting and diving through the air, they passed through the tunnel and beyond the traps with supernatural ease.

Tarrant allowed a smile of satisfaction to stretch his own reanimated flesh. "Now she has someone to keep her company in this awful place."

Lightning flashed again in the killing tunnel, knocking one of the resurrected Odessa soldiers out of mid-air. Mira raised her head, knowing without seeing that her ordeal was far from over, and caught a brief glimpse of the approaching foes in the instant before they burst from the tunnel.

She moved as if to flee, but pulled back from the feint, charging instead toward the pack. No longer motivated by human reasoning ability, the zombies were not easily fooled. Hell-bent on adding her to their ranks, they did not attempt to form strategies for snaring her with the least amount of effort. They simply threw themselves at her with rabid ferocity. For all their supernatural energy, however, they still had the bodies and mass of men.

Mira crouched, coiling for a serpentine strike in the instant before the revivified Montero pounced. As soon as he committed to the lunge, she side-stepped, assaulting him with feet and fists as he flew helplessly past. When he recovered from the thwarted attack, spinning around to pounce once more, Mira had his gun.

The captured machine pistol in Mira's hands bucked frenetically as a torrent of nine-mil spewed from its barrel and chewed into the undead neo-Nazi. Blood and flesh exploded from exit wounds as Montero staggered back, but the bullets seemed to have no real effect on their target.

Montero's troops were likewise uncowed by the assault and charged toward her with single-minded voracity. Mira swung the MP5 to meet this new front, fully aware that Montero was already regaining his footing on her flank. The kinetic energy from the bullet impacts caused some of them to falter, but the rest surged forward, heedless of injury. A moment later, the machine pistol stopped bucking, as the bolt slid home on an empty firing chamber.

Her short-lived defensive plan had served its diversionary purpose; it had given her time to think. She knew she could not hope to overpower these reanimated cadavers as she had Mann's desiccated remains. Worse, she was wounded, perhaps gravely so, and it was only a matter of time before blood loss led to fatigue and eventually unconsciousness.

But beyond these immediate concerns, there was a greater issue that she could not simply push into the background: Aimes—the original grave robber Tarrant—had control of the complete Trinity and intended to use it for an act of incomprehensible evil. His delusions of vengeance, fed by the god-like powers of the joined relic, had led him to sever all ties with humanity. It was not unreasonable to imagine him rending the very planet. Mira knew she had to escape, not simply to preserve her own life, but perhaps every life on earth.

She threw the spent gun at the head of the nearest attacker and then dove under his grasp. Bowling into the midst of the zombie pack, she gained an instant in which they confusedly reversed and stumbled over one another in their haste to seize her. She used that moment well, crossing the laboratory to the first tunnel trap.

The dismembered remains of two victims lay at the far end of the steel corridor. The trap had remained sprung, not resetting because of the lingering weight on the pressure sensitive floor. The blunt edge of several sets of spring-loaded knives presented a grid-like obstacle, though less daunting than the tunnel leading from the Trinity vault. Mira raced into the corridor, diving and rolling through the blades like an expert gymnast, but the Odessa troops were still close on her heels.

As she passed the hunks of flesh and cloth—all that remained of the ill-fated Bolivians that had chased her and DiLorenzo—she reached down and snagged a discarded gun from the floor. It was an old .357 Magnum, slightly discolored and pitted with corrosion, but packing a full load of bright brass shells. She hefted the weighty firearm, not even noticing that the hand which had gripped it previously was still moving on the metal floor, and dived through the final set of blades.

She tucked her head down and landed in a forward roll that brought her to her feet in a low crouch, with the Magnum extended in a two-hand grip before her. Despite her expectation that some of her enemies would be alive and waiting in the cavern alongside the underground river, she was momentarily dumbfounded by what she saw.

Two men, one dressed in a stained, white linen suit and the other in the rough garments of a laborer, stood in mute disbelief over three motionless forms in dark fatigues. It took a moment for Mira to realize that the latter group were Odessa soldiers, snuffed out by Aimes in the same act that had slain Montero. The two Bolivians took advantage of that brief lapse in her vigilance to raise their weapons against her, but before a shot could be fired, the three dead men suddenly began moving.

"*Madre de Dios,*" gasped the man in the suit. If the invocation was sufficient to expiate a lifetime of criminal activity, then Rafael Delacortes went straight to heaven a moment later. The three dead soldiers fell upon the cocaine baron and his hireling, beating them savagely and twisting their heads almost completely around, before tossing lifeless bodies aside to concentrate on their true foe. At the same instant, Montero and the rest of his group broke from the tunnel like a pack of wolves, rushing to attack Mira from behind.

Mira snapped off three quick shots with the Magnum, each a perfect head shot that knocked down the three most recently awakened members of the undead army. Though the back of each man's head had exploded like an overripe melon, they were back on their feet before Mira could take even a step. At the same time, the two slain Bolivians began to stir, rising to join the ranks despite shattered limbs and torn muscles that left their heads hanging like pendants against their torsos.

For the first time in a long time, Mira felt the icy stare of the Grim Reaper. She wasted no further effort battling the unvanquishable foes, but instead turned toward the staircase landing off to her left. Two more corpses, victims of the earlier gun battle, were stirring to life as she hurtled past. She reached the stairway in a few bounding strides, but even as she began ascending, surging up three treads at a time, she knew that the worst was yet to come. High above her, the sound of old bones scraping on stone signaled the return of the fortress' original guardians.

As the last of Turner's mercenaries hauled himself out of the old elevator shaft, Rachel Aimes turned toward her adopted father. If his return from the underworld had created a minor rift between them, then his current status had transformed it into a chasm. To say that he was no longer human was a ridiculous oversimplification. Still, there was something to be said for backing the winning team.

Tarrant stood with his back to the group of hired soldiers, impassively gazing at the road ahead. The enslaved New York City policeman, whose role in the drama Rachel barely grasped, hung a few steps away as if impaled on an invisible fishhook. As soon as the last man was up, Tarrant started forward again without a word.

The loosely organized party moved at a jog along the upper promenade above the parade ground, quickly finding the stairway that led up to the turbine access tunnel and the geyser exhaust vent. None of the mercenaries had paid attention during the initial hasty descent, and all were now relying upon Tarrant to lead them out. He did not disappoint. Like a drop of mercury following the course of least resistance, he seemed to flow up the narrow tunnel, rising effortlessly on the fixed rope left behind by Mira Raiden and hastening up the steep passageway.

"Look at that old guy go," remarked one of the hirelings, not completely comprehending their leader's supernatural enhancements.

None of them even noticed the groaning noise of the steam chamber as internal pressure pushed the riveted steel walls to the breaking point.

Mira had only reached the next level of the redoubt before discovering the enormity of the odds stacked against her. It was impossible to discern a single human shape in the mass of reanimated remains that was spilling from the corridor into the stairwell. Though the staccato steps of Montero and his pack were still audible over the din, perhaps only a hundred steps below but closing fast, she turned back. She had gone only a few paces when the swarm engulfed her.

Because they were little more than bones held together with brittle strands of mummified sinew, the individual members of the undead army had little potential to cause injury. Despite being outweighed and outmuscled however, the mindless corpses crowded together like the sea, flooding down the steps intent on literally drowning Mira beneath a combined mass of dust and bones. Skeletal fingers tugged at her hair and clothing, but were unable to seize firm hold. She fought the vanguard of the swarm with well-placed kicks and punches, never slowing in her descent, but it wasn't enough. Her legs were swept from beneath her and she tumbled down the carved stone steps.

Suddenly, none of that mattered.

Unable to contain the swollen mass of super-heated water vapor, the steel containment chamber and the surrounding cavern burst apart along a dozen different fracture points. Observers as far away as Ouros saw the side of the mountain explode skyward in a gray column of steam and dust. The rock face Mira and the others had climbed to access the steam vent was completely gone, blasted into pebbles and chunks of dirt that were either blown into the sky or swept down the mountain in the subsequent mud flow.

At the controls of the old Viet Nam era Huey helicopter, Rachel Aimes felt the cataclysm as a wave of thermal turbulence, requiring her deft touch to avoid a loss of control. Already more than a quarter-mile away from the zone of destruction, Rachel and her cohorts were hardly inconvenienced by the destruction of the mountain and the hidden Nazi fortress inside.

Mira was not so fortunate.

The entire cavern lurched violently, pitching her away from the chattering horde, down more steps. She barely felt the bruising impact, however. Her senses were attuned to the unceasing vibrations in the steps and walls. Though she didn't know exactly what had happened, she knew that the tremor was only a harbinger of what was to come. Even the threat of relentless undead monsters paled alongside the very immediate reality that she might be forever entombed beneath the collapsing mountain. Beating off a renewed assault, she struggled to her feet and hastened downward.

An abrupt wind chased down the stairwell, a hot breeze that carried a noise like thunder. She beat her way past Montero and the Odessa zombies, spurred onward by a growing realization of what was beginning to happen.

The groaning and pitching of the cavern continued, redoubling in intensity. Weakened by a honeycomb of human excavations, the peak began to collapse inward. As the weight of debris accumulated to critical mass on the uppermost levels hewed out by Mann's slave laborers, the floor gave way, triggering a chain reaction of destruction. Withal however, the annihilation of the Nazi redoubt was insignificant when measured alongside what was occurring deep beneath the mountain.

The explosive release in the bowels of the earth had forever altered the geyser. Displaced by tons of debris, the tributary of the underground river that had supplied water to the geothermal phenomenon no longer flowed through to its original destination. Instead, the full volume of the subterranean torrent was diverted into the main channel, increasing its volume by nearly seventy-five percent. The hydraulic force of so much water in the already weakened caverns hastened the total destruction of the cave network.

Mira hit the landing at the base of the stairwell in a controlled headlong plunge. She could feel the effects of injury and fatigue slowing her reflexes and clouding her judgment. Every step was a battle, both with the risen dead and her own human frailty. She struggled onward, acutely aware that the underground river was now in the grip of a flash flood. Behind her, a similar roar of water thundered down the stairwell, heralding the approach of a second deluge.

With the last of her reserves, she broke from the grip of a dozen animated corpses in varying states of decay, and sprinted toward the precipice above the river. Her destination swayed wildly, high above the surging waters, snapping back and forth with every tremor. She scrambled up the wooden platform and without hesitation leapt out over the raging torrent.

Her outstretched fingers snared a handrail on the sliding door to the tram vehicle. Even as she closed both fists around the smooth metal, she felt the car lurch away, as if trying to escape from her grasp.

The first wave of zombies plunged, lemming-like, from the platform and were swept away by the flood. But as the car swung back toward the platform, those who followed learned from the mistake of their predecessors. Mira felt the subtle impact of loose bones and old flesh striking her body and falling away, or impacting the metal and glass exterior before tumbling to the same fate. In the corner of her eye, she saw Montero and the other neo-Nazis striding through the sea of walking mummies, eager to take their turn.

Pulling up slightly, she lifted her left hand to the simple latch bolt securing the door and pushed it open. As the cable swayed back toward the platform, she swung her left foot up into the car, then pulled herself inside the antique conveyance. Even before she landed, some of the squirming zombies joined her inside, tearing at her with shriveled fingers.

Mira ignored them momentarily, focusing instead on turning off the flow. Bracing her back against the floor of the car, she pushed the door closed with an abrupt kick. As the sliding panel slammed shut, it cleaved a yellowed skull in two.

As the zombie mass was unable to immediately reinforce its numbers, Mira quickly gained the upper hand, tearing arms and legs from bony torsos and scattering teeth and skulls with deft kicks. However, while the shattered remains on the floor fell still, the briefly restored force of life departed, the outside of the tram grew thick with the undead. Like maggots on meat, zombies swarmed over the car, shutting out the dim light with their wasted bodies and the tattered remnants of prison clothing and Wehrmacht uniforms.

Over the noise of bones scraping on glass, she could hear the pounding of boots on the roof of the car, likely Montero and his men adding their superior strength and dexterity to the attack. Yet, there was nothing more she could do. Dropping to the floor in exhaustion, she waited for the inevitable.

What she could not see was the sudden rush of muddy water that exploded from the stairwell, driving ahead of it enormous chunks of rock as effortlessly as matchwood. In the blink of an eye, the dead returned to their previous condition, smashed into oblivion by the collision. The surge caught the tramcar an instant later, ripping it from its cable like rotten fruit from the vine, and tossed it into the turbulent flow.

Mira was hurled mercilessly about the interior space, barely able to discern which way was up. One of the windows exploded inward, struck by a piece of debris in the flood or perhaps a low hanging rock in the river tunnel, but surprisingly little water crept in. For some time the unguided vessel surged through uncontrollable spins and plunges before the ferocity of the flood diminished. The tram somehow stayed upright, riding the current like a gondola.

Mira barely noticed.

As soon as the sensation of constant upheaval relented, she settled onto the sloshing floor and fished a flare from her pack. The sudden light hurt her eyes and offered little help in illuminating the area beyond the small car. Outside, there was only darkness and the awareness of swift motion. It mattered little; she was no longer in control of her destiny.

The last radiant sliver of the setting sun vanished below the horizon, turning the green water of the Pacific Ocean almost black. In the azure twilight that followed, only the silhouette of cresting waves could be distinguished on the dark surface. There was no one to notice the strange shape, like an enormous beer can crumpled and cast aside by a slovenly giant, that breached the surface off the Chilean coast.

It would be nearly twelve hours before the object, caught in the tailings of the El Niño current as it pushed northward, would drift into the tidal zone to be thrown up onto a rocky beach in the first light of dawn. Nestled inside the battered tramcar, Mira slept on, oblivious to the fact of her own survival.

FOURTEEN

It was raining in the Sherpa village of Namche Bazaar. To be more precise, it was raining heavily on the entire Indian subcontinent. The vestiges of a late season monsoon had pushed up against the barrier of the Himalayas and stopped, dumping torrential rains on the mountain nations of Nepal and Bhutan and most of Eastern India. Mira had seen nothing but rain for two days. She unconsciously tugged the heavy coat of yak wool closer about her shoulders as she stared through the streaked window into the stormy night.

Only four days had passed since the debacle in Bolivia. It had taken the better part of the first two days just to escape the remote section of Chile where she had washed up following a hellish ride through the underground river and the subsequent disgorging from the belly of the sea. The tram gondola had retained enough air to remain buoyant and burst immediately toward the surface.

Thirty-six hours after washing up on the beach, she boarded a chartered floatplane to Santiago. There, she changed to a commercial carrier bound for Rio de Janeiro, Brazil, connecting to Miami, Florida, then New York, then London. An Indian Air flight destined for Calcutta was her next connection, after which she had to rely once more on smaller chartered aircraft to reach her ultimate goal in timely fashion. Somewhere between New Delhi and Katmandu, the rain had started.

Two small lights, like the glowing eyes of a nocturnal creature, appeared in the gloom beyond the windows of the smoky inn where Mira was now lodged. She squinted, fixing her gaze on the lights, and spied a second pair close behind and drawing near. With a tight-lip expression that almost passed for a smile, she moved toward the door and stepped out into the punishing downpour.

Despite the heavy raindrops, she welcomed the chance to breathe something other than the wretched fumes of burning yak dung. Though the fuel source was in abundant supply and used extensively by the Sherpas to heat their homes and cook their food, the acrid smell could not by any stretch of the imagination be mistaken for wood smoke.

Two mud-caked Range Rovers gradually came into view and pulled up in front of the inn. There were no other automobiles to be seen. No one who lived in the village owned a car, and the regional bus had not made an appearance since the start of the monsoon. Mira hastened toward the vehicles, eager to greet the drivers. Although swathed in layers of brightly colored, cold-weather gear, she had no difficulty identifying an old friend.

"Andy!" she cried, her voice cracking with unexpected emotion as she threw her arms around him.

Andrew Banks, a gruff former Special Forces shooter and small arms trainer, and one of the few people from her days at the Farm whom she recalled with fondness—and whose cell phone number she still remembered—stood in shocked paralysis at the intensity of the embrace. When she finally relaxed her grip, he managed an uncomfortable smile. "You're looking a bit worse for wear, kid."

"You don't know the half of it."

Banks' forehead creased in an unspoken, concerned inquiry, but she offered nothing more. One explanation would surely lead to another and another, and there simply wasn't time for that.

She had contacted him directly from South America, begging a favor for old time's sake. Banks had continued to work as a trainer and armorer for the Agency even after Mira's division had closed its doors, and he still had the wherewithal to equip her for the task ahead. What he did not have, however, was sufficient motivation. For that, Mira would have to ask a favor from someone she did not count as a friend, someone who would demand those explanations.

The second driver stepped forward with hand extended. He neither expected nor received an embrace. "Hello again, Mira."

"Jack." She accepted his handclasp deferentially, unable to completely forget their last face-to-face meeting, or his ultimatum. With the closing of her section, all Agency assets had been redistributed, and Mira Raiden was an asset that had fallen into Jack Carlson's lap. Though skeptical of the paranormal nature of the projects in which Mira had worked, he nevertheless recognized her talents. "You've been forged for one purpose," he had told her. "You belong in the field. So either get these quaint notions of good guys and bad guys out of your head right now and go back to doing what you do best . . . or you're out."

Back then, it had been an easy choice. Carlson and the Agency had nothing to offer but a means of livelihood, and once the strings were cut, she had proven herself more than adequate to that task.

When she had called Banks from Chile, begging for help, he had promised only to try. On her second call from Miami, he had told her what the price of that assistance would be. The kind of help Mira needed could only come from the Agency—from Jack Carlson, and his terms had not changed.

But hers had. It wasn't just about Mira Raiden anymore. She was now prepared to make any sacrifice to prevent her former benefactor from unleashing hell on earth.

She had not expressed her needs in those exact terms, however. Yet, Carlson understood that Walter Aimes had gone rogue and tried to kill his former pupil and he was left to believe that her intentions were merely to exact revenge. Mira did not elaborate on the greater peril; Carlson would not have believed her anyway. It was enough for him that the former Agency behaviorist was on his way to China, and that Mira was willing to silence him by any means necessary.

"Well," she said, breaking the uncomfortable silence of the reunion. "Let's have a look at the Christmas presents."

Banks turned and opened the rear hatch of one of the Range Rovers. The cargo space was half-filled with sundry items, spare clothes for Mira and foodstuffs. He looked around, needlessly checking for spying eyes, and then raised the key fob, hitting the buttons in a sequence that triggered musical tones reminiscent of "Yankee Doodle." The carpeted floor of the cargo area abruptly began moving, lifting up on telescoping posts, to reveal a small arsenal of weapons and ammunition packed in foam.

"Very clever."

"Child's play," scoffed Banks with false modesty. "It's completely invisible to customs inspectors, and the foam is treated with a chemical that masks the scent of nitrates from the security dogs. Had to cut the gas tank down by half to make room, and all that weight plays havoc with the mileage, so you have to fuel the beast up every time you pass a gas station."

Mira let her eyes wander over the selection. Banks had, it seemed, left nothing behind. She bypassed the larger weapons. She didn't doubt that she might need the firepower, but firepower would have to be sacrificed for the sake of mobility. She skipped over the M4 carbine and the long tube of a Stinger missile launcher, but took one of the relatively portable single-use M-72 LAW (light anti-armor weapon) rockets. She slipped the stubby, compact weapon in her backpack and went back to looking. Almost without thinking, she stuffed in a grenade launcher, which both looked and functioned like a fat-barreled sawed-off shotgun, and ten forty-millimeter grenades, and then picked up a Desert Eagle. The chrome-plated handgun, manufactured by Magnum Research, was the undisputed king of automatic pistols; the largest semi-automatic handgun in existence. Depending on the load, it could reputedly tear a human target in half. Mira extended her arm, sighting down the barrel, and found the foresight lined up on Carlson.

The department director swallowed nervously. "Don't screw this up, Mira. Nothing leads back to us, understand?"

"I remember how the game works, Jack." She donned a new shoulder holster, into which she stuffed the Desert Eagle, now loaded, along with several spare magazines.

"Good. I'm looking forward to putting you back to work."

"I wish I could say I was looking forward to working for you, but we both know what a lousy liar I am." She hefted the backpack onto one shoulder and turned to Banks, her tone and demeanor softening. "I appreciate this, Andy. It means more than you'll ever know."

The gruff old soldier returned an earnest smile, then tapped a button on the key fob, activating the mechanism to return the smuggling compartment to a secure position.

"Keys, please."

Carlson tossed her an identical fob with the key to the second Rover, and she caught it in the air, striding toward the driver's side door.

Banks' voice was uncharacteristically emotional as he offered his final exhortation. "Be careful, kid."

She shook her head gravely. "'Careful' won't get the job done."

The rain remained her companion through most of the night, but the massive Range Rover plowed through the treacherous mud bogs with little difficulty. In the heated luxurious interior, it was easy to forget that she was traveling through a harsh, dangerous environment.

Four days without dodging bullets, to say nothing of the relentless undead, had afforded her a chance to make a partial physical recovery from the injuries sustained in her harrowing escape, but somehow sleep had eluded her. There was simply too much to do and the clock was ticking.

She knew that Tarrant—the name Walter Aimes reminded her too much of his betrayal—was nearby. She could sense the presence of the Trinity at an instinctual level. More than that, she had heard a rumor—spoken almost like a ghost story— about a strange group of foreigners that had entered the country on a chartered aircraft, passed like wraiths through customs without so much as opening a passport, and helped themselves to trucks and equipment. There was little question in her mind about the identity of these strangers.

By her best guess, she was more than half a day behind them, but there were several factors in her favor. Unlike Tarrant, who would have to rely on second-hand directions from a conceivably uncooperative DiLorenzo, she would be following a course burned into her memory.

The Trinity might have imbued Tarrant with god-like powers, but it could not convey upon him divine wisdom. His inexperience and limited knowledge about the region through which he now blazed a swath of destruction, perhaps coupled with the belief that nothing could stand in his way, had caused him to forsake the path of least resistance in favor of a more direct, if less accessible, route. Rather than crossing into Tibet at the open border town of Kodari and making the circuitous journey on well traveled and somewhat maintained surface roads, at elevations low enough to be free of snow, Tarrant had betrayed his ignorance by moving his group overland through Namche Bazaar and then commenced an arduous off-road trek along the Sherpa trail to Lobuche, where he turned northeast following the path of the Khumbu glacier.

In the worsening weather, moving through some of the roughest terrain on the planet, it should have been an impossible journey, but somehow a path had been opened. Mira could almost taste the memory of the Trinity's power reaching out to reshape stone and ice to the whim of its new master. Her own affinity with the relic confirmed her suspicion that Tarrant was now traveling in a virtually straight line toward his goal.

As she gained elevation, the rain became snow, threatening to choke the road ahead. In the rutted drifts, however, she could read the tale of her foe's progress. The accumulation in the treads revealed that a pair of large vehicles had pushed through the treacherous pass less than two hours before. The tires of the Range Rover had little trouble digging down to the packed snow to find traction, leaving her to wonder if she might actually catch up to her rival before he reached his destination.

She did not overtake the other party by the time sunlight from beyond the Himalayas gradually illuminated the world to the east. The storm front passed during the night, making progress easier. Late that afternoon, the trail led to the heavily secured border with Tibet.

The tire tracks of the preceding vehicles were barely dusted with fresh snow, forming parallel lines leading without interruption to the border fence and beyond. Mira stopped the Range Rover, just out of view of the high gun tower overlooking the pass, and stepped out into the winter landscape. She would make no less of a target approaching the frontier on foot, but perhaps the watchful eyes of the sentries would be fooled into thinking that she was merely a curious Sherpa, investigating the damage to the fence. Sherpas rarely jaunted about in Range Rovers.

As she hiked closer to the barrier, staying in the hard pack where Tarrant's trucks had passed, she got her first good look at the fence itself. A huge section of the chain-link metal weave had been cleanly excised, leaving the remnants to either side supported only by the snowdrift. She was now in full view of both the guard tower and a larger shack erected just beyond the fence, but there was no sign of activity. It was only upon reaching the physical border that she began to understand the eerie stillness.

There were two dark shapes in the snow to either side of the parallel tire tracks. Each step closer reinforced her certainty that the unmoving forms were bodies. The uniform-style, cold-weather gear worn by the dead men confirmed that they were soldiers in the army of the People's Republic of China, but there was no sign of a struggle or of any attempt at resistance. The Chinese-made Type 56 rifles remained slung over the shoulders of the corpses.

Mira could almost picture the men approaching Tarrant's truck, curious but not particularly concerned, and then simply dropping dead from a mere whisper of a thought amplified to fatal proportions by the ancient artifacts the old grave robber wielded.

She let the mental image slip away to lie beside the fallen soldiers, and turned back toward the Range Rover.

Tarrant's trail continued northeast under the shadow of the great mountain, gradually climbing to an altitude of more than 5,000 meters. Even if she had not already known his ultimate destination, it became glaringly evident as the track blazed by both his trucks and the irresistible might of the Trinity curved toward the Rongbuk glacier.

For millennia, the glacier had carved across the face of the mountain, scouring its stony visage to plow a valley more than ten miles long and a mile wide. It was in the midst of this severe, yet strangely beautiful, place that Buddhist monks had established a place of meditation.

For more than four hundred years, hermits had come to contemplate the austere majesty of the Himalayas, residing in caves and building small huts. In 1902, the Rongbuk monastery had been established, and while it possessed neither the size nor grandeur of the palatial religious complexes in the capital city of Lhasa, it remained a noteworthy destinations for pilgrims, as well as for a new breed of ascetic travelers: the mountaineers. The North Face route to the summit, along which famed climber George Mallory had disappeared after successfully reaching the highest place on earth, could only be reached after passing through the Lhakhang of Rongbuk.

The annexation of Tibet by the communist Chinese government, and the subsequent persecution of the native residents and their religion, had spelled the end of Rongbuk's notoriety, and the monastery was all but destroyed during the Cultural Revolution. Over the years, however, the Chinese government had learned the value of tacitly permitting a degree of religious freedom in order to keep tabs on the adherents, and a program of reconstruction had been instituted at Rongbuk. At the same time, a desire to capitalize on the interest of Western travelers had prompted the communist leaders to make both the monastery and the North Face route into a tourist destination.

What neither the secular policy makers in Beijing nor the devout monks of the Tibetan plateau realized was that the Rongbuk valley had been a focal point far longer than anyone realized, and for reasons that were scarcely imaginable.

The fortress-like Lhakhang stood out from the face of a cliff overlooking the valley almost as if it had been carved from the very rock of the mountain, not unlike the ruins of Petra in Jordan. Mira found Tarrant's trucks abandoned near the foot of the path leading up to the ruins of the monastery. The vehicles had been haphazardly discarded, as if their previous occupants believed they would no longer have need for wheeled transportation. Mira parked the Range Rover alongside, and after savoring a final moment of artificial warmth, exited into the bitter cold of the Rongbuk Valley.

The steps leading up to the main entrance were surprisingly clear of accumulated snow, but tiny chips of glacier ice born on the wind like grains of sand pelted her face as she made the ascent. She hugged the Yak hair garment close to her face, staying near the cliff wall, and hastened toward the relative shelter of the buildings.

But for the air, nothing moved in the monastery. Frayed and faded prayer flags snapped in the gale that roared down from the summit, but there was no indication that anyone now lived in the complex. Mira did not know if the stillness was Tarrant's doing—if he had massacred the residents of Rongbuk as mercilessly as he had dealt with the soldiers at the border crossing—or if there was a less macabre explanation, but the stillness remained ominous.

It was not her limited grasp of Tibetan Buddhism that guided her through the maze of terraces, rooftops and courtyards that formed the monastery complex, but rather the scent of something far more ancient.

High above the residences, on the path that continued up the valley toward the north face of Everest, was the *chorten* of Rongbuk—the circular reliquary adorned with emblems of the sun and moon to symbolize the enlightenment of Buddha's teachings. Nearby, adorning a sheer wall of metamorphic schist, the painted eyes of the deified Siddhartha Gautama gazed from a background of yellow ochre, as if to scrutinize all those who ascended the heights to gain such illumination. It was this latter feature that commanded Mira's attention. Centering herself between the stony gaze, she studied the cliff face, probing the unyielding surface with her fingers.

The wall was solid.

Mira frowned. She knew that she had reached the threshold of Agartha, and that this was the doorway through which Tarrant had passed. She had visited this place in her mind's eye—seen it as it was in the prehistory of the world, unrefined by monks and craftsmen—and knew that the only portal into the ancient city was sealed behind this slab of native rock. Yet the wall showed no sign of disturbance. Tarrant had indeed opened the door, but he had used a key—the Trinity—and locked it up tight afterward.

Recognizing that there would be no subtle means of breaching the portal, Mira turned away and put some distance between herself and the painted cliff. Given enough time, she might have been able to figuratively pick the lock, but time was something she didn't have. She elected to employ a more straightforward approach.

A spring-loaded catch allowed the hinged barrel of the M-79 grenade launcher to fall open, after which Mira loaded in a single stubby, bullet-shaped cartridge. She snapped it shut and without further consideration sighted on the round dot between the decorative eyes—the *ajna chakra*, symbol of the metaphysical third eye that can see into the spirit realm and glimpse the future—and pulled the trigger.

The spherical, forty-millimeter grenade armed itself as it flew toward the target. As soon as it struck the rock face, the armor-piercing charge released a jet of fiery metal plasma that burned into the schist, rendering it molten in the instant before the high explosive payload detonated.

A blast of smoke and thunder rocked the monastery and echoed between the valley walls, triggering a series of crushing avalanches across the face of the mountain. Fragments of stone pelted the chorten and crashed down onto the roofs of the buildings in the complex. In the moments following the explosion, Mira could hear the shrill siren of the Range Rover's alarm system on the valley floor, triggered by the severity of the concussion. These secondary effects of the grenade, however, were of little interest. An eager smile touched her lips as the smoke cleared to reveal a ragged vertical seam torn open in the sheer rock face, and beyond it, a shadowy void. It would be a tight fit, but the doorway to Agartha was open once more.

The mountain groaned again, and Rachel Aimes hugged her arms tight across her chest. Despite having left the frigid air of the glacier behind, the subterranean environment through which they now traveled, unlike the humid tunnels of the Bolivian Nazi fortress, remained as chilly as a refrigerator. One of the drawbacks to her adopted father's straightforward approach to travel was that it afforded little time to shop for the appropriate clothing. For his own part, Tarrant seemed unaffected by the temperature.

Of course he's not bothered, she thought with a hint of irony. *He's dead.*

The rest of the group, however, seemed likewise unperturbed by the cool underground air and the breeze that seemed to rise up from the abyss far below. Turner and his mercenaries were too macho to give any outward indication that they felt discomfort, and the New York City detective was oblivious, trailing along like a mindless automaton. Rachel forced herself to relax and continued onward.

At first, the rumblings of the mountain had heightened her anxiety. But after the first hour of trekking through the ancient city, accompanied by the ticking and creaking of tons of earth, she had come to realize that the mountain was by no means a sleeping lump of rock; it was a living thing. And while the noise of countless fault lines sliding and flexing gave the impression that the whole network of caverns might collapse at any moment, there was absolutely no evidence to suggest that there had ever been a cave-in.

This time, however, Tarrant stopped in his tracks, and everyone behind him froze in place, fearful that their worst claustrophobic fears were about to be realized. The old grave robber said nothing, but merely turned his head as if listening for whispers on the wind.

"What is it?" Rachel asked, nervously.

Tarrant turned slowly, his answer a barely audible question. "Mira?"

"That's impossible." Rachel was surprised by the intensity of her denial, but she heard Turner echo her sentiment.

"No way," he said, making a dismissive gesture. "Nobody got out of that place. She's buried."

"No." Tarrant spoke softly, deliberately. "She did. I wonder why I didn't feel her presence sooner."

"She's here?" Rachel still couldn't believe it. "She followed us all the way here?"

Turner shook his head. "Well, can't you just . . ." He

snapped his fingers and made a noise at the back of his throat.

"She's left me no choice." Tarrant managed a sad smile as he closed his eyes, tightening his grip on the second Trinity. "Good-bye, my dear."

FIFTEEN

As she struggled through the fissure, Mira felt a chill creep over her extremities that had nothing to with the wintry wind that perpetually buffeted the valley. Her heart began involuntarily racing, and beads of perspiration condensed on her forehead as her ability to breathe abruptly vanished. Panic gripped her, and this was doubly unsettling because she rarely experienced trepidation on such a visceral level. She struggled to draw breath, but it was as if the weight of the mountain was squeezing the air from her lungs. Spots began to swim across her vision as her strength fled, and she sagged in the grip of the stony crevice, unable to pull herself through.

In the descending twilight, a familiar gleam of light materialized before her—one of the Trinity crystals—and she reached out to it with her mind. The image coalesced but remained intangible, like something reflected on a pane of glass, and Mira saw not only the relic she had so briefly possessed, but also the face of her tormentor.

The man she had once known as Walter Aimes, or rather his astral presence, stood in the darkness before her, with his right hand squeezing the life from her heart. Invisible lines of power snaked into her like the roots of an invasive plant, to draw away her vital force.

Her reaction was instinctive. She thrashed impotently to free herself, foolishly expending what precious little energy remained. Tarrant had slain Montero and his neo-Nazis in this fashion, and had probably dispatched the Chinese border guards in the same way. He wielded the complete Trinity. How could she hope to defend against that?

And yet, she did not completely give in to her fear. The Trinity was no longer completely foreign to her. She had felt its power more than once. Was it too much to believe that she could also tap into that ancient power to save herself?

Two can play that game, Walter.

She reached out to Tarrant, her hand more a psychic

projection now than a physical one, and touched the talisman in his hands. As soon as she made contact, the constriction around her heart abated and her foe's dismay became palpable.

They struggled to wrest control of the Trinity from one another in a moment of time that seemed to occupy an eternity. The physical distance that separated them prevented Tarrant from stamping out her life force, but also denied Mira total control of the relic. She knew that while the deadlock endured, Tarrant was moving closer to his ultimate goal. A stalemate was not acceptable.

She turned her attention to the piece of the Trinity that was not joined physically to the others, the one that had started it all, the relic that had belonged to Atl'an. She could see it clearly now, beating the rhythm of life in the old grave robber's chest cavity. How he had known that surgically implanting the talisman in his cadaver would revive him, she could not guess, but one fact was glaringly apparent: the Atlantean talisman was the only thing keeping him alive.

Impulsively, she released her hold on the joined Trinity and made a grab for the pulsing, cracked crystal of its counterpart. Not recognizing his peril, Tarrant redoubled his attack, and as the darkness crashed over her once more, Mira wondered if her gambit had failed. With the last of her awareness, she tightened her grip on the Atlantean Trinity and pulled with all her might.

Tarrant's cognizance of the immediate threat arrived with a tortured shriek, and he abruptly severed the astral connection, ceasing the assault in an instant. The tendrils of his attack were wrenched from her soul with the exquisite pain of a sliver removed from a festering wound. She hovered on the verge of collapse, held upright only by the embrace of the rock walls on either side, but she had succeeded in driving back the attack.

Suddenly, she felt her breath slip away once more. Unable to defeat her head on, her enemy had instead turned his power against the mountain. With a creaking noise, the split halves of the crevice began moving together, filling in the gap caused by the grenade. Tarrant was using the Trinity to seal up the doorway once more.

Frantic, Mira squirmed in the tightening embrace, grasping

the rough stone to propel herself forward ahead of the slow but inexorable collision. Her outstretched fingers abruptly closed on air—she was almost through—but the width of the fissure held her shoulders so that she could barely turn her hands to grip the outer edges. With an unrestrained cry of determination, she heaved herself forward. The yak wool coat was torn from her back, shredded on the ragged surface of the fractured stone, to lay bare the skin underneath to similar punishment. But it was enough. Lubricated by blood and the sweat of her exertion, she slipped free, virtually exploding into the darkness inside the mountain. The stone sealed itself behind her, leaving only a jagged crack to mark the place where she had made her forced entry. The torn remains of the wool over-garment protruded from the cleft, fixed beyond hope of removal.

"Is that the best you can do, Walter?" She tried to sound defiant, but her trials had left her breathless. The old grave robber had almost won, had almost killed her with a power she barely understood. In a face-to-face confrontation, she might not be so fortunate. And now he knew she was coming.

A frown creased Tarrant's undead visage. Rachel knew him well enough to recognize that behind his imperturbable mask, his rage was growing. He faced Turner. "Take your men. Hunt her down and kill her." Offering no further explanation, he resumed walking. Only DiLorenzo followed immediately, his steps exactly synchronized with his psychic captor's.

The mercenary laughed noiselessly, then leaned close to Rachel. "Never send a god to do a man's work," he said, winking conspiratorially.

Before she could reply to his quip, he nodded to his companions, who as one shouldered their rifles and turned back the way they had come. Rachel shook her head, still trying to comprehend exactly what had happened, how Mira had somehow survived what she believed to be an irresistible power, then raced after her father.

Although she had witnessed the birth of Agartha in a vision, Mira could not help but be amazed at the scope and grandeur of the forgotten city. Unlike the cities built by the three brothers, Agartha had not been laid to waste in the global cataclysm. Rather, its inhabitants had simply deserted their dwellings and sealed up the mountain, preserving its splendor in a timeless stasis.

The subterranean metropolis was nothing like the Nazi redoubt in Bolivia. Whereas the German architect had utilized existing caverns and exploited countless laborers to hew out connecting tunnels, leaving behind chisel scars and walls scorched by high-explosives, the singular methods employed by Agartha's builders had left every visible surface smooth and polished, and on a scale to dwarf Mann's underground fortress. In spite of, or perhaps because of, its abandonment, the terrace upon which Mira found herself and the vaulted roof high above conveyed a gravity to rival the mountain beneath which the ancients had founded their empire.

The doorway from the Rongbuk monastery opened onto the lowest of a series of terraces—twelve in all—which ascended like a corkscrew to the highest point in the excavation, more than a thousand meters overhead. Each of the tiers was a city in itself. The primary platform was over a mile in diameter and formed the foundation for a myriad of structures whose purpose had long been forgotten. Exquisitely grained metamorphic rock, polished schist and marble established the boundaries on three sides, while the remaining edge overlooked a vast chasm—the axis around which the levels of the city spiraled, culminating at the Trinity temple. It was no coincidence that Hindu and Buddhist philosophies had established thirteen levels of existence in the universe. The abyss—the lowest level—was remembered in the collective human consciousness as unlucky thirteen. Or simply as Hell.

The apex of the dome was crowned with a sheet of white quartz, likewise refined to glassy smoothness, which radiated a faint illumination. Mira had seen the crystal in vision, shining with near solar brilliance as it amplified the Trinity's energy to provide light and heat to the city's inhabitants, but now there was only a hint of that former glory silhouetting the tallest towers, which vanished altogether as she activated a chemical lightstick. Her field of view shrank to the reach of the greenish tube, a sphere of light roughly thirty feet across.

She took off at a sprint, angling away from the wide promenade that skirted the edge of the chasm and moved into the heart of the city. Her psychic familiarity with the subterranean metropolis allowed her to navigate the labyrinthine streets with a surety that she hoped would give her an advantage over Tarrant. At the very least, she would be less vulnerable to sniper fire here in the narrow footpaths, than on the broad walkway at the edge of the terrace.

She remembered the city's genesis as if she had actually lived through the centuries of its development, and its mysteries were second nature to her. The ascending tiers grew progressively smaller as they rose, in keeping with the social order established by the original Trinity kings. Sheer walls nearly two hundred feet high separated each terrace, and the only way to pass from one to the next was a stairway, situated in a temple at the base of each platform. Agarthan citizens endeavoring to reach the next level had to study for years—even an entire lifetime—in order to learn the carefully guarded secret that would unlock the temple gate and permit passage to the next level.

Because she had touched the Trinity, Mira intuitively knew the solution to each of those puzzles. She also knew that there was no other way to make that transition. The stairways were a natural choke point, and if Tarrant was planning an ambush, she would be most vulnerable there. Because there was nothing she could do to alter that fact, Mira put her faith in her guns and in herself, and entered the first temple.

Tarrant's group had attained the fourth level of the city before Mira's arrival prompted the grave robber to divide his forces. While Tarrant pressed on toward his appointment with destiny, Turner led his party of hired guns back along the esplanade to the head of the stairs leading up from the third stage. He also recognized that the stairs would be the ideal place to catch their prey, but where was the fun in that?

"Boys, I'm in the mood for a little hunting. What do you

say we run this bitch down?" He grabbed one of his subordinates by the arm. "Wait here. If, by some miracle, she makes it past us, take her out."

The man nodded and dropped down into a prone firing position, bracing the stock of his AR-15 semi-automatic rifle against his shoulder as he propped himself up on his elbows. He peered through the M-64 holographic close-quarters combat sight, following the progress of Turner and the other gunmen with the targeting dot as they proceeded down the long staircase and out of his view.

The young mercenary felt a twinge of jealousy as he watched them go; why had he been the unlucky choice to remain behind? Still, he reasoned, Mira Raiden had proven to be a pretty resourceful adversary. Maybe she would make it past them, giving him a chance to make the kill shot. He smiled in eager anticipation and flipped off the safety.

Even if his attention had not been transfixed upon the stairwell, he still might have failed to notice the figure creeping through the darkness to his rear. So swiftly and silently did it steal upon him, at no time did the hunter realize that he had become the hunted, and when the attack came, there was not even time for him to scream.

The only sound in the darkness was the crunching of bones.

The first puzzle was a simple reading test. At the foundation of Agarthan society—as with many civilizations that would follow—there had existed a caste of laborers; some would have called them slaves. Although it was not explicitly forbidden, no effort was made to educate those who dwelt on the lowest level of the city. If any desired to better themselves, to reach the next step, they would first have to learn to read. The key to unlocking the gate that guarded the stairway was the ability to comprehend a question, carved in the hieroglyphic language of Agartha. Surrounding the gate were dozens of tiles marked with similar glyphs. Some were actual words, others nonsensical lines, and only by selecting the tiles that correctly answered the question could an aspirant gain the freedom to move to a better life on the next terrace.

Mira did not have to study the characters to render an interpretation. Her knowledge of Agarthan evolution included an intrinsic familiarity with its language, both written and spoken. The question roughly translated as: "What is the source of life?" The answer, she knew, was "the Mother." She quickly located the tiles that spelled out that answer in the tongue of the ancient ones, and pressed each one into the wall. Deep inside the stone, an ancient lock mechanism opened, and a system of counterweights caused the stone gate to rise like a portcullis. Breathing anxiously, Mira ducked under the solid slab as it slid into a recess and charged toward the stairs beyond.

Her enemies were not lying in wait on the landing above, but she did not take much comfort in this fact. The long climb had left her exhausted and she slowed her running pace down to a tortured walk. She paused on the final step, observing the second level of the city in the green-tinged glow of her chemlight as she struggled to catch her breath. Because she was underground, it was easy to forget that she was more than five thousand meters—roughly three miles—above sea level, much higher than the mountain in South America where Mann had built his stronghold. The altitude thinned the air, making every sort of exertion into an ordeal, and could even cause fatal swelling in the pulmonary system and the brain. Mira drew scarce comfort from the knowledge that her enemies were confronting the same conditions. She very much doubted that Tarrant would feel any sort of distress. Forcing down a copious amount of water from her canteen, she headed for the next gate.

This level of the city, like the first, was given over to rather ordinary and featureless architecture. Literacy represented only a small step in the order of Agartha, elevating those on the second stage more in a physical sense than a social one. The only real difference she noted was that the broad step upon which those unremarkable buildings sat was about one third smaller than the first. It took her only a few minutes to catch a glimpse of the pagoda roof of the gate temple towering over the rest of the blockish edifices. Heartened by her progress, she increased her pace.

Suddenly, a loud cracking noise began to reverberate across the abyss. Mira recognized it instantly as gunfire—distant, but unmistakable. Reflexively, she dropped into a crouch, flipping her chemical flare away as she drew her Desert Eagle. Because she had no idea where the shots had originated, she turned on her heel, one leg extended for balance, and scanned for a target. A movement, just a shadow suddenly projected in the glow of the discarded chem-light, caught her eye, and she swiveled toward its source, triggering the enormous Magnum.

The gun barked in the stillness, spitting flame and brass, and bucked wildly in her grip. Mira walked her fire toward the place where she thought the shadow's caster had stood, and caught a glimpse of something scrambling through the darkness. A tortured squeal reached her ears over the ringing noise of the shots, and she knew her bullets had wounded more than just the slumbering stone.

Something moved behind her—she felt its presence more as a premonition than anything else—and she twisted around to meet this new threat. Her intuition saved her life, but the warning came a moment too late. A heavy, indistinguishable shape bowled into her and sent her sprawling. The impact jarred loose the grip of her left hand and knocked the breath from her lungs, but she retained her right handed hold on the weapon and brought it to bear. The pistol spoke again as she pumped the trigger.

There was another howl, much closer, and in the muzzle flash, Mira could see the outline of the assailant that rushed toward her. Her shots, at point blank range, could not have missed, but the shrieking behemoth did not relent. She tried to roll out of the way, even as she emptied the pistol, but again she was a split second too slow. The lumbering shape crashed into her and pinned her to the stone floor.

The impact further stunned her, and for a moment she could mount no defense against the flurry of blows or the scratching of claw-like fingers against her extremities. But the assault weakened and ceased almost as soon as it had begun. Mira felt the splash of hot arterial blood soaking through her clothes as the quivering mass of her attacker became motionless, his full weight settling upon her.

As the odor of burnt cordite began to dissipate, Mira felt the full force of the aggressor's stench, both in life and death, and knew that the hulking shape did not belong to anything remotely human.

The sound of continuous gunfire in the distance reminded her that the peril had not passed, but now at least she understood the reason for the shooting; her enemies were doing battle with the same creatures she had just fought. She couldn't find it in her heart to pity the loser of the outcome, but a twinge of concern for the catatonic DiLorenzo crept to the surface. She doubted anyone in Tarrant's party would raise a hand in his defense against the strange creatures.

Pushing and squirming from beneath the heavy, motionless carcass, she managed to free herself. She immediately slammed a fresh magazine into the pistol and swept the area for a new target, keeping low behind the corpse of the slain beast. Nothing.

Relaxing her guard only a little, she studied the form of the creature that had attacked her.

It was unquestionably primate, but larger even than the mountain gorillas of Central Africa. The simian face, fixed in a snarl upon death, resembled the fierce features of a baboon, but its pelt was a shaggy mass of orange and black stripes, now streaked with dark blood. Mira knew exactly what it was.

No concrete proof of their existence had ever surfaced, but more than a few credible sightings had been recorded, even in the modern age. Its name was taken from two words in the language of the Sherpas: *Yah*, meaning rock, and *Teh*, or animal. It was a name given to creatures that existed in the legends of the Himalayas for as long as anyone could remember; demons that left the abyss to walk among men, ravaging their herds and frightening children.

She had killed a *yeti*.

Hefting the pistol in both hands, she walked backwards until she had a building directly behind her. The presence of the yeti was not something the Trinity had prepared her for. At no point in the vision of Agartha's genesis that she had experienced, did these legendary creatures make an appearance. Their origin lay in some other niche of history or evolution. Yet at some point, the species had found its way into the chasm deep beneath Everest. Perhaps the great cavern had not been completely sealed after all.

The significance of it was not lost on her, and she wondered what other surprises lay in store.

As she skirted along the perimeter of the building, then darted across a narrow avenue to put yet another structure at her back, she had the nagging suspicion that there was something else about the encounter with the yeti that had escaped her notice. She heard sporadic gunfire, presumably from the next level of the city, but was not herself attacked again. It was only as she entered the pagoda, triggering the tiles to answer a second, more difficult question and open the next gate that she realized what she had been missing.

The yeti had free run of the city. In the visitation she had shared with DiLorenzo, the security of each level had been absolute. Even now, the mechanisms that guarded the stairwells were active. It was highly improbably that the ape-like creatures had randomly solved the riddles in order to come and go as they pleased. There had to be another way to reach the upper levels, and anything that might give her the edge in her race to intercept Tarrant was worth pursing. She turned from the open portal and made her way back into the streets.

She retraced her steps to the place where she had fought the giant beast. It still lay where it had fallen, undisturbed by others of its species. Mira did not approach but instead walked in a wide circle, scrutinizing the smooth street surface underfoot in the glow of her chemical light. She soon found what she was looking for: a spray of red slowly drying on the glassy floor. A few steps away, she saw a scattering of drops—the blood of the first yeti she had fired at and only wounded. Maintaining constant vigilance with the Desert Eagle drawn and ready, she followed the spatters that marked the trail of the injured yeti's retreat.

The path veered sharply away from the route she had taken

to the stairwell, leading directly toward the massive overhanging cliff on the side of the tier opposite the chasm. As she drew close to the imposing stone embankment, she observed another instance where her familiarization with the city had been incomplete. The solid wall of rock was not solid after all. Imperfections in the rock, seismic fractures, and erosion from subterranean streams and glacial melt, evidently occurring after the abandonment of Agartha, had left the massif a veritable Swiss cheese of natural tunnels. The metamorphic rock—sandstone transformed by the heat and pressure of continental collisions—was riddled with holes, some no more than pockmarks, but others large enough for her to stand in. The trail of blood led directly into one.

Mira hesitated. The wounded yeti would likely flee to its lair, but was that where she wanted to go?

"Let's be logical about this," she murmured, barely aware of her own voice. It made sense that the creatures would dwell in the lower reaches of the massive cavity. Even underground, the air was thin at higher altitudes. Moreover, the plenitude of sightings of the so-called Abominable Snowman near populated areas seemed to confirm that the yeti had discovered a way out of the Agarthan cavern unknown to its original builders, and that exit was almost certainly in the depths below. Therefore, the route taken by the wounded beast would probably lead, not to the uppermost levels of the city, but down into the abyss.

She moved away from the tunnel, scanning the wall for another opening that bore the signs of continuous travel. Almost a hundred meters further down the wall she sound what she was looking for: a tiny niche at shoulder height that was littered with tufts of orange and black hair and smelled of animal excrement.

There was a scratching noise behind her and she whirled, the barrel of the Desert Eagle seeking a target. Something was moving near the corner of one structure, but it was clumsy and obvious. Over the pounding of her own heartbeat, Mira could hear labored breathing. It didn't sound like one of the yeti

A familiar figure abruptly stumbled into view. It was the hulking mercenary she had first seen in the sky above the New

York museum. His clothing was torn and soaked with blood, and there were streaks of red on his face like handprints. His eyes were wild and his head jerked spasmodically in every direction, searching the shadows as if fearful of an attack. He still clutched his AK-47, thrusting it forward randomly to engage targets that existed only in his imagination. When he squeezed the trigger, nothing happened. Either the weapon had jammed and the man had not attempted to correct the problem, or he had fired off all his ammunition. That he still lived after an encounter with the fierce ape-like beasts suggested the latter.

Mira lifted her own weapon, unsure of what sort of threat the traumatized mercenary presented. The motion caught his eye and he swung the assault rifle toward her. "You." He spat the word of recognition disdainfully. He was not as incoherent as she had first believed.

"I don't believe I've had the pleasure," she replied warily, her finger ready on the trigger. It had not escaped her notice that the man had not actually attempted to fire the empty weapon at her, and she wondered if it might not be possible to reach through his delirium to find an ally. "I'm sure you know my name, but I didn't catch yours."

The man seemed mildly surprised at her forbearance. "It's Turner."

Mira nodded. "Well, Mr. Turner, it looks to me like your employer isn't paying you quite enough."

He laughed humorlessly. "That's for damn sure."

There was movement in the shadows behind him, but Mira kept her stare fixed on the mercenary. "Maybe it's time you rethought your loyalties."

"And work for you? Think you can pay more?" His tone was insincere, as if he was merely curious.

"You don't actually believe Walter will reward you," she countered. "If you stick with him, you'll end up like Montero."

"The Nazi? Hah. He deserved what he got."

"Maybe," Mira conceded. "But men like Walter don't make a habit of keeping their promises."

"You don't get it, lady." Turner advanced a step, a hint of menace twisting his visage. "When he gets what he's after, he's going to be top dog. King of the world."

"That will never happen," she replied, her tone flat and certain.

"You think you can stop him?" Turner moved forward again, his intent beyond question. "That's what ain't going to happen."

The shadows stirred again. Mira extended her pistol, the muzzle aimed directly at his right eye. "Are you sure you won't reconsider?"

Turner did not stop, but as he took another step, he let the spent Kalashnikov rifle fall to the ground. "You won't shoot an unarmed man."

She didn't argue his assertion. "I won't have to."

The yeti began moving as soon as the AK-47 rattled to the ground, crossing the distance in a flash. Turner saw the flicker of movement in Mira's eyes. He did not comprehend that her statement was not a threat, but rather a warning, until it was too late. The charging creature scooped up the fallen weapon and swung it like a club. There was a sickening crunch as the wooden stock made contact with the mercenary's shaved skull. In a frenzy of bloodlust, the simian ignored Mira and continued pummeling Turner's motionless corpse.

She pulled herself up into the tunnel, distancing herself from the carnage, but did not turn her back on the preoccupied yeti until it was no longer visible. "I'm sorry we couldn't work something out," she said under her breath, and then hurried down the passage.

SIXTEEN

The tunnel was nearly vertical in some places, like a chimney, and Mira had to brace herself against the narrow sides in order to make upward progress. She found this encouraging, however, for as long as she was going up, she was moving closer to her goal. After what seemed an eternity of climbing and crawling, she came to an opening that overlooked a higher portion of the subterranean kingdom.

It took her only a moment to recognize where she was—the eighth level of the city. The terrace was considerably smaller than the first two. Only a select few ever gained access to the highest levels of Agartha. The disc-shaped shelf was only a few hundred meters across, and occupied only by a single, palatial structure. Situated closer to the crystal light source, the floor of the terrace had at one time been cultivated into a magnificent garden, but centuries in the dark, scoured by the winds rushing up from the chasm, had left it as barren as the rest of the underground empire.

The eighth level had been the secular capital of Agartha. The citadel had served as an administrative headquarters, overseeing the day-to-day needs of the population on the seven tiers below, and also housed the highest court to which the citizens might appeal for justice. Only the three Trinity bearers, who resided on the tenth level, held greater authority, but they were rarely bothered to resolve civil disputes.

The transition to the ninth level established the segregation between the worldly and mystical spheres of Agarthan culture. Although essentially living in a theocracy, with absolute power in the hands of their spiritual leaders, the residents of the underground kingdom, for the most part, had little interest in religious mysteries. The ninth terrace housed a seminary where an elite few studied the power of the Trinity and debated the true nature of the figure known only as the Wise Father. As an additional security measure, the means to unlock the gates leading to the tenth and eleventh levels, the eleventh tier being itself the final gate, were known only to the three.

Mira recalled all these details in the few seconds it took for her to pull herself from the narrow cleft and descend spider-like to the floor below. She scanned the open floor, searching both for signs of yeti and Tarrant. Her heart sank when she saw movement in the shadows above, on the ninth level. Her gamble to beat the old grave robber to the Trinity temple had been in vain; Tarrant was within final striking distance of his objective.

Despite the rarefied atmosphere, she took off at a sprint and crossed the distance to the unsecured entrance to the palace complex. Although the corridors and courtyards seemed as familiar to her as the buildings of the Farm complex where she had been raised, she found herself hesitating at each junction. The thin air was causing her to feel disoriented and slowing her reflexes.

She paused before the ornate gateway that guarded the next ascension, trying to calm her racing heart and jangled nerves. At this level, the temples and their security mechanisms were not simply locks that kept out the uninitiated, but also traps designed to punish those who did not correctly grasp the mysteries of Agartha and its rulers.

Once more, the means to unlock the gate was found in a series of tiles and a question requiring an exact answer. Without her intimate knowledge of the city and its rulers, Mira could not have begun to guess at the correct solution, much less understood the riddle. So alien was the culture and lifestyle of the hidden city that there was no frame of reference in the modern world. She did not waste the mental energy trying to fathom what she read, but simply selected the appropriate tiles and waited for the gate to rise.

By the time she reached the top of the stairway, she could see three figures moving along the next flight of steps, advancing to the tenth level. She couldn't make out individual features. If she had been able to, she might have tried shooting Tarrant at a distance, despite the questionable accuracy of a pistol at that range. But DiLorenzo was almost certainly one of those distant shapes, and she wasn't ready to risk killing him to stop her foe. Not yet, at least.

She was gaining on them—of that she was sure—but there was no way to tell whether she would be able to intercept Tarrant before he reached the Trinity temple. The small trio was not moving rapidly, but their destination was already within reach. The remaining tiers of city were the smallest yet, requiring only a few minutes of walking from one side to the next. She lost sight of them as she negotiated the passageways through the Agarthan seminary to the gateway shrine, and by the time she set foot onto the next flight of stairs, Tarrant and the others had already moved onto the tenth level.

Prior to dividing their kingdom, the three members of the triumvirate had chosen to make their permanent home two steps below the crystal pagoda, in a mansion that occupied the entire breadth of the terrace. The enormous structure was primarily utilitarian; the Trinity wielders had no need to impress their subordinates by displaying an opulent lifestyle. In fact, very few citizens ever saw the palace where Sham'b'Alla, Le'Mu and Atl'an ate and slept. None of those few who did would recognize that the manor had been hewn from living stone according to a very familiar pattern. Mira instantly recognized the circular layout, with three crystalline spires spaced equidistantly around the perimeter, in an enormous representation of the joined Trinity.

The stairs to the next level rose directly from the center of the palace, spiraling around a pillar of quartz crystal. She could easily distinguish Tarrant from his daughter and DiLorenzo, halfway up the flight and advancing at a steady pace. Without hesitating, she sighted down the barrel of the Desert Eagle, tracking the undulating motion of his head for a few seconds, then squeezed the trigger.

The gun thundered in her hands, the recoil traveling up her arms to buffet her torso. At the same instant, she saw Tarrant's head snap sideways as an equivalent amount of kinetic energy was delivered in the form of a .45 slug, and he disappeared from her view. She recovered her stance before the last echoes of the report fell silent and drew a bead on Rachel Aimes, but before she could fire, the blond woman ducked for cover. DiLorenzo stood in place, unmoving.

A moment later, the stubby barrel of Rachel's PDW protruded from the edge of the stairs and unleashed a random burst. The shots gouged chips of marble from the palace roof but were otherwise ineffectual. Mira nevertheless sought concealment before answering the volley with a single well-placed shot that grazed the edge of the step where Rachel was hiding. The weapon disappeared as its shooter retreated.

Without warning, DiLorenzo turned on his heel and marched to the open edge of the spiral staircase. For a moment, Mira feared he might walk right off the precipice, but he came to an abrupt halt with the tips of his toes protruding out into space, and stood there, gently swaying.

"That wasn't a very nice thing to do, Mira." The detective spoke, but the voice was not his own.

Mira breathed a rare curse. That Tarrant had survived was unfortunate, but somehow not really surprising. All along she had suspected that the Trinity implanted in his chest would grant the old grave robber almost total invincibility. In order to beat him, she was going to have to separate him from the Trinity, and that would mean getting a lot closer.

"Careful who you shoot," chided Tarrant, using DiLorenzo like a ventriloquist's dummy.

She caught a glimpse of activity behind the enslaved policeman—Rachel Aimes, identifiable by her mane of lush, blonde hair, staying close to the inner limit of the stairway, but resuming the ascent. Mira couldn't see Tarrant, but it stood to reason that he was also on the move. DiLorenzo remained on the outer edge, but turned and began climbing as well, keeping pace with his captors and serving as a human shield.

Mira dashed from her place of concealment and hastened to the gate temple. Even here, in the heart of the Trinity bearers' residence, there was a security device to limit access to the uppermost levels. The gate was closed. The device had reset itself after Tarrant's passage. With almost automatic efficiency, she keyed the tiles to unlock the portal, and continued onward.

She raced up the spiral, taking two steps at a time, her head and heart pounding from the exertion at altitude. Dark spots began to float in front of her eyes, but she did not relent. If she lost this race . . .

As she neared the end of the flight, she ducked down to keep her head below the level of the floor for as long as possible. Then, when she could conceal herself no longer, she sprang forward, arched her body into a dive and tucked into a forward roll. Through the rush of blood in her head, she couldn't tell if anyone was shooting at her. As soon as her feet made contact with the quartz-tiled floor she took off running again, scanning for a target. It took her a moment to realize that the expected assault had not materialized. Still wary, she skidded to a halt and looked again.

This stage of Agartha's ascension was unlike any that preceded it. No one had ever lived here, and on the rare occasions when the three Trinity bearers visited, it was only in order to progress to the next stairway and the pagoda temple on the ultimate level. The eleventh tier of the city was nothing but a final gateway; the last test before a worthy initiate might enter the abode of an earth-shaking power.

Unlike the other levels, which had been hewn out of solid stone, the eleventh floor was an intricate machine, with numerous working parts. The floor was arranged in a grid of hexagonal spaces, each about three feet across, with the appearance of masonry tiles. At the center were three elephantine statues, which Mira immediately thought of as Sphinxes—bestial shapes poised like reclining lions, but with feminine faces—surrounding the gate controls. As before, one would have to enter the appropriate code in order to continue. Tarrant had evidently done so, for several of the hexagonal segments of the floor had risen in a chain to form the final flight of stairs leading up to the Trinity temple, and the undead grave robber was nearing the top.

Unhesitatingly, Mira charged toward the steps, heedless of any other threat. But even as her foot touched the first six-sided column, it began retreating back into the floor. She bounded to the next, then another, but the mechanically activated stairs were collapsing beneath her faster than she could run. As her boots touched the fifth step, that column began sinking. The next tread was chest high for a moment, but before she could vault up onto it, it also began settling. The step upon which she had halted dropped until it was flush with the rest of the floor and then stopped with a jarring thump. In a matter of seconds, the entire sequence of columns had returned to the original configuration, leaving her once more on the floor of the eleventh level. She caught another glimpse of Tarrant, standing on the final tier high above, gloating over his victory in the race.

She now became aware of DiLorenzo, no longer of any use to Tarrant, standing motionless at the center, as though imprisoned by the trio of sphinxes. Suspicious, Mira moved toward him, her gun aimed at his heart. If Tarrant could speak through the detective's mouth, what else was he capable of? She didn't want to have to kill him, but in the larger picture, his life was but one of billions that were now imperiled by her enemy's imminent victory.

DiLorenzo suddenly crumpled as if, puppet that he was, his strings had been cut. Rachel Aimes was standing directly behind him, her machine pistol aimed at Mira's heart.

Mira twisted to the left even as flame spat from the barrel of Rachel's gun. The report of the shot thundered an instant later, but the bullets had already sizzled through the air where Mira had been. Rachel's aim followed her, but Mira returned fire as she dove sideways, behind one of the massive sphinx statues.

Only when she was crouching defensively did Mira feel a stinging on her right upper arm where one of Rachel's shots had grazed her. The enemy had drawn first blood in a battle to the death. That was never a good omen.

She knew she had to keep moving, both to keep Rachel off guard, and to maintain her own momentum. Abandoning the solid cover of the statue, she rolled across several of the hexagonal tiles toward a second sphinx, taking pot shots at Tarrant's daughter. As she did, she caught a flash of gold— Rachel's hair—and corrected her aim, emptying the pistol as she completed the roll. She reloaded and was up and firing again almost instantly.

Overwhelmed by Mira's unflagging resistance, Rachel was

driven back. Like her foe, she attempted to use the statues for cover, but she was less agile than Mira and less able with her weapon. A constant barrage of slugs kept her moving when she should have been firing, and the few shots she did manage to get off were wildly off-target. When her magazine fed its last shell, she fumbled to reload. Mira seized the advantage, cutting a path away from the ring of statues to flank Rachel and pin her down. Suddenly fearful, for perhaps the first time in her life, Rachel threw the useless H&K pistol at Mira and ran.

Mira ducked reflexively, narrowly avoiding the projectile, and drew a bead on the blonde woman's retreating back. Rachel had a good head start and was weaving at random intervals, but Mira kept firing. At least one of her shots struck the mark, and Rachel staggered as she approached the edge of the terrace and then pitched forward, disappearing from sight.

Mira did not pause to savor the victory. Wheeling about, she raced past the sphinx guardians to the center of the level. DiLorenzo had not moved, but she could tell by the steady rise and fall of his chest that there was still life in him. His fate was important to her but not the highest of priorities. Reviving him, if that was in fact possible, would have to wait. She moved past him to the upraised dais and scanned the tiles for the sequence to activate the stairway.

The final code, like the others before, was burned in her memory. Through the fog of fluctuating adrenaline surges and altitude-induced fatigue, she could still see the hands of the original Trinity bearers as they tapped out the password that would raise the stair-like columns from the floor, while keeping the final security measure in a dormant state. Nevertheless, she moved with extreme caution, scrutinizing the writing to make sure she was seeing it correctly, before actually pushing the tiles.

There were nine characters in the ancient word, and as soon as she depressed the last one, she turned on her heel and raced for the first step, anxious to end Tarrant's fiendish scheme once and for all.

But nothing happened. The floor remained unchanged.

Tarrant's mocking laughter trickled down like gray rain. "Sorry, Mira. Had to change the locks. Hope you don't mind."

Mira felt her breath slip away as the old grave robber turned from his vantage high above and disappeared, eager to keep his appointment with destiny. He had beaten her, and there wasn't a thing she could do about it. Yet, it was not the fact of Tarrant's impending triumph that now left her virtually paralyzed with dread, but rather the distinctive sound of stone sliding on stone that signaled the activation of the intruder defense system.

SEVENTEEN

Mira had once tried to explain to DiLorenzo how the antediluvian cultures had been more technologically advanced than even modern society. She had witnessed ample evidence to support this statement, both in the simple mechanisms that regulated the gates at each level—really nothing more than the most basic applications of engineering: wedges and levers, pulleys and counterweights—and in the incomprehensible manifestations of the Trinity—psychic visions and the reanimation of dead corpses.

The latter phenomena were prime examples of the axiom that in a sufficiently advanced culture, science and sorcery would become indistinguishable. Though she could not explain it, Mira knew that everything she had witnessed derived from the advanced science of this forgotten civilization, knowledge that the Wise Father had passed along, and which was embodied in the relics, rather than mercurial whims of the gods and demons and of superstitious mythology. This afforded some small comfort; science, no matter how mind-boggling, still had certain incontrovertible rules. One of those rules established that for every agent, there was a reagent, an antidote to every poison.

In the simplest possible terms, the Trinity functioned by reorganizing atoms of carbon and other elements into molecular replicas of itself. In the argot of modern science, it created nano-machines. It communicated with these on an electromagnetic wavelength almost identical to human Beta waves—the nervous impulses generated by the brain during REM sleep, when dreams occur. A side effect of this was the psychic white noise, which interfered with the naturally occurring, but now for the most part, completely dormant psychic abilities of nearly every human being on earth. But sometimes the output was not white noise, and the Trinity could directly interface with a human mind, downloading its memory, as it had done with DiLorenzo and Mira in the Nazi redoubt. In the hands of a sentient user, this conduit for data transfer could be used for mind-control and even astral projection.

The Trinity was not itself sentient, but rather a computer with a default program, simple directives, foremost of which was self-preservation which, in the absence of an intelligent operator, was downloaded into the nano-machines. It was in this way that the Trinity could reanimate organic matter long after electro-chemical activity had ceased and cellular decay begun. While not changing the outward appearance of the transformed material, the molecule-sized computers networked together to take over the functions once controlled by the central nervous system of a living organism. It had done so for Mann, turning him into an undead automaton with a simple instinct to protect his piece of the Trinity, and it had done so for the man once known as Walter Aimes. In the case of the latter, enough of Tarrant's memories and personality traits had been preserved to give the impression that he had simply come back from the dead. In reality, that was not the case. Though he himself was not aware of the distinction, the old grave robber was in fact a walking mass of microscopic machinery.

The triumvirate, possessing a deeper grasp of the Trinity's functions, had used the talisman not only to carve out their kingdom, but also to protect it. The Trinity vision had advised Mira of the consequences of failing to unlock the security code to disengage each trap, nothing so mundane as spring-loaded scimitars or electrocution chambers. Despite the forewarning, she still experienced an instinctive incredulity as the last line of defense rumbled into action.

The three figures that guarded the center of the eleventh level of the underground city were not simply inanimate statues, but complex machines programmed to activate if someone attempted to access the pagoda without entering the appropriate keying sequence. Their response would be absolute. No opportunity to explain or apologize would be given.

The trio of sphinxes moved with a swiftness that belied their stony composition, but they remained slaves to their programming, unable to think spontaneously or predict the behavior of their prey. In the instant it took for them to turn and face her, she launched into motion, springing away from their gaze.

In mythology, there were abundant tales of creatures able to strike a person dead with a single glance, but those legendary gorgons and basilisks were in actuality based on ancestral memories of these ancient devices. In her peripheral vision, Mira could see the crystal eyes of the sphinxes, glowing brightly as they released a constant stream of amplified light. Though invisible to the human eye, the streams of focused brilliance could cut through living tissue like a surgeon's scalpel. If one of those needle-thin beams touched her, death would be instantaneous.

There was a weakness in the program, however, which she was quick to exploit. The sphinxes did not track their targets visually; their eyes served only as emitters for the laser-type weapons. In fact, the three animated statues were not independent at all, but linked to the same operating system that monitored the gate devices and had enabled Tarrant to raise the stairway columns out of the floor. It was no accident that the surface of the eleventh level had been arranged in a grid of perfect hexagonal tiles. Each cell was a pressure sensitive mat which now served to alert the security system to her location. Only by staying in constant motion, running in broad circles, could Mira hope to avoid the deadly stare of the guardians.

The sphinxes did not simply turn their heads to follow her, but also began moving from tile to tile like pieces on a chessboard, trying to trap the opponent's queen. Their movements were predictable but their pursuit was tireless, and Mira could feel fatigue settling into her limbs after only a few seconds of running. It was time, she decided, for the queen to go on the attack.

She circled wide, drawing the pack into a tight group then cut toward their flank. The abrupt maneuver put two of the guardians momentarily out of the picture, blocked by the third. As it pivoted toward her, she fired at its humanoid visage. The large caliber bullets struck like hammers, chipping at the stony face, but ricocheted away, seemingly without causing anything but cosmetic damage. The sphinxes did not relent.

Mira didn't either. Correcting her aim, she fired again and again until one of the lights winked out, then the other.

For a moment, the sphinxes seemed to hesitate as their collective programming sought to interpret this unexpected development. The disabled unit broke away from the others and veered toward the center, away from Mira and out of the way of the other two.

Mira shifted her aim toward the nearest of the remaining pair, and without stopping, unloaded into its face. As she hastened to replace the spent magazine, she noted with satisfaction that a second set of deadly eyes had been blinded.

She made another sudden turn and angled toward the now impotent sphinx, keeping it between her and the last fully operational defender. Even as the defanged guardian tried to get out of the way, Mira targeted the head of the last sphinx and opened fire. Round after round slammed into the carved countenance, blasting away chips of stone and shattering the delicate network of crystals that formed the matrix for the laser-like weapon.

As the brilliance vanished, Mira skidded to a halt and fought to catch her breath. The guardian shook its head as though actually feeling the pain of a wound, then swung its deformed face toward the tile where she had come to rest. It was the first time she had actually looked directly at one of the sphinx-like automatons since their waking, and she was mildly surprised by the attention to detail its craftsmen had employed. But for the vacant area, where her bullets had chewed away the eyes to reveal scarred stone, she might easily have believed it to be a living thing. The smooth face undulated like flesh as the lips curled into a fierce grimace. She heard the scrape of stone moving against stone behind her as the rest of the trio fixed her location and began walking toward her. Only then did Mira realize that the battle was far from won.

Tarrant did not linger to watch the results of his tampering with the gate mechanism. Whether Mira somehow succeeded in defeating the ancient booby trap mattered little now. Even if she triumphed, the pagoda on the twelfth level was literally beyond her reach.

He had experienced a strange pang on witnessing the demise of his adopted daughter. It occurred to him that he ought to have felt something more; grief perhaps, or rage at Mira for having been the instrument of her death. It was the total absence of emotion that troubled him more than any sense of loss.

What have I become? He wondered. *What will I become?*

Turning away from his vantage, he strode toward the massive edifice that solely occupied the ultimate level of the subterranean empire. Although there was an obvious similarity to the architecture of the many Oriental cultures that had followed the abandonment of Agartha, there was an unmistakable element of pyramid design in the high, vaulted roof of the structure. Tarrant was certain that the design had more to do with functionality than aesthetics.

The talisman he carried had been reacting to the proximity of the temple for some time. In fact, from the moment he had used it to unlock the gate near Rongbuk monastery, it had been trembling with anticipation of its return to the temple. He was envious of its absolute sense of purpose. It seemed that with each passing day since his resurrection, he found it harder and harder to tap into the passions which had propelled him through an entire life spent searching for this very place, for this very moment.

There had been times when the thirst for revenge had abated. Although he had ever been grooming Rachel, the only one of his many surrogate daughters that he actually brought into his life, to be his strong right arm in a grand, if ill-defined scheme, to locate Mann's lost U-boat, he had grown to love the role of father more than he expected. But always the embers of the vow, made the day of Mann's act of betrayal, smoldered in his heart, and when Mira Raiden called him from the Panamanian jungle, describing her discovery of an Atlantean refuge city and the existence of the Trinity, he knew the time had finally arrived.

But now, at the moment of triumph, his obsession fled

him. He still understood the purpose that had brought him here, but could not wake the slumbering rage that gave it meaning.

Don't question it, he told himself. *You know what to do, just let it happen.*

Beneath the towering apex, the altar was a featureless hexagon of crystal. He was drawn to it, as iron to a magnet, and without being fully aware of his actions, extended the hand that held the two joined pieces of the Trinity until the relic was directly over its center. The white quartz slab began to shimmer, pulsing in time with the light from the twin gemstones mounted in the talisman. There was a gentle tugging, as though an unseen hand was trying to take it from him, and he relaxed his grip. Immediately, the Trinity flipped horizontal and hovered directly above the altar. He felt a similar tugging in his chest, but it soon relented, and he understood that his mere proximity was enough to satisfy the requirements of the Shrine's ancient architects. The entire mountain seemed to come to life, as if a missing fuse had been restored to close a long dormant circuit.

This is the moment I've lived my life for, Tarrant thought. *Revenge against the offspring of those who betrayed me . . . And I can't for the life of me remember what it was I wanted to do.*

He knew he had only to give shape to his desires—to merely imagine a thing, and it would happen—but that simple action proved elusive. Retribution was purely an intellectual concept with no underlying emotion to incite him to bring the desire to fruition.

Don't think about it. Let it happen.

He put his hands out over the tabular surface and felt the amplified energy, like a mild electrical shock, dancing across his undead fingertips. Then he let himself fall forward until his palms made contact with the altar.

For a moment, he thought he might come apart, that the power surging through his limbs might rend him to atoms. But because his resurrected flesh was also a manifestation of Trinity technology he endured, and after an instant of unspeakable pain, was lucid once more.

"Vengeance is mine!" he roared, his words reverberating

throughout the hollow mountain like a peal of thunder.

Then nothing.

He instantly felt foolish for having the audacity to speak the words attributed to God himself. *How droll*, he thought. *How cliché. The question is: what are you going to do about it?*

He searched his memory, trying to find a better answer. It was one thing to have the intent to ravage the world, but quite another to become the architect of such ruin. There was only one event in his frame of reference that seemed to correspond to what he had planned for so many decades, and he drew his inspiration from the words of the man who had made it all possible. The quote, attributed to J. Robert Oppenheimer, the lead scientist in the development of the first atomic bomb, was itself a paraphrase from another holy book, the *Bhagavad Gita*, in reference to the Hindu deity Vishnu, and it was that mythic figure, rather than the mushroom cloud of the Manhattan Project, that entered Tarrant's thoughts as he repeated Oppenheimer's words: "I am become Death, the destroyer of worlds."

The Trinity harmonized with the image in his mind and instantly complied, transforming his flesh into the thing he had always believed he wanted to be.

Oh, yes. Now I remember.

Mira felt the tremors of Tarrant's transformation and knew that the race was over and her enemy had won. Yet she was still alive, and while there was life, there was hope.

She rolled forward, evading the rush of the nearest sphinx as deftly as a bullfighter, and brought her gun to bear. The guardian's momentum carried it past her, exposing its rear to gunfire, but the incessant stream of bullets had little effect. The animated statue lumbered about for another pass, even as the other two began to careen in her direction.

Because of their mass, the sphinxes' attempts to run her down were not unlike being chased by automobiles. Once their momentum was invested in a charge, there was little they could do to alter course in response to her evasive tactics. Yet despite her agility, she was at a severe disadvantage. She could not run forever, and even if she could, it would matter little. Tarrant was minutes, or perhaps only seconds, from laying the world to waste.

She saw that the creatures had lined up for a concerted attack, with two moving in from one side and the third intending to pass between them from the opposite direction. It was a clever strategy; no matter which way she tried to run, at least one of the sphinxes would be able to veer off and stomp her into oblivion. Whatever artificial intelligence guided the guardians, it was, like an advanced chess computer, learning from its mistakes.

I can learn, too, Mira thought, holstering her pistol and facing the lone sphinx moving in from her right side. She started running, aiming herself directly at the rampaging figure. It was only about twenty yards away and would close that distance in a matter of seconds, but it abruptly slowed in response to Mira's sudden offensive, while the pair from behind her increased their speed, still trying to time the precise moment of their engagement. It was exactly what she had hoped they would do.

Instead of trying to dodge the triple-headed charge, Mira maintained her head-on collision course with the lone sphinx, forcing it to slow to what was barely a walking pace. She could feel the vibrations of the remaining guardians as they drew closer from behind, but they were of little concern. If she did not change her course, they would pass by without touching her.

The sphinx seemed to grow larger with its approach. She had not been quite so close to one of them since the battle had started. Her timing would have to be perfect. At the last possible moment, she made her move, not left or right, but up, jumping as high as she could to plant her foot on its breast.

If the charging guardian had been moving any faster, the transfer of kinetic energy at the moment of impact would have broken her bones. As it was, the shock that traveled through the soles of her feet, jarring her entire body, felt like a parachute landing, and she had to struggle to keep her balance as she continued moving.

Her own momentum nearly carried her all the way over,

and she had to throw herself flat on the sphinx's broad back into order avoid crashing back down onto the floor. She spread her arms and legs wide to stabilize herself against the violent tremors of the monster's ponderous movements.

Confusion overcame the sphinxes. Their enemy had effectively vanished, but the collective consciousness that governed them reasoned that she still had to be there somewhere. As the creatures milled about aimlessly, it began analyzing the input from the pressure sensitive floor pads, trying to figure out where Mira had gone.

She didn't doubt that the guardians would eventually realize that one of them was marginally heavier than the others, but then getting off the game board was only the first step in her hasty plan. Her bullets had done little more than tickle the stony creatures, but there were other weapons in her arsenal. She delved into her backpack and brought out the grenade launcher.

The other two sphinxes had passed by in the instant of her leap, and had continued some distance before slowing and commencing a sort of holding pattern. She took aim at the most distant of the pair. They were both closer than she would have liked, perhaps too close. The fuze mechanism of the grenades required them to travel a minimum of ten meters before arming. Still, there was no guarantee that the explosive would go off at such close quarters. Of course, if it did, the shock wave from the detonation might very well kill her.

Nobody lives forever, she thought mordantly, and pulled the trigger.

As the spherical bomb hurtled toward its intended target, Mira rolled sideways and dropped back onto the floor. All three guardians abruptly ceased moving and swung their heads in her direction. Then one of them ceased to exist.

The explosion shook the entire level, and reverberated down the chasm. A deadly hail of stone fragments radiated away from the blast, driven by a wall of air compressed to the hardness of concrete. The force knocked both of the surviving sphinxes down, and Mira felt as though she had been punched in the gut, even though she had taken cover at the last instant. For a moment, smoke occluded her view of the damage, but as it cleared, she saw an enormous crater where one of the guardians had stood. Before it could recover, she scrambled onto the back of the nearby sphinx and reloaded.

Two to go.

The thing Tarrant had become was only peripherally aware of what was occurring on the penultimate level below. The spider-web fractures that had crept up the stone walls, hinting at the possible collapse of the cavern, mattered little to it. Agartha was merely the womb from which it would be birthed in order to annihilate all life. If the mother did not survive, it was of little consequence.

The figurative pregnancy, however, had not quite come to term. The Trinity, in answer to his final directive, had begun augmenting that original shell, stripping raw material from the city walls and reorganizing it into a simulacrum of organic matter in order to feed the embryonic monstrosity.

He had grown. Already his bulk had filled the pagoda, splitting apart the weakened polygonal walls. Remarkably, the ruin of the temple did nothing to halt the metamorphosis. The relic had served merely as a catalyst, commencing the chain reaction, and was no longer necessary to the final outcome. But the volume of the structure's interior was not the limit of Tarrant's evolution; he was going to have to be a lot bigger if he wanted to rip lightning bolts from the sky in order to ravage entire continents. The transformation had barely begun.

A second sphinx disappeared in the aftermath of another high-explosive grenade. The orderliness of the eleventh tier was gone now, replaced by broken stone and blast craters. In addition to the shattered remains of the two guardians, large chunks of the ceiling and walls had crashed down onto the lattice of tiles, shattering the sensitive grid and effectively blinding the remaining sphinx. It meandered away from Mira and headed for the largest of these sensory voids, incorrectly reasoning that she must be hiding there. A moment later, a chunk of rock the size of a pick-up truck dislodged from somewhere overhead and erased it from existence. The impact caused a ripple effect, and the floor beneath Mira's feet pitched and rolled, throwing her about like so much refuse.

Although the peril of the guardians was gone, Mira would have preferred that to the danger she now faced. The collapse of the cavern was a random game of chance, and it would take only one unlucky moment to end her life. She recognized that her grenades had contributed the geological instability, but knew that there were other factors at work. She didn't even have to look to know that something Tarrant had done with the Trinity was tearing Agartha apart.

DiLorenzo had not moved since his collapse. Mira sprinted to the center area where he lay and knelt at his side. "Wake up, sleepy head."

He shifted in response to her insistent prodding, but did not stir. She frowned and drew back her arm to slap him. Before she could deliver the blow, however, a sudden impulse prompted her to lower her hand and dip her head down until they were face to face. "Let's try this first, sleeping beauty."

Her lips met his, and for a moment he remained as unresponsive as a department store mannequin. Then his eyes flew open and he jerked away involuntarily, his sleep-dimmed eyes squinting to come into focus.

"Mira? Damn, did I pass out again?" He raised his head gingerly. "You changed your clothes. . . . Did you just kiss me?"

In spite of the urgency of their situation, she laughed. "I was afraid you hadn't noticed."

"Oh, I noticed. Remember, I'm a detective. Powers of observation." He grinned. "I've been having the strangest dream. . . ."

His eyes darted past her and grew wide as he began to realize that he was no longer where he thought he was. "It wasn't a dream, was it?"

As if to underscore his revelation, a noise like a sonic boom rattled the cavern. The terrace that had previously been occupied by the pagoda split in two, with one half shearing away and sliding toward the next level down.

The slab that calved from the larger mass was itself the size of a small mountain, and if the sound of its tearing loose was loud, then there was no standard of comparison for the noise that accompanied its crash. Another undulating wave rippled across the floor, throwing tiles about like dust motes.

As the tremor rolled toward them, Mira threw her arms around a barely comprehending DiLorenzo and held him tight. The floor lifted beneath them, then abruptly dropped. Mira felt a sharp pain in her ribs, and for a moment, could not draw breath, but in the instant before their collision, she saw something else had descended from the twelfth level; a towering shape that moved independently of the avalanche of stone. Her glimpse lasted for only a heartbeat before a tremendous cloud of dust engulfed them, completely blinding her, but it was long enough for her to recognize the gigantic figure.

"No," she said, when the din subsided and the only sound she could hear was DiLorenzo coughing. "It's no dream. It's a nightmare."

EIGHTEEN

Though the creature he had become was only in its infancy, Tarrant had already grown to colossal proportions. He was now arguably the most massive living organism that had ever existed, surpassing the greatest whale in the ocean and even rivaling the tallest Sequoia redwood. The latter comparison seemed more appropriate to his anatomical structure, for his body no longer resembled anything mammalian. As he grew, trying to match the vision of Shiva he had imparted to the Trinity, his physiology raced to adapt. A human heart, with a volume of less than half a liter, could scarcely supply blood to the extremities of an entity that was now over three hundred feet in height, so it had to grow, bulging and stretching deep within the recessed hollow of his chest cavity. Likewise, in order to distribute essential oxygen and other nutrient through a circulatory system more than a thousand times longer than that of a normal human, his blood supply had to increase, and did so rapidly as his skeletal structure also expanded and changed in response to the new biological imperative.

The bipedal design which served Homo sapiens so well was impractical for this new life form. No less than six legs now sprouted like tree roots from the base of its towering trunk, spreading out like fingers to give it stability. Tarrant's head and face had all but disappeared, for the evolutionary alterations that were remaking the landscape of his body had caused little change in his brain, and therefore required no commensurate growth of the cranium. His eyes however had grown larger, migrating to the front of his torso, and beneath them two ragged nostril holes, covered by a thin membrane, pulsated with each gargantuan inhalation. His mouth was gone, because he no longer needed to eat or digest food for growth or sustenance. Instead, several brilliant tendrils of energy, like violet lightning bolts, coruscated from his body to atomize raw matter from the cavern floor and walls and transform it into the base material for his continuing regenesis. His redundant digestive tract had already atrophied and been assimilated by his reconfigured anatomy. Likewise, his organs for speech—a pitifully inefficient means of communication for a creature of his psychic puissance—had shriveled away.

The changes were not limited to the physical. His elevation to god-like status had wrought equivalent changes to his ego. Though cognizant of where he was and what had transpired in the journey to this pinnacle, he was only marginally aware of the two figures huddled on the floor below, covered in the dust of the city's ongoing collapse. They were as insignificant to him now as insects.

It had not yet crossed his elevated mind that some insects have a deadly sting.

DiLorenzo gaped in disbelief at the mountainous pillar of flesh that shifted ponderously across the shattered floor, certain that what he was witnessing was some kind of hallucination triggered by the choking cloud of dust or a lingering after-effect of his long catatonia. His credulity was further taxed when a series of loud explosions occurred right beside him. Mira was shooting at the thing.

"What are you doing?"

She didn't look away from her target, but shouted her answer through clenched teeth as the Desert Eagle rocked in her grip, spitting lead at the monstrosity's eyes. "Everything I can!"

The bullets seemed to have no effect on the creature, vanishing into the black orbs like rocks thrown into the ocean, but as Mira paused to reload, a thundering voice resonated inside their heads. "Still here, Mira?"

"You didn't think you'd get rid of me that easily?" she shouted back, and resumed firing.

Tarrant gave an apathetic grunt then pivoted his tremendous bulk so that his eyes were no longer exposed. Six tentacle-like protrusions unfurled from the crown of his trunk. Each ended in an over-sized, but in every other way perfectly recognizable, human hand. Electricity arced between the fingertips as the arms fanned out, then leapt out in a blinding discharge against the sheer wall of the cavern. The sound of lightning, ionizing the atmosphere, was as loud as a jet engine.

"What the hell is he doing?" shouted DiLorenzo, shading his eyes.

"He's tunneling! Trying to get out!" She stared at the gun in her hand, her mind racing to form a strategy for fighting the towering creature. Tarrant, or whatever he had become, was still a living thing and as such could be killed. Marquand Atlas, wielding a piece of the Trinity in the Panamanian tomb, had gone down from a single bullet wound. Yet, even when her former benefactor had walked on two legs, a round from the Desert Eagle had barely tickled him. She would need something a lot bigger if she was going to take him down.

She holstered the pistol and reached for her backpack. Her fingers found the grenade launcher she had used against the guardians, but she kept digging until her hand closed around a larger cylindrical object. "This will do," she murmured, too softly for even her own ears to hear.

DiLorenzo did not recognize the weapon until she folded down the handgrips and pulled out a second tube telescoped within the first. It was something he had seen only in movies, a single-use missile launcher. Mira raised the device to her shoulder and took aim. Before pulling the trigger, she glanced over at him. "Better get down."

Startled out of his dumbfounded paralysis, he dropped to the floor and covered his head in the very instant that she pulled the trigger. The dry chemical propellant in the rocket motor ignited with an explosion that was itself like a bomb going off. DiLorenzo felt the percussive slap in the pit of his stomach, and for a moment thought that the warhead had detonated. He raised his head in time to see the projectile streaking toward the Tarrant-thing, trailing a finger of white smoke and a wave of blistering heat. Before he could cover-up a second time, the missile completed its journey.

To his surprise, the warhead did not erupt on impact. Instead, the arrow-shaped rocket pierced the skin of the colossus and kept going. DiLorenzo's dismay was short-lived, however. A second detonation, mostly felt rather than seen, shook the cavern as the high-explosive payload was triggered a millisecond after contact.

A pillar of smoke, like a seventh arm, erupted from the creature's trunk as a section of living tissue the size of a freight train engine was vaporized deep within. Simultaneously, a telepathic screech rattled through DiLorenzo's head, and he realized that for better or worse, Tarrant had finally noticed them.

The monster whipped around, its orbs blazing with fury. Centered below the eyes was a dark wound like a gaping maw, a crater of scorched tissue and shattered bones that seemed to reach all the way through the huge beast. Yet despite the severity of the trauma and the torrent of blood that now cascaded onto the floor below, Tarrant's presence was undiminished. There was more rage than pain in his strident disembodied outcry. "Oh, Mira. Now you've done it!"

Mira threw the spent rocket tube away. "Run!"

Since he didn't know which way to go, DiLorenzo chose to follow her lead. His head instantly began pounding as he ran, but a surge of adrenaline pushed him through the effort. In the corner of his eye, he saw something descending—one of the creature's humongous arms—to smash them into oblivion. Insect-like, they scurried from the path of destruction in the nick of time, and felt a blast of displaced air at their backs an instant before impact. The ground pitched beneath their feet as a tremor rippled out from beneath Tarrant's open palm.

Mira kept running, but glanced over one shoulder both to check on DiLorenzo and to determine where the next blow might fall. At the same time, she reviewed the options that now remained. The LAW missile had been the most powerful weapon in her arsenal, and while it had done a considerable amount of damage, her enemy was nowhere near defeated.

Another of Tarrant's hands began to fall just ahead of them, as if the mutated titan was trying to anticipate their movements. Mira cut hard to the left, adjusting course at the last possible second to avoid the crushing strike. DiLorenzo almost missed her maneuver, but she grasped his shirt collar and yanked him along a whisker's breadth ahead of the collision.

Like mice seeking shelter under an elephant, she steered them closer to the monstrosity. As they drew near the towering mass, she saw that the blast crater from the missile was already beginning to heal. The same biological mechanism responsible for Tarrant's runaway growth was also quick to efface any wound. For the first time, she began to wonder if it would be possible to kill him.

The answer hit her like a slap and she skidded to a halt.

"What?" DiLorenzo shouted, lost somewhere between incomprehension and panic.

"I've got an idea." She unlimbered the grenade launcher and showed it to him. "Do you know how to use one of these?"

He nodded. A similar version of the weapon was used by the New York City police for riot control to shoot CS gas canisters and less-than-lethal munitions such as rubber bullets or beanbags.

She passed it over along with a handful of forty-millimeter grenades. "I need you to get his attention."

"Get his attention," he repeated, as if reciting a grocery list. "Meanwhile you will be . . . doing what?"

She reached down to her lower leg and drew her boot knife. "Surgery."

DiLorenzo stared at the knife, then at the grenades in his own hand. "You're kidding."

Tarrant's root-like feet began shifting as he lifted his massive bulk and commenced relocating in an effort to expose the bothersome duo hiding in his shadow. As he moved, his arms fanned out above them, with blue fire dancing at his multiple fingertips.

"Go!" Mira shouted the admonition as she herself broke away, veering back out into the open. "And for God's sake, don't shoot me."

DiLorenzo started to follow, but the suddenness of her decision, coupled with his own hesitation, had given her an insurmountable head start. He remained where he was a moment longer, still debating what to do, and his indecision saved his life. Lightning from Tarrant's hands licked at the stone floor and scorched a furrow between where he stood and where Mira ran.

Though he had no idea what Mira was planning to do, DiLorenzo knew she was counting on him to . . . what had she said? Get his attention? For the moment, Tarrant's awareness seemed to be fixed on Mira, the ever-present monkey wrench in the works of his grand scheme, and if something wasn't done to distract him, Mira would be blasted to cinders.

DiLorenzo ran in the opposite direction, trying to get the necessary range to implement the grenade launcher. It didn't take long. Despite his bulk, Tarrant was moving rapidly away in his pursuit of Mira. The detective found a heap of rubble for concealment, then knelt and fitted a grenade into the launcher. Aiming just a little high, he let one fly.

If Tarrant heard the hollow pop of the gunpowder primer in the firing chamber, he gave no indication. But when the tiny explosive ball hit and erupted, blasting a second crater in his flesh, his psychic bellow was deafening.

"Oh yeah," DiLorenzo muttered, ducking down behind the impromptu barrier. He slid another shell into the launcher. "That got his attention."

Mira had managed to put herself on the opposite side of the creature from the detective. Her goal had been to reach the fractured rock wall where part of the twelfth level had broken away. It was a dangerous place to be, especially if DiLorenzo failed to distract the monster from its single-minded determination to stomp her out of existence. As it was, she was barely staying ahead of the thunderbolts, and wondered if the old grave robber wasn't intentionally missing in order to herd her toward a literal dead end.

As soon as the first grenade blew, she sensed a lull in the intensity of the pursuit. Tarrant hadn't forgotten about her, but he also knew that she had not been the one to sting him this time. His torso whipped back and forth, scanning the floor to find DiLorenzo without losing track of where Mira was. She knew she might not get a better chance.

A second blast struck close to one of the grotesque eye

orbs, smashing it and spilling a torrent of ocular fluid down the creature's chest. This time, the screams were equal parts frustration and agony, and the remaining eye burned with fury as it scanned the ruined floor for the impudent mortal who dared to menace it so. It was just the break Mira needed.

She scrambled over the shattered rubble and immediately began climbing the ragged wall. The broken stone was by no means sheer, an easy climb by comparison to the cliff face she had negotiated in order to gain access to the Nazi fortress in Bolivia, but the circumstances under which she made this ascent were far more extreme.

Tarrant lofted his arms overhead, his reach extending almost to the uppermost reaches of the ceiling. The energy arcing at his fingertips illuminated every crevice of the cavern like a spotlight. Mira squinted against the sudden brilliance and looked away. She could hear stone shattering and the hum of electrical discharges behind her, but focused her concentration on the sensory input from her fingers as they sought out handholds in the schist, expecting at any moment to be swatted off the wall like a fly. However, Tarrant's attention had indeed been diverted and as he scoured the floor to find DiLorenzo, she finally reached the shattered remnants of the highest level of the city.

The circular terrace had broken nearly in half, and the division seemed almost surgically precise. It took her a moment to reconcile what she was seeing with her implanted recollection of the pagoda. It was like looking at a cross-section of a memory. And right in front of her, less than three steps away, was the crystalline altar and two-thirds of the Trinity.

She glanced over her shoulder and down. Tarrant still searched the floor for the detective, who wisely was keeping his head down. The Trinity continued to hover before her seductively.

She moved closer to the altar, feeling subtle resistance of its energy field. Part of her wanted to destroy it, and with it, all the future schemes of men like Tarrant, yet she knew she would not. It was a tool, which might also be used for good instead of evil. Her fingers pushed into the invisible matrix to touch the ancient talisman.

The blow caught her completely off-guard, and the abrupt translation from standing before the Trinity to lying sprawled on the hard floor several feet away from where she had been left her momentarily dazed. As she rolled over, trying to clear the cobwebs, she caught a glimpse of her assailant moving in to follow up on the blind-side assault. A booted foot that slammed into the side of her head punctuated her astonished recognition.

She let herself go limp, trying to absorb most of the energy of the blow, and rolled away. Despite her last-moment preparations, the impact left her ears ringing and her vision blurred, but she retained enough sense to flip over to a seated position, with one arm raised to fend off the next attack. A tall, bloodied, blonde nightmare wavered before her like a mythic Valkyrie ready to send her to Valhalla. Through the fog in her head, she could just hear the strident accusation.

"You ruined everything," Rachel Aimes screamed. "Can't you just die?"

Mira couldn't tell if Rachel was a Trinity zombie, brought back from the dead for one last battle, or if the woman was simply as relentless and determined as she was. Nor could she begin to grasp how Rachel had managed to recover from her fall and gain the twelfth level ahead of her. And at just that moment, she didn't care to ask.

Rachel moved swiftly, but despite being on the ground Mira's position was more defensible. She deflected the next kick, and lashed up with her own foot, striking her opponent in the knee. Rachel's leg folded beneath her and she went down. Mira sprang onto the other woman's back and delivered a chopping blow to the base of Rachel's neck. She only got one good hit in before her larger and stronger foe bucked like an enraged animal beneath her and pitched her aside.

Rachel was on her instantly. Mira felt her head snap back as her hair was seized, but she flipped backwards, twisting free, and continued through a second reverse handspring that ended in a low crouch ten feet away. Rachel whirled and charged again, but this time Mira was ready.

At the moment of contact, Mira stepped aside and pivoted

on her left foot as she brought her right leg around in a roundhouse kick that connected solidly with the back of Rachel's head. The added momentum impelled Tarrant's daughter forward, arms waving like windmills as she stumbled toward the precipice overlooking the abyss. Rachel fell to her knees at the edge, but it wasn't enough to stop her headlong plunge.

Panting to catch her breath after the unexpected combat, Mira approached the precipice and looked over. In defiance of all reason, Rachel Aimes clung to the sheer wall, her fingertips just barely hooked on the lip. Mira felt a grudging respect for her foe's tenacity.

With an almost superhuman effort, Rachel began hauling herself back up onto the smooth rock floor. "I'll tear your heart out, you bitch!" she snarled.

"Not exactly a profound choice of last words," replied Mira, raising an eyebrow. "I was hoping for something a bit more philosophical."

What Rachel's next utterance lacked in eloquence was made up for in decibels. She was still screaming as Mira wrestled the Trinity from the altar several seconds later. The chasm was deep and it took quite a while for her to reach the bottom.

DiLorenzo turned his head cautiously, moving as little as possible. He could feel the intensity of Tarrant's lightning on his back, and although he was covered in dust and debris from the geological upheaval going on all around, he was certain the god-like monstrosity would at any moment spot him and smash him to a bloody pulp.

He had done his part, distracting the thing long enough for Mira to do whatever it was she had planned. Whether she was successful or not, he couldn't begin to guess, but he knew his own time was limited.

The creature wasn't invincible. He knew he had done more than just scratch it with the two grenades he had fired, and he still had three more in reserve. If he could just hit a vital area, it might be enough to end the threat once and for all. But how many chances would he get before the thing fixed his location and roasted him with a lightning bolt?

The towering pillar of flesh loomed directly over him, the arms spread out now like fiery tree branches, and suddenly streams of argent fire were spilling down onto the floor, striking at random targets, but in such rapid succession that the explosions seemed to be everywhere all at once.

DiLorenzo's fingers tightened around the grenade launcher as he gathered his courage. *It was a good effort, Mira. Sorry it didn't work out.*

From her new vantage, Tarrant seemed even bigger. Mira thought maybe he was still growing. It was time to do something about that. His one eye was turned elsewhere, still presumably looking for DiLorenzo, and she knew she might not get a better opportunity. Holding the knife in her right hand, she backed away, putting several steps between herself and the edge, then took off running.

Her leap described a high arc out over the rubble of the collapsed section of the twelfth tier. She dropped nearly sixty feet in a parabolic descent before slamming into the solid mass of Tarrant's trunk. As she lit, she drove the blade into the tightly stretched skin, and clung to the haft.

The knife caught in the solid muscle tissue, arresting her fall long enough for her boot soles and fingernails to find a purchase. If Tarrant felt the sting of her knife in his flesh, he gave no indication. Although the growth of his skin was commensurate with the rest of his evolving physiology, it was nevertheless stretched to its limits, and her fingers tore through it like paper, exposing twisted muscle fibers the size of hawsers. Using the blade like an ice axe, she worked her way up and around the undulating mass.

The wound from the LAW rocket had begun healing, but remained an open and deep tunnel into which Mira did not hesitate to plunge. Yet, this weak spot in the monster's flank was not her primary goal; what she sought would require a little more effort.

She abandoned the idea of cutting through the cable-like strands of muscle that sheathed Tarrant's new form, not because to do so would have been so difficult as to be impossible, but because it was unnecessary. Although the fibers were themselves dense and impenetrable, they were held together only by a thin fascia, which she pulled effortlessly apart to create a narrow cavity. Drawing a deep breath, she plunged head and shoulders into the gap. A moment later, she was gone, completely swallowed up inside the creature's living flesh.

DiLorenzo rose to a kneeling position, trying not to think about the holocaust that was raging all around, and fitted another grenade into the launcher. If he failed with the first shot, he might not get another, so his movements were deliberate and careful. Locking the barrel in place, he raised the gun to his shoulder and pointed up into the center of the fiery mass. But as his finger began to squeeze the trigger, the lightning abruptly ceased flowing from Tarrant's fingertips, and the cavern was plunged into darkness.

DiLorenzo blinked. He could still faintly see the red glow where Tarrant's conflagration had liquefied sections of the stone floor, but this afforded scant illumination to his light-scorched retinas. Somehow the sudden night was more disconcerting than the raging inferno had been. He swallowed and then resumed his preparations to fire the grenade.

"What are you up to, Mira?"

Tarrant's voice rumbled in his head like the crushing of boulders, and he jerked his finger away from the trigger. Was Mira still alive? It didn't seem possible. Yet, whatever she was doing, it was enough to distract Tarrant from his apocalyptic display of power. He blinked, straining his eyes to find her in the crushing darkness.

His night vision was just returning when a faint green glow appeared high overhead. He squinted, trying to look around the bright spots that still swam in front of his eyes, and was able to distinguish the source of the illumination. It was a chemical light stick and it was moving against the surface of the atrocity Tarrant had become. DiLorenzo strained harder and could just make out the silhouette of a person moving against the dark backdrop of the blast wound.

"Mira!" He was unaware that he had shouted, but his exclamation rang loud in the unexpected silence.

The light tube abruptly fell and with it the dark shape that he now knew to be the unstoppable Mira Raiden. She tumbled from the crater, bouncing along Tarrant's trunk until she rolled out onto the floor and lay prone, unmoving. In spite of the ominous threat still hovering above, DiLorenzo left his place of concealment and raced toward her. Before he could reach her, however, she began to stir, and rose to her hands and knees. Her head remained down, her face all but invisible behind a mask of blood and dust.

"You didn't really think you could kill me, did you?" Tarrant's voice was full of menace. He lifted his arms once more, and the sun seemed to rise over Agartha as baleful lightning leapt from his fingertips. He let the electricity build, as if by increasing the potency of the final blow he might erase all memory of the woman who had so nearly foiled his plans.

"Kill you?" Mira raised her head, looking up into his one good eye. "You're already dead."

In her left hand, she held a blood-streaked circlet of silvery metal, adorned with a single gemstone which, despite being marred by an ugly crack, pulsated with brilliant light.

Though he no longer had any sort of facial expression, Tarrant's shock was plain. "No. Wait. . . ."

Mira flipped Atl'an's Trinity into the air and in the same motion drew her Desert Eagle and fired. The .44-caliber round finished what she had begun in Panama, pulverizing the crystal completely.

Tarrant's denial was instantly silenced as the flow of Beta waves to his reanimated cells ceased. The power building at his extended fingertips abruptly leapt toward the ceiling in a single cataclysmic discharge, then the darkness instantly returned. Although the three Trinity segments working in harmony had triggered his transformation, it was the artifact stolen from the museum that had given him back his life, and now, as simply as throwing a switch, it had been taken away. There was no lingering protest, no thrashing death throes. The undead grave robber was simply gone.

The pillar of lifeless flesh remained upright for a few moments before it gradually began to tilt. Once gravity seized hold, the creature's empty shell pitched over like a felled tree. The lower portion of the trunk slammed into the floor, creating yet another tremor, but the upper half extended out beyond the edge of the terrace and kept going. Tarrant's carcass slid serpentine toward the precipice, and in a matter of seconds vanished into the abyss below, where he joined his daughter and at long last delivered the price of his diabolical promise.

NINETEEN

There was no time to savor the victory. Mira snatched up the fallen chem-light and rushed to DiLorenzo's side. "Follow me!"

The detective fell in behind her without questioning her urgent command, focusing on the green lamp held over her head. She immediately led the way to the spiral stairs, which descended to the tenth level. As they started down the steps, DiLorenzo felt the first droplets of chilly water on his face.

"It's raining!"

"Not rain," Mira called back. "Tarrant melted the ice frozen in the rock matrix."

"Why am I thinking that's a bad thing?"

"At the risk of sounding like Chicken Little, when the ice melts, more than just water is going to start falling."

DiLorenzo looked around skeptically. In the limited cone of illumination from the chem-light, it looked as though Mira's prediction had already come to pass. Rubble from Tarrant's rampage and their own explosive weapons littered the stairs and had visibly damaged the roof and walls of the lone structure on the tenth level. Yet, as if to chastise his incredulity, a chunk of quartz the size of a bus broke loose from the central dome and fell majestically past them, a trail of ice and water droplets glittering around it like a comet tail as it sailed into the dark chasm. After that, it seemed as though a cork had been removed.

Within moments, the floor was awash in several inches of water, and over the rushing noise of the deluge that poured down from above, they could hear the impact of solid matter letting go from the ceiling and demolishing in seconds structures that had stood undisturbed for ten millennia.

Like Mira, DiLorenzo had a preternatural familiarity with Agartha, which Tarrant had exploited during the detective's thralldom, wringing not only the layout of the city, but also the codes to release the gates to each successive level. Now, as he fled back through the changing landscape, down stairways and avenues that were as familiar to him as the borough of Manhattan, he found cause to question Mira's navigation. Upon reaching the eighth level, she had veered away from the direct path through to the next tier and headed toward the outside wall.

"This isn't the way out."

"The front door's been locked," Mira replied, a hint of irritation in her tone.

"But that's the only way in or out." He splashed to a stop beside her, facing the sheer cavern wall. He followed the line of her pointing finger to a dark recess in the wall. "I don't remember anything like that."

She fixed him with a wry smile. "That's why you have to trust me."

The cavern continued coming apart as they threaded through the narrow paths of the yeti, and the devastation was by no means limited to the twelve terraces of the city. Seepage from the frozen slopes was flooding into the venous passages through which they fled, pushing them along like driftwood in the flood. The torrent was bone chilling, but the groaning of the cavern's collapse supplied an adrenaline edge that kept them moving despite uncontrollable shivering.

Beyond the tunnel junction where Mira had first deviated into the footsteps of Agartha's new inhabitants, the journey ceased to follow any sort of intentional route; they simply traveled the path of least resistance. From that point, the subterranean channels never revisited the main cavern, but wandered ever closer to the surface, until at long last, they were vomited into the Himalayan night.

The flow of water across the surface of the glacier had left it as smooth and slippery as glass. Yet even here, separated from the collapse of Agartha by tons of stone, the echoes of that disaster were felt. Monstrous crevasses were opening up along the glacier, while towering seracs broke apart and came crashing down all around.

Mira managed to snare DiLorenzo's pant leg and pull him into a shared embrace, but there was little else either of them could do until the slope leveled out. Somehow, they survived the harrowing journey and came to rest on a flat shelf overlooking yet another broken field of ice, scoured by the same monsoon that had chased Mira across Nepal.

"We're on the south face!" Even though she still hugged him closely in an effort to pool their body heat, she had to shout to be heard over the shrieking wind. The moisture in their clothes was already stiffening into ice crystals. "I think this is the Khumbu icefall!"

"What's the good news?" answered DiLorenzo through chattering teeth. He was trying to be flippant, brash in the face of this new peril. It was false bravado, yet his comment earned a faint smile. Before she could answer, however, they both heard a shrill cry that had nothing to do with the weather. It was echoed several times, and seemed to be coming from all around.

"That was the good news," she finally replied, drawing the Desert Eagle from its holster. Her flesh of her fingertips froze instantly to the metal grips and she abruptly realized that she might not be able to count on the weapon to protect them from the gathering of yeti that had likewise been forced out of the subterranean kingdom and onto the ice. She pulled loose from his embrace. "We've got to find some shelter!"

DiLorenzo nodded, but when he tried to move his limbs, he felt himself curl into a ball, hugging his arms to his chest as his entire body was wracked with shivers. He opened his mouth to apologize, but the wind stole his words away. Recognizing that she would get no help from him, she reached down and gripped his collar with her own stiffening hands. The fingerless leather gloves she wore afforded little protection against the cold, but it was better than nothing.

Crouching low against the wind, she pulled him across the new ice toward a sculpted ridge beyond the icefall. The upswept drift afforded some protection against the wind, but it wasn't nearly enough. And another round of howls from the yeti reminded her that the elements were not the only enemy grouping for an attack.

Through the descending fog, DiLorenzo was barely aware

of being shoved into a niche in the ice, hidden from the storm. He felt strangely calm inside the shelter. Mira was still bent over him, blocking most of the wind with her body, and after a moment he felt her thrust something into his arms. "Think warm thoughts, detective."

"It's M-M-Mike."

He thought maybe she was smiling, but he was having trouble keeping his eyes open. After a moment, he heard her talking, but not to him. "Get a fix on this loca—"

Her sentence ended abruptly and was followed by the roar of a firearm discharging. The sound repeated and then there was only the wind. DiLorenzo struggled toward the surface of consciousness, but his efforts were in vain. Darkness overwhelmed him and he heard nothing.

Several times he drifted back almost to alertness only to be turned away by the harsh reality of his surroundings. After a while, the wind died down and there was silence within and without. Still he did not wake.

At some point, a sound like the beating wings of a dragon crept into his dreams. The noise grew and deepened, but the dragon failed to appear in his mind's eye, and he dared not look with the eyes of his body, for fear of what he might find.

"This is it," a voice cried from the darkness. "These are the coordinates."

"That's her sat-phone," called another. "Look. Over here. There's someone buried here."

He tried to shrink back so that they would not find him, but it was too late. Hands closed around his arms and drew him into sunlight.

"It's not her." The observation was filled with contempt.

"No, but I'll bet it's the guy she was chasing after." He sensed the speaker drawing closer. "Where is she?"

"Banks, look, in his hands . . ."

The exclamation jolted DiLorenzo closer to lucidity, and he opened his eyes. He did not recognize the two men who held him erect, but their amazement compelled him to look down at his own hands. They were curled into frozen claws, holding an object tight against his chest.

It was the remaining pieces of the Trinity, still joined, still faintly pulsing with energy.

"Mira . . ." The name tumbled from his lips, but he couldn't find any more words.

"Where is she? Where is Mira?"

"She . . ." He looked down at the Trinity again, but couldn't remember how he had come to possess it, or what had happened to Mira. The awful realization of his ignorance washed over him like vertigo, and he sagged in their arms. Before he could speak again, the darkness swelled around him, and he couldn't stop falling. . . .

EPILOGUE

Mira sped through the darkness, fleeing the pursuing yeti and the icy grip of hypothermia. There was a chance she might escape the former peril, but in doing so she had all but sealed her fate by the latter. She was lost now, and her intuition told her that every conceivable path led to failure.

The Desert Eagle was gone, not that it would have made much difference. She couldn't have pulled the trigger anyway. At some point during the night, as the cold stole the feeling from her nerves, the sheer weight of the pistol had ripped it from her grasp, tearing chunks of frozen skin from her fingertips.

Dazed she staggered onward because there was simply no other alternative.

Mira.

The voice did not surprise her. In the context of her situation, it seemed perfectly reasonable that she would hear disembodied voices. But when it repeated again and again, it occurred to her to wonder to whom the voice belonged to. It wasn't DiLorenzo. It certainly wasn't the man she had always known as Walter Aimes. She didn't believe in God, Jesus or guardian angels. So who did that leave?

Mira, this way! Hurry!

The voice was not truly audible; it would be impossible for her to hear speech. Even the howls of the yeti were indistinguishable from the shriek of the wind. Yet the words were nevertheless distinct. She could even tell from which direction they came and altered her meandering course ever so slightly in order to heed its call. *His call*, she thought. *I know this voice. . . .*

And then she saw him, standing before her, perfectly visible despite the gloom of night and the impenetrable shroud of blowing snow. His arms were spread in welcome, beckoning her onward. *Mira. Come to me.*

"Curtis." The whisper was snatched away by the gale, and

for a fleeting instant she felt a profound sadness. Her dead had come for her, which could only mean that . . . *Well, it was a good ride.*

And then through the haze of her despair, she felt his firm grip as he pulled her into his warm embrace, and her fear fled away.

Rest now, Mira, he whispered solemnly. *You have begun to accomplish the will of the Wise Father, but there is much yet to do in the Great Work.*

TO BE CONTINUED...

EMISSARY
A Mira Raiden Adventure

PROLOGUE: SILENCE

The damage was catastrophic.

The nine-millimeter bullet, deformed by the ricochet, was already tumbling as it slammed into his eye, smashed through the orbital bone, and burrowed a chaotic path through the temporal lobe of his brain. The shock of the injury left him almost instantaneously paralyzed, even before the real effects of the wound became manifest.

The specific regions of his brain damaged by the bullet were not critical to life support; with immediate medical treatment, he might even have survived with only limited impairment. However, the secondary effects of the trauma—a hydrostatic shock wave that rippled through the surrounding tissue, the subsequent swelling of his brain that would in short order cause his gray matter to extrude through every orifice—would probably, under the best of circumstances, be fatal to an ordinary human.

But then he was no ordinary human.

How long he lay there without conscious thought, he could only begin to guess. He gradually became aware of maggots squirming in the ruined flesh of his eye socket, and assimilated them without conscious thought, drawing nutrition from their protein to begin the rebuilding process. It was all he could do; he could not move, he could not breathe. He could only lay in the darkness, trapped in the prison of his own rotting flesh.

They came for him nearly a week later. He was aware of them, felt their presence and thereafter their touch, but they were closed off to him. Their speech reverberated against his eardrums, but the damage to his brain did not allow him to process the nervous impulses into something meaningful.

Nevertheless, those impulses were traveling through him. His brain was listening to his nerves, and soon it would begin repairing the pathways that would allow him to communicate with and begin repairing his decaying corpse.

A setback. Just as his remaining eye, began to interpret light— an intense glare filtered through the opaque membrane of his eyelid—the invasion began. His nerves flared with searing pain, then just as quickly were overcome with a chemical numbness. It was, he would later realize, formaldehyde.

He was being embalmed.

The darkness returned with a vengeance.

Yet, the flickering flame of his life would not be extinguished. Even as the transfusion of embalming fluid ended, his body began to repair itself again. The preservative chemicals were broken down at an atomic level, and useful molecular components were redistributed to nourish the restoration process while toxic elements were shunted into the lipid cells that sheathed his torso and extremities.

Time passed and his nerves began once more to transmit information, but there was no light to guide him. After days or perhaps weeks, he suddenly felt the impulse to breathe, but his lungs refused to inflate. At some deep intellectual level, he correctly recognized that he had been placed in a vacuum-sealed container—a coffin—but his reactions were purely primal, instinctual. Like a trapped animal, he began to kick and scratch and claw. His hands found the outer limits of his prison. The soft, silky cushioned liner swiftly fell to pieces beneath his clawed fingers, revealing the smooth unyielding metal of his casket.

Without consciously thinking to do it, he brought his knees up close to his chest and placed his feet flat against the unseen lid of the coffin. Then, with a mighty, silent heave, he flexed his legs and pushed.

It should not have been possible for the aluminum capsule,

sealed with lead solder and negatively pressurized, to be opened by the mere brute force of a human, but then no mere human would have been alive under such conditions to begin with. After a moment of struggle, the metal buckled slightly and that was enough to break the seal. Air whooshed into the cavity and with the equalization of pressure, the thin line of molten lead broke free in several places. The lid, hinged on one side, banged noisily against the side of the coffin, then the stillness returned. The darkness remained absolute.

Nevertheless, that first breath of fresh air—that first moment of true life—worked wonders for his cognitive faculties. His memories were still a mosaic of fractured recollections, but then that was to be expected when one's brain held several millennia of life experience. He knew enough to recognize that his casket was situated in some kind of crypt, and that once he found the exit to his tomb, he would emerge once more into the light. He did not hesitate to begin groping for the walls of the enclosure, and after a few minutes isolated what felt like a doorway, blocked by slab of cool stone. Another violent shove broke the marble loose from the portal.

Even as the barrier tumbled down the ornate steps leading from the crypt, light filled his world. It was night, and the sky was overcast blocking out the stars, but after months in absolute inky blackness, the brilliance of the orange-hued ambient glow—the lights of a distant city reflected in the low clouds—stung his eyes. Both eyes. No trace of his maiming remained.

He staggered forward, breathing deeply like a man who has just escaped drowning, and then was abruptly racked by a spasm of nausea. Vile green vomit erupted from his mouth and nose; a greasy mixture of body fat mixed with the toxic residue of the embalming fluid.

In spite of the discomfort, as the chemicals were purged from his body, he felt stronger, more alive. He barely recognized his own flesh. The skin of his fingers, which had once been as plump as sausages, the result of centuries of unashamedly living well, now hung in great slack folds over bone and sinew.

I have lived too soft for too long, he thought. That changes now.

His sensitive eyes detected movement, an undulation of light and shadow; someone was coming. Animal instinct prompted him to shrink back into the darkness of his crypt, but his wiry muscles tensed in preparation as the approaching figure came into view. It was a single individual wielding only a flashlight; a caretaker, no doubt coming to investigate the tumult. He waited until the silhouette paused to examine the cracked marble slab at the base of the steps, and then struck with the swiftness of a wild predator.

The smell of terror enveloped the caretaker like a miasma of poisonous smoke in the instant that his throat was torn open, but he did not cry out or struggle; he was dead before his conscious mind knew what was happening.

Later, as the first gleams of predawn twilight began illuminating the sky, the man who had emerged from the crypt pushed away the remains of his repast. His heightened metabolism had sped the nutrients of his meal to every part of his body, restoring both the full functionality of his organs and muscles and his overall sense of vitality. His memories were returning, and with them his sense of purpose.

He pawed through the torn and stained remains of the caretakers clothing, finding a wallet with a few small bills and more importantly, a slim cellular phone. He flipped open the latter item and punched in a sequence of digits.

"This is Wallace Vaught." The voice that answered was more alert than he would have expected given the hour, which could only mean that his contact was in a different time zone, further to the east.

"It's me." His vocal cords were tight from disuse and his voice gravelly and all but unrecognizable.

"Who is this?"

He was not used to having to explain himself to underlings, but it was evident that Vaught—a simpering sycophant whom he found useful, but in every other way intolerable—would not be able to connect the dots based on a mysterious early morning phone call.

"I'm going to give you a bank account number, a number that only you and one other man know about." He rattled off a sequence. "That should tell you who I am. I need you to withdraw…take it all. We're going to need it. Then come and get me."

There a long silence at the other end, then finally: "Can it be?"

He ignored the question. "I need to know if the Trinity is safe."

"The Trin… My god, of course you wouldn't know. It was stolen."

"Stolen?" His voice cracked with rage. "Who?"

"No one is sure. It only just happened. It was on display with the other artifacts, but someone switched it for a replica. Mira Raiden is looking for it."

Mira. The very thought of the woman amplified his wrath exponentially, but the anticipation of revenge tempered his response and his steely calm returned. "Come and get me Wallace. Hurry."

"Where are you, sir?"

He turned in a circle, gazing at his surroundings for some hint of his location in the landscape, but saw only his crypt, a squat marble structure modeled after the Roman temple of Vesta at Tivoli, set on a perfectly manicured lawn in the midst of a grove of cherry trees that were already giving up their leaves to Autumn. His eyes finally came to rest on the inscription above the door of the crypt. Two simple words in perfectly executed block letters, no date, no explanations:

Marquand Atlas.

"I'm right where you left me."

Mira Raiden sped through the darkness, fleeing the pursuing yeti and the icy grip of hypothermia. There was a chance she might escape the former peril, but in doing so she had all but sealed her fate by the latter. She was lost now, and her intuition told her that every conceivable path led to failure.

Her gun was gone, not that it would have made much

difference. She couldn't have pulled the trigger anyway. At some point during the night, as the cold stole the feeling from her nerves, the sheer weight of the pistol had ripped it from her grasp, tearing chunks of frozen skin from her fingertips.

Dazed she staggered onward because there was simply no other alternative.

Mira.

The voice did not surprise her. In the context of her situation, it seemed perfectly reasonable that she would hear disembodied voices. But when it repeated again and again, it occurred to her to wonder to whom the voice belonged to. It wasn't DiLorenzo. It certainly wasn't the man she had always known as Walter Aimes. She didn't believe in God, Jesus or guardian angels. So who did that leave?

Mira, this way! Hurry!

The voice was not truly audible; it would be impossible for her to hear speech. Even the howls of the yeti were indistinguishable from the shriek of the wind. Yet the words were nevertheless distinct; she could even tell from which direction they came, and altered her meandering course ever so slightly in order to heed its call. His call, she thought. I know this voice….

And then she saw him, standing before her, perfectly visible despite the gloom of night and the impenetrable shroud of blowing snow. His arms were spread in welcome, beckoning her onward. Mira. Come to me.

"Curtis." The whisper was snatched away by the gale, and for a fleeting instant she felt a profound sadness. Her dead had come for her, which could only mean that… Well, it was a good ride.

Through the haze of her despair, she felt his firm grip as he pulled her into his warm embrace, and her fear fled away.

Rest now, Mira, she heard him whisper. You have begun to accomplish the will of the Wise Father, but there is much yet to do in the Great Work.

But then, as she slid toward the darkness of final release, the specter evaporated, revealing a different visage, one she did not immediately remember.

"Mira." The man had to shout to be heard over the tempest. "Things ended badly between us last time. I hope we can make a fresh start."

The sardonic voice, like the face, was unfamiliar, but she knew immediately who he was. A cry ripped past her frozen lips as the darkness mercifully claimed her.

ABOUT THE AUTHOR

Sean Ellis is the author of several novels. He is a veteran of Operation Enduring Freedom, and has a Bachelor of Science degree in Natural Resources Policy from Oregon State University. He lives in Arizona, where he divides his time between writing, adventure sports, and trying to figure out how to save the world.

Visit him on the web at
www.seanellisthrillers.webs.com